A River Through Two Harbors

Books of the Two Harbors mystery series
by Dennis Herschbach

Convergence at Two Harbors, 2012
Seven Graves, Two Harbors, 2013
A River Through Two Harbors, 2014

A River Through Two Harbors

Dennis Herschbach

NORTH STAR PRESS OF ST. CLOUD, INC.
Saint Cloud, Minnesota

Dedication

To: Abby, Ande Kate, Berit, Eason, Elsa,
Emma, Emma, John, Martin,
Olivia, Roman, Tyler

May you find peace and love
growing among the thorns of life.

Cover photo by Diane Hilden

Copyright © 2014 Dennis Herschbach

ISBN 978-0-87839-719-8

First Edition: June 2014

Printed in the United States of America

Published by
North Star Press of St. Cloud, Inc.
P.O. Box 451
St. Cloud, Minnesota 56302

Special thanks to Elizabeth Brunsvold and Laurie Bammann for doing the preliminary reads of *A River Through Two Harbors*. Your comments, suggestions, and encouragement were invaluable.

Thanks, also, to the folks at North Star Press for making this publication possible.

And especially to my wife, Vicky, who was patient while I hibernated in my study, struggling to create this story, thank you. I am truly blessed to have you in my life.

Preface

Until the Europeans came to North America, prostitution was nearly unheard of among the Indian Nations. As a matter of fact, in their culture women were held in very high esteem. All that has changed in the last hundred years, and today, Native American women are preyed upon in unprecedented numbers.

Here is a list of facts recorded in an article written by Christine Stark, a Native America woman and researcher, that appeared in the August 4, 2013, issue of the *Minneapolis Star Tribune*.

- Native American women are the only group who are predominantly assaulted by men outside their race. And in prostitution, the vast majority of pimps are white or African-American.
- Trafficking of Native women is rampant in northern Minnesota. Native American women and teens are coerced and groomed into prostitution through gangs and organized crime.
- The Duluth harbor is notorious among Native people as a site for the trafficking of Native women and teens, including First Nation women and girls brought down from Thunder Bay, Ontario, to be sold on the ships.
- Native women, teen girls, boys, and even babies have been sold for sex on the ships.

A River Through Two Harbors is fiction, but as with much fiction, it is based on truth that is, in some cases, overly dramatized but in others perhaps understated. The river in the title is not literal. It contains no water, only women and girls, victims who are transported down Highway 61 and pass through Two Harbors on their way to the Duluth harbor, and it seems no one much cares.

Chapter
One

DEIDRE JOHNSON STEPPED OUT of her patrol car. On its sides was stenciled SILVER BAY POLICE. As she walked across the paved road, she pulled on a heavy jacket to ward off the frigid November wind that sliced down from the northwest, and she turned up the collar of the coat to protect the back of her neck.

George Swenson, a longtime acquaintance, was waiting for her, his shoulders hunched against the cold and his hands covered with heavy leather mitts lined with wool inserts.

"Mornin'," she called out to George, who stood leaning on the railing of the bridge she had just driven across. "Your call was forwarded by our answering system. Something wrong?"

George didn't move. "I'm not sure, Deidre, but I thought I better give you a call. I was taking my morning walk, and came this way. When I was crossing the bridge, I stopped to look at the stream. Looks like something got hit by a car and was thrown down there." He pointed at the riverbed. "Just a deer, probably. There's no animal down there, but it might have crawled off and is hiding nearby. Thought maybe you could put it out of it's misery if its still alive."

By that time Deidre was standing beside George, and they looked down at the streambed twenty feet below. A trickle of crystal clear water gurgled as it washed over time-worn boulders, and ice sheets had formed in places where the water flowed more slowly.

It had snowed the night before, and an inch or so of white powder dusted the exposed rocks and ice.

"That's an awful lot of blood," George commented. "Whatever's down there is probably dead by now."

Deidre shrugged. "A little blood on fresh snow spreads a long way. You'd be surprised how little it takes to make a scene look pretty gruesome. Is there any sign of an animal being hit on the road, fur or tracks on the roadside, any blood up here?"

George shook his head. "I looked while I was waiting for you, but couldn't see anything. I didn't climb down the bank. Thought you wouldn't want anything disturbed until you found out what's there."

Deidre nodded. "Well, I guess I better take a look. Will you stick around until I get back up? Those rocks look pretty slippery, and if I fall and break a leg, it'd be nice to have some help." She sort of chuckled but knew it could happen.

Deidre eased herself around the edge of the bridge railing and began picking her way down the slippery bank. The closer to the bottom she came, the more the hair on the back of her neck began to prickle, not necessarily from the cold wind.

On the shelf of ice near the stream edge she saw an impression in the snow. It wasn't recognizable, but she could see a trail leading away as though something had been dragged up under the bridge. She was right. There wasn't as much blood as it had seemed when she and George looked down from above. It was enough, but probably not so much that whatever animal was pitched over the railing would have died of blood loss. The drag marks were stained crimson, marking the direction of movement.

Deidre bent down to take a closer look at the trail, and her heart flipped, momentarily skipping a beat. She squinted and looked again, stood up, and inhaled deeply.

Damn, she thought. *Why did I ever take this job?* "Shit!" she said out loud.

George heard her curse and leaned over the railing. "Find something, Deidre?" he called down to her.

"Nothing yet," she hollered back to him, and then she stooped down to get a better look at a small handprint in the snow.

2

Deidre called the State Highway Patrol dispatcher. "This is officer Deidre Johnson, Silver Bay Police. If you have any troopers in the area, I can use some backup on the outskirts of town. I'm on Highway 3 at the bridge spanning the creek. Follow the road that leads out of town and joins Forest Highway 11. Just before they reach the city limits, they'll see my squad car. This is an emergency, so have them come as quickly as possible."

She fumbled taking the flashlight from its loop on her belt, and tentatively flashed the light into the dark recesses under the bridge abutments. The beam wasn't strong enough to penetrate all the way into the shadows. Just then she heard a siren approaching, and Deidre decided to meet the trooper before proceeding further. Subconsciously, she didn't want to face what she feared would be found at the end of the drag marks.

It was a struggle for her to climb the steep bank to the road, and after several slips and by grasping the few shrubs growing from the rocks, she was able to get close to the top. The two men grasped her hands and helped her up over the edge of the river bank.

"Hi, Cliff," she said to the state trooper. "Glad you were close by. It didn't take you long to get here."

She turned to George. "Thanks for taking the time to call this in. I don't think you want to stay around to see what's down there. I'd appreciate it if you wouldn't talk to anyone about what you've seen, because we'll need as much time without distraction as we can buy." She looked him square in the eye. "You know this town. People look for any excitement, and the last thing we need is a crowd."

Deidre suspected George had planned to meet his cronies at the one coffee shop in town for their daily gossip session, but George could tell by the tone of Deidre's voice that this wasn't the time to argue. As he was leaving, another state trooper arrived. George hurried off. Before the trooper could get out of her car and put on her jacket, Deidre called the county sheriff dispatch and asked that they reroute traffic away from the bridge area.

"Cliff, will you come down there with me?" she addressed the first trooper. "And, Kathy," she said, turning to the second, "will you make sure that no one passes this way. Maybe put up some crime tape to cordon off this area," she asked of the newly arrived officer.

As Kathy sprinted to her car, Cliff and Deidre began a careful descent to the stream below, only this time she ventured further under the bridge while Cliff covered her move. She shined her light into the angle formed where the bridge bed met the bank.

"Oh, no!" The words left her mouth before she could stop them.

"What'd you find?" Cliff knew whatever it was, it wasn't good.

"Follow my tracks so we don't trample any more area than necessary. I don't want to face this alone, Cliff."

He picked his way to where Deidre was standing, and shined his light at the same spot that she had lit up. He wasn't prepared for what he saw, and he involuntarily gasped.

"Oh, my God," he moaned. "Who in the world would have done this?" The two stood silent for a moment, letting his question go unanswered.

Finally Deidre could speak. "Let me climb up there and check, but I don't think there is any doubt she's dead. The frost crystals on her skin mean she's cold, probably frozen in place, but for the record, we better be sure."

Deidre climbed to where the body lay and removing her glove, felt for a pulse. As she expected, the body was as cold as the rocky ground upon which it lay. Deidre retreated to where Cliff waited.

"If you will, I'd like you to stay down here until I can call in some more help."

Cliff nodded and again Deidre began the climb to the road, but this time her feet felt heavier than before. Her first call was to the Twin Cities of Minneapolis and St. Paul.

"Good morning. Minnesota Bureau of Criminal Apprehension. This is Mary speaking. How may I direct your call?"

"I'd like to speak with Dr. Judith Coster, if she's in."

The receptionist needed more information. "May I ask who's calling?" Her delay irritated Deidre, but she managed to keep her voice level.

"This is Deidre Johnson. Dr. Coster and I worked on a case in northern Minnesota a little over four years ago. Please connect me with her. This is official business."

"Certainly," Mary complied rather abruptly, maybe sensing that Deidre would not take no for an answer.

The phone rang twice. "Hello. Dr. Coster speaking."

"Hi, Judy. This is Deidre Johnson. How are things with you?"

"Well, Deidre. What a surprise. It's been what, six months since we last talked? I'm doing really well. My work is caught up, and I've had a week to drink coffee, gather my thoughts, and do some reading. What about you, enjoying retirement?"

Deidre cleared her throat. "I wish. A few weeks ago, the Silver Bay Counsel asked me to fill in for their one full-time police officer, Dan Butler, who needed elective surgery. They said it'd be for six weeks. I said yes. Wrong answer. I started about five weeks ago. Now I'm up to my eyeballs in something too serious to handle alone. I really need some help and in a hurry. Is there any chance you can come here right away?"

"What's so urgent it can't wait until tomorrow?" Judy wanted to know.

It took only a couple of minutes for Deidre to explain what she had found under the bridge and that she was still at the scene. She explained she was pretty much on her own and didn't want to move the body until she had help collecting evidence. The detail of what Deidre found overwhelmed Judy.

"I can be out of here in a half hour, be up there by one o'clock this afternoon. Do you need anything else?"

"I was hoping you'd see if Melissa could join us. I'd appreciate the two of you working with me." Deidre silently offered a prayer to no god in particular.

"I don't know her schedule, but after I tell her what you've told me, I'm guessing she'll drop everything and come along for the ride. Better go now. See you in a few hours."

Next, Deidre hit the speed dial on her phone and heard it ring once before an automated system answered.

"You have reached the Duluth District office of the FBI. If you know your party's extension, please say it now. Otherwise, hold for the operator to handle your call."

Deidre said, "Four six seven." She hated talking to computers. The phone rang three times, and Deidre was prepared to leave a voice mail after a beep when she heard a familiar voice.

"Good morning. This is Agent Ben VanGotten. How can I help you?"

"I think I'm beyond help, but I wanted to call you about tonight."

"Hey, Deidre. What's up, girl? I was just sitting here thinking about you."

Deidre smiled. "You were, were you? Well, I was thinking of you, too. I'm afraid I'm not going to make it to your place tonight for supper. Something really tragic happened here, and there's no way I can escape for the evening. Dr. Coster, and I hope Melissa, of the BCA, are on their way up to Silver Bay. Should be here around one or so."

Deidre went on to repeat the story she had told to Judy. Ben listened without saying a word. When she finished her story, she heard him sigh.

"The girls were so excited last night when I told them you were coming for supper, I could hardly get them to go to sleep. To them, you're Cinderella, Mary Poppins, and a fairy godmother all rolled into one. They're going to be disappointed. Can we reschedule?" he asked.

"For sure—for sure," she answered, "but I can't set a definite day until I get this cleared up. I'm hoping that won't take too long. Tell the girls I miss them, and I think of them every day. Tell them we'll have a really fun day as soon as my job here is done. They're so delightful, I wish we could see each other more often."

"I wish you could too, but for now we both have work to do. Thanks so much for calling. I hope all goes well when Dr. Coster and Melissa arrive. Give them my best, will you?"

"Sure will. Sorry about tonight. I was looking forward to a happy evening with you and the girls. Take care now. Bye."

Deidre heard a click as Ben hung up, and she buried her phone in her jacket pocket, then walked over to Kathy.

"It's too cold for us to stand out here until the BCA arrives. Let's take shifts while the other two warm up in the vehicles. Kathy, will you take the first shift? I'm about frozen, and Cliff's been out in the weather for a while too. What say we switch off guarding the site every fifteen minutes? Sound okay?"

Kathy nodded her approval, and Deidre retreated to her police car. She started the engine and turned on the heater full blast, trying to push out the cold that had permeated her being to her core. She leaned forward and put her forehead on the steering wheel, and with her eyes closed, thought of what she would be missing in Duluth that evening.

Chapter
Two

AFTER DEIDRE'S FIANCÉ, John Erickson, had died in her arms, tragically murdered in a drive-by, Deidre pretty much went into seclusion. She sold her house in Two Harbors and moved to an isolated cabin located on a plot of land nearly surrounded by the Superior National Forest. It was a wonderful piece of property, forested with a dense stand of hundred-year-old red pines. Her cabin was on a high bluff overlooking Cedar Lake, and, much to her liking, the driveway was almost a third of a mile long. With the help of her friend who owned Terry's Bar, they had installed a heavy steel gate with an alarm attached to it. She had a dog and her service revolver, and she felt safe living alone.

Now, after over four years of mourning, the deep sting of losing John had begun to subside, and finally she took some interest in living. She even found joy in spending a few days at a time in Duluth. It was on one such trip early last summer that she quite literally bumped into Ben, her friend from the FBI.

They had been classmates in high school, but Deidre developed quite a dislike for him because of his macho ways. They both attended the same police academy and had developed a mutual dislike for each other, a bitterness that was only exacerbated when Deidre, in retaliation for his harassment, broke his foot in a training exercise.

Then, as fate would have it, they were both hired as deputies by the Lake County Sheriff's Department. When the sheriff they served under retired, the two adversaries ran for his office, Deidre defeating Ben in a hard-fought election. Ben went so far as to file an unfair labor complaint against her.

Gradually, the ice between them thawed, and five years ago, in a shootout involving terrorists, Ben had saved her life. The result of his quick and assertive actions led to an appointment with the FBI. He and Deidre remained friends, but their paths seldom crossed. They hadn't seen each other for a well over a year.

Deidre remembered the early summer day she had decided to drive to Duluth, take in a play at the local theater, and stay in a lakeside hotel. As she was walking down Superior Street with her head down, her mind was a thousand miles away. Suddenly, she was hit with a jolt as a vary large person struck her, almost knocking her off her feet.

She felt a strong hand grip her shoulder, and she was about to cry out when she looked up and saw the face of the person who had delivered the body check.

"Ben!" she exclaimed, surprised to see someone she knew. "Ben, you almost took me out. I guess we both must have been pretty deep in thought. Geeze, I'm sorry I wasn't watching."

"No. No, it was my fault. I was in a rush and not paying attention. Deidre, you look great. How you doing—I mean are things kind of back to normal for you? Hardly a day goes by that I don't think of you and John. I still remember the look in your eyes the night of his visitation. I honestly didn't think you were going to make it, but it's good to see a sparkle in your eyes again."

"You know, Ben, things are good. I'm happy where I'm at, and the pain's subsided, but I'll always miss him. What can I say?

"How's your family? Okay, I hope." The minute the words left her mouth she knew that wasn't the case.

Ben's face became like a stone mask. "You haven't heard, then? Jenny died a year ago in August."

Deidre's gut knotted, and she couldn't force words from her mouth. Here she had been telling him about her missing John while his wounds were far fresher and more raw. She looked into Ben's eyes and saw nothing but pain.

"Jenny was having some problems earlier in the summer. She was experiencing quite a bit of back pain, but that wasn't unusual for her, just a little more intense. When the pain became too strong, she visited her doctor, who ordered a CT scan. They discovered she had advanced ovarian cancer.

"I did some research and discovered the one-year survival rate for that disease is only seventeen percent, so I prepared for the worst. She died three months later."

Deidre finally found her voice. "Ben, I had no idea. I'm so sorry I wasn't there to comfort you. News doesn't always reach me up there in the woods. How are your girls doing?"

"Okay, I suppose. They have a hard time understanding why they don't have a mother anymore, but we manage. My folks still live in Two Harbors, and they help out as often as they can. The girls are with me most of the time, but I'm afraid I don't quite have a mother's touch."

Deidre toed a crack in the sidewalk. "Tell you what, if you ever want to get away, let me know. I'd enjoy babysitting them."

Ben perked up. "Are you sure you'd like to do that? Because if you're serious, I'll take you up on your offer. Two of my buddies are going camping next weekend in the BWCAW to do some fishing. They invited me to go with, but I said I couldn't get away. If they still have room, I'd really like to get out with them."

And so plans were made. The next weekend Deidre drove back to Duluth and located Ben's home in a comfortable neighborhood off Woodland Avenue. She rang the doorbell and heard the rush of feet running on the other side of the door.

Ben answered. "Come on in, Deidre. We're just about set here."

Deidre spotted two blond heads peeking around the doorway behind their father.

"Come on, girls. You remember Deidre, don't you? She's a friend of mine."

The girls, four-year-old twins, cautiously approached from either side of Ben, each holding onto one of his legs. Deidre knelt down so she was at their level.

"My, you have beautiful hair. Did your daddy make those braids?"

They nodded and looked at the floor.

"Well, he did a really good job. You'll have to show me how he does it. Which one of you is Maren?"

The twin with a red ribbon in her hair smiled and lifted her shoulders as she buried her head behind her father's knee.

"Well, you must be Megan," Deidre said to the other girl whose hair was held back with a blue ribbon.

"Here, I have these for you." Deidre had bought two small dolls before she came, and she took them from the store's bag. "Would you like these to play with?" she asked. "I'll bet you have other dolly things. Would you show me?"

Without saying a word, the twins took her hands and led her to their room where they showed off their other dolls, a cradle, and all of the paraphernalia little girls collect. She sat on the floor. In minutes the girls had warmed to her, forgetting about Ben.

By the time Ben was ready to leave for the weekend, Deidre had made two fast friends. They hardly gave their father a notice when he hugged them and said goodbye.

Deidre couldn't believe how quickly they bonded, and the weekend sped by. She, Maren, and Megan colored with crayons, played games, and went to a nearby kiddy park. But the hit of the time they spent together was when Deidre played a DVD of *The Sound of Music*. She and the girls sang along with the music, mimicking the parts played by the children and pretended they could yodel.

All too soon, as far as Deidre was concerned, Ben returned from his fishing trip. He suggested they go out for pizza before Deidre had to leave. By the time the meal was over, she felt a part of the family.

"Thank you so much," Ben expressed his gratitude. "I needed to get away for a couple of days, and there's nothing more therapeutic for me than getting out in the woods. Thanks again."

The twins hugged her and begged her not to leave, tugging at her heart like nothing had done for a long time.

"Tell you what . . . why don't you have your daddy drive up to my cabin some day soon? We can go swimming, he can fish in the lake while we make him supper, and you and I can spend the day together."

The little girls jumped and clapped their hands. "Can we, Daddy?" they begged. "When can we go to Deidre's?"

Two weeks later Deidre found herself mothering the little ones, and she felt a deep love growing for them. That was the beginning of a summer of healing for all four of them, Deidre, Ben, Maren, and Megan. By autumn they were making a habit of spending at least one day of each weekend together.

Now, as Deidre warmed herself in her police car, she regretted having said she would act as a replacement for the officer while he recovered from shoulder surgery. She didn't want to break her date with Ben and his daughters, but she had no choice. She looked at her watch and stepped back out into the cold.

"My shift," she said to Cliff. He had been standing in the cold for fifteen minutes, Kathy was still trying to warm up after her turn, and Deidre felt the sting of the northwest wind pierce the fabric of her coat and cap. In minutes, her fingers were tingling, and then they became numb.

The rotation continued until nearly one o'clock. Deidre was standing her shift, making sure the crime scene was observed constantly while they waited for the BCA to arrive. She heard the vehicle approach before she saw it and was relieved to see the marked SUV pull to a stop on the other side of the bridge. Deidre met its passengers halfway across the span.

Judy Coster, forensic anthropologist, held out her arms and hugged Deidre while Melissa Sobranski, BCA investigator, put her arm over Deidre's shoulders. It was good to see her friends again.

"We thought you'd hung up your spurs. What made you change your mind?" Judy asked.

Deidre shrugged. "Boredom. A moment of weakness. Who knows? I sure never expected this. I signed on for six weeks to fill in while the regular officer, Dan, recuperated from shoulder surgery, rotator cuff. Then this had to happen."

By that time, Cliff had left his car and joined the three women. Deidre made the introductions and urged, "We better get this over with before dark. That gives us about four hours of daylight.

"I haven't called in Search and Rescue to pick up the body. Didn't want anyone monitoring the call and showing up. The less interference, the easier this is going to go. I'll warn you, it's not pretty down there."

"From what you told me on the phone, I think this is going to be a tough one to handle," Judy said. "Well, lead the way. The sooner we're done, the faster we can get in where it's warm."

The investigators sorted through some items in their SUV, evidence collection bags, a camera, marker flags, and whatever else they figured they'd need. The bank was too steep to climb up and down very many times.

Deidre led the way. When they reached the bottom, Melissa began to take samples from the blood smears. Deidre pointed out the handprint in the snow, and Judy photographed it as Melissa prepared to make a cast of the imprint.

She sprayed it with a special kind of wax to seal the surface, and then poured in a concoction that would set up.

"Let's move ahead and give this time to solidify. We can come back to pick it up."

Deidre shined her light into the dark area under the bridge's bed. "I think we should take our time getting up there and scour the ground for anything of interest. That way we won't walk on any evidence and have to figure out what it was later."

The women made their way shoulder to shoulder, stooped over at the waist, their eyes searching every inch of ground as they slowly moved forward.

"I don't think we're going to find a thing," Melissa opined. "It looks like the victim crawled up there without any help. To me, it looks as though she were pitched over the bridge railing onto the ice and was left for dead. I am guessing after her attackers left, she revived enough to crawl up there." Melissa shined her light in the direction the crawl marks led.

"I agree," said Deidre, "but I think we still have to take every precaution. We can't really know what happened until we reach the body."

And so their progress was slow.

"Oh, the poor thing," Judy exclaimed when they were close enough that their flashlights lit up the body. Melissa let out an expletive.

"I know," Deidre said, shaking her head. "Senseless, isn't it?"

Huddled in the shelter formed by the river bank and the roadbed of the bridge was the frozen body of a young girl curled in the fetal position. She was bluish, and ice crystals hung from her skin. They could see she had moderately long black hair, and her eyes were closed, so they could see her heavy eyelashes. She looked to be about thirteen or fourteen years old, and she was totally naked. It was as though she were sleeping peacefully, except for the ice crystals.

"I'm surprised," Judy said, her face screwed in a grimace. "There's so little blood up here. It doesn't appear that she bled out."

"Well, something killed her. Deidre, why don't you call for transportation to Two Harbors. They don't have a funeral home in Silver Bay, and we'll have to transport the body to where it can be thawed. It'll be a while before we can perform an autopsy. Possibly then we'll have some answers."

Deidre dialed the number of Search and Rescue, and after a brief conversation, she turned to her companions. "We'll have a vehicle arriving in fifteen minutes and bringing some help. In the meantime, let's go up top and see what we can find. Cliff and Kathy will help us, and we can make a pretty thorough search of the area before anyone else arrives."

Before starting up the bank, Melissa collected the cast she had made of the hand imprint. "I'd be surprised if this is anyone's but the victim's," she mumbled to herself as she struggled up the steep slope.

Chapter
Three

THE FIVE OFFICERS, two state troopers, Deidre, and the two BCA members walked side by side across the bridge, their heads bowed, eyes scanning the ground for anything out of context. Their first sweep revealed nothing, so they turned and reversed their direction, this time moving closer to the side of the bridge over which the victim had been hurled.

"Here! I just spotted something metallic when the wind kicked up a flurry of snow," Deidre shouted. She stooped and gently brushed away the powder with her gloved hand, picked up a brass object, and held it so the afternoon light shone on it.

"It's a key," she excitedly announced to the group. "And there are letters stamped onto the top." She turned the key to catch the waning afternoon sun.

"RRR. Do you suppose that stands for some railroad line?" She turned the key over in her hand, and the others came closer so they could get a better view.

"It doesn't look like its been used for quite some time," Cliff offered his opinion.

Melissa contradicted. "Look closer. See those fine scratches in the patina. It's an old key that wasn't used for a long time, but I think someone has recently fit it into a lock, although not often."

Cliff bent so he could look closely at the key. "You know, you're right. It's really tarnished, but up close, there are scratches on the side, and you can see that the teeth are a little shiny. But I don't recognize those letters. Nothing around here would have those initials. The only old railroad was the DM&IR. Reserve Mining had their own line and so did the docks at Taconite Harbor further up the shore. They were built in the '50s, but the initials don't jive. Do you suppose those are someone's initials?"

"Could be," Judy said. "But whatever this is, it's about the only significant clue we have. Why don't you bag it, Deidre, and lock it in your car."

As she was bent over with her head in her patrol car, Lake County Search and Rescue pulled up, and her friend Scott got out.

"Hi, Deidre. Thought you'd decided to retire."

"So did I. Just filling in until their officer recovers from rotator-cuff surgery. You probably know him. Dan Butler?"

"Oh, sure. Dan. I know him well. He's a good man," Scott added. "So now you've got yourself up to your neck in another tough one. What's the story? I don't see anything." He looked around to see what he missed.

"Under the bridge, but I'm warning you, it isn't pretty. Be prepared."

Scott and two other members of the rescue squad followed Deidre down the bank, with Judy and Melissa close behind. The six of them gathered under the bridge, and Deidre shined her flashlight under the abutment.

"She's up there, but I don't think it's going to be easy. She's curled in a ball, and frozen solid. Maybe the best way is for two of you to lift her and the third keep her from rolling down the bank into the river. You might as well leave the stretcher here. It'll only get in the way. You'll see what I mean when you get up there."

The men nodded.

"Go ahead of me. I'll hold the light so you can see."

The three Search and Rescue members began the climb with Deidre behind as she had said.

"Oh, shit!" Scott muttered. Deidre couldn't make out what the other two said. "What's wrong with people? She's just a little girl, probably as old as my seventh-grade daughter." Then he stood looking, shaking his head. Finally he came out of his trance.

"Okay, guys, let's get this over with."

Together, the three burly men approached the body. They bent down to pick her up, one on each side and one on the down side of the bank. As they made their way down the steep grade and maneuvered past Deidre, she was stopped by the sight of tears freely flowing down their cheeks.

In the direct light of day, Deidre could see that the girl's body was covered with bruises and scratches. Her back looked as though she had been flogged, and on the side of her face that was visible, Deidre saw a large welt under her eye. Everything was silent, the very sound of their footsteps muffled by the loose snow.

They gently laid the girl's body on the stretcher and tried to devise a plan so she wouldn't roll off while it was raised to the roadway. While they were strategically placing straps around her, Melissa and Judy climbed to where the body had lain. Deidre could see them on their hands and knees, trying to find the smallest clue.

By the time they finished, the Search and Rescue crew had worked their way to the top and had placed the stretcher into the back of their truck, which was equipped to serve as an ambulance.

"Wait a second," Judy panted as she came up the river bank. She bent over for a second to catch her breath. "Is there any way to keep the back of the vehicle cold so the body won't thaw? I'd like to be present while the process takes place."

Scott looked at the others and shrugged. "Sure, we can do that. Bundle up boys. It's going to be a cold ride to Two Harbors."

Deidre and Melissa watched as they pulled away from the scene with windows rolled down and the heat turned off. Judy was riding in the back, bundled against the cold, her hands thrust deep inside the pockets of her parka.

"I think you can go now," Deidre said to the highway patrol troopers. "Thanks so much for your help. I'm not sure how you do it, patrolling these lonely stretches of highway by yourselves. I'd be worried every time I made a stop that the driver was going to turn out to be somebody dangerous."

"The nature of the beast." Kathy shrugged in resignation.

They said goodbye and wished Deidre luck with the investigation that they knew was not going to be simple. She looked at Melissa. "If you don't have a place to stay, why don't you come to my place for the night? I'm alone—except for my dog, and he doesn't bite. We can get up early and head into Two Harbors in the morning and find out how Judy's faring."

Melissa called Judy on her phone to see if she needed help, and Judy assured her that nothing exciting was going to happen while the body thawed. She was going to stay at the mortuary that also served as the county morgue to keep an eye on the process, but she'd see them in the morning.

"Let's stop and get something hot before we leave town. I'm about frozen to the core and could use some caffeine," Melissa said as she involuntarily shivered. "Do you have any good coffee shops in town?"

Deidre laughed as they walked toward their vehicles. "If you look on the Internet for eating places in Silver Bay, you'll find only one listed, Northwoods Cafe. The info says its a local coffee klatch hangout. We've missed their daily breakfast and lunch specials. When we get there I'll fill you in on the town's history."

In five minutes they were at the shopping center, the only one in Silver Bay. As they entered the warm confines of the small shop, several patrons turned their heads to look at the two women coming in from the cold.

George was there and appeared to be holding court at one of the tables, because all eyes were glued to him. When he looked up and saw Deidre, his eyes widened, and he stopped in mid-sentence.

"Deidre. Good to see you're finished with whatever you were doing." His face flushed, and he averted meeting her gaze. "Well, boys, I better be getting home. My wife'll be wondering where I've been. I'm usually home by noon. See ya, guys. Deidre." George nodded to her as he pulled a stocking cap low over his ears.

Deidre and Melissa chose a table in the far corner of the room, as far away from the rest of the customers as they could, although every time they looked up, they could see the patrons looking at them as if seeking clues about a mystery.

Deidre gave Melissa a brief history lesson of Silver Bay, how it hadn't even existed before 1954, how it was built by Reserve Mining for its workers, and how the company had dictated who could live where and what businesses could exist. She went on to explain how the community had boomed, reaching a peak population of nearly four thousand in 1960, almost all of them young families with children.

"I remember when their school was bigger than the one in Two Harbors, graduating two hundred per class." Deidre explained. "Then disaster hit when the company was charged with violating the River and Harbors Act of 1899. That's the oldest piece of federal environmental legislation on record in the U.S. It makes it illegal to dump waste of any kind into navigable water without a permit. I guess they didn't have the proper permits or something."

They ordered when the waitress came by before Deidre continued. "Anyway, a few years later the taconite plant closed, and residents were forced to seek employment elsewhere. It did reopen under different management, but the workforce really dropped. Our population is pretty stable at around eighteen hundred. Now too many of the residents are past childbearing age, so the school's taken a big hit. I think they have about thirty-five students per grade. It's sad."

Melissa asked, "So that's why you agreed to fill in while Officer Butler's out? This is kind of a sleepy community, out of the way, and you thought not much could go wrong?"

Deidre smirked. "Yeah, that's why. Guess I was wrong, huh?"

They had each drunk two cups of coffee and were warmed up. "Let's go," Deidre suggested, and she and Melissa walked out the door, feeling the glances cast their way as they left.

*****

As Deidre followed the driveway to her cabin, Melissa scrunched down in the seat so she could see the tops of the massive pine trees. The private road to Deidre's place traced a serpentine path through the woods, following the route of least resistance. Bumping over the rutted, dirt road for a half mile, Deidre pulled up next to her rustic home.

"Look at that view," Melissa exclaimed as she stepped out of the car and looked across Cedar Lake. It was partly frozen, and what ice had formed was covered with snow. Its pure whiteness intensified the lake's blue-black in the evening sunset.

"This is perfect," she said in awe of the setting.

Just then Deidre's dog came bounding around the corner of the building, and Melissa stooped to ruffle his ears. "And I see you even have a roommate," she said as she lavished attention upon him. "What's his name?"

"That's Pete. I named him after a friend of mine who lives even further in the sticks than I do." She laughed, obviously happy to witness Melissa's approval of her living conditions.

The two women entered the cabin with Pete leading the way. He headed straight for his dog dish and immediately set to crunching dry dog food, his tail wagging in delight that his master had returned home.

Their breath hung in clouds of condensed vapor, and Melissa shivered. "Don't you have a furnace?" she wondered.

"Oh, I've a small propane heater, but I don't use it unless I have to. I'll have a fire going in the woodstove in two minutes. It'll heat up quickly. I'd leave my jacket on until then if I were you."

Deidre balled up a few sheets of newspaper and crammed them into the stove before stacking a few pieces of kindling on top. She struck a match and lit the paper, which burst into flame. After adding a few sticks of split maple, she closed the door, and the stove came to life. Soon the red enamel of the Vermont Casting heater turned a deep burgundy as it became hot, and Deidre shed her coat.

"Why don't you hang your jacket over here. In a few minutes, it will be so warm you'll even want to shed your heavy sweater."

Melissa looked at the logs that formed the walls of the structure, then looked overhead at the beams supporting the roof. "This is like something out of a Terry Redland painting. I can't believe it. I could stay here forever."

Deidre busied herself, deciding what to fix for supper. "It's beautiful, but I tell you, it gets old after a while, lonely." She looked at Pete who turned his head to stare at her. "Sorry, Pete, but sometimes you just don't fill the bill."

Pete wagged his tail and came over to rub his head against Deidre's leg. She reached down and patted his neck.

"Well, enough of that. What would you like for supper? How does tube steak and sauerkraut sound?" She held up a ring of kielbasa sausage.

"Sounds good to me," Melissa answered. "Especially if you have some wine to go with it."

"That I have." Deidre reached under the counter and came up with an unopened bottle of chardonnay. "This is a good one, my favorite."

By the time the sausage and kraut were heated, the cabin was almost too warm inside and Deidre opened the kitchen window a couple of inches. It had become dark, and a full moon had risen over the lake. In the distance a pack of timber wolves began their serenade. Melissa felt the hair stand up on the back of her neck.

"No need to worry," Deidre reassured her. "They won't come near humans. They're too smart to have anything to do with our species." She halfway meant what she said.

After supper, the two friends sat on cushions in front of the glass doors of the stove. They were mesmerized by the yellow and blue flames of the burning maple, and Pete lay with his head resting on his paws. Every so often he would twitch in his sleep, then look up, trying to orient himself.

"So, how are you doing, Deidre?" Melissa asked, concern in her voice.

"Okay, I think, at least until this happened. I vowed I'd never put on another badge again."

Melissa swirled the wine in her goblet. "That wasn't exactly what I was talking about," she pressured. "I mean, how are you coping since John's death? How are you surviving?"

Deidre watched the fire, and tears formed in her eyes. She shrugged. "I'm doing about as well as I can, I think. Most days I look forward to getting up in the morning, and I really am happy living up here. Do you remember Ben VanGotten?"

"Of course. He was the FBI agent who was a high school classmate of yours. What about him?"

Deidre cleared her throat. "Ben's wife died a little over a year ago. She was such a lovely woman and a terrific mother. Did you know that she and Ben had twin girls? They're four years old. Anyway, Ben told me that she was diagnosed with stage four ovarian cancer and died only months later."

Melissa broke in, "What does this have to do with how you are holding up?" She calculated that Deidre was trying to change the subject.

"I volunteered to baby sit the girls if Ben wanted to get away sometime, and he took me up on my offer. He went camping for a weekend, and I watched the little ones. I guess I fell in love with them the first day. Now, Ben and I try to get out and do something with them every Saturday. We take in a movie or sometimes go to a museum. They treat me almost as if I'm their mother."

Deidre paused to let the emotion subside. Then she continued. "Ben brought them up here a few times. We went fishing. A couple of times they've stayed overnight, and we built a bonfire and toasted marshmallows. They're so much fun, it's hard for me to leave them."

"And what about Ben?" Melissa looked at Deidre expectantly.

"What about him?" She answered a little too quickly. "Oh, wait a minute. It's not what you think. We're just good friends, and his daughters need a female around to balance being with Ben all the time." She blushed and got up to pour another glass of wine.

"If you say so," Melissa said with a laugh, which made Deidre blush all the more. "On a work-related note, are you all alone in this job?"

Deidre was glad the subject had changed. "There's a part-time officer on weekends. He's quite a guy. Jerry looks like everyone's grandfather with his gray hair and moustache. But he's surprised more than one suspect. He's retired from the Minneapolis Police Force where he was lead detective with the drug unit. One time a young man tried to take a swing at him. Jerry had him on the ground and handcuffed in less than ten seconds. Other than that, though, a town the size of Silver Bay can't afford to have round-the-clock service, so you might say I pretty much work alone."

Melissa looked at her with concern. "How much longer before Dan Butler returns to duty?"

"The end of next week. Then I can take my bows and turn the case over to him. I only wish he'd been able to come back to work before this happened. I didn't need this."

Melissa knew she was pushing it a little when she asked, "What if the case is still active? Do you think you can walk away from it?"

"Just watch me," Deidre answered emphatically, then downed the last swallow of chardonnay.

Melissa smiled. "Then you can spend more time with Ben and his daughters."

"Exactly," Deidre shot back and then caught herself. Again her face turned red, and she got up, poked at the glowing embers in the stove and added two sticks of split firewood.

Melissa laughed, enjoying Deidre's discomfort. "Well, I'm glad you two are just friends."

Deidre sat back down on the floor cushion. Pete came over, his tail wagging, and laid his head in her lap. She scratched behind his ears, and the lab closed his eyes in satisfaction. Soon he was wheezing as he slept.

"We're good friends, and I don't think it'll ever be any different. He loved his wife deeply, and I loved John the same way. Right now, I think we're two injured people who need each other's company."

Melissa stared at the logs that had burst into flame and said nothing. The two women sat for a half hour in silence, Deidre petting Pete's head and Melissa savoring the last of her wine.

Finally Deidre announced, "I think we better turn in. Judy expects us in Two Harbors by nine o'clock, which means we have to get up at six-thirty. I'll get you a down comforter. I warn you, though, it'll be cold in here by morning. The fire will have gone out, and I'm not getting up to stoke it in the middle of the night. We can build a fire to take the chill out of the air before breakfast, which by the way will be pretty simple: oatmeal, toast, and coffee."

Deidre helped Melissa make up her bed and both of them retired for the night.

She thought she would fall asleep immediately after a difficult day and all the wine she'd consumed, but she was mistaken. Every time she closed her eyes she saw the pathetic figure of the body they had removed, and she tossed and turned. Once, she lifted her head and looked at the red numbers on the face of her digital bedside clock. One o'clock, and Deidre did the math: only five and a half hours until the alarm would go off.

When it seemed she had just fallen asleep, she heard the buzz of her clock, soft at first but gradually increasing in volume until she couldn't stand it anymore. She reached over and shut it off, her eyes still closed, and swung her legs over the side of the bed. The cold floor jolted her, and she opened her eyes. Pete came into the room, looking at her with an urgency that said he had to go out. A cold blast of air hit her in the face when she opened the door, and she became fully awake.

Deidre's head ached, from lack of sleep she thought. Certainly it wasn't from the wine she had consumed the night before. She started a fire in the stove. By the time she had the coffee pot on the kitchen range, she could feel the heat beginning to radiate into the cabin.

She heard Melissa's feet make contact with the floor. "My God, is it always this cold in the morning?"

Deidre laughed. "No, sometimes it's a lot colder. Let's fix breakfast and eat before we clean up. By then the cabin will be warm, and we'll be able wash, brush, and flush in comfort."

Melissa didn't object.

Chapter
Four

NEITHER WOMAN SAID A WORD as they traveled down Highway 2 toward Two Harbors, each absorbed in her own thoughts. Finally, Melissa spoke. "What do you think Judy is going to find when she examines the body?"

"I can only guess," Deidre answered, shrugging. "My thought is the girl was at a party and had too much to drink, or got into some bad drugs and ended up dead. At least that's what her friends may have thought. They panicked and dumped her body so they wouldn't be implicated.

"I suppose she might have been violated by male party goers while she was passed out. Because she was frozen in a fetal position, it was difficult to determine the full extent of her injuries. Some of the bruises we saw might have been the result of her being thrown into a car and then off the bridge.

"But, there are so many other possibilities. I don't know. We do have that key we found. If we can figure out what RRR stands for, it'll make our job a heck of lot easier."

"I have a bad feeling about this one," Melissa said, rubbing her temples. She had gotten no more sleep than Deidre. "I don't know what it is, but I can't buy into the idea that this is the result of a party gone bad. I wish I could tell you why, but I don't know. We're trained to follow the evidence and not go with our gut feelings, but right now, my guts are telling me a lot."

"Like what?"

"Why wouldn't her friends help her?"

Deidre was silent for over a minute. "I have a friend who's an EMT. He told me one time he and his partner were called to a party where someone had fallen off a balcony. When they got there, the party was still going strong, and everyone was pretty wasted. The young man who had fallen was lying on the ground, and no one was paying any attention to him. They were too busy partying to care about him. All my friend and his partner could do was load him in the ambulance and take him into the hospital. Not one of the partiers even asked how he was doing. He said when you're at one of those bashes, you have no friends. I still think we're looking at the consequences of an underage party."

"Yes, but in your friend's case, somebody at the party took the time to call 911 or else the EMTs would never have been alerted. Right?"

Deidre had to agree.

"So if this isn't the result of a pit party gone bad, what is it? There isn't much else that goes on in this neck of the woods that would end up with a young girl naked and dead."

They passed a roadside sign that read TWO HARBORS, POP. 3,750, and Deidre said, "Well, we'll know more in a few minutes after we've talked to Judy. I wonder if that poor girl's body has thawed yet."

Melissa, so deeply in thought that she really hadn't heard Deidre's comment, didn't answer. They pulled up behind the funeral home and walked up the steps in silence. Deidre pushed a button that rang a buzzer inside the building, and a solemn-faced funeral assistant opened the door.

"Hi, Deidre. Dr. Coster said you'd be getting here about now. She's downstairs, still sitting by the cooler where we hold bodies before embalming. I think she only slept in spurts last night and could probably use a fresh cup of coffee. There's some in my office if you want to take a cup to her."

Deidre thanked him and filled a mug with the steaming brew. Then she and Melissa descended the stairway to the lower level where bodies were delivered into an underground garage and receiving area.

Judy was seated on a stool, looking haggard and emotionally exhausted.

"You look worse than a mouse that's been toyed with by a cat," Melissa remarked as Judy looked up. "Didn't you sleep at all last night?"

"Not much, only a few short naps in between examinations. Because it wasn't frozen to the core, the body is almost completely thawed. I somewhat expected that, because it hadn't lain in the cold for more than several hours before being found."

Deidre looked at her disheveled friend with concern. "Here, we brought you a cup of fresh coffee. Take a minute to drink it before we get into the nitty-gritty of what you've found."

Judy sipped the hot brew and closed her eyes. She held the cup in both hands and inhaled the aroma, then took another sip.

"Why don't the two of you sit down. I'm afraid you're not going to like what I have to tell you. This is more than a teenager who got herself into a bad situation."

Deidre and Melissa pulled up chairs and sat so the three were looking at each other. Judy took a long swig of the coffee before continuing.

"I'm certain that the victim was tortured before she was thrown off the bridge. Evidently those who assaulted her thought she was dead and had no fear that she would live to ID them." She took another gulp of coffee and sighed.

The others waited for her to say more, but after a few seconds, they realized she was struggling to talk.

Tears formed in Judy's eyes, and she cleared her throat. "There is a strange mark on one of her ankles. The skin has been rubbed raw, rubbed off, really. There are less grievous abrasions on her wrists. She has several lacerations on her extremities that could have been made by being beaten with a thin rod of some kind, some of them fresh, some of them partially healed."

She took one last swig of coffee, emptying the cup. Deidre and Melissa sat in stunned silence as Judy continued. "She has bruises over most of her body, and her breasts appear to have been pinched by some sort of implement, especially her nipples." Judy stopped and took a deep breath, unable to continue.

"Do you have any idea what caused the mark on her ankle?" Deidre asked in a subdued voice.

"Only one thing. She was forced to wear a shackle for an extended period of time. The marks on her wrists were from some kind of restraint, possibly plastic ties, that were recently placed there. I have no doubt this girl, this child really, was held captive by being chained up. If I could get my hands on whoever did this, I'd gouge his heart out, if I could even find one."

She stared at the floor, and the others waited, not knowing what to say. Judy continued.

"On top of it all, the signs are pretty conclusive she was strangled. There are marks around her throat consistent with the grip of someone much larger than she. The whites of her eyes were marked with numerous petechiae. They are areas of bleeding caused when small blood vessels rupture, a common sign of asphyxiation, or in this case strangulation. I can't imagine what this pathetic waif suffered at the hands of an incredibly cruel person—or persons."

"Have you finished your examination of her body?" Deidre asked, her voice quiet as though she were in church.

"No," Judy answered. "But that was what I found as of two hours ago. I'm guessing I can finish now." She reached for the handle of the cooler in which the body was stored.

Melissa had sat silently, her eyes closed and head bowed, while Judy described her findings. She opened her eyes and looked up. "Was she sexually assaulted?"

Judy paused before opening the door. "I couldn't tell for sure. The body needed a little more time to thaw so I could examine her genitals, but I think we can proceed now. I'm quite certain what we are going to discover, though."

She opened the door and pulled a sheet-draped gurney from the cubical. The three stood motionless, not wanting to remove the cover but knowing they must. Judy gently folded the sheet down to the dead girl's waist, then folded the bottom up, and lifted the cover off. They looked at the naked body in horror.

Yesterday, they had seen it curled in a fetal position, and they knew the sight wasn't going to be pretty, but neither Melissa nor Deidre were prepared for the small, broken body lying on the table before them.

For what seemed a very long time, they stared at the pubescent body. The girl was young enough that her breasts appeared to not be fully developed and her nipples were still forming. Deidre surmised her age to be only about thirteen or fourteen, perhaps only twelve, because her pubic area was so sparsely covered with fine black hair.

"What kind of animal did this?" Melissa mumbled, not expecting an answer.

Deidre shook her head.

Judy gently separated the legs of the corpse, and moved so she could have a better view. She turned on a small tape recorder, and began speaking. "The subject has severe bruising on the inside of the thighs." Deidre assumed she had already recorded what had been discovered on the rest of the body. "I am now spreading the *labia majora.* There appears to be bruising consistent with being roughly manipulated. Several tears are evident in the tissue, and the *labia minora* are similarly traumatized."

She turned off the tape recorder and reached for her camera. After taking several close up photos, Judy turned to Melissa and Deidre. "There's no doubt this girl was sexually active. From the bruising, I'm almost positive it wasn't consensual. That really doesn't make much difference, because at her age it would still be considered rape."

Melissa and Deidre were too stunned by what they were witnessing to say anything. Judy turned on her tape recorder and began again. "I'm inserting a speculum into the vagina of the corpse and proceeding with an internal inspection. The vaginal walls are badly bruised. A three centimeter hematoma is visible on the posterior vaginal wall consistent with blunt force trauma from a foreign object. The cervix is badly bruised, showing lacerations around its circumference."

She turned off the recorder, and took several vaginal swaps with what appeared to Deidre to be oversized Q-tips. Using a camera designed to take internal pictures, Judy snapped several shots of what she had observed, removed her tools of examination and stepped back from the table as she removed her gloves.

"There's no doubt in my mind but that this girl was sexually tortured, then strangled, and her apparently lifeless body thrown from the bridge onto the ice. She must have revived enough to crawl up under the abutment where she died and subsequently became partially frozen. Judging by the time you found her, Deidre, and by the partially frozen condition, she died about four o'clock yesterday morning. I'll do more research concerning the temperature night before last, but that is my guess right now. Do you have any questions or observations? Otherwise, I'll put her back into the cooler."

Deidre had enough sense about her to ask, "Have you taken fingerprints? And how about DNA samples?"

"The prints are over there." She motioned toward the counter. "Her blood samples are in vials in the refrig. The swabs I just took are in case the perpetrator left some of his semen in her. There were no samples of skin under her nails. I was hoping she'd put up a fight and scratched whoever did this, but it appears she was so overpowered that she had no chance."

After a moment, Judy said, "This is one case I want to see solved. Someone has to pay for this atrocity." She took a moment to compose herself before continuing. "Preliminarily, I think she may be a little older than what she looks, but only by two or three years. Her third molars, what are commonly called wisdom teeth, haven't begun to erupt, but her second molars are completely emerged. That usually occurs when a child is between twelve and thirteen years of age. In this case, there is some evidence, chips and signs of wear that would indicate to me she may be fifteen or sixteen. I'll know better when I can do a more thorough exam in my lab."

"Is there anything else you can tell us?" Deidre questioned, pain evident by her facial expression.

"It's far too soon to tell, but just between the three of us, I believe this girl is Native American. She has the characteristic high cheek bones and other facial bone structures. Also, and it's difficult to tell because of her bruising and having been frozen, but her skin has the coloring of that ethnic group. When we do the blood work, we can tell a little more. If she is type O, that would support my theory but not prove it. Eighty percent of indigenous people have that type. A significant number, fifteen percent, are type A. That is also a factor to consider. But only four percent are type B, and less than one percent are type AB. If she turns out to be either of those, odds are she is not Native American."

Deidre mulled the figures for a second. "Well, that would be a starting point, I suppose."

Melissa had been strangely silent through the entire examination of the body, and all she did was nod. Judy respectfully replaced the drape over the body and wheeled it back into the cooler.

None of the women wanted to go to lunch, their appetite killed by what they had just witnessed. It was as though their senses were numbed.

"Is there anywhere we can meet and discuss what we've just seen, where we can lay out a plan of attack? I think we all need to talk about this and get it out of our system. I'm talking about a plan of action, but also about the fact that we need a catharsis," Judy stated. Her posture showed how emotionally drained she was. "Deidre, is there an place where we can be alone, where we can talk openly and let out our feelings in private?"

Deidre was flummoxed by the question. She thought, *We need a place where we can't be overheard, and where we won't be interrupted. But we need somewhere that's comfortable, where we can feel at ease about sharing our feelings.* She remembered a case four years earlier when she had visited with a pastor in town. She had met with him and his wife in his study. "I think I know where we want to be," she said as she reached for her cell phone and punched in a number. She listened to it ring until a man answered.

"Hello. This is Reverend Jackson speaking. Can I help you?"

"Pastor, this is Deidre Johnson. How are you?"

"Deidre, I was just thinking of calling you. You know Naomi is in her third year at the U. She e-mailed me this morning with the news that she has been selected by Hazelden, the rehab clinic in the Cities, to do her internship during spring semester. She wanted me to tell you. She had lost your cell phone number."

The pastor's daughter, Naomi, was instrumental in Deidre's being able to break up a drug ring operating out of the Superior National Forest. While in high school, she had fallen into the life style of a user, and Deidre had helped her set her life back on the right track. Now, she was attending the University of Minnesota, majoring in psychology and social work with an emphasis on drug counseling.

"Great news, Pastor. I'm so happy for you and Mrs. Jackson. You have every right to be proud of her. But, Pastor, I need a favor. Two friends and I need a quiet place where we can have a very private meeting, someplace comfortable. Your office immediately came to mind. Is there any chance we can use it for a couple of hours this afternoon?"

Reverend Jackson's answer was immediate. "No problem. I'm making hospital visits in an hour, and my wife's volunteering at the nursing home. Come over right away so we can visit a few minutes. It's been a while since we've seen each other. You can have the run of our home. No need to cram into my office. Use the living room."

Deidre remembered how comfortable and inviting their home was. "Perfect. See you in about fifteen minutes."

Chapter
Five

THE JACKSON'S HOME HAD a feeling of order and well being. After what the women had just observed, they needed a place where they could find a modicum of peace.

Pastor Jackson hugged Deidre, who introduced him to Melissa and Judy, but after a few minutes of small talk, he had to leave to make his rounds. In the living room, they found a pot of hot coffee and a plate of cheese, crackers, and other snacks waiting for them. Deidre thought how lucky Naomi was to have parents who were so terrific.

Her mind returned to the day she had brought their daughter, Naomi, home after catching her using cocaine. She remembered how supportive her parents had been. She also remembered the boy they had caught with Naomi that day, Gerald Colter III, and how violently his father had reacted. She wondered what had happened to that young man.

The three of them plopped down into the living room chairs, each with a cup of coffee in their hands. Judy spoke first. "Deidre, you said you're serving in a temporary position as a Silver Bay police officer. How long before the person you are replacing returns?"

"A week from today. Then I'm through. He's a good man, and I'm confident he'll do a good job. Why do you ask?"

"Just wondering," Judy answered, still deep in thought about the body she had so recently examined.

"Even though I'm not going to be on this case much longer, I'd like you to help me set up a plan of action. I wasn't prepared for anything this severe when I agreed to fill in for six weeks," Deidre said.

"But before we begin with that, I think we should process our own feelings. I know I for one am so deeply upset with what we've seen I can hardly think of anything else. I'm angry, enraged that anyone could be so cruel. It brings back feelings for the need for revenge I experienced when John was murdered, and I don't like it. Do you have the same thoughts, or am I the only one?"

Judy cleared her throat, and Deidre and Melissa waited for her to say something. Seconds slowly ticked by, and finally she was able to speak. "Last night, as I watched her frozen body relax and I could see the extent of her injuries, I wept. No one should ever experience what she went through. And, yes, I thought of doing the most despicable things to the person or persons who did this. Then, while I was waiting for more thawing and while I had a chance to process, I realized that an eye for an eye would accomplish nothing. In fact it would reduce me to the level of the perpetrators. I came to the revelation that the only way to rise above his or their level is to seek justice. The revenge will come at their own hands."

After another long pause, Judy continued. "When we catch the parties involved, and we will, they'll be prosecuted, and their freedom will be taken from them. Death of any kind would be too swift and complete. I think that to rot in prison for the rest of their lives would be a far more fitting punishment than even a slow death. That thought makes me more intent on doing a thorough job and catching whoever could possibly be this animalistic. That isn't the right word. Even animals behave better than this."

The three women sat silently staring at the floor, studying the carpet pattern. After a minute or so had passed, Deidre raised her head. "Melissa, you haven't said a word since viewing the body. Your posture tells me there's a lot going on in your mind. Can we help with anything?"

Tears rolled down Melissa's cheeks, and she dabbed at her eyes with a tissue. She tried to talk, but choked on her words. Deidre and

Judy watched her swallow hard and clear her throat. "I'm not sure I can get the words out," she struggled to say. "I have a daughter, Jessica, who's fifteen years old."

The two other women thought they knew what was coming next, but they were completely floored by Melissa's next words.

"She always was a difficult child to deal with, especially after I divorced her father. It was not an amicable settlement, and I was awarded full custody of Jessica. Her father had visitation rights, but we never saw him after the decree. That hurt her more than I can possible imagine. As she became older, she was almost uncontrollable. Her mood swings became so erratic I took her to a child psychologist, but she balked at that idea every step of the way and, in the end, refused to cooperate.

"When she was eleven she ran away from home, and it took me four days to locate her. She was staying at a friend's house in one of the suburbs. Her friend's sixteen-year-old sister had been left in charge while their parents were on vacation.

"Six months later, we had words when she refused to see her therapist, and she ran away again. That time it took us a week to track her down. Once again she had moved in with a friend whose parents had little interest in what was going on in their child's life."

Melissa blew her nose, and tried to continue. Deidre sensed that there was more to the story.

"Over the next two years, Jessica's behavior became a pattern of running away, followed by bouts of contrition and then depression. Still, she resisted treatment of any kind. Her psychologist recommended we take her to a psychiatrist so we could get a handle on her depression, but she refused to cooperate. Said she wasn't nuts.

"Two years ago, when she was thirteen, she ran away for a final time. As hard as we have tried, we haven't been able to find her. Every time I think of her, I have this image in my mind of her being on the streets alone and, inside, I die."

Melissa's face cracked into a contorted grimace somewhere between a failed attempt to choke back her tears and the desire to openly weep.

Stunned, Deidre and Judy stared at her. Then Deidre got out of her chair, knelt beside her friend and colleague, and placed her hand on Melissa's knee. Looking into her red-rimmed eyes, Deidre said, "I can't imagine the pain this has caused you, but you still have hope. We're here for you when you need us, always remember that."

"Thanks. I know you are. I appreciate your kindness, but this case is really disturbing me, more than can possibly be imagined. I'm afraid I'll have a difficult time retaining any sense of objectivity."

After several minutes of silent contemplation, Melissa stood.

"Excuse me a few minutes. There's something I've decided to do." She walked out of the room, and Deidre and Judy were left to discuss how they could help their friend, who they thought had gone to the bathroom to splash cold water on her face. Time dragged, and Melissa was gone almost twenty minutes. She was more in charge of her emotions when she returned to them.

"I've just gotten off the phone with the director of the BCA, my immediate boss. I told her what we've discovered and also told her about my dilemma, my feelings. I told her I was struggling with this case."

"Did she have any suggestions?" Deidre wanted to know.

"At first she just listened to my story. Then we talked about what can be done. I told her you'd be finished with your assignment as of next week, Deidre, and I suggested you be hired by the BCA. It'd be on an as-needed basis, specifically to continue investigating what we have found. I explained your role in the seven-graves case and gave you my highest recommendation."

Deidre was shocked. "I don't know what to say. Maybe I should ask what her reaction was."

"She remembered you from when you, Judy, and I worked together." Melissa sort of laughed. "She remembered that you were the one who gave most of the interviews from the burial sites in the woods. In fact, she asked if you were the one who looked so 'earthy'?"

In spite of the gravity of the situation, Deidre had to smile at that comment. "I know I said I could leave the case," she told her friends, "but after seeing what we saw today, there is no way I can walk away from this horrendous murder. I wouldn't be able to sleep at night, wondering what was happening. Okay, I'm in."

"I think this is for the best. You know this area better than anyone from the Cities. You know the people, and you're very good at what you do. Thanks for being willing to continue. The BCA will notify the county sheriff what your role will be. Do you think he'll be all right with us taking most of the responsibility on this one? Do you know him?"

"We're very close friends. You know him, too. Remember Jeff, Jeff DeAngelo, my deputy who was on the dig with us when we unearthed those seven graves. He was talked into running for sheriff after I resigned and won hands down. I can't think of anyone I'd rather have by my side than Jeff. He'll be fine with the idea of my working the case, I know he will."

Judy spoke up. "I have a little more work to do: collecting samples, taking a few more photos, and giving the body one more examination for anything I may have missed. I've arranged for transport to my lab at the Bureau where I can do a more thorough job. Deidre, I'll have the report to you first thing next week, although the tox screen will take a little longer. For now, why don't you and Melissa spend some time together while I finish up. It's a long ride back to Minneapolis, but if we can get out of Two Harbors by five o'clock, we can make it home by eight-thirty or nine tonight."

With that, Deidre and Melissa decided to go to a local restaurant, Blackwood's Bar and Grill. The place had spacious booths that afforded privacy. They could drink coffee and talk while Judy went about her grizzly business.

Chapter
Six

DEIDRE LAY ON THE FLOOR, her back propped against three large cushions. The cabin was cozy, and a fire in the wood-burning stove shone through its glass windows. Her dog, Pete, was curled up, just near enough so she could scratch his ears. Whenever she stopped, he would raise his head and thrust his nose under her hand, forcing her to resume stroking him.

Deidre was so absorbed in her thoughts she was nearly oblivious to her pet's presence. She had bitten off a huge chunk of responsibility this afternoon. She knew that, but she also knew she would never have been able to walk away from the murder she had discovered the day before.

"Well, old boy, here we go again," she mused to Pete. His reaction was to roll his eyes upward and look lovingly at her. "What's it like living in a world where you get fed every day, get to sleep anytime you want, and don't have a care in the world, or if you do, you don't seem to remember?" Pete reacted by rolling on his back so she could scratch under his front legs.

Deidre looked at the clock on the mantle behind the stove. Seven o'clock. Ben would be home. She punched in his number on her cell phone. She was relieved to hear his voice.

"Hi, Deidre. When I didn't hear from you today, I thought you must really be slammed at work. How's it going?"

"Too long of a story to talk about on the phone, but I've got an awful lot to tell you. Any chance we can get together tomorrow? I miss the girls, and I'd like to bounce some thoughts off you, if you don't mind being my sounding board."

She could hear Ben reprimand one of his daughters, and she smiled at the image in her mind. "Sorry about that. What do you have in mind? My place or yours?"

"How about yours. I'd like to get out of the woods for a day or two. Maybe it'll give me some perspective, give my mind a chance to clear itself. Tomorrow's Friday. I have a few things to clear up in the morning, but I can be in Duluth by about five. That okay?"

"That's great. Can't wait to see you, and neither can the twins. They've been standing here the whole time, and you can probably hear their ruckus right now."

Deidre hung up the phone and let pleasant thoughts of Ben and his twin daughters wash over her tired mind. Tomorrow would be a better day.

*****

SHE WOKE AT SIX the next morning, not well rested after having gone through a series of nightmares. After eating a hurried breakfast of yogurt sprinkled with granola and a steaming cup of coffee, she kenneled Pete in the back of her SUV and drove to work.

In five days, Dan Butler, would be back on duty, and Deidre would be working for the BCA. By that time Dr. Coster would have her report ready, and she would have a better idea where to begin. Until then, Deidre was going to catch up on some minor paperwork and prepare the office for Dan's return. He probably would be relieved to learn that the BCA wanted to handle the case and that Deidre would be the one working the investigation. She made arrangements for the part-time officer to spell her later in the day. By noon, Deidre was ready to make the trip to Duluth, and she eagerly anticipated spending time with Ben and the twins.

On the way through Two Harbors, she drove toward the courthouse, a majestic old building with a towering silvered dome that stood like a beacon in the center of town. Next to it was the law enforcement center, and Deidre parked in front of it, walked up the stairs as she had done so many times when she was sheriff, and stopped at the security window. Jaredine, the dispatcher on duty, buzzed her into the outer office of the sheriff's department.

"Deidre, great to see you," Sheriff DeAngelo exclaimed as he jumped up from his chair. "Man, it's been way too long. How you doin'?"

"Things were going great until day before yesterday. That's what I want to talk to you about, Jeff. Any chance we can visit in your office? This is kind of a touchy subject right now."

"Hey, sure, no problem. Grab a cup of coffee, and come in." He led the way, holding the door for his former boss. "I think I know why you're here, Deidre. We heard something real bad's happened in Silver Bay. Have a seat, and tell me what's going on."

Deidre sat down and took a sip of hot coffee before she began.

"We had an ugly murder three days ago. I suppose all murders are ugly, but this one is way past ugly. A teenage girl is involved, and all I can say is you're lucky you didn't have to see it. That's why I'm here. You remember Judy, Dr. Coster, who helped us with the seven-graves case. I called her and Melissa in on this one. Judy's finished her exam, and the body's been shipped to the BCA building in Minneapolis. We couldn't ID the body from the evidence we had."

Jeff interrupted. "Of course I remember them. Now there are two competent persons. You three made quite a team."

Deidre smiled. "Yeah, we're just regular Three Musketeers. Anyway, I wanted to give you the heads up about the investigation. The BCA's assuming jurisdiction in this case. The body was found within the city limits of Silver Bay, but their force has such limited resources, there's no way they can lead the charge. Because of my knowledge of the area, I've been hired by the BCA to handle the investigation of this murder. Jeff, I told them I didn't think that'd be a problem between us. I hope I was right."

Jeff leaned back in his chair and steepled his finger tips. "A problem? The only problem is that you aren't sitting in this chair, and

I'm not your deputy. You were the best sheriff this county ever had, and I still regret you didn't fight that bugger of an attorney, Gerald Colter. He's still pushing his way around the courthouse, causing trouble. It seems he's always just a step from crossing the line with his tactics. Just the other day, we thought we had him for witness tampering. Then, on the stand, the witness reversed her testimony, saying she had misunderstood what Mr. Colter had said to her. She recanted the statement she had made to us.

"But enough of that garbage. Deidre, it's good to have you back on our team. Just tell me what I can do to help."

Deidre felt one burden she had been carrying lift. "I thought you'd feel that way, but I couldn't be sure. Thanks, Jeff, for your vote of confidence. I promise I'll keep you in the loop, but right now I've got to get to Duluth. Ben's little girls are waiting for me."

"And how about Ben?" Jeff asked, a knowing smile on his face.

Deidre felt her face blush, and she so wished she could control that reaction which had plagued her since childhood. "Come on Jeff, you know better than that. We're just good friends."

All Jeff did was smile and nod.

*****

DEIDRE KNOCKED ON THE DOOR, but didn't wait for Ben to answer. She hardly had time to step through the doorway when two four-year-olds jumped into her arms.

"Are you going to stay here tonight, Deidre?" they questioned in unison.

Before she could answer, Megan asked, "Did you bring Pete with you?"

"Yes, and yes." She scooped up the girls, one in each arm, and started for the living room while Ben stood back, a broad grin on his face.

"It's good to see you so chipper," he said. "The girls were awfully disappointed when you couldn't make it the other night. It's great you're here for them." He left the room for the kitchen where he had mac and cheese on the stove for supper.

"You know I'm not much of a cook, but we try," he hollered from the other room. Deidre could hear him placing silverware and plates on the table. The sound of milk being poured into glasses followed, and then the familiar call, "Come and get it."

The twins jumped off Deidre's lap and pulled her by her hands into the dining room.

"I get to sit by Deidre," Maren called dibs.

"You don't have to worry. I'll bet Dad set the table so one of you can sit on each side of me during dinner," she reassured them.

The meal was accompanied by laughter and funny faces, and Megan and Maren clung to Deidre the entire time. Dessert was gingerbread men that Ben had bought at a local bakery. The girls played with them, pretending that they could run as they recited, "Run, run as fast as you can; you can't catch me, I'm the gingerbread man." Then they would pretend they were the fox in the nursery rhyme and bite a part of him off. The game continued until there was nothing left of their gingerbread men.

Deidre looked at them with so much love and caring that her eyes became teary. "What's the matter, Deidre," Megan asked, looking confused. "Are you sad?"

She hugged them close. "No, I'm so happy, I can't keep it all inside me," she said. Ben coughed and began clearing the table.

The four of them played games until eight o'clock. "Okay you little imps, time for bed."

"I'm not an imp," Maren declared, her hands on her hips.

"Oh, yes, you are," Ben exclaimed as he swept her up and started up the stairs. Deidre followed with Megan.

"Will you tuck us in, Deidre?" They asked in unison. Deidre drew the covers up to their chins, brushed the hair back from their faces with her hand, and kissed each girl on her forehead.

"Sleep tight, my little ones," she said.

Megan spoke up, "Daddy always says, 'And don't let the bedbugs bite'," and she giggled, as she wriggled deeper under the down quilt.

Ben flicked off the light switch, and the room took on a warm glow from their Cinderella nightlight that shown dimly from the wall outlet in the corner of the room.

"Good night, my little ones," he said as he partially closed their bedroom door.

Deidre was glad the girls had been put to bed so early. She needed time to talk out yesterday's events with Ben, and as they sat on opposite ends of the couch, she told him about the BCA's offer to have her join their force, if only for this one case. He agreed that she was the right person for the job, and he wished her well.

The rest of the time they talked about Megan and Maren. It was evident they were two loved little girls, and Ben let Deidre know how much they loved her.

For an instant, Deidre wished Ben would move closer to her, but she forced that thought from her mind. She was here because of two little girls who had no mother, plain and simple. Anything else would complicate the matter and possibly destroy a good thing.

The two adults talked until midnight. Finally, Ben announced, "I think we'd better get some sleep. The twins'll be awake and raring to go by seven o'clock. Be ready for them to come wake you. I told them they could."

Deidre made her way to the spare bedroom upstairs and readied herself for bed. She could hear Ben rummaging in the room down the hall, and then the house was quiet. She slept well that night, knowing tomorrow would be filled with the antics of two needy little girls.

She was still sleeping when Megan and Maren barged into her room and jumped onto her bed.

"Deidre, you're still here!" they cried out in delight. "Daddy said we could wake you up, and so we did. Is that okay, Deidre? Is it?"

Deidre rolled onto her back and forced her eyes open. Then she grabbed the two tykes and pulled them close to her.

"Of course, it's okay. I have waited all week to do this," and she kissed each of them on the cheek. "Just give me a chance to get the sleepies out of my eyes." She rubbed her eyes to clear her vision.

"Come on, let's get some breakfast made so we can go sliding. I think we're going to the hill by Chester Creek. But first, I have to get dressed. You scoot to your rooms and have Daddy get you ready. I'll see you downstairs in a few minutes."

Deidre hurriedly brushed her teeth and combed her hair. No need to be too fastidious to go sliding with two little girls. For the rest of the day, she left her troubles behind and lost herself in the fun they were having. Time passed too quickly.

At six in the evening, she left Ben's for her wilderness cabin but not before squeezing Megan and Maren tightly. Before she drove away, she and Ben hugged briefly, the way friends do. By eight o'clock, she was home, had the fire kindled, and was ready for bed.

Tomorrow she would try to relax. The next day was work. As she was falling asleep and in a dream state, she felt Ben in bed beside her. She woke with a start to find she had her arms wrapped around her spare pillow. She fluffed it into shape and placed it under her head.

She dreamed of Megan and Maren, not a good dream, but a frustrating dream in which she was trying to shield them from an unknown danger. What was so frustrating was that she couldn't identify what it was.

Chapter
Seven

ON MONDAY, DEIDRE FOLLOWED her familiar routine getting ready for work and traveled into Silver Bay. She drove across the bridge under which the body had been found. It had snowed three inches while she was in Duluth on Friday night, and a snowplow had come through with its blade down and had rolled back a windrow of snow, scraping the bridge deck clean.

That takes care of any evidence we may have missed, she thought.

She stopped her car, got out, and looked over the railing. The river was frozen more than it had been. Only a narrow channel was still open in the middle. The fresh snow covered everything, erasing all signs of the tragedy that had occurred. Deidre wished that the ills of humankind could be so easily obliterated. She stood staring from the bridge for several minutes before getting back in her car and driving to her office in the police station.

After checking messages, Deidre took a ride around town. It was a sleepy day. Gray clouds blanketed the sky, and a few tardy townspeople were clearing snow from their driveways. There was no wind, and smoke rose straight up from chimneys in the crisp November air.

It took her an hour and a half to make her rounds. Ascertaining that all was well, she returned to the station. A fax was waiting for her in the machine on a stand in the corner of the room. She picked it up and thumbed through the pages, four of them.

To: Deidre Johnson, BCA Investigator
From: Dr. Judith Coster, Forensic Anthropologist/Examiner
Re: Jane Doe, recovered in Silver Bay, November 20, (The year was smudged, so it was illegible.)

The following report concerns an examination of a young girl's corpse found frozen under a bridge in Silver Bay, Minnesota. The body was discovered by Officer Deidre Johnson of the Silver Bay Police Force on Wednesday, November 13, at approximately 7:30 A.M. She notified the BCA at 8:45 A.M., requesting the help of an investigator and a medical examiner. Both arrived at 1:00 P.M., and the body was removed from the scene at 1:51 P.M.

It was found to be frozen from exposure to the elements for a minimum of nine hours. The core temperature at the time of removal from the scene was 47 F. The outer layers of skin and deeper flesh of the extremities were deeply frozen. The extremities could not be manipulated.

The body was not allowed to thaw during transport to Two Harbors, and the examiner accompanied the body the entire trip. The Lake County Search and Rescue Team arrived in Two Harbors at 2:34 P.M, at which time the deceased was transferred to a gurney and moved to the confines of the morgue, where it was allowed to slowly thaw over the next eighteen hours. The examiner made observations during that time. Below are her findings listed chronologically as the body was able to be manipulated as it thawed. November 13 3:00 P.M.

The nude body of what appears to be a post-pubescent female is curled into a tight fetal position with knees drawn up to chest and arms wrapped around its thorax. Hair is black, shoulder length, and appears to be natural color. There appear to be no puncture wounds consistent with gunshot or stabbing. The face is badly bruised. The upper lip is swollen and a three centimeter gash follows the upper left lip-line. A five-centimeter hematoma is clearly visible under the corpse's right eye. Upper arms are covered with contusions and a hematoma six centimeters in diameter is evident on the left buttock. The upper thighs show evidence of bruising. The body was returned to a cooler kept at a constant temperature of 40 F.

November 13 4:00 P.M.

The victim's eye lids could be retracted. Upon examination, the sclera was found to have numerous petechiae indicative of manual strangulation. The limbs are not able to be extended and the body is still in a curled fetal position.

Deidre continued to read the hourly recordings, many of them reiterating that the body remained too curled on itself to make further evaluation possible. The notation for the 1:00 A.M. observation said that the girl's body was beginning to thaw to the point where the fingers and hands could be manipulated.

Judy noted that she was able to procure scrapings from under the corpse's fingernails, but upon gross examination, she could see no signs of skin or other evidence.

As she read on, the report seemed to be a macabre script for a horror movie. The problem, Deidre was all too aware, was that she was reading about a real life incident and a human being whose life had been traumatically taken from her.

Finally, she reached the time that she and Melissa had joined Judy, and Deidre recognized the report of what had been observed by the three women.

Following the hourly log she compiled while the body thawed, Dr. Coster, Judy, attached several more findings to the report. Deidre read more.

A blood sample was tested, using the ABO system, and the subject is type O.

Deidre remembered the statistics Judy had quoted at the morgue: nearly eighty percent of indigenous people were of that type. One more miniscule clue for her to add to her meager list. The report continued.

After further review of the victim's dental condition, it was found that her third molars (wisdom teeth) were nearing the point of eruption, indicating her probable age as between sixteen and eighteen. Her dental condition was excellent with no trace of having worn braces. The upper left first premolar has an amalgam filling, as does the lower right second molar. The most pronounced anomaly is that her permanent lateral incisors are missing and the gap they would have left is filled by a shift forward of the posterior teeth.

The epiphysial plates of the distal and proximal ends of her radii are not ossified. Neither is the medial end of the humerus. It was noted that the distal end of the humerus was in the late stages of ossification, a process that occurs at approximately sixteen years of age in females.

The victim has straight, naturally black hair. Her skin appears to be of a darker shade, as are her nipples, areolae, and peritoneal skin. She has ample eyelashes, also black, and shaped eyebrows with evidence, signs of eyebrow plucking, that at one time her brows nearly met over her nose.

X-ray analysis of her bone structure revealed the absence of superacondyloid processes, a boney growth found anterior on the humerus. Its presence would have indicated the bone of a Caucasian. X-rays taken from differing angles of that bone reveal that it is somewhat flattened in cross-section.

Taken individually, each factor is not definitive. However, taken collectively, indications are that the victim was a sixteen-year-old Native American female. From the data and from the geographical location of where the body was found, the tribe to which she belonged might theoretically be Cree.

Deidre used a yellow marker to highlight areas of the report she would return to for more thought. On a page, separate from the report was a note from Judy.

Deidre,

When I returned to the Twin Cities, I was so emotionally involved with this case that I couldn't take the weekend off. An assistant and I stayed in the lab until we finished enough of the exam to enable me to make a preliminary report. More info will be coming as I discover more about this girl. Go catch whoever did this!

Judy

By the time Deidre had read the report and pondered some of its implications, straightened her desk, and filed the report for the day, it was nearly 3:30, close to quitting time. She heard the outer door to the station open and heard someone stamping snow off boots. She came around her desk to meet whoever would be opening the inner door.

"Dan," she greeted the officer for whom she was filling in. "Good to see you, and no sling. That must be a good sign."

Dan grinned from ear to ear. "All healed and ready to go. Actually, I've been going stir crazy having to stay inside with nothing to do. I wasn't supposed to walk on slippery surfaces until I was healed up. They're afraid I'd slip and fall and tear things up again. I'm sorry you got tangled up in such a mess, but on the other hand, I'm relieved I was away. You've got far better connections than I do to handle this sort of case."

"Then you know of my recent hire by the BCA?" she asked.

He plopped into an office chair. "I'm more than happy. I'm just a small-town cop content doing what I do. I'll be here to help you anyway I can, but, believe me, I know this is way out of my league. From what I hear, you have some pretty big guns backing you up. Go to it with my blessings."

This was exactly what Deidre had hoped for, but she hadn't been sure how Dan would react. She poured a cup of coffee for both of them and sat down in another chair, not the one behind Dan's desk.

Dan spoke first. "I feel so good, Deidre, and restless. Is there anyway I can come in tomorrow? You could help me get up to speed on what else has happened while I've been out. Maybe we could even ride around in the patrol car a bit, just to let me get my feet wet."

Deidre beamed. "That's an offer I can hardly refuse. Seven tomorrow morning? Let me ask you this. If you feel comfortable being back, is there any chance I could take off at noon? I've got a couple of things I'd like to do tomorrow away from town."

"I think I can manage that," Dan said, his eyes sparkling at the thought of being back on the job, his job.

Chapter
Eight

DEIDRE COULD HEAR THE RUSH of feet from inside when she rang the doorbell. "Deidre's here. She's here, Dad."

She didn't wait for them to answer the door. When she walked in, Megan and Maren threw themselves into her arms, smothering her with kisses.

"Are you staying with us tonight?" they asked in unison.

Deidre continued to hug them. "I sure am. Maybe we can play a game tonight before your bedtime. What would you think of that?" She placed them on the floor, and the girls ran upstairs to their room.

"I want to play checkers," Maren announced. "No, let's play Old Maid." Deidre could hear them arguing even after they had cleared the top of the stairs.

She looked up to see Ben standing in the kitchen doorway, a smile on his face. "Well, it's obvious who counts around this house," he scolded, but with a laugh.

Deidre went over to him and gave him a hug. He was almost a foot taller than she and had to stoop to get his arms around her. "I'm glad you called this morning. It was good to hear your voice. Glad we can spend a few hours together before you have to leave for the Cities. Did you bring Pete along? I'm always happy to put him up for a day or two, and the girls love him. They treat him like a person, and he doesn't complain a bit."

The evening was what Deidre needed, providing her a diversion from the task ahead. The four of them played Old Maid and Chinese Checkers, laughing and teasing each other. At eight o'clock Ben announced that it was bed time for little girls, and amid much whining and cajoling, he and Deidre ushered them off to bed. Deidre tucked in one, then the other, kissed them on their foreheads, and quietly closed their bedroom door. As she and Ben tiptoed down the stairs they heard, "Good night, Daddy. Good night, Deidre. See you in the morning," followed by giggles and then silence.

When they were alone downstairs, Ben poured each of them a glass of wine, and they took their usual places at each end of his couch. Deidre took a sip of her wine before she said anything.

"I love those girls like they were my own. I find myself thinking about them so often, wondering what they're doing, if they miss their mom, if they'll remember her when they're older." She took another sip, and wiped away a tear that rolled down her cheek.

"They were so young when she died." Ben rotated his wineglass in his hand. "They talk about her, but I don't know how much they remember. Sometimes I think what they think they remember is actually coming from the pictures I have sitting around."

"And you, Ben . . . what about you? Are you finding your way? Deidre looked at his face.

"It's getting better, easier. This is a new normal. I . . . we are getting used to it. But I do miss Jenny."

Ben and Deidre sat in silence, nursing what was left of their wine. Finally, Deidre took one last swallow and got up.

"We'd better get some sleep. You have work, and I have a trip to Minneapolis in the morning. Good night, Ben, and thanks for all you're giving me."

She rinsed out their glasses while Ben collected the games they had played. Together, they climbed the stairs, and he gave her a hug of thankfulness before going into his room.

*****

DEIDRE LISTENED TO THE RADIO during her drive to the BCA. She made the same trip so often it was becoming routine, and by nine she was walking into the central office. She needed no introduction.

The receptionist recognized her instantly and ushered her into Melissa's office.

"Good to see you made the trip safe and sound," the detective greeted her. "The director, Erin Goodman, is waiting for us next door. She's a great boss. I'm sure you'll enjoy meeting her."

Melissa walked out of the room and motioned for Deidre to follow. She knocked on an office two doors down the hall from her own.

"Come on in," Deidre heard the alto voice call out from inside the office. Melissa opened the door, and they were met by a burly figure. Erin grabbed Deidre's hand and shook it.

"You must be Deidre. I've wanted to meet you for the longest time. Here, take a seat and let's talk." She swung a chair away from the wall with one hand and plunked it down for Deidre, who was rather awed by the larger-than-life presence of her new boss.

"I've read your report of finding the frozen body of a girl under a bridge in Silver Bay," Erin began with no preamble. "I also read Dr. Coster's report of her examination of the victim. This has the makings of something the media would consider sensational. It'd sell a lot of papers and airtime. Let's try to get it wrapped up before that happens.

"Now, Deidre. I've already done some footwork from my end. Dr. Coster implied the victim may be of First Nation descent," she expounded, using the preferred term of the indigenous Canadian people. "Specifically, she indicated Cree. Judy is seldom far off the course, so this is where I want you to begin." Before Deidre could respond, Erin continued in her commanding voice. "We ran her fingerprints through our data base and drew a blank. DNA takes a little longer to work with, but in a few days we'll have results on those tests as well. I suspect that won't help us ID her either if she's from Canada.

"So here's where you will begin. I spoke with the Grand Chief of the Nishnawbe Aski Nation, Henry Musio. Here is the address of his office."

She handed a piece of paper to Deidre, who noted the city was Thunder Bay, Ontario, Canada.

"The Nishnawbi are Cree and have an excellent social organization. Their police system is second to none. Henry's phone number is at the bottom of the page. Call him when you are ready, which I'm assuming will be day after tomorrow, and he'll have the head of the force's Guns and Gangs Unit present for your meeting.

"As of now, we're going to concentrate on finding the identity of our victim, and you're going to start by following Dr. Coster's supposition that she's Cree. If that turns up nothing in a few days, then we'll get our heads together and find other threads to follow.

"Do you have any questions?" Before Deidre could even shake her head, Erin said, "Good. Now if you'll excuse me, I have a meeting with the state Attorney General."

Melissa took the cue and got up from her chair. Deidre followed suit, but as they were leaving, Erin's parting shot was, "Oh, and Deidre, good to have you on our team."

As soon as they were out of earshot, Deidre turned to Melissa. "Is she always like that?"

Melissa laughed and put her arm around her colleague's shoulder. "Sometimes she is more abrupt. Don't worry. I could tell she likes you. If you ever need someone in your corner, Erin's the person you want there. She'll defend you to the last man standing and still have the energy to make sure you're okay. Believe me."

Deidre shrugged, accepting what Melissa said. But she knew Erin would accept nothing but her best and would want results yesterday, if not sooner.

"Come on. It's lunch time. Let's collect Judy from her lab and grab a bite to eat. Seems the three of us do our best work over food," and she grabbed Deidre's elbow, leading her down the hall. "Something tells me we're going to be seeing quite a bit of each other over the next several weeks. By the way, Erin gave me some directives to pass on to you.

She spoke to the Lake County sheriff this morning before you arrived. Your office will be set up in the Lake County Law Enforcement Center next to the courthouse. By tomorrow morning a private phone line will have been installed. You'll have a secretary, Jill Dobers I believe is her name, who starts work the day you do. Also, you'll have your own fax machine, copy machine, and computer.

"As you can probably guess, Erin wants you on the job tomorrow morning at seven and wants a meeting set up with the Grand Chief for Friday. That shouldn't be difficult to arrange. She's already done the ground work, and he is expecting your call. An official SUV has been delivered to Two Harbors, and you have a designated parking spot. By the way, you do have a passport, don't you?"

Deidre's head was spinning because of the pace at which everything was happening, but she had enough sense left to nod an affirmative. By that time they had arrived at Judy's office, she stepped out to greet them. "Hey, thanks for giving me a heads up. I have my desk cleared, at least temporarily, so let's go."

The three women made their way to a cafeteria that served several office buildings in close proximity. Deidre looked outside as they traversed a skywalk and was grateful they didn't have to brave the mid-November cold. The temperature hovered around the ten-degree mark, and a stiff wind blew from the Canadian northwest. At this rate it was going to be a long winter.

They moved through the assembly-line cafeteria, selecting what suited their tastes, and after finding a table in a somewhat secluded spot, they settled in to fill their bellies.

"I have no other findings to give you," Judy announced. "I wish I had better news, but we have a few things to go on. I'd bet my next paycheck I'm right about the girl's ethnicity. Hope you get some results in your search."

For the rest of the time, the three talked about non-forensic topics: how their jobs were going, if the legislature was going to come through with funding for their department, how their personal lives were playing out.

"Deidre," Judy wanted to know, "Any man in your life since we last visited?" She laughed as Deidre's face turned red.

"Even if there was, I don't think I'd tell you two gossips." She laughed and winked at Melissa.

Too soon their meal was over, and Deidre headed up I-35 toward Duluth. She was so lost in thought that before she realized it, she was at the crest of Thompson Hill, more than six-hundred feet above the fresh-water ports of Duluth/Superior.

The frigid November air was perfectly clear, and she took in the panorama of lights laid out in perfect squares of city streets. Red dots, taillights of cars, moved at what seemed a snail's pace far below. The arch of the Blatnik Bridge was clearly visible with its span delineated by halogen lighting, and ships were lit up like Christmas trees as they sat in their berths, waiting to be loaded with iron ore pellets, grain, or containers destined for overseas cities. Deidre never ceased being surprised by the grandeur of the sight.

In little more than a mile, the road descended to lake level, and she made her way through Duluth in short order, stopping at Ben's long enough to pick up Pete. Twenty miles later she was in Two Harbors, still forty minutes from her cabin in the woods.

It dawned on her this was never going to work. She'd have to move back to Two Harbors until her assignment was over, a thought that troubled her a great deal. By the time she reached home, it was ten-thirty at night, and she stood outside her cabin, looking at the stars and soaking in the magnitude of what she too often took for granted.

After a few moments, the chill of the night filtered through her winter jacket, and she was forced to go inside.

"Come on, Pete, time to get the place heated up. We've got a lot of work waiting for us." Pete cocked his head to one side and looked at her as though he understood.

Chapter
Nine

DEIDRE'S ALARM RANG AT 5:30 a.m. She pried her eyelids open, but when she threw the covers back, she found that the woodstove had not had time to burn itself out. The floor around it was still toasty against her feet. She didn't bother to put another stick of wood in its firebox. She would be out the door by the time the cabin cooled off.

She dressed and didn't take time to make a cup of coffee, thinking she'd stop at the convenience store in Silver Bay to save time. She arrived at her office in Two Harbors before seven. On the first floor of the Law Enforcement Center, toward the back, it looked as if someone had cleaned out a storage closet to make room for her.

Two desks cluttered the small space, evidently one for her and one for her secretary, Jill. On a stand in the corner sat a fax machine/copy machine. There were no windows. Deidre felt sorry for Jill, who would spend the great majority of her time in the cubical-sized space. At least Deidre would be out in the field most of the time, but everyone had their own problems to deal with, she thought. Nevertheless, she would remember to be extra considerate of Jill's situation.

As she was arranging items on her desk, her secretary reported for work. She walked in unannounced, her rainbow-dyed hair in a flyaway mess, and extended her hand to Deide. "Jill Dobers, your secretary. You must be Deidre. I've heard so many good things about you and have been looking forward to working for you since they assigned me this job. Now, what can I do to get us started?"

Deidre hadn't given the subject one thought. "Gosh, I'm afraid I have nothing for you to do yet. I just got here myself and have nothing organized."

Jill looked around. "Well, for starters, we need a coffee pot. Regular or decaf?"

"Regular."

"Good. If we're not going to get a charge out of it, why bother? Okay, what's the most pressing thing on your plate this morning?"

Deidre thought for a moment. "I have to organize my desk, then make some kind of living arrangement for myself while I'm on this case. After that I have to call the Grand Chief of the Nishnawbe Aski Nation in Thunder Bay to set up an appointment to meet with him and the head of their Guns and Gangs Unit tomorrow. If I can get that much done today, I'll be lucky."

Jill looked around the room again. "Leave the organization to me. You get yourself situated as far as living accommodations are concerned. When you get back, I'll have made your appointment with the chief."

Deidre looked at her, shocked at the woman's efficiency. It was only seven-fifteen, and already she felt like something good was going to happen.

"Well, don't just stand there, I've got things to do," Jill said, asserting her secretarial authority. All Deidre could do was leave the office.

She checked upstairs, hoping her friend Jeff was done with his morning report session. He was, and when he saw her enter the outer office, he rushed to give her a hug. "Diedre, you don't know how good this makes me feel. It hasn't been the same since you left. Everybody says so. It's good to have you back in the building. I've got some things for you." Jeff motioned for her to follow him into his office.

"Have a seat for a minute or two." He reached into his desk and grabbed a set of keys. "BCA dropped these off yesterday. The SUV is out back. It's black and has the agency logo stenciled on its side doors. Also, they left a credit card for your use to charge gas, lodging, meals, and anything else pertaining to your investigation. Make sure you give Jill all your receipts. She'll tally them and send them in for you. Here are your credentials," he said as he handed her a badge and an ID tag."

There was a handwritten note with the ID. *Didn't have time to get these to you yesterday. Took the picture off our records. Hope it's okay. Good hunting. Erin Goodman.*

Deidre smiled at the curtness of the note, and she could picture Erin hurriedly scribbling it on a piece of paper.

"Jeff, I hope this job is short lived. I don't know if you have much information about what we found under that bridge in Silver Bay, but we need to get to the bottom of this as soon as possible. It's the worse case scenario you can imagine."

Jeff's face told her he knew. "I'm glad you're the one working this." was all he said. Deidre stood to excuse herself, and Jeff looked her square in the eye. "I mean what I said."

The SUV was out back, just as Jeff said it would be, and Deidre crawled into the driver's seat, adjusted the mirrors, and turned the key. She hoped the vehicle's heater was a good one.

Leaving the parking lot, she turned right and then left onto Waterfront Drive, continued to Highway 61, then turned left. She was heading to her old neighborhood on Ninth Avenue. When she reached Seventh Street, she turned down a familiar alley and pulled up behind Inga Olson's house. It had been over a year since the two of them had visited. As she walked up the shoveled walkway, she glanced at the house next door, her house, the one in which John had been gunned down.

For an instant, the memory of that night hit her full force, but before she could dwell on its impact, Inga was at the door, holding it open and calling out, "Deidre Johnson, my word, get in here before you freeze to death. Child, what are you doing in Two Harbors this time of the morning?"

Deidre stomped the snow off her boots on the outside door mat, then removed them in the entry. She walked into the kitchen and sat down at the table. Inga was already taking down two tea cups and had placed a plate of peanut butter cookies on the table.

"Oh, it's good to see you. How have you been, my dear?"

Deidre looked at the older woman and was surprised to see that she didn't seem to have aged at all since the last time they met.

"I'm good, actually very good. Life has taken me down a road I never dreamed I'd go. But right now, I'm up to my eyeballs in a problem."

She went on to give a thumbnail sketch of why she was in Two Harbors. Inga seemed surprised Deidre was back in law enforcement but stated her approval, saying that she had too much to offer society to be stuck in the woods.

"Inga, I could use your help for a little while. I need a place to stay for a few weeks, and I'm wondering if my old room is still empty. I'd pay you room and board, and there wouldn't be any wild parties at night. Promise." She laughed at her own joke.

The older woman became animated. "I can't believe we might have time to spend together. It'd be almost like old times, only under better circumstances. Of course you can stay, for free."

Deidre laughed at her exuberance. "No, the BCA is footing this bill. You'll be paid well. I'll see to that. It's okay then?" Inga's reaction was more than a reward for Deidre. "I'm going to my cabin for the night and then to Thunder Bay tomorrow. But I should be back tomorrow night. If I pull in at ten, ten-thirty, is that too late?"

"Heavens no! You know my sleep habits. Nothing's changed since you were my neighbor. Deidre, it's great to be able to spend time with you again. I'll have a light snack ready for you when you get here."

Deidre knew what Inga's "light snacks" were like. She anticipated a wonderful stay, even if she gained a pound or two.

"One more thing, I have a dog, a pretty big one, I'll need to bring with me. Is it possible he could stay here?"

Inga looked surprised. "I'm allergic to dog dander, but years ago my husband had a hunting dog. He fixed a wonderful kennel off the garage. You never noticed, I'm sure, because I've planted clematis, which climbs the fence. It looks like an arbor most of the time. Your dog would have access to the garage that has an insulated sleeping area. We can put a heat lamp in there if you'd like."

And so that problem was taken care of with little fuss.

Deidre was back at her office at ten o'clock. When she entered the room, she couldn't believe the change. Coffee was brewing in a pot on a stand Jill had scrounged from another office. The desks had been rearranged to make for a better traffic pattern. A calendar covered the surface of her desk, and a coffee mug stood full of sharpened pencils, highlighters, and pens ready for use.

Deidre sat down in her swivel chair and saw a note neatly printed on a legal pad. *You have an appointment tomorrow at 1:15 P.M. with Henry Musio, Grand Chief of the Nishnawabe Aski Nation (NAN).*

On a separate card was listed the chief's name, the name of the head of the Nation's Guns and Gangs Unit, as well as the address of the chief's office. She looked at her desk calendar. Neatly printed in ink on the square for Friday, November 22, was the same notation. Deidre couldn't believe what she was seeing. Just then, Jill walked in the room, and Deidre noticed that, with her hair under control, she had numerous piercings in each ear.

"Well, what do you think?" Jill asked. "Will this arrangement do? I've called the border patrol to facilitate your getting through customs. Both sides are aware you'll be coming through about nine tomorrow morning. You'll still need your passport, but you should get through without a hitch. You can bring a gun with if you're packing, but they'll want the serial number and the number of your permit. "I notified the head of NAN's Gun and Gang Unit so he knows the nature of your visit. He said to bring a copy of Dr. Coster's report. I asked that he set up a separate meeting with the tribal police so you can request what assistance you would like. That meeting is at three o'clock. You should be back to the US border by five, which should get you home to Two Harbors no later than seven-thirty, nine if you stop for dinner along the way. If that's your intention, where would you like to eat supper? I'll call ahead and make a reservation for you."

Jill stood looking at Deidre, an expectant smile on her face. Deidre was flummoxed by her efficiency. "I-I really hadn't thought

64

that far ahead. I'm planning on having a snack with a friend when I get back to town. Let's skip stopping for supper. I'd just as soon get home. By the way, thank you for all you have accomplished today. I hope I can provide enough for you to do so you don't become bored."

"Oh, don't worry about that. I always find enough to do to make time fly. Did you find a place to stay? If you want me to, I can track down a decent place for you to lodge. I've plenty of connections. Did I hear you own a dog? If you do, I have a friend in Knife River who owns a pet care service. She'll walk your dog once a day, make sure it's fed, watered, and will spend and hour with him so he doesn't get lonesome. Would you like me to take care of that?"

Once again, Jill stood with the same expectant smile on her face.

"Uh, that would be fine. His name's Pete. He's a black lab and will be staying at Inga Olson's place on Ninth Avenue."

"Thank you for all your help. I don't know how you've gotten all of this done in such a short time, but thank you. Naturally, I won't be in tomorrow. Do you want the day off?"

"Oh, no," Jill answered. "I'll find plenty to do. Still have some equipment to get, and somebody better be here to answer the phone if you receive an important call. I'll set up your e-mail account. Do you want me to set up Facebook for you? It might come in handy if you want to contact a large number of people at one time. How about Linkedin?"

Deidre turned down the social networking sites but knew she'd need an e-mail account. "I'm going to leave early today," she told Jill. "I have some packing to do at my cabin, and I want to be rested for tomorrow. I can cut across on Highway 1 to Highway 61. Then it's a straight shot to the Canadian border."

Jill nodded. "Remember, you can't take your dog across the border unless he has a veterinarian-signed paper showing all his vaccinations are up to date."

Deidre smiled to herself. *Is there anything she doesn't think of?*

Chapter
Ten

IT WAS STILL LIGHT WHEN DEIDRE drove up her access road and stopped near the backdoor of her cabin. Pete came bounding out of his dog house and slathered her with affection. She ruffled his ears and talked baby talk to him. He raced away, his excitement getting the better of him. Deidre laughed as he plowed through six inches of snow, slipped on a hummock and rolled over three times before gaining his footing.

That night the cabin felt especially cozy, and Deidre disliked the thought of having to abandon her paradise, if only for a few weeks. But she remembered the body she'd found, and all remorse vanished. She had a job to do, a compelling job, and she would do it well.

Deidre was on the road by seven-thirty the next morning. Her trip to the Pigeon River International Bridge, the border between the United States and Canada was uneventful. She pulled into the Canadian customs check point with her passport in hand. The guard checked her ID, stamped her document, and ran his finger down a list of names attached to his clip board. His finger stopped mid-way down the list, and he waved her through. No matter that he hadn't asked if she had a gun in her possession, she had not felt the need to bring one with her.

On November 22, the sun didn't rise until after seven o'clock, and it hung only a few degrees above the horizon. Deidre looked at her watch—ten-thirty. She calculated she had about six and one-half hours of daylight remaining, which meant she'd be driving home in the dark, something she didn't relish. The thermometer in her car registered minus four degrees outside, a record for this day.

Will-o'-the-wisps of steam rose from Lake Superior like specters that danced and swirled. They were the result of contact between the arctic-cold air and the surface of warmer lake water. The winter sun shining through the haze made the scene seem even more inhospitable.

By noon Deidre arrived at the port city of Thunder Bay, the Canadian counterpart of Duluth/Superior. In the distance she could see towering grain silos standing along the harbor docks. Rime-covered boats were being loaded, many of them "salties," ships that would be traversing the ocean to distant continents.

She stopped at a small cafe and ordered a sandwich and a piece of carrot cake. When the waitress returned with her order, she remembered she had forgotten to order coffee. The waitress returned with a scowl, a cup, and coffee pot. She set it on the table and left without saying a word. *So much for your tip*, Deidre thought. But when she made ready to leave, she left a toonie on the table. A two-dollar tip was more than what was deserved.

From the cafe, it was a twenty minute drive to the NAN office, at least that's what her GPS indicated. But the instrument hadn't counted on a traffic accident at one of the intersections, and so Deidre was delayed for a half hour. She arrived at the front desk with barely five minutes to spare.

After checking her credentials, the receptionist led Deidre to an office down the hall, knocked on the closed door, opened it a crack, and announced Deidre's arrival. She heard a man's voice say, "Send her in," and the receptionist motioned for her to enter.

Henry Musio greeted Deidre warmly, taking her extended hand with both of his. He was in his mid-forties, was tall and very good looking.

"Your secretary called yesterday, asking if we could meet today. She's a very persuasive lady. I'd like to meet her sometime." He chuckled, and Deidre instantly thought she would like him.

"Come, sit down so we can talk. The head of the Guns and Gangs unit will be here anytime now. Our meeting is back to back with one he had scheduled, and he may be running a little late."

Chief Musio had just uttered the words when someone knocked on the door. A man who resembled the chief in many ways walked in without waiting for an invitation.

"This is Joseph Walkin. Perhaps there's significance to his name." Henry laughed at his own joke, one she figured Joseph had heard more than once.

Joseph shook Deidre's hand, while he looked squarely in her eyes as if judging her spirit. Henry sat and motioned for them to do the same. "Your secretary said you had information that might be of interest to our tribal counsel, information about a homicide in your town. What assistance will you be expecting from us?" His tone was not at all condescending, only matter-of-fact, and Deidre felt no veiled hostility.

She removed a folder from her briefcase and opened it, producing copies of Dr. Coster's report. Before handing it to the men she reviewed how she had found a naked body huddled under a bridge, and briefly explained the condition of the corpse. Then she handed them the copy.

Deidre anticipated that they would question why she was interested in the Nishnawbe Aski people and had highlighted Judy's supposition that the victim may have been of Cree Indian ethnicity. Henry spoke before he looked at the paper Deidre handed to him. "Your secretary faxed these to us yesterday. She included a note saying you were prepared to begin working on this today, and requested we do some footwork before you got here. She sent copies of the girl's fingerprints, as well as the examiner's x-rays of her dentition, and she indicated you'd be willing to stay an extra day if needed. The two of you make for an extremely efficient team."

Deidre didn't have time to answer, which was all right, because she wouldn't have known what to say. Henry and Joseph paged through the report and concentrated on the areas she had highlighted.

"We understand why you want to speak with us. Are you aware that at the present time more than six hundred Nishnawbe Aski women, what you would probably call Cree, are missing, many presumed dead, many presumed to be trapped in the sex trade?"

Deidre's jaw dropped. She had no idea the problem was so extensive. Joseph continued. "The average—*the average*—age they enter the sex trade is fourteen, with some as young as ten."

Henry's jaw muscles bulged as he fought to control his anger. He said, "Many are girls who come from dysfunctional homes. Others have run away for trivial reasons, and some are literally kidnapped. They are transported down Highway 61, a river of bodies flowing to Duluth, where they are sold to sailors onboard the ships in the harbor. Many are taken overseas, servicing the sailors on the boats throughout the journey. Many are thrown overboard as the journey nears its end. Estimates are that a supplier realizes profits of over $250,000 per year."

Henry leaned toward Deidre. "Are we interested in what you bring us? Absolutely. Will we cooperate? To the fullest. Is this an isolated case? It's the tip of the iceberg."

With those words he went silent, but Joseph began to speak. "There are few statistics to support what Henry's told you because most of the victims are killed before they can speak out. Thunder Bay's police spokesperson has gone on record saying he isn't aware of any problem. However, the Ontario Provincial Police, headquartered in this city, recognizes the crimes against our people. The Royal Canadian Mounted Police, the OPP, and the Canada Border Services struggle to combat human trafficking, but still, it's a trade that flies under the radar. The wilderness border is as porous as a sieve. Anything can leak through, especially in the summer when the waterways are open to tourist canoe traffic. What can we do to help you in your investigation?"

Deidre sat in deep contemplation for several moments. "You can begin by helping me find out if our dead girl is from your nation, and if she is, what her history is. If we do find an answer to that question, then we must find out how she reached the town of Silver Bay. Finding that answer, we must then locate the party or parties who brought her to Minnesota. Then we go after the killer or killers."

Without realizing what she was doing, Deidre was formulating the sequence of a plan she would follow to the end of the case. Her dead girl deserved to be heard in a court of law, if only by the silent testimony of her wounds and death.

"We appreciate your desire to move forward on this issue as quickly as possible. The information from your secretary was passed on to NAN's chief of police, Charles Freeman. He'll meet with you at four o'clock today, and I believe he has some answers for you. Joseph will accompany you to his headquarters and help you find your way around. Charles is a good man, hard working, and very intelligent. He is eager to meet you and to seek your cooperation on this case. Is there anything else I can do to facilitate your work?"

Deidre sensed the meeting was over and stood to leave. She extended her hand. "No, not right now, but I hope the lines of communication will remain open between my office and yours."

The grand chief smiled warmly as he held Deidre's hand for a moment. "After speaking with your secretary over the phone, I don't think I have a choice."

Joseph Walkin escorted Deidre through the maze of hallways to his car, and together, they rode to the NAN police headquarters. On the way, Deidre phoned Inga to tell her not to expect her home that night. Then she called her friend, Terry, who owned a bait store a few miles from her cabin and asked him to stop by and check on Pete and to give him some food and water. Even if she was done with her meeting by early evening, she didn't want to drive one hundred-fifty miles home in the cold and the dark. By the time she finished her calls, Joseph had parked his car in an underground garage. They took an elevator to the fifth floor of the headquarter building.

Again, she followed Joseph through a maze of hallways until he walked into one of the offices. The receptionist looked up from her work. "Joseph, how are you today?" Not waiting for an answer, her gaze swung to Deidre. "And you must be Deidre. Welcome to Thunder Bay. Your secretary called and left a message for you. She has made reservations for your stay tonight at the Valhalla Inn. It's only a few minute's drive from here, and is one of our best lodgings for the money. You'll be comfortable there."

Deidre was beginning to wonder if Jill was some sort of psychic. She wasn't accustomed to having someone being one step ahead of her all the time. She smiled and took the paper from the receptionist.

Joseph was holding the door to the inner office open and motioned for Deidre to go in first. A black-haired man stood by his desk, a welcoming smile on his face. Deidre thought he looked like a man who could have modeled for one of those calendar pictures of a Royal Mounted Policeman.

"Deidre, so good to meet you. I feel as though we've already met. Your secretary faxed me a brief bio of you. Your work experience is more than impressive, and I, for one, am delighted to be able to work with you. I'm equally impressed with your secretary's initiative. She pointed out what might be most useful to meet your needs. You're lucky to have her working for you."

Deidre found herself mumbling something about being grateful for her assistance, but she really wasn't quite sure.

Charles, the NAN chief of police, bypassed any small talk and got down to business.

"We know your schedule's tight, so let's get to the point. You're aware, I'm sure, of the monumental problem our staff is facing, and it's taxing our resources, both in personnel matters and financially. For decades, centuries would be more accurate, our women and girls have been preyed upon by men who have used them as prostitutes. But the problem has become increasingly more sinister because they are being coerced in more systematic ways by gangs and criminals. There are so many girls missing, it's difficult for us to stay abreast of the situation. Fortunately, we have made considerable progress since receiving Dr. Coster's report yesterday."

With that news, Deidre became acutely focused on his words.

"Of the six hundred some missing females registered in our files, our computer system was able to quickly select those between the ages of fourteen and nineteen. That brought the number of possible leads down to three hundred forty-seven. Selecting those who had type O blood, further narrowed the search to three hundred twenty-six. Considering height, we narrowed the field to one hundred eighteen. We were getting closer."

Deidre was getting fidgety in her chair, and she wished that Charles would skip the process and tell her what they had found, but he continued. "Next, we checked the dental x-rays you sent us against the records of the one hundred eighteen. Unfortunately, most of our missing women and girls come from conditions of extreme poverty. Many have never seen the inside of a dentist's office, and so no records exist for them."

Deidre's hopes began to plunge.

"In our case, we were lucky. Your victim comes from a moderately successful family. In her record file was a complete set of dental x-rays. Fortunately for us, unfortunately for her family, we found a perfect match."

Charles handed a paper to Deidre. "This is the information you're looking for."

She quickly scanned the page. *Name: Anna Joyce Woodsong.* Deidre read more. *Age: 16 yrs. 9 mo.* Judy had nailed this one perfectly. *Height: 160 cm., Weight: 50 kg.*

She wasn't used to metric measurements, but a rough calculation mixed with a little guesswork led her to the figures about five feet three inches and a weight of about one hundred ten pounds. That seemed to fit the corpse, although she appeared to be much lighter than one-ten.

There were other data on the page, but Deidre's eyes were too full of tears to read.

Joseph cleared his throat. "We've located Anna's parents, and they'd like to meet with you this evening. Charles will accompany you to their home and sit with you during your meeting. I'm sure there are questions you'll want to ask her parents, but we ask that you be respectful of their feelings and their heritage. They are solid people who have been held up as an example by our people, but they are hurting deeply right now."

"I know what they're feeling. You needn't worry about my ability to respect them. I've been there myself," she said as she wiped her eyes with a tissue. "I'll be gentle with my questioning."

*****

AFTER RETRIEVING HER SUV and checking into her hotel, Deidre ate a light supper before Charles arrived to take her to visit Anna's parents. Neither of them said much on the way, each facing his and her own sense of dread over the uncertainty of how the visit would go.

He pulled into the driveway of a modest home. "This is it. Before we go in, I think you should know that her parents are keenly interested in their heritage and in preserving some of the old ways. Not that they're trying to live in the past. They're very progressive. They simply want to preserve their native language and some of the traditions. Under other circumstances, you'd find them to be interesting people."

They walked up the sidewalk, and Joseph rang the doorbell. It was answered by an attractive woman who looked to be in her late thirties. Deidre could see a distinct resemblance between her and the picture of her daughter she'd seen back at Charles's office.

"Come in, please," she invited them. Deidre noticed the lady's hands were trembling, and her voice quivered. She and Joseph removed their shoes in the entry and followed the victim's mother to the living room.

"This is my husband, John Woodsong. I'm Mary. Thank you so much for taking the time to come to our home." She sat down next to her husband, and there was a moment of awkward silence. No one seemed to know what to say.

Finally, Anna's father cleared his throat. "We understand you have confirmation our daughter has been found dead."

Deidre shuffled her feet. "I was called to a suspicious site in the town of Silver Bay last week. It appeared that something had been struck by a car and thrown off a bridge. When I investigated, I found your daughter's body under the bridge. I called in experts from the Bureau of Criminal Apprehension of the state of Minnesota. Their medical examiner, who is also a forensic anthropologist, determined that her death was a homicide. She also believed the body to be that of a Nishnawbe Aski girl. That's why we contacted the NAN officers, to seek their assistance. From their forensic data, a positive identification was made."

Deidre waited for a response, and another long period of silence followed.

"Did she suffer?" Mary asked. She held her head high as though bracing for a slap across her face.

Deidre didn't tell the whole truth. "I think death came painlessly."

She thought it probably had. Hypothermia would have set in and the girl drifted into death. Deidre was not about to go into what had transpired before death released her from her torment.

Anna's father asked, "Was she badly broken from the impact of the car?"

Deidre took a deep breath. "She wasn't hit by a car. I'm sorry if I left you with that impression. Unfortunately, your daughter was accosted by an individual or individuals and was left for dead." She didn't go into details. Mary began to weep into a towel she had been worrying. John clenched his teeth so hard the veins in his neck stood out.

"I have a few questions to ask you, if you're willing to share with me." She needed information, but she also wanted to move the conversation in a different direction.

"How long ago was it that your daughter disappeared?"

Mary Woodsong tried to speak, but each time she would begin, the words were cut off by a sob. Finally, she shook her head and looked at her husband.

John was able to speak, although he had to stop repeatedly and take a deep breath. "It will be six months tomorrow." He paused to control his voice, then continued speaking, looking nowhere. His eyes were blank. "We had an argument that day. I insisted that she go to tribal classes that night to study our native language, but she wanted to go to a concert with friends. I said, 'No.' We had words. She didn't come home for supper, and we thought she had gone off with friends to the concert, but later that night we called her friends. They said the last time they saw her she was walking alone on a path in the park by the lake.

"We called the NAN police, but they found no trace of her. We haven't seen her since." He paused again. "When can we see her body?"

"I'm not sure. Your daughter's remains are at the BCA lab where they are still looking for clues as to who her killers might be." She wasn't lying. "Here is the number for their central office. They'll have the details you need." She handed a card to Mary. Do you know if your daughter had any involvement with older men?"

Mary glanced at her husband. She said, "No, I'm sure not. Her friends were all her own age. She was a good girl, officer, no trouble at all. It's just that she was exerting her independence lately. She was growing up and wanted to make her own decisions."

Deidre nodded her understanding. "Do you know anyone who might have wanted to hurt your daughter?"

"No one. She was popular and friendly with everyone. Why would anyone want to do this to her? And how did she end up in the States? Do you have any idea?"

Deidre had to admit that she didn't, but in her mind she made a vow she would find the answers.

"I want you to know that I appreciate your taking the time to visit with me," she told the grieving parents. "I won't say I know how you feel. I'm sure your pain must be beyond comprehension. I promise you I'll do everything I can to bring your daughter's killer to justice. I also promise to keep you up to date on what we're discovering. I may not be able to divulge everything we're doing for the sake of the investigation, but I'll be in contact on a regular basis. Again, thank you so much, and I'm sorry for your loss. I'm sorry."

Joseph stood up, and Deidre followed suit. John escorted them to the door. As they were walking away, they heard his fist pounding on the inside of the door.

"That was difficult." Joseph agreed.

Sleep did not come easily for Deidre that night. She dreamed she was chasing a formless figure through the woods, but the snow was knee deep, dragging at her every step. She dreamed that she finally collapsed, exhausted, while the figure lurked in the shadows of the tree line.

By six the next morning, she had packed her few belongings and checked out of the hotel. The ride home was long.

Chapter
Eleven

Pₑₜₑ barged out of his dog house when she drove up her driveway. He stood waiting, his tail wagging exuberantly and his ears perked expectantly. When Deidre opened the car door, he almost crawled into her lap.

"Well, aren't you the perfect welcoming committee," she laughed as she scratched his ears. If dogs could smile, Pete did.

"Come on, boy. Let's get you some food, and then I have a call to make. What do you say we take a trip to Duluth this afternoon?"

It was early afternoon when she pulled into Ben's driveway. By then the day had taken its toll. Deidre had logged over two hundred miles on icy, winter roads, had skipped lunch and had put herself through an emotional wringer, wondering where to go next in the investigation. She needed a friend.

Before she could exit her car, Megan and Maren burst from the door, running down the sidewalk in their stocking feet, oblivious to the cold.

"Girls! Girls, get back here and put on your jackets and boots," Ben shouted, but they were deaf to his voice.

Deidre swooped them up in her arms and carried them back to the house. Pete was left in the backseat, trying desperately to join the excitement. The children were deposited safely in their father's arms, and Deidre returned to let Pete out. He immediately checked the shrubbery to see what other dogs had been around, then left his yellow mark on a juniper bush protruding above the snow.

They all went inside. Pete, being comfortable with the place, lay down on his pad in the corner of the entry, and Deidre took the twins from Ben.

"Oh, I've missed you girls so much," she said as she kissed each girl. "I could just eat you up," and she made a snuffling noise as she pretended to nibble on their cheeks.

The girls giggled and twisted as though they wanted to escape, but they didn't really want to be put down. Ben stood in the background, looking on.

"Okay, you two hunyucks, let's give Deidre some air."

Megan retorted, "We're not hunyucks."

"Oh, yes, you are," Ben shot back, and he tucked each child under an arm as he carried them into the kitchen. They squealed with delight. It was Deidre's turn to watch, and she thought, *If any children have a shot at a good life, it has to be them.* She smiled at the unforced expression of love she was witnessing.

After a quick snack, Ben suggested they go to the Duluth Zoo. A sliding hill had been prepared, and for any donation to the Zoo's coffers, children could play all day.

They packed up four inner tubes Ben had stored in the loft of his garage and bundled the girls against the cold with bright colored scarves ready to drape around their chins as they careened down the hill.

Conditions were perfect, hard packed snow, crisp air, and not a huge crowd to slow their fun.

"Come on, Deidre, I'll show you how we do this," Maren urged Deidre to follow her to the brink of the hill. "We line up our tubes this way," and she placed the rides side by side. "Megan, that one is yours," and she pointed to the one at the far end.

"No, that's not fair!" Megan spat out. "I want to be in the middle." Maren ignored her sister's complaint.

"Daddy, you get this one. Deidre, you get to be next to Daddy, and I'll be on the other end." That arrangement placated Megan.

"Now we all sit in our own tube and hold each other's hand," and she plunked down in her spot, reaching for Deidre.

When all were ready, Ben gave a slight push to get them started down the hill, and the chain of sliders picked up speed until the snow beneath them was flying past. Near the bottom of the hill was a man-made mogul, and the string of sliders hit it at top speed. In rapid succession, they were catapulted in the air, separated from their tubes, and ended up in a heap on the snowy ground.

Megan picked up a handful of snow and rubbed it in her dad's face. He, in turn put his cold, wet fingers down the back of her neck, and she squealed in delight. For an instant the four wrestled on the ground, trying to untangle their arms and legs. Deidre found herself entwined with Ben, and for a moment they stopped laughing.

Then Ben, with a forced laugh, said, "Sorry about that. My bad," and he got up, dusted the snow off his clothes, and started up the hill.

Deidre was in the middle of saying, "Oh, think nothing of it," but she was speaking to the back of his head by that time, and she doubted if her heard.

They played in the cold for over an hour, until the twins hair was stuck to their sweaty foreheads, and Ben and Deidre were getting chilled to the bone.

"Time to go, girls. Deidre's had a long day, I'm cold, and it's time to make supper."

They left the hill amid gripes and complaints echoing from the backseat of Ben's van. Pete was waiting to be let out, and he immediately re-marked his favorite bush before wanting back in the house. He plopped down on his pad, stretched full length before curling up, and closed his eyes.

"You must be tired and cold," Ben said to Deidre. "Why don't you take a hot shower and then a nap. We'll wake you for supper, and we can spend the evening watching a movie. The girls love the movie *Cars*. We have our own copy. Afterward, if you want to talk about it, you can tell me about the case you're working."

*****

Deidre stood under the hot spray, letting the core of her body warm, letting her body relax, if only for a few blessed minutes. Somehow, she was having a difficult time washing away the memory of that brief moment when she and Ben lay in a tangled heap on the ground. Then she put it from her mind. *Not going to happen*, she thought.

She dried herself off and was standing in front of the full-length closet mirror. The scars on her chest were still very visible, probably would be for the rest of her life, but they didn't bother her. It was the scars inside of her that mattered, the ones in her mind that no one could see. She reflected back to the day more than four years ago when Ben had saved her life.

Although she remembered nothing about what happened after she was wounded by a terrorist, Deidre had been told Ben had shot and killed her assailant before he could put another bullet into her prostrate body.

She had just put on her panties when the bedroom door was thrown open. Megan and Maren burst into the room.

"Oh, sorry," they started to say, and then stopped in their tracks. "What's that?" Maren asked, pointing at the scar. Megan stood with her mouth open.

Deidre closed the door. "I had an accident one time."

"Was it a big owie?" Maren wanted to know.

"Yes, it was a big owie."

"Does it still hurt?" the twins asked in unison.

"No, not at all. Sometimes it itches though."

"Do you want us to scratch it for you?" Maren offered.

"No, it doesn't itch right now."

"Can I touch it?" Megan timidly asked.

"If you want to." Deidre knelt down and each girl took a turn running their fingers over the healed wound. Their touch was gentle, almost like a butterfly landing, Deidre thought.

"Does Daddy know you have this?" Maren inquired.

"Yes, your daddy knows about it."

"Has he ever seen it?" Megan wanted to know.

Deidre laughed. "Well, I certainly hope not." By this time she had put her bra on and was pulling on a sweater.

"I'm going to take a short nap. Do you want to lie down with me?"

The girls crawled onto the bed, one on each side of her. They lay perfectly still for ten seconds, then Megan popped up.

"Is it time to wake up?" she asked.

"Yeah, is it time to wake up?" Maren echoed.

"No, I need a little more rest. Why don't you girls go down and play with Pete. I'll bet he needs his ears scratched."

"Okay," they answered as they slid off the bed.

Deidre heard them shut her door and heard their feet as they raced down the hall. The next thing she heard was a knock on her door.

"Deidre. It's six-thirty. I have supper on the table. Do you want to eat, or should we let you sleep?"

She rubbed the sleep from her eyes and tried to clear her head. She went to the bathroom sink, splashed some cold water on her face, and straightened her hair until she was satisfied with what she saw in the mirror.

After supper, Deidre helped Ben clean the kitchen while the girls dressed Pete in a dolly bonnet and tried to feed him from a dolly bottle. The doleful look in his eyes said, *Please get me out of this.*

Ben set up the DVD player and everyone sat on the couch, Megan and Maren wedged between the adults. Before the movie started, Megan looked up at Ben.

"Do you know that Deidre has an owie?" she innocently asked.

Ben smiled at her. "Yes, I know about her owie."

"Well, have you ever seen it?"

This time Ben had to laugh. "No, I've never seen it."

"Well, we have," Maren smugly stated. Then as children do, they shifted their attention to the TV.

"Is the movie almost ready?"

*****

DEIDRE'S EYES POPPED OPEN the next morning as if waking from a nightmare. For an instant she was confused, and it took a moment for her to oriente herself to her surrounding. Her heart beat returned to normal, and she looked at the digital clock glowing on the night stand. Six-thirty. At that time of year it was still dark until 7:00.

The house was dark and quiet, and Deidre put on her robe, quietly made her way downstairs, let Pete out to inspect his personal shrub, and picked up the Sunday paper that had been delivered in the early morning hours.

She made a cup of tea in the microwave and sat down to peruse the front page while she sipped the brew. Her attention was immediately drawn to an article with lesser headlines.

MINNEAPOLIS JUDGE ARRESTED IN PAY FOR SEX SWEEP

Members of the Minneapolis Police Vice and Racketeering squad executed a nighttime raid on Saturday morning. They were acting on reports of girls as young as thirteen being prostituted at an undisclosed four-plex in Edina.

One officer, who spoke off the record, said the public would be shocked at what was discovered, but for the time being, names are being withheld to protect those who are innocent.

At that point Deidre bristled. "And to protect those who have buddies in the system," she said out loud. But she continued reading.

Separate information provided by a reliable source has indicated that the multi-unit housing complex is owned by an individual long associated with crime in the city, and that four girls, all under the age of sixteen, were handed over to Social Services.

Our informant told us only one customer was in the facility at the time of the raid. He was identified as District Judge Tony DeMarcus, longtime member of the Twin Cities legal scene.

Deidre sat staring at the paper, her mind refusing to let her forget the sight of Anna Woodsong's body huddled under the bridge. She thought it would be a long shot if there were a connection between the judge and her victim, but the article triggered thoughts about the murder.

At that moment, she contemplated a visit to Judge DeMarcus to ask him about his knowledge of the organization he had been patronizing. She knew he'd be hostile, knew he'd refuse to see her, knew he wouldn't incriminate himself. But perhaps, she thought, he might be encouraged to reveal some clues if she approached him with a hypothetical case, speaking as Bureau officer to judge.

Before she could form a plan, chaos erupted when the girls, leading Ben, spilled into the kitchen.

"We're having pancakes for breakfast. We always have pancakes on Sunday. Do you? Do you want chocolate sprinkles on them? We do. Daddy makes pancakes with smiley faces. Have you ever had a pancake with a smiley face?"

The questions came at her so fast, Deidre didn't have time to answer.

"Calm down, girls. Give Deidre time to wake up." He looked at her and laughed.

That evening, Deidre left Ben's as the sun was setting. It was four-forty-five, and by the time she got to Inga's, the early winter night would have arrived. Again, she was forced to drive in the dark. On the way home, she made a mental list of what she would ask Jill to do in the morning.

Chapter
Twelve

DEIDRE ARRIVED AT HER OFFICE fifteen minutes early, hoping to gather her thoughts and start the day with a cup of coffee. As she made her way down the hall, she could see the lights were on, and she could smell coffee brewing. She felt as though she were late for work.

"Good morning Boss Lady," Jill said as Deidre made her way to her desk. "How'd the meeting go with the Grand Chief?"

Deidre didn't quite know how to react. On the one hand, she was irked at Jill's informality. But on the other hand, she couldn't fault the woman's efficiency. "Thanks for setting up a motel room for me. It was nice to not have to deal with that. Much appreciated." Jill caught the point that Deidre hadn't answered her question and didn't press the issue further.

She poured Deidre a cup of coffee, and asked, "What do you want me to do today? I'm at a loss for work this morning, unless I rearrange the office furniture, but there are only four corners, and it won't make much sense to rotate what we have." She smiled expectantly at Deidre, who tried to smile back.

"Send off official letters of thanks to Grand Chief Musio, Joseph Walkin, and Charles Freeman for their support. Then I'd like you to do some research on a district judge in Minneapolis, Tony DeMarcus. Find out as much as you can about a raid on a four-plex in Edina last Saturday. It involved teenage prostitution. Contact the Minneapolis police for what information they'll give you. Play the BCA card.

For a moment Deidre watched Jill scribble in shorthand. "I'm going to Duluth today to interview a boat captain I know, and it might take awhile. He's an old Norwegian. Nils is his name. He's a pretty lonesome guy, and it's hard to get away from him once you start visiting. But he knows a lot about the harbor and boats. I want his perspective on what the harbor was like twenty years ago."

Jill jotted down what Deidre ordered. "The drafts of thank you letters are in the folder on your desk. Read them over. Make any changes you want. I'll have final copies ready for your signature when you return."

Deidre read through the communications. "I can't see a thing I'd change. I'll sign these, and you can get them in the morning mail." She left the room shaking her head in amazement.

On the way out of town she stopped at the Holiday gas station on the southwest end of town. As the meter on the pump turned to double digits, Deidre was thankful she had a company credit card. This case was going to burn up a lot of gasoline, she thought.

When the tank was full and she collected the receipt, Deidre pulled onto Highway 61, heading back to Duluth. Deep in thought, she crossed over the French River and was almost to London Road in Duluth. The speed limit was thirty and when she looked at the speedometer it registered forty-five.

Lucky I'm in a marked car, she thought but nevertheless let her vehicle coast to the prescribed limit. In about two miles she turned onto I-35 and picked up her pace. Ten minutes later she was at the Fortieth Avenue West exit where she left the freeway. Another three blocks and she was at Nils' home. She had visited regularly when she lived in Two Harbors, but it was a long drive from her cabin to Duluth, and her visits had become infrequent.

When she knocked on the door of his cottage, she heard a thin voice call out, "Come on in. The door's open."

Nils had been a captain of a Great Lakes ore boat for years, but to look at him now, one would never guess he had guided those thousand-foot behemoths through narrow passageways. These days, Nils was relegated to sitting in a wheelchair and letting others serve him.

"Deidre Johnson," he croaked as his milky eyes attempted to focus on her. "What are you doing visiting a dried up old prune like me? Don't ya know the neighbors will be talking if we meet like this?" He cackled at his own joke.

"Let them talk, Nils. If I lived closer, I'd ask you to go steady with me." That made Nils laugh until he had a coughing fit, and it took him several seconds to get his breath back.

"Just the thought of that almost killed me," he said, and laughed again.

"Nils, I came by to have a talk about something serious. Sorry to have to get to the point this way, but I need to tap into your knowledge of the harbor."

Nils became silent. Then he murmured, "Yes, the harbor. Well, I guess I can tell you a few things about that place. But nothing recent. I haven't been able to get down there for years. Don't even get to sit by the canal and watch the boats come into port."

Deidre noticed the faraway look in his eyes. "This isn't a pleasant subject for me to talk about, but when you were captain, did prostitutes ever get smuggled on board the lakers?"

Nils shifted his position in his chair, and Deidre could see how thin and useless his legs had become.

"Not that I would ever allow it, or any other captain I knew. We had strict rules about that. If any hand was caught trying that stunt, he was immediately fired. If anyone did succeed on a captain's watch, the captain was written up and docked wages. A second incident of that nature led to dismissal. I never knew of a captain losing his job because of such an incident."

In a way, Deidre was relieved by what Nils told her.

"Of course, what sailors did in port was their own business. We had no control over that. I know many of the sailors weren't angels. Rumor was they met prostitutes in empty railroad box cars parked by the docks in Two Harbors. A whorehouse on wheels, you might say." Nils sort of snickered. Deidre didn't laugh, so he continued. "No, we kept pretty close tabs on that sort of thing. Course things changed when the St. Lawrence Seaway opened in 1959. I had just been promoted to captain that year and remember well the day the first salty arrived to take on a load of wheat at the Superior terminal. Now *they* were a different story. In fact, I was told that some, not all mind you, but some of their captains encouraged prostitutes to come aboard as a reward for the crew. Port security said they tried to prevent it, but I don't think they tried too hard. I suspect some money exchanged hands under the table."

"Tell me, Nils, do you know of any women not allowed to leave the boat once the ship was ready to leave the harbor? Did you ever hear of any of them being kidnapped?"

Nils went silent for a moment. "I really can't say one way or another. You see, it was as though our crews and theirs lived in two different worlds. We didn't speak their language. They didn't speak ours. I think the girls sort of watched out for each other, kept each others' backs. One of them might know. 'Course I don't know any of those ladies. Most of them are dead by now, I suppose."

His gaze drifted to his window where he could see the dried stems of hollyhocks moving in the wind. Then he continued. "I do know this— things were getting a lot rougher on the docks by the time I retired. That was after the shipping season ended in 1979." He paused. "Now I'm ninety-three. Not much time left, but I had a good life. I'm content where I'm at and with where I'm headed." He smiled winsomely at Deidre, and it almost broke her heart to hear her great-uncle talk that way.

"I'm glad to see you're at peace, Nils, but I have one more question. If I wanted more answers to the questions I asked, who would you say I should look up?"

Without hesitation he answered. "You'd want to see William Ojannen. He served under me when he first joined the fleet. Worked his way up the ranks same as I did. He became captain the year I left and retired in 2010. But you'll have a tough time catching up with him. He spends his winters in Florida. I don't know where exactly, but you should be able to find out."

Deidre wrote down the name with a notation beside it. "Nils, can I do anything for you before I leave," she asked.

"Wheel me over to the window so I can wave to you when you go. Oh, and, Deidre, happy Thanksgiving if I don't get a chance to see you before then."

Deidre walked to her SUV carrying a load of guilt for having neglected the old man the last few years. She made a vow to spend more time with him. Before she stepped into her vehicle, she turned and waved at the sallow figure in the window. He waved back with his bony hand.

*****

DEIDRE WASN'T QUITE SURE of what to expect when she returned to the office. What arrangements would Jill have made?

"Hi, Boss Lady," she was greeted. "I've got the info you wanted about the judge. It's in the file on your desk. The Minneapolis police are being pretty tight lipped about the raid. Seems they're going to be stepping on some pretty big toes, and they don't want unofficial reports leaking out before they're ready. Need anything while you read what I have for you?" She smiled her expectant smile, something that was beginning to unnerve Deidre.

"Yes, I need William Ojannen's phone number. He worked on the Great Lakes fleet of ore boats until 2010 and now lives in Florida, at least during the winter. Where he stays summers, I don't know."

"Gotcha, Boss Lady. I'll get right on it."

Deidre didn't know what to say, so she sat down, picked up the folder , and began to read Jill's report.

Judge Tony DeMarcus
- *one of 62 judges in the 4th district of Minnesota*
- *age 59*
- *graduated William Mitchell Law School 1976*
- *first elected to position November, 1999*
- *married, three adult children*
- *home address: 1300 Lake Calhoun Drive, Minneapolis, MN 53211*
- *Notes: During early years of his judgeship, was noted for being strict but fair. Since 2006 has shown leniency toward certain cases,*

especially those involving the sex trade. Since then, he has thrown out three cases on grounds of insufficient evidence. Also dismissed two charges of assault brought against suspected drug dealers.

Deidre's thoughts were interrupted by Jill.

"Sorry, Boss Lady, unless you can raise the dead, you're going to have a tough time getting any info from William Ojannen. He died six months ago. Fell off a ladder and broke his neck. You'd think at his age he'd have known better. Anyway, he won't have much to give you."

Deidre still wasn't sure how to respond to this working arrangement. What could she say, the woman was more than competent.

"I ran off a copy of a Google map for you. It has instructions for getting to the judge's house on Lake Calhoun. If you leave now, you can be there by four and still have time to make it back tonight."

It was as if Jill had read her mind. She *had* planned to try to meet the judge.

In a half hour she was in her car and on her way to Minneapolis, realizing the road was becoming all too familiar. She stopped at Tobie's, a legendary stop on I-35 midway between Duluth and the Twin Cities, ordered one of their famous caramel rolls and a cup of coffee to go, and was back on the road in fifteen minutes.

Juggling the coffee and the sticky roll, she managed to drive at the same time. Deidre mulled over what she would say if she had the opportunity to see the judge. She didn't want to call ahead to ask for an audience, knowing the phone would probably be hung up, if it were answered at all.

No, she wanted this visit to be a surprise. She thought if she could catch him off guard, she might have a chance.

Jill's map and directions were easy to follow, and she maneuvered the streets with no problem. A little after four in the afternoon, Deidre pulled over to the curb near 1300 Calhoun Drive. She didn't want her BCA emblem to be noticed so she made sure she parked down the block.

As she neared the front door of his house, she could hear the shrill voice of a woman screaming obscenities inside, but she couldn't quite catch every word.

"You lying bastard! Don't you come close to me. I've put up with your philandering long enough. No! Don't you ever touch me again you . . ." Deidre couldn't make out what the last word was, but she could guess.

She hesitated before ringing the door bell, and during that moment's hesitation, the door flew open, and a very angry woman, her jacket open and flapping in the November cold, stormed past. She carried a suitcase in each hand.

Janelle DeMarcus, Tony's ex-wife-to-be, stopped in front of Deidre. "You blond bimbo, are you lining up to see the judge already? Well, go to it, you little tart, and have a good time with that worn out old SOB. You'll find out he's not much good in the bedroom, or anywhere else."

Janelle spit on the ground as if trying to get a bad taste out of her mouth, threw her stuff in a van, and peeled out of the driveway.

The judge stepped to the doorway, a drink in his hand. He teetered for a moment and then hurled the glass at the speeding van. It fell short and shattered on the concrete.

"Who the hell are you," he barked at Deidre, looking at her through bleary eyes.

"My name is Deidre. I'd like to come in if you don't mind." She smiled as sincerely at the drunk as she could.

The judge cursed and said, "I don't want to talk to anybody. Get lost." But then he looked again at the petite blond who stood on his doorstep, smiling innocently at him.

"Oh, hell, come on in. Maybe we can get to know each other."

Tony DeMarcus poured himself another drink, and flopped down in an expensive leather chair. "So, what do you want?" he slurred.

"Judge, I need some legal advice. I—"

Before she could continue, he broke in. "Leave the SOB. That's what he is, an SOB. In fact," and he pointed his drink at Deidre, "we're all a bunch of SOBs." Tony took a long swig from the glass and went silent, staring at the floor.

"Judge," Deidre tried again. He reacted as though he had forgotten she was there, jerking upright and trying to focus his eyes on her.

"Wha?" he asked. Deidre figured she better get to the point before he passed out.

"Judge, I have a hypothetical situation I'd like your advice about. From your years on the bench, are you familiar with anyone who might be connected to a prostitution ring in Hennepin County?"

The judge looked at her through narrowed eyes. "Hell, yes. This county is filled with crime. Every year, we try more cases than all the rest of the state. Walk down Hennepin Avenue any night of the week, and then ask me that question."

"Well, then, hypothetically speaking of course, do you have any judge friends who might be involved with prostitution?"

"Hypothetically? I suppose one or two might be." He drained his glass and reached for the bottle to pour another.

"If I were talking to one of them, do you think he'd be able to name some names of the pimps involved?"

The judge shifted his feet. "Maybe. Might there be anything in it for me if I say yes?"

Deidre smiled sweetly at him. "Might be, judge. But what would your friend have to tell me?"

"I think he'd say, 'Billy Evers.'"

"And where would he say I'd find this Billy Evers?"

The judge leered at Deidre. "He's in jail."

With those words he drained his glass, began to make a move toward Deidre from his chair, and fell flat on his face, passed out.

"Sorry, Judge, I guess that's all you're going to get. And you're wrong. Not all men are a bunch of SOBs."

She let herself out of the house, not bothering to rouse the inebriated judge, and climbed into her SUV. Deidre was getting ready to call Jill, but her phone rang while it was in her hand.

"Hi, Boss Lady. It's Jill."

Deidre was about to recite her rehearsed script about respect, authority, and protocol, but Jill cut her off. "I've found the names of three people charged with prostituting women and let off by Judge DeMarcus. DeJohn Franklin appeared before him four years ago. The judge ruled the evidence against him had been compromised and dismissed the case. The prosecuting attorney went ballistic and received a stayed sentence for contempt of court. Mr. Franklin was killed in a drive-by shooting last December, so you won't have to interview him."

All Deidre could do was listen and take notes. Jill continued. "The second is Trenton Williams. He appeared before DeMarcus two years ago. Same situation, same results. The judge declared the evidence inadmissible, much to the chagrin of attorney. Evidently, Trenton left the city after his release, because two months later he was arrested in New York City. He was convicted of aggravated assault with a deadly weapon, attempted murder, and kidnapping. He's serving a twenty-year sentence in the Downstate Correctional Facility in Fishkill, New York."

Jill concluded, "Not only would it be time consuming to interview him, it also might not be productive, because he's been in jail for over a year and a half."

Deidre still couldn't get in a word.

"The third is more interesting. His name's Billy Evers. Four months ago, his case was dismissed by our favorite judge, but he was arrested on a different warrant a couple of days ago at the same time the judge was caught with his pants down. Billy is in the Hennepin County Jail, and his arraignment hearing is set for nine tomorrow morning. You'll never guess who his attorney is—Gerald Colter II, a Two Harbors attorney. I thought you might try to see Billy this evening, if he'll talk to you. You might even want to hear Mr. Colter's argument in the morning, so I've booked a room for you at the Marriott. You might as well be comfortable while you're there. Got a pencil? Here's the address." Deidre wrote down what Jill dictated.

"So, anything else you want me to do before you get back tomorrow afternoon?"

Deidre was still writing. "No. No, this is fine. I'll see you around two or three tomorrow."

"Bye, then," and Deidre heard Jill disconnect the phone.

She was not quite sure how she was going to handle the whirlwind who camped in her office, and as she drove, she brooded on the problem. By the time she arrived at the Hennepin County Jail, she had come to the conclusion that Jill had done exactly what she, Deidre, would have asked her to do. It was just unnerving to have Jill do everything before she was asked.

She presented her identification to the guard manning the metal detector in the entry and was allowed to pass through. It was a long shot. Billy Evers probably wouldn't talk to her anyway, but she was here and might as well try.

To her disbelief, when she made her request known, she was escorted to a room divided by a glass partition. She sat in a wooden chair opposite a speaker mounted in the glass, and she saw movement in the hall leading in from the other side. A man who looked to be about thirty-five sat down opposite her on the other side of the glass.

"I'm Deidre Johnson, an investigator with the BCA. Are you Billy Evers?" Deidre asked, staring directly into his eyes.

"I am.

"Can I ask you a couple of questions not related to your case?"

"You can, but I can't guarantee I'll answer them."

"How well do you know Gerald Colter?"

Billy thought for a full ten seconds. "Well enough to call him."

"Have you ever been to Duluth or up the North Shore?"

Billy grinned and took his time answering. "No, can't say I have."

"How did you know to call Mr. Colter to be your attorney."

Again a long pause. "His name's in the phonebook."

"And you just happened to pick the Two Harbors phonebook?"

Billy smirked. "Good as any."

"Do you know anything about the trafficking of women to the sailors on the boats in Duluth?"

Billy's face went blank. "I suppose it could happen."

Deidre knew she was getting nowhere, that Billy Evers was mocking her. "Where were you two weeks ago tonight?"

Billy shrugged. "I'm a busy man. Do you expect me to remember that far back. If I had my calendar, I'd check it, but they're kind of fussy about those kinds of things in here." He squinted at her. "Say, you're pretty good lookin' for a cop. Doin' anything tonight? I thought we might get together, say sevenish." He laughed at his attempt to be funny.

Deidre glared at him, wondering if she should get up and leave or say what she felt like saying.

"Anything else? Otherwise, I'm bored." Billy motioned for the guard to take him back to his cell.

Deidre left, wishing she hadn't been so foolish as to get into a peeing contest with a skunk. When she got to her hotel, she was thankful for Jill's foresight. The hot shower relieved some of her tension, and she set the alarm for six-thirty the next morning. It would be good to observe Gerald Colter II in action.

She was seated in the courtroom at nine o'clock the next morning and heard the bailiff call out, "All rise." The judge, a stern looking woman with graying hair and heavy, black eyebrows stomped to her place and sat down.

The bailiff read from a script. "The case of *William Evers versus the State of Minnesota*."

The judge addressed Billy. "You are charged with being complicit to prostitution, to contributing to the delinquency of a minor, and with having sexual contact with a minor. How do you plead?"

Before Billy could answer, his attorney, Gerald Colter, sprang to his feet. He stretched out his arm and adjusted his shirt cuff so his expensive Rolex watch glinted in the light for everyone to see.

"I am requesting that all charges against my client be dropped, Your Honor. If you will take a brief moment to scan the police report, I'm sure you will agree that Mr. Williams has never been involved in such practices as the warrant against him charges today. That woman assured him she was over eighteen, and he took her at her word. Secondly—"

The judge cut him off and stared at him over the rims of her glasses. "That will be enough, Mr. Coulter. From your outburst, I assume you mean to plead not guilty. Am I correct?"

Colter was not cowed, and he glared back at her. "You are correct in that assumption. I will, however, further request that my client be released without bail. He resides in Minneapolis, has relatives in this area, and has three children. Obviously he is not flight risk and has assured me he wishes to clear his good name of these charges."

The judge continued to stare impassively at the attorney. "Bail is set at one hundred thousand dollars. Until that is paid or until this case is scheduled for trial, Mr. Evers will be remanded to the Hennepin County Jail." She hammered her gavel. "Next case."

Gerald Colter glared at her as though he thought he could intimidate her.

Once a bully, always a bully, Deidre thought.

Deidre watched Colter gather up his papers, and as he looked back at the courtroom observers, he spotted Deidre. His eyes widened and his nostrils flared, but he gave no other indication he saw her.

Chapter
Thirteen

DEIDRE GLANCED AT HER DESK CALENDAR. On the square reserved for November 28, Jill had placed a turkey sticker, its tail fanned out in full display. Thanksgiving was only three days away, and Deidre could hardly wait.

Ben had called and invited her to spend the day with him and the girls. He said his mother and father would be there as well, a thought that unnerved her somewhat. Also his brother and sister-in-law, as well as his sister, her husband, and their two children, ages ten and twelve would be present.

She almost declined the invite, but she had nowhere else to go and had no valid excuse to be alone on a holiday.

Now, she was happy she had accepted. Each of the twins sent her an invitation scribbled in their four-year-old hand, and Ben had asked her to come the evening before to help him prepare the meal.

Her desk phone rang, and she absentmindedly picked up, her mind still on Thanksgiving Day.

"Deidre, this is Jeff. I'd have come down to your office to see you in person, but things have been a little hectic here this morning. Dan Butler called me a few minutes ago to report something, and I thought you'd be interested in hearing about this. A cabin owner to the west of Palisade Head told him someone broke into one of the old cabins at the Head's base and is squatting there. I'm going to investigate. Will be leaving in a few minutes. Here's the kicker. A few people have caught a glimpse of this mystery person. It's a girl, they're pretty sure, but she never lets them get close enough to be positive. She seems to be more animal than human, always slinking from sight, never allowing anyone to approach her. And . . . she seems to fit the description of the girl you found dead."

Deidre could hardly believe what Jeff was saying. Sheriff Jeff DeAngelo, the man who had been elected to her former position was a dear friend, and she knew that if he called, he had already done some checking to make sure it wasn't a wild goose chase.

"When are you leaving?" Deidre asked.

"I'll swing by your office in five minutes. We can take my squad. No reason for us to drive separately."

Deidre told Jill where she was going and asked her to check on what clients Gerald Colter II had in the Twin Cities in the past four years. She'd have to search court records for that information. Jeff knocked on the office door, then poked his head in. "Ready?" he asked.

Deidre had her winter jacket and boots on. "How much snow is up there?" she asked, referring to Palisade Head.

"They had a good dump the night before last. I'd say about a foot."

Deidre knew the area they were going to visit well. Palisade Head, a massive rock outcrop on the shore of Lake Superior, was a sheer cliff dropping straight down to the boulder-strewn shore. Geologists estimate that it was formed over a billion years ago, when a fissure opened in the earth's surface and untold amounts of lava oozed from the crack. Now it stood over three hundred feet above lake level.

It was a popular tourist site. Although dangerous, sightseers could virtually walk to the edge and look over. In the past, there had been accidental deaths resulting from someone losing their balance and falling from the precipice. Some were probably not accidental. When she was sheriff, she had been called to investigate two of those deaths.

With the recent snow accumulation, and taking into account the minus-ten wind chill factor, Deidre was sure no one would be on the Palisade today. She calculated they would have a half-mile trudge to the abandoned cabin, find the homeless person, talk her into coming back with them, and take her to the women's shelter in downtown Two Harbors.

Jeff parked his SUV on the side of the road opposite a nearly hidden driveway, and they began slogging through the snow. Deidre was forced to pull up the hood of her parka to shield her face from the frigid winter air. Their breath crystallized as soon as it left their mouths, and the cloud of frozen moisture scattered in the wind.

A few yards in, they were surprised to find a set of tracks in the snow. "Someone else must know about this place," Jeff commented. "It looks like they came in from the driveway to the south. Maybe it's a neighbor come to check on the girl."

Deidre was too cold to answer. She plowed on with her head bowed against the wind. It took them twenty minutes to reach the tumble-down cabin. When they did, they could see the tracks they had been following veered to the left, heading up the grade toward the cliff.

Wood smoke rose from the cabin's chimney, and Deidre noted several trails leading from the door. Evidently, the occupant had been here for a while and had been scrounging the forest for firewood.

She stepped onto the open porch and knocked on the door. "Anyone in there?" No one answered. Deidre pounded harder, and the unlatched door swung inward.

The deserted cabin was rustic. It held that characteristic odor of a building that had sat empty for a long time—a mixture of dust and stale air mixed with the aroma of wood.

A crumpled overcoat lay in a heap on the bed, evidently having served as a blanket. A mostly empty bread wrapper sat on the table, but they saw no other signs of food. Except for the coat and plastic wrapper, the cabin would have appeared unoccupied.

"A set of tracks leads up the slope," Jeff called from outside. "It looks as though whose ever tracks we saw coming in joins them. One must be following the other."

Deidre went to where Jeff stood, looking at the intersection of the two sets. "The set we saw are the most recent. They were made on top of those leading from the cabin. There must be two people squatting in the building."

Jeff and Deidre began following the trail. It was terribly difficult, because the slope to Palisade Head was almost too steep to climb, the snow was nearly knee deep, and the icy air seared their lungs as they gasped for oxygen. Deidre reflected that their trek was easier than that of the people they were following, because their predecessors had somewhat packed a trail. She hoped they were gaining on the pair.

At one spot along the climb, the wind had made an unobstructed sweep across the terrain, and the snow was packed so hard they could walk on its surface. Jeff stopped. "Deidre. Look!"

She knelt to get a better view. The tracks diverged enough that she could make out individual prints. One was a boot track. It was large and had a tread pattern much like Canadian pacs would leave. Deidre compared her boot size to the markings in the snow, and surmised it had been left by a man's foot. The other track grabbed her attention.

"What do you make of this?" she asked looking up at Jeff.

"Whoever made these smaller tracks wasn't wearing boots," he solemnly observed. "It looks like feet wrapped in cloth or rags. And look there."

Deidre looked ahead to where Jeff pointed. She could see faint pink stains left in the snow. "Is that blood?"

She moved to where Jeff indicated. "We better get moving. I don't think the two we are following are together. By the looks of it, this person is clearly in distress."

Deidre picked up the pace, speaking over her shoulder. "You're right, the first set of tracks has no distinct edges, and the blood we saw was seeping through whatever is on her feet."

She realized she had unconsciously made the assumption they would find a man chasing a small woman.

Her lungs ached from sucking in the cold. She was almost ready to tell Jeff she needed a rest, but they were too near the top to stop now. Through the trees she could see nothing but sky, and she assumed they were nearing the crest of the cliff. Then they heard muffled sounds of a scuffle in the snow. There were no shrieks or screams, only grunts and groans as though the fight was too life-and-death for wasted energy.

Jeff signaled to Deidre he was going to circumvent the scene and come up from the other side. He motioned for Deidre to come from the other direction. She veered somewhat to her right and moved toward the sounds of the struggle. The snow made it possible for her to move silently.

She pushed aside the balsam boughs and grabbed for her service revolver. Her hand fumbled as she tried to clear it from under the layers of clothing she wore, and on the other side of a small clearing, she observed Jeff standing, his pistol in hand and pointed at the two people.

Near the edge of the cliff, they were clasped in a death grip. A large man was clearly attempting to throw the other person off the cliff to a sure death on the rocks three hundred feet below.

Deidre could make out a girl's long, black hair flying in the wind. Her arms were clasped around the man's waist, and her legs were entwined with one of his. She was barefooted, and Deidre saw that whatever rags had been wrapped around her feet had come loose and were lying in a bloody heap in the snow.

"Get your hands up, now!" Jeff shouted. ""NOW!"

The man was so intent on what he was trying to do, he was oblivious to the fact that the law enforcement officers had arrived. He kept edging closer to the brink and kept trying to pry the girl's arms and legs from him. He would peel off one of her arms, and then try to untangle her leg, but whenever he let go one appendage and reached for another, she would clutch at him again. There was no way he could throw her over the edge without being pulled over himself.

All this happened in an instant, and Deidre realized that Jeff was rushing the frantic duo. She became aware she was doing the same. Jeff arrived first.

"Let go of her!" Jeff bellowed, and the man looked up in surprise, a momentary look of panic in his eyes. He relaxed his grip on the girl and involuntarily stepped back. In the same instant, the girl let go of the man.

The smooth rocks on the top of the Palisade were covered with a thin coating of ice. For a second, the man's arms windmilled empty air.

With one curse and a loud groan he disappeared over the edge. What seemed like a minute later but must have been only seconds, they heard a thud as if a sack of flour had been dropped on a concrete floor.

Deidre moved toward the girl but stopped in her tracks when she looked into her eyes.

The waif backed closer to the drop, and Deidre couldn't help notice the snow turning red beneath her bare feet.

"Please, stop," Deidre begged in a soft voice. "We're police and want to help you."

The girl shook her head over and over, a wild look in her eyes, and moved even closer to death. Jeff moved to the other side and attracted her attention. He put his gun in his pocket and held up both hands as a sign that he meant no harm.

Deidre had seen cornered wild animals, and the girl reminded her of one. She was so frightened she couldn't speak and only made a mixture of whimpers and snarls. Deidre could see utter panic in her eyes and was fearful the girl would leap, preferring death to being taken alive.

Jeff spoke in as reassuring a voice as he could. "We're here to help you. Whatever it is you are running from, we can protect you. Please believe me."

He kept moving, not toward her but enough to keep her attention focused on him. Jeff kept his hands in the air, showing her that he had no bad intentions, all the while speaking softly. The girl seemed to have forgotten about Deidre's presence. While Jeff held her attention, Deidre silently moved into position between her and the cliff. Finally, she remembered Deidre and spun to make a dash for the edge.

Deidre was nearly in position. She lowered her shoulder and made a forceful tackle. No way was she letting the slight frame elude her grasp. Together they fell in the snow.

The girl didn't utter a sound but fought like a wildcat, biting and scratching as only a deranged person could. Jeff wrapped his arms around her, pinning her arms to her torso. Still she struggled, kicking and writhing so that Deidre could hardly subdue her.

Finally the girl collapsed, totally spent. Deidre had seen this happen to animals. When they sensed all was lost, they would enter what she could only describe as a stupor, waiting for the end to come.

Deidre took off her jacket and wrapped it around the girl's shoulders. Jeff did the same but wrapped his around her feet. She placed the girl's head in her lap, and curled her body over it, trying to be a shield from the bitter wind that whipped from the northwest. She could feel the slender body trembling, and she thought it wasn't from the cold. The snow turned yellow beneath where the girl lay, and Deidre realized the poor thing had urinated.

Steam and the smell of ammonia rose in the brittle air.

"Hold her, Deidre. I'll phone for help," Jeff said as he fumbled out his cell phone with shaking fingers numbed by the cold.

Deidre tried to comfort the child, whispering in her ear that all was going to be fine, even though she didn't believe it. The girl lay perfectly still, her eyes open but seeing nothing. She had lost all ability to communicate. For a moment, Deidre thought she had died but noticed a slight rise and fall of her chest.

Jeff finished his call and joined Deidre in trying to protect the frail girl from the elements, but by that time, all three were reaching the point of succumbing to hypothermia.

It seemed like an eternity while they waited for the expected help to arrive. She and Jeff hovered over the girl, crowding their bodies together to conserve body heat. In actual time, within five minutes of Search and Rescue receiving the call, they were on the road. Ten minutes later they were at the entrance to Palisade Head.

Deidre heard the whine of a snowmobile motor start up. It grew louder, and she knew that within a very short time help would arrive, bringing plenty of blankets, she hoped. She could see flashes of yellow through the brush, and Scott, the head of Lake County Search and Rescue, came into full view.

"My God! What happened here?" He looked around, as another snowmobile pulling a sled arrived.

"Quick, get those blankets over there," he ordered the driver of the other rig. "We've got two more sleds coming. What else do we need?"

Jeff said, "I'm afraid you'll need your rappelling gear. I hate to ask this of you guys, but there's another person down there." He pointed to the edge of the cliff. "I doubt if there's much hurry, but we need to retrieve his body. Deidre and I need blankets and something hot to drink. Has the ambulance gotten here yet?"

Scott spoke into his two-way before answering. "I heard it coming when I left the staging area down below. It should be waiting."

The other driver took three heavy wool blankets to Deidre, and the two of them wrapped the covering over the limp body. Deidre was able to put her parka back on, but nothing could stop her shivering. Jeff did the same.

The four of them gently lifted the unconscious girl and laid her on the sled. Three straps were laced over her to prevent her from being dumped out on the way to the parking lot below.

"Jeff, this is your county," Deidre said. "You don't need me taking over your jurisdiction. I'm going to hitch a ride down to the road and accompany this girl in the ambulance. As soon as you can, will you stop by my office and let me know what's going on with that guy down there?"

Before Jeff could respond, she hopped on the machine behind the driver, and they slowly made their way down the trail. On the way, they met two more members of the squad coming up. She didn't envy them their job.

Chapter
Fourteen

"What happened up here, Jeff?" Scott wanted to know.

"When we got here, some guy looked as though he was trying to throw that girl off the cliff. Deidre and I startled him. He slipped and fell himself. He's down there somewhere, I know that. No one's ever survived a fall off this ledge. He went over right there." Jeff pointed to a place where the scuff marks in the snow ended in empty space.

The two most recent members of Search and Rescue to arrive were busy belaying ropes to a large tree. They strung out the lines, threw the coils over the edge, and watched them disappear. They were rewarded by a tug on their end. The ropes were secured and hung down the side of Palisade Head.

Jeff watched them strap on their harnesses, and he was thankful there were people with enough courage to hang from the side of vertical rock walls. He knew he couldn't have done it. They slipped the steel rings of their harnesses over the ropes, looped the end of it under their thighs and around their backs and began the three-hundred-foot descent to the bottom.

In minutes, Scott received a call on his hand-held radio. "Scott, lower the stretcher down. No need to hurry. Not much left of him."

Scott and the other team member dragged a heavy wire and conduit stretcher to the edge, rigged a rope to it, and lowered it to those who waited below. While the men at the bottom were doing their job, he, Jeff, and the third man fixed an electric winch to a tree in preparation for lifting the dead weight to the top.

They had just finished when they felt a tug on the line, and a voice on the two-way said, "You can start bringing him up. Go slow so we can guide from here, but it's tough going. The entire cliff face is coated with two inches of ice. This will take awhile."

A half hour later, Jeff spotted the hand of one of the climbers reach over the edge, and then his sweaty head emerged.

"Once is enough for today," he gasped and rolled over on his back in the snow. It took the combined effort of all to haul the stretcher onto flat ground. Jeff was glad the crew had completely wrapped the body with a blanket.

It took them another twenty minutes to haul up the lines and coil them neatly away for the next time, but eventually they rode the snowmobiles down to the road. As expected, the ambulance was gone, but it didn't matter.

*****

DEIDRE WATCHED AS THE EMTs carefully placed the stretcher in the ambulance. "Careful," one warned the other. "We don't want to trigger a sudden cardiac arrest."

He turned to Deidre. "Are you riding with?" She didn't need a further invitation and climbed in the back of the rig.

As the ambulance slowly lumbered away from the road leading to Palisade Head, the paramedic took the girl's temperature. "Ninety-four degrees," he announced with little inflection in his voice. "Respiration, ten. Heart rate thirty-six and irregular."

Deidre realized his comments were being recorded. He continued. "I'm applying heat packs to her neck, thorax, and groin areas." She watched as the EMT placed chemically activated heat pads around the girl's chest, under her armpits, and near her pubis.

She watched as the EMT cut away the girls clothing, exposing her groin. She diverted her gaze to the girl's face. *She could be the twin of Anna Woodsong,* she thought. *Same hair color, same facial features, same body shape. This is more than a coincidence.*

By that time the ambulance was speeding down Highway 61 toward Two Harbors with its lights flashing and its sirens screaming.

They reached a passing lane, and Deidre was relieved to see the lone vehicle on the road swerve to the side and stop. They sped by without having to change lanes.

In twenty minutes the ambulance pulled into the emergency bay of Lakeview Memorial Hospital, and two attendants ran out to meet them. One was guiding and the other pushing a gurney. The girl's limp body was wheeled inside, Deidre following closely behind.

"Deidre, good to see you," the charge nurse said as she walked by, not breaking stride. Deidre followed behind without invitation.

The nurse began to hook the patient up to all sorts of sensors. On a monitor screen, Deidre saw her temperature register first: ninety-five degrees, up one degree since they left the Head.

Another lead was attached to her index finger, Oxygen level: ninety-four percent Deidre's eyes were fixed to the monitor. Respiration rate: fifteen. Another lead. Heart rate: forty.

The orderly had stripped away the clothing from the victim, and she lay naked on the bed. Deidre's eyes were fixed on her breasts. They were small, and her brown nipples were nowhere nearly fully developed. *She can't be more than fourteen,* Deidre surmised.

The ER nurse began fixing EKG patches to strategic spots: one under the girls left breast, another on the side of her ribcage, another above her breast near her collar bone.

Deidre watched as she palpated the girl's thorax on the right side of her sternum, feeling for her ribs. When the right spot was found, she stuck a lead connection there. Finally, a lead was placed on each arm and her leg.

When the nurse was done, ten wires fed impulses to the monitor, and Deidre could see a series of peaks and valleys etched on the screen by an invisible stylus. Even without medical training, she could observe that every few beats an irregular peak was recorded. Sometimes it was missing, at other times it was too soon, and sometimes it was higher than the others.

An LPN inserted a urinary catheter, and Deidre saw a bag attached to the side of the bed begin to collect an amber solution. Then the girl was covered with a warming blanket.

An ER doctor who looked like he was hardly old enough to be out of high school entered the room and observed the cardiogram as it was being made.

"I want a 1,000 mil, ninety-nine-degree normal saline drip started. Do not leave her side, and call me when it has been totally infused." He left the room without saying another word and ignored Deidre.

The nurse hurried away, leaving her alone with the girl she had rescued. Tears came to her eyes as she looked at the helpless child laying on the table, and she tugged the blanket up a little higher in a feeble effort to help.

A med tech came in, carrying her tray of tools. She broke open a packet and produced a needle attached to a tube. She palpated the girl's forearm, located a vein near her wrist, and inserted the needle into a virtually non-existent vein. Deidre winced when the needle went in, but the tech matter-of-factly taped it in place, flushed it with saline, and left the room. On to the next patient, Deidre imagined.

Her nurse returned, carrying an IV bag, and with no hesitation hung it on a stand and connected it to the port the med tech had inserted. Deidre could see fluid begin to drain down the tube into the girl's thin arm.

In fifteen minutes the bag was nearly empty, and the nurse retreated to the main desk for a few seconds. She returned with the ER doctor.

By now, the monitor registered a temperature of ninety-eight degrees. The EKG had fewer anomalies, and her heart rate had risen to fifty-five.

"I think she's coming out of the woods," the doctor stated, relief evident in his voice. "Looks like we won't need a saline lavage. Young people always respond quicker than the elderly do. By the looks of it, she's been through a lot."

He turned to Deidre. "Are you the adult in charge of this juvenile?" he said with an accusatory tone.

Deidre shook her head. Then she identified herself, producing her badge. She went on to explain the happenings leading up to the girl having been brought to the ER.

"Will I be able to speak with her in the morning?" she queried.

"Possibly. However, I've called in a child abuse specialist. There's a pediatrician who works out of the Cities, Mark Hrovich, who's hired by the state to investigate this type of case. He'll be here this evening to make an assessment of the patient's condition. Your request will have to go through him.

"You can wait for him tonight or see him in the morning before he returns to Minneapolis. Either way, it'll be his call."

Deidre opted to wait until morning. She wanted to check with Jeff, and she surmised he might have returned to his office.

*****

JEFF STUCK HIS HEAD into the emergency room. "Is she alive?" he questioned, expecting the worst.

Deidre filled him in on what she knew. "I need a lift back to the Center. Will you give me a ride?"

After Jeff pulled into his parking space, the two of them walked to his office together.

"What do you think, Deidre? There must be a link between that girl and your murder victim. There seem to be too many similarities to ignore. Between the two of us, I think we have our hands full."

Deidre paused when they reached his office. "I know you're understaffed, but I think it might be wise to place a guard at her hospital door. I can't believe her assailant is the only person who wants her dead. I may be overreacting, but whatever is going on is not going to stop. I'm sure of that."

108

Jeff looked at her in surprise. "I hadn't even thought along those lines, but of course, I didn't have anything to do with the murder you discovered a couple of weeks ago. And you're right. Better safe than sorry. I'll have a deputy up there in a short while."

"Thanks for catering to me. How about you? Have you found out anything about the guy who went over the cliff?"

"So far, not much," Jeff answered, shaking his head in puzzlement. "As you can imagine, his body was pretty broken up from the fall, but he did have a wallet in his pocket with an ID. His name's Jason Leder. The interesting thing about him, his address is Thunder Bay, Ontario. I ran his name through our data base. I'm pretty sure he's not a U.S. citizen."

That information took Deidre by surprise, and she saw another thread to her case form. The coincidences kept piling up. *Another job for Jill*, she thought. On her way home to Inga's, she phoned her office.

"You have reached the office of BCA Officer Deidre Johnson. This is Jill Dobers, her secretary, speaking. How may I help you."

This was the first time Deidre had heard her answer the phone and was startled at her professionalism.

"Hello," Jill said again, wondering if her caller had hung up.

"Oh, sorry, Jill," Deidre said, a little embarrassed at being taken aback. "This is Deidre."

"Hey, Boss Lady. How are you? I worried about you when I heard there was a problem on Palisade Head. You okay?"

Again Deidre was slow to answer. She hadn't expected Jill to be concerned about her welfare. "Uh, oh, I'm fine. Just really tired. I know it's late in the day, but could you run a check on a Jason Leder. He lives in Thunder Bay." She gave Jill the street address. "We're pretty sure he's not a U.S. citizen, so you might begin with the Thunder Bay authorities first. I'm going home and try to get some rest. See you in the morning."

"Bye, Boss Lady. Take care of yourself. We need you on this case."

Deidre had to smile as she closed her cell phone, ending the call.

Inga had some kind of hot dish on the stove, and its aroma made Deidre's mouth water.

"Deidre, I was hoping you'd get home in time for supper. You must be cold and hungry after such a long day. Sit down." Inga pulled a chair out from the table and motioned for her to sit. The table was already set. Inga dished a helping of food onto both plates. Heat rose from the concoction of hamburger, potato chunks, sliced onions, and carrots smothered in some kind of tomato sauce. She sliced thick slabs of bread from a loaf fresh out of the oven, and poured a cup of steaming coffee.

Over supper, Deidre shared with Inga the story of her trek up Palisade Head, but she gave no information about why she was up there or what she had found, only that it had been bitter cold and hard work.

"I'm going to lie down on the couch, if that's okay. I'd like to grab a few minutes of sleep. Wake me in a half hour. We can talk more this evening."

She curled up and pulled a down lap robe over her. After a few minutes she flipped over, trying to get comfortable, but images she could not erase from her mind kept her from rest. A half hour later, Inga gently placed her hand on Deidre's shoulder. She hadn't slept a wink.

"Do you want to wake up, dear?" the older woman asked.

Deidre reluctantly sat up. "I couldn't sleep, Inga. I think I'm going to check on someone in the hospital. She got up and pulled on her parka.

"I don't think I remember a November this cold, ever," she said as she closed the outside door behind herself.

*****

DEIDRE RANG THE BUZZER, and was admitted to the ER entryway. "Has Dr. Hrovich been here," she asked at the nurses' station.

"He's with a patient right now. Do you want me to tell him a relative is here?" The nurse was young.

"No, that's all right. I'll wait for him to finish. My name's Deidre Johnson. I'm with the State Bureau of Criminal Apprehension. I want to learn what he has discovered about the girl we brought in today. How is she doing?"

"She's stable," the receptionist answered, noncommittally. "There's hot coffee in the waiting room."

Deidre filled a cup and sat in a chair, looking off into space and seeing nothing. The next thing she knew, the nurse was touching her shoulder. "Dr. Hrovich would like to speak to you in the conference room."

Deidre looked at her watch. An hour had passed since she took a seat, and she was glad she had set the cup of coffee down before falling asleep.

A kindly-looking man rose to greet her when she entered the conference room. "Hello. I'm Mark. Before I tell you what I've discovered, may I check your ID? Just a precaution."

After Deidre had produced her badge and picture ID, he motioned her to sit opposite him at the end of the table. He placed his fingers to his temples and closed his eyes for a minute. "I don't quite know where to begin, except to say that we are dealing with one of the worst cases of abuse I have ever witnessed. We might as well begin with some very unusual bruising I found. There is little doubt but that she was manacled by her left ankle to prevent her from escaping. The marks left by the ring are unmistakable. Bruising would indicate she was handled very roughly, although I couldn't find evidence of her being beaten by any specific object such as a club or a whip."

He paused again to massage his temples.

"She has been sexually abused. Evidence points to repeated assaults. And, also, she tested positive for gonorrhea. If that isn't enough, her feet are lacerated from running through snow and over ice while barefoot. Her hands show signs of frostbite, and she's extremely malnourished. Like I said, this is about the worst case of abuse I've seen in over ten years on this job." He shook his head and went back to kneading the sides of his head. Deidre saw a tear trickle down his cheek, and he blew his nose on a tissue.

"Will I be able to speak with her in the morning?" Deidre wanted to know but not wanting to sound pushy, considering the girl's condition.

"You can try. I'll still be here, and we can see her together. However, I must warn you that right now she's so traumatized that she's in a stupor. She doesn't respond to any stimuli, not sound, not lights, not even pin pricks. She has totally withdrawn into a world somewhere else. I'm sorry. I wish I could give you more."

Deidre drove home in the cold. It was beginning to snow heavily, and she thought it was shaping up to be a long winter.

Chapter
Fifteen

THE MORNING DAWNED CLOUDY but warmer, the temperature hovering near the freezing mark. Last night's snowfall amounted to about three inches of the powdery white stuff, and already water was beginning to drip from the eaves of houses. Deidre drove straight to the hospital to check on the girl she had rescued.

She entered through the main entrance and found the information desk. "May I help you," the volunteer asked.

"Yes, I'd like the room number of a young lady admitted yesterday afternoon. Her room probably has a guard at the door."

The volunteer looked through her list of patients. "I need to know the nature of your visit and see your ID before I can release that information. Something pretty dangerous must be going on. I've never had a request like this before."

Deidre produced her BCA badge along with her photo. The volunteer examined the plastic cards intently before handing them back. "She is in room 218. Check in at the nurses station before going to her room."

Deidre took the stairs. She remembered how slowly the elevator responded and knew she could get there faster by walking. She turned left down the hall and stopped at the nurses' station. A nurse was so intent on his charting that he didn't raise his head. After waiting a few seconds, Deidre cleared her throat, and he quickly looked up. "I'm sorry, can I help you," he asked, keeping his finger on the page where he had been writing.

"I'd like to visit the patient in room 218. The person at information said to check with you first."

"No visitors allowed. Dr. Hrovich's attending her. He left word that only a Deidre Johnson is to be allowed to see her." Deidre could see in his eyes that he connected the dots. "Are you Deidre Johnson?"

Deidre smiled at him, thankful that the doctor had not forgotten. "I am. Can I go to her room now?"

"Just a moment please. I need to see your official ID and your driver's license." She produced both, pleased that security was tight.

"Go ahead. Hers is the last door on the right." He motioned the direction for Deidre to go.

The door was marked by a deputy sitting in a chair outside the room, and Deidre nodded to him as she reached for the doorknob. He leaped from his chair. "I'm sorry. This room is off limits," he ordered, and his hand moved to his hip.

He was a young man hired after Deidre's resignation as sheriff, and it hadn't dawned on her he had no clue who she was. "It's okay. I'm Deidre Johnson. I'm with the BCA. Doctor Hrovich's expecting me."

"I'm sorry, ma'am. I'll have to see your ID before I can let you in."

Again, Deidre had to fumble through her pocket for the required proof of who she was. The deputy knocked on the door and opened it for her. "Sorry about the stop, ma'am, but orders are orders."

Deidre was a little miffed by the ma'am part. Suddenly she felt old.

Doctor Hrovich was sitting in a chair, staring at the girl. When he looked up, Deidre noted the dark bags under his eyes. He looked as though he hadn't slept at all.

"Hello, Ms. Johnson," he said, not bothering to stand. "Have a seat so we can talk. I'm leaving in a short while, but I'll have a report sent to you tomorrow. In the meantime, we have to decide what we're going to do with this child. I'm quite sure she's of Native American descent. At least her physical characteristics point in that direction. She's been terribly traumatized, so much so that she has completely withdrawn into her own cocoon. Look at her."

Deidre had avoided looking directly at the motionless form lying under the sheet. She forced herself to look. The girl lay on her right side, knees drawn up to her abdomen, her arms wrapped around her chest. Her chin was drawn down onto her sternum, and every now and then her feet twitched in spasms.

What was most disturbing to Deidre were the girl's eyes. They were wide open but not blinking, expressionless, and to Deidre it appeared that all spark had left them. She looked like a breathing corpse.

"I don't know what it'd take to bring her back to this world, or if that is even possible anymore. Last night, I told you about her physical problems, but I can't look into her mind. I'm recommending she be moved to a hospital in Duluth, to a psychiatric ward. She needs the intensive psychological care they can offer. Even then, I'm not sure what can be done. She'll recover from the physical abuse, but I have to believe her mind will be scarred forever."

He sighed deeply and then sat still.

"I need to do a couple of things, doctor. First, I need to finger-print her, and second, I need to have a buccal swab taken for a DNA test. Can I do that?"

"No need," he responded. "The sheriff was here last evening after the guard was posted, which, by the way, is prudent, I believe, not only to keep intruders out, but also to not allow her to leave if she should revive enough to try an escape. Anyway, he took prints and a sample for testing last night. He seems like a good man."

"The best," Deidre said in a quiet voice.

The doc continued. "Part of my job is to testify in trials involving child abuse cases. Catch whoever did this, and I'll crucify him from the witness stand."

He sat in silence, looking at his patient, and then forced himself from his chair. "I've got to be going. I'm set to testify at one o'clock against a father who intentionally scalded his two-year-old son. Who spawns these bastards I'll never figure out."

Doctor Hrovich left the room without saying goodbye. Deidre followed him out the door.

*****

"Good mornin', Boss Lady," Jill's chipper voice sang out as Deidre entered her office. "I've got some info for you that I think might wake you up."

Deidre was getting used to her secretary's greeting. At least she didn't rankle at the words anymore. She poured herself a cup of coffee. "I hope it is better news than I've had so far this morning."

"Yesterday, you asked me to check on this guy, Jason Leder. You were right. He has Canadian citizenship, but that hasn't stopped him from having a record here in the U.S. Check this out." She handed Deidre a piece of paper, and she quickly scanned down the sheet.

June 2, 2006. Implicated in prostitution case—Dismissed from Minnesota 4th District Court.

September 9, 2008. Implicated in child pornography case—Dismissed from Minnesota 4th District Court.

December 18, 2009. Implicated in prostitution case—Dismissed from Minnesota 4th District Court.

July 22, 2010. Arrested with juvenile female in car—Charged with contributing to the delinquency of a minor—Dismissed from Minnesota 4th District Court on technicalities.

There were a few other minor infringements recorded: speeding, disorderly conduct, running a red light. Deidre ignored those, but she focused on the pattern of offenses that fit the case she was tracking.

Jill interrupted her thought. "Now here's what you'll want to hear. The judge in each of the possible sex cases was none other than your friend, Tony DeMarcus. Not only that, but Leder's attorney in each case was the same person, Gerald Colter II. He's the one who represented Billy Evers the time he dodged the bullet and got off without so much as a slap on the wrist. Remember him? He lives here, in Two Harbors."

"Oh, I remember him all right," Deidre said, disdain dripping from her words, but she didn't elaborate. "Tell you what, Jill. It's almost noon. Why don't you take the rest of the day off. Tomorrow's Thanksgiving, and you probably could use the time to get ready. I'm heading to Duluth to spend the evening with a friend and his daughters, and I won't mind getting an early start. That okay with you?" Deidre realized she had just asked permission of her employee to leave work early.

"I don't have anything planned for tomorrow," Jill said. "I'll catch the evening community church service, and do some reading tonight. I'll watch the Macy's Thanksgiving Parade on TV tomorrow and then some football. Maybe read a little more."

"Don't you have family?" Deidre queried.

There was an uncomfortable pause. "Not around here."

"Well, rest up. My guess is we'll have some heavy lifting on Monday. See you then."

The women left the office together, and Jill locked the door behind them.

Chapter
Sixteen

DEIDRE RANG THE DOORBELL at Ben's home, and she heard the thump of running feet as the twins raced to be first to the door. She hadn't called ahead to let them know she was arriving earlier than they had planned. Ben would be at work, and the sitter was not expecting her. The door was flung open.

"Deidre!" the girls shrieked in unison.

Deidre stooped to their level, and they wrapped their arms around her neck so tightly she could hardly breathe. She kissed each on the cheek and tried to walk away, but they continued to hang on her, one on each leg.

The sitter stood back, smiling. She had met Deidre several times and knew how the girls loved her.

"Is it okay if I'm a little early?" Deidre asked. "I needed to get away from work for a while."

The sitter laughed. "You're a savior. I've got a ton of company coming tomorrow, and I sure can use some extra time to prepare." Then she thought, "Oh, you *are* staying aren't you?"

It was Deidre's turn to laugh. "You couldn't force me to leave. Anyway, I think you'd have to battle these two," and she ruffled the twins' hair. They looked up at her, grinned and hung onto her legs more tightly.

After the sitter left, Deidre got down on her knees to be at twin height. "Well, what are we going to do until your daddy gets home?"

"I know. Let's play dress up," Megan suggested. "How about you be the mommy, and Maren and I will be your kids."

"Well," Deidre hesitated. "How do we play this game?"

Very confidently, Megan continued. "Let's pretend you have been with us al-l-l-l," she dragged out the sound, "day long. That means that when Daddy comes home, he'd like to see the table set. Let's do that."

So far everything sounded pretty safe, and the three of them busied themselves setting place mats for four, arranging the silverware, although Deidre wasn't quite sure on which side of the plate the fork was placed. It took almost a half hour to complete the task.

"So what are we going to do for food?" Deidre wanted to know.

"Oh, we can do what we usually do," Maren chimed in. "Pizza!"

Deidre laughed. "How about we fix something really fancy for when your daddy gets home?"

"I know." Megan's eyes lit up. "Peanut butter sandwiches!"

"Okay," Deidre agreed. "We'll make super peanut butter sandwiches. And how about a salad."

"Ahh, do have to?" the twins complained in unison.

Deidre ignored their complaints. "Let's get busy, so the food is ready when Daddy comes home. We'll surprise him with a special meal."

"I know what would really surprise him," Magan volunteered, her expression serious.

"What's that, dear?"

"I think he'd be really surprised if you hugged him and gave him a bi-i-i-g kiss, and said, 'How was your day, honey?'"

Deidre was totally blindsided, and she felt as though this had been a perfect setup. Finally, she responded. "Well, I bet that would really surprise your daddy. What do you think he'd do if I did that?"

Maren jumped in on cue. "I think he'd be happy."

Deidre sat on a chair. "Come 'ere, you two." She placed one child on each knee so she could look into their eyes.

"Your daddy is a special man, and he loves the two of you very, very much. You know, I think right now two women in his life are enough for him. When he comes in the door, why don't you run up to him and give him a big kiss on the cheek and say, 'Daddy, I love you so much. Come and see the special dinner we made for you.'"

They looked at Deidre a second or two through their large, blue eyes. "Okay." They both slid off her lap. Deidre breathed a sigh of relief.

"Megan, you get out the toaster, and, Maren, you find the bread. When you've done that, show me where you keep the peanut butter."

In seconds the girls had produced the items.

"Okay, now we need a fry pan."

"A fry pan?" the girls squawked. "Why do we need a fry pan for peanut butter sandwiches?"

"Wait and see." Deidre opened the meat keeper in the refrigerator and found an opened package of bacon.

In minutes, she had several strips sizzling in the pan. The girls began making toast, stockpiling the browned pieces in the warm oven. Deidre threw together a special salad.

"Come on, kids. Let's make some dessert." With their help, she made instant chocolate pudding and topped it off with fresh raspberries she had brought with her from the grocery store in Two Harbors.

"Now, we make our sandwiches." She helped them smear on a generous spread of peanut butter and showed them how to layer the crisp bacon strips."

"Do you think Daddy will like our sandwiches?" Maren wondered.

Before Deidre could answer, they heard Ben stomping the snow from his boots before he stepped into the entry. The girls went flying to meet him.

"Daddy!" they cried in unison and jumped into his arms.

"We're having peanut butter sandwiches for supper," Megan proudly announced.

Maren added, "With bacon. Do you think you'll like that?"

Ben kissed his girls, all the while looking at Deidre and smiling. "You're early. It's so good to see you."

"We wanted Deidre to kiss you when you came home, but she's too bashful," Maren announced, and Ben looked embarrassed.

"I see. What have you three been talking about while I've been at work?" He gave each girl a pat on the head, then hugged them close.

Something snapped inside Deidre when she saw the way that Ben related to his daughters. For an instant she saw the body of Anna Woodsong and the battered child in a hospital bed. She burst into tears, sobbing uncontrollably.

Ben took two steps and was in front of her. She wrapped her arms around his neck and buried her face in his chest, her body convulsing as she tried to get hold of her emotions. Ben held her and stroked her hair with his free hand.

"What's wrong?" Megan asked, perplexed.

Maren gently placed her hand on the back of Deidre's leg. "Daddy'll fix it, Deidre. He can fix anything."

That made Deidre sob all the more.

It took several minutes before she could speak. She blew her nose on a tissue and dabbed her eyes. Then she realized Ben still held her, and she slowly pushed away.

"Oh, I'm so sorry, girls. I must have scared you. It's just," and she paused to form her words without beginning to cry again. "It's just that you make me so happy I had to cry tears of happiness. Do you understand what I'm trying to say."

Both girls nodded, but their eyes told the truth. They had no idea why Deidre had burst into tears. She wasn't sure, herself, what had happened.

"Come. Let's eat." she said, painting a smile on her face.

Ben said grace while they held hands in a circle at the table.

"Um, one of my favorites. Peanut butter and bacon sandwiches. I'm sure glad you made me two, because I am so-o-o hungry." He took a bite of the sandwich as though it were made of the finest shaved sirloin steak.

"I think this is the best peanut butter-bacon sandwich I've ever eaten." The little girls beamed. "And this is the best salad I've had, too." Deidre laughed.

After dessert was finished and the table cleared, Deidre and Ben played Chinese checkers with the kids, helping them to spot the correct moves. Then Ben got out a book and they all sat on the couch, Megan and Maren between Deidre and Ben. It was a kids poetry book, *My Rollaway Bed*, about a little girl's magic bed that took her to adventuresome places at night.

"Okay, bedtime," Ben announced when he finished the last page.

"We want Deidre to tuck us in," they sang out in unison.

"Ben carried Maren and Deidre carried Megan up the stairs to their room, and Deidre pulled the covers up around their chins, giving each child a squeeze and a kiss goodnight.

"I wish you lived here all the time," Maren said, a look in her eyes that could only be described as a plea.

Ben turned on their nightlight, and the grownups returned to the living room.

"A glass of wine?" Ben asked.

"That'd be great. After my scene a while ago, I think I need more than that."

"Tough day, huh? Anything you can tell me?" Ben knew there were times in their business when a person simply needed to verbalize the baggage they were carrying.

Deidre tried to explain the feelings that had overwhelmed her when she broke down. She explained about the condition of the dead girl and the blank stare of the girl she'd helped rescue. Then she said she had such a feeling of fear for Megan and Maren that it had completely blindsided her. For an instant, she said, she had visions of the twins being violated in the same way, and it seemed far too real for her to face.

Ben listened intently, not interrupting once. He knew Deidre had to get this off her chest. When she finally went silent, he spoke.

"Sometimes I get those same feelings when I watch them at play, but then I realize I'm giving them all the love I can right now so when they're older they don't go looking for something they never had growing up. When I become fearful for them, I remind myself I must have faith that what I'm doing with them now is laying the foundation for a lifestyle that'll help them avoid some of life's pitfalls. I know they'll make their own mistakes along the way, but all I can do is direct their lives so those mistakes aren't so tragic that they can't overcome the consequences."

After a pause, he added, "I hope you realize that you're having a profound influence on them, Deidre. I'll be forever grateful for what you're doing. I believe they're going to have good lives. But thank you for sharing. Sometimes it's good to talk about our problems. Kind of like *The Sound of Music* . . . then they don't seem so bad."

Deidre laughed.

"Here's to you, Deidre, my friend, my daughters' idol, and a very, very wonderful person."

Deidre blushed and lifted her glass in the direction of his. "Thank you."

*****

THANKSGIVING DAY WAS SNOWY. Deidre was sitting at the kitchen table, coffee cup in hand and looking out the window, when the twins peeked around the doorway at her. Sleep was still in their eyes, and their hair stood out from an accumulation of static electricity. They came running to her.

"Do you feel better today?" Megan wanted to know.

"We don't want you to be sad, Deidre," Maren chimed in.

She got down to their level and hugged them. "You girls make me happy. So happy I could just eat you up," and Deidre pretended to nibble on their ears. They squealed in delight.

"What about Daddy?" Megan asked. "Does he make you happy?"

123

Deidre was beginning to sense a pattern developing. "Well . . . I think friends make us happy, and your daddy's my friend, so, yes, he does make me happy." She paused a moment, then playfully wrestled with the girls. "But not as happy as you imps do."

The girls giggled and tried to tickle Deidre.

By eight o'clock, everyone was dressed. Breakfast had been served, and the holiday was about to get started.

Ben had ordered a complete dinner from a supermarket nearby, and at mid-morning he picked up all of the fixings. It was complete with roast turkey, mashed potatoes and gravy, dressing, everything.

His brother, Cal, and his wife, Vickie, arrived shortly after he returned from the store, and introductions were made. A few minutes later, Ben's sister, Stephanie, and her husband, Bill, rang the bell and entered without waiting to be invited. They were followed by their two pouting pre-teen kids. With the exception of those two, Deidre was warmly accepted.

Ben's parents arrived a half hour late because of the heavy snowfall. That mattered little, because all they had to do was heat the meal in the in the oven or the microwave and serve it. The table had been set hours ago, and there was not much to do except visit and eat.

Deidre answered the door, and Ben's mother looked quite surprised to see Deidre there. Evidently, Ben had forgotten to tell his parents that a guest would be joining them.

"Deidre," his mother said, and the eaves of the house were not the only thing with ice cycles hanging from them.

"Hello, Mrs. VanGotten, or can I call you Rebecca?" Deidre cordially asked.

"Either way is fine," the older woman answered in a non-inviting way.

Ben's father extended his hand. "Hi, Deidre. Jim is fine for me. It's good to see you again. Ben didn't tell us you'd be joining us. Did you drive through the storm to get here this morning?"

Before Deidre could answer, Maren piped up. "Oh, no, she stayed here last night."

Rebecca's left eye brow almost reached her hair line. She glared at Ben. He said, "Good to see you, Mother. Here, let me take your coat. In fact, there's something I want to show you in the other room."

He took his mother's arm in his hand and led her away, leaving Jim and Deidre standing awkwardly in the entry.

"Hey, how are my two favorite girls," Jim called to the twins, warming the room with his exuberance. He pulled two small, wrapped gifts from the pocket of his overcoat. "I've got these for you. Let's sit over here on the couch, and you can open them."

The girls clamored onto the sofa, one on each side of Jim, while Deidre went to the kitchen and busied herself, although nothing needed attention at the time.

"Deidre, look what Grandpa brought us," she heard them call to her from the living room. She decided she couldn't hide in the kitchen all day and went to see the girl's gifts.

"Isn't this pretty?" Maren asked, lifting her chin so Deidre could see the gold chain necklace and tiny charm hanging from it. Deidre squatted so she could get closer for a better view. It was an angel, its eyes cast down as though looking from above at something. Megan had an identical necklace.

"Grandpa says this is to remind us that we have an angel looking out for us. Do you think that's true, Deidre?"

Deidre'd had no religious upbringing during her childhood, and she had seldom darkened the door of a church. "You listen to what your grandpa says. He must be right." At least she hoped he was.

Rebecca and Ben entered from the other room, she daubing her eyes. Ben had a stern look on his face.

"I think it's time for us to break out the hors d'oeuvres, don't you, Mother? I'll help with the wine, and we can visit for a while before the meal. Deidre, will you give me a hand in the kitchen?"

They were gone only a few minutes and returned with Deidre carrying a plate of fancy deli appetizers and Ben carrying a tray of wine glasses for everyone. The twins got sparkling grape juice, and the adults, either red or white wine. When everyone's glass was full, Ben raised his to make a toast.

"Here's to family and friend. To my lovely daughters, and to the memory of their mother. Here's to the future. May it be full of good times spent together, peace, and to a blessed year for all of us."

"Here, here," Jim echoed, and they all took a sip from their glasses. Deidre had tears in her eyes, as did everyone except the girls, who felt grownup to be included in an actual toast.

The meal was served and, as was to be expected, everyone ate too much, groaning when the pumpkin pie was served and complaining they couldn't eat another bite. But they did.

As the adults savored a last cup of coffee before giving up, Rebecca tried her best to make small talk. "I don't know when the last time was that I saw you, Deidre. Perhaps it was when you and Ben were running against each other for sheriff."

Out of the corner of her eye, Deidre saw Ben signal his mother to stop. The woman had begun to dig herself a hole, but she didn't know how to stop. "Of course, after you won the election, Ben talked about you several times. Everything good, mind you."

Deidre laughed. She remembered the rocky relationship she and Ben had when they were in high school together, when they had attended the law enforcement academy together, and especially when she was his boss. That was ancient history now, and she was enjoying seeing Ben trying to corral his mother's tongue.

Deidre offered, "Neither Ben nor I are the same persons we were then, Rebecca. I'd trust my life to your son. He's is a true gentleman, a wonderful father, and a great person. I think both of us would like to forget the past. Don't you think that would be best?"

Ben's brother, Cal, tried to calm the waters. "Of course we all change. Don't you remember when you tried to stop me from seeing

Vickie? And look how you love her now?" He winced when Vickie stepped on his foot under the table. "But that's in the past. So let's enjoy the day and being together." He thought he better shut up.

Rebecca shifted uneasily in her chair. "Of course, dear. It . . . I mean, it is a little awkward for me. Jenny hasn't been gone very long, and Ben's so vulnerable right now. I worry about him and the girls." She swallowed hard.

Deidre understood vulnerable. "Rebecca, believe me, I'm not taking advantage of your son or his situation. We're just very good friends. I love your granddaughters more than you can imagine. Someday, I hope Ben finds someone who can be their mother, but for now, I'm trying to help out."

"And doing a wonderful job." Ben interjected. "Mom, let it rest now."

Jim changed the subject, asking Ben if he had been ice fishing yet. Stephanie asked Deidre where she was working, and the talk became more relaxed.

At the end of the day, Ben's parents, his siblings, and their families, said goodbye. His mother gave Deidre a cursory hug, but whispered in her ear, "Thank you for being kind to my grand-daughters." She turned and walked out the door ahead of her husband.

When they left, Ben said, "Well, that went well, don't you think?" He laughed, and Deidre never asked what was said between him and his mother in the other room.

By Sunday afternoon, Deidre had to begin thinking about returning to Two Harbors and her job. She was ready to get on with the investigation, but it was difficult leaving.

Chapter
Seventeen

"Mornin', Boss Lady," Jill greeted Deidre. Her voice lacked its usual upbeat tone, and her face made Deidre think the weekend had not gone well.

"How'd Thanksgiving work out for you?" Deidre asked, thinking she might gain some insight into her secretary.

"Like any other weekend, I suppose. I did a lot of reading and spent time with my two cats. They miss me when I'm at work. Other than that, I volunteered at the women's shelter so the staff could spend time with their families. Not a happy place to be on a holiday."

Deidre didn't push the issue. "I suppose not. Anyway, are you ready to get to work? I've got some things I need done as soon as possible."

Jill nodded.

"First, make an appointment for me to see that attorney, Gerald Colter, this morning, the earlier the better. Second, I want to set up a meeting in Thunder Bay with Henry Musio and Charles Freeman. Tell them I'll drive up this afternoon, if they can see me on such short notice. Contact Sheriff DeAngelo and see if he's available to meet with me when I return from Mr. Colter's office."

Deidre paused to let her finish taking notes. "When you get those meetings set up, will you please call the hospital in Duluth. Request the name of the physician who'll be treating the abuse victim we rescued. When you obtain that info, have the BCA director request a copy of the girl's medical records be made available to me for my investigation."

Jill perked up with the knowledge she would be busy. Deidre retreated to her desk and the computer. She had just begun to run

Jason Leder's fingerprints through the national database when Jill placed a note on her desk.

You are set to meet Gerald Colter at 8:30 this morning. Good luck!

Deidre smiled. In their crowded office, Jill could have spoken across the room. The girl was a hard one to figure out.

She looked at her watch, 8:10. "Gotta go. I think I'll be back within an hour. If not, call the police." She laughed and saw Jill grin back.

It was only a few minutes ride to Colter's law office, and Deidre arrived five minutes early. The receptionist at the outer desk asked her to have a seat, saying that Mr. Colter would be with her as quickly as he could manage.

Deidre picked up a copy of the Duluth newspaper and sat down opposite the young lady. She peered over the top of the paper as she held it in front of her face. *I'd expect his receptionist to look like this. Wonder if they are real or fake? She hardly looks eighteen.* In her mind she continued to make observations until she ran out of critical thoughts.

As she waited, her mind wandered back to when she was sheriff of Lake County and when a public meeting was held after the seven-graves incident. Her teeth involuntarily ground together.

After she and her partner had picked up his son, Gerald Colter, III, on suspicion of drug abuse, Colter, the attorney, made life miserable for her, humiliating her at the meeting, organizing a recall election, and literally forcing her from office.

Deidre took a deep breath, shifted in her chair, casually glanced over the front page headlines, and turned to the comic section. She checked her watch: 8:52, nearly a half hour late.

Finally, the receptionist announced, "Mr. Colter will see you now." She got up from her desk and opened the door to his private office.

Gerald Colter rose from his chair, a forced smile on his face. "Deidre Johnson, how pleasant to begin my day by meeting with you."

Deidre wanted to punch him. She smiled back, as best she could.

"What's this I hear that you're employed by the BCA? That's quite a step up from sheriff of Lake County. I suppose there must be a reason for your promotion."

Deidre was becoming more than annoyed. "And that reason is why I'm calling on you, Mr. Colter," she snapped.

"There's no reason we can't be civil. I was only making small talk, but then, if I remember correctly, you always were a little defensive. So, what is it you want from me?"

Deidre sat down without being invited. The attorney took the cue and took a chair diagonal to hers. "I want information about one of your former clients," she began.

"And who might that be?" he asked in his usual patronizing manner.

"Jason Leder. Do you recognize the name?"

"Leder. Leder." He rolled the name off his tongue as though he were trying to conjure up an image of the client. Finally, he shook his head. "No, I can't say I do. Of course I'd have a file on him if I ever did represent him."

Deidre was so exasperated that she began to curse but caught herself, nearly biting her tongue. "You represented him in *four* cases involving alleged sexual infractions ranging from prostitution to a possible sexual encounter with a juvenile. Does that help your memory?"

Again Colter appeared to be wracking his brain for an answer. After several seconds, his brow furrowed, and he said, "I'm sorry, I just can't place the man's name."

Deidre pressed on. "Last week Judge Tony DeMarcus was arrested in a prostitution sting in Edina. Now do you recall anything?"

With the mention of Judge DeMarcus's name, Colter blanched. "I did read about that in the paper. But what does this have to do with me? I'm only a small-town attorney. Most of my cases would be considered penny ante by big time lawyers."

Deidre knew she was beginning to strike a nerve and smiled at the man. "What it has to do with you, Mr. Colter, is that the records show you represented Jason Leder four times in a fourth district courtroom, and in each case, Judge DeMarcus presided. Not only that, in each case Mr. Leder got off almost totally free. You might be interested to know that last week, the day after he was arrested, I spoke with the judge at his home."

Colter squirmed in his chair and ran his fingers through his hair. "Did you get your information about this man, Leder, from the judge?"

Deidre noticed beads of sweat were beginning to form on his brow. "I'll be honest with you, Gerald," she said, using his familiar name to further show she was in control. "Your name didn't come up during our conversation. What I told you is in the public record."

Visibly, Colter exhaled the breath he had been holding and relaxed somewhat. Deidre didn't want to let him off the hook that easily. "We've established that you represented Jason Leder four times in cases involving sex offenses. We also have a connection between you and Judge DeMarcus, if only that he heard your arguments, although, most people would question the fact that in all four cases the defendant got no real punishment." She could see Colter's fingers clenching the arm rests on his chair. "Which gets me to the point of my visit. I want to know what your relationship was to Jason Leder."

"You should know that information is protected by attorney/client privilege. I can't divulge what was said between us or why I was hired for his case."

Deidre pounced on the crack in his statement.

"Oh, so now he's your client. Funny how quickly your memory repaired itself. Is there anything else you want to tell me about him?"

Gerald Colter's eyes narrowed to slits, and he spit his words out. "I'm required by law to hold any information relative to our conversations in strict confidence. Yes, he was my client, and yes,

DeMarcus was the judge each time. I had no control over that. Is there anything else?"

"Yes, Jason Leder died in a struggle on Palisade Head. Would you like to know what the struggle was about?" She didn't give him time to answer. "He was assaulting a girl who doesn't appear to be much more than fourteen years old. Your client's dead. Now, is there anything you want to tell me."

The oily smile reappeared on the attorney's face. "I know you law enforcement people are not well versed in the legal aspect of the law. Let me fill you in. In 1998, the Supreme Court heard a case, *Swindler and Berlin vs. United States*. Perhaps you've heard of it? Kenneth Starr— I'm sure you recognize that name—subpoenaed notes taken during a meeting between a Vince Foster and his attorney. Nine days after the meeting, Mr. Foster committed suicide. Mr. Starr wanted the notes to be admitted as evidence in his investigation, saying there was precedence to negate the attorney/client privilege in certain cases. The argument went all the way to the Supreme Court, which ruled in favor of the plaintiff. So you see, Ms. Johnson, the attorney/client privilege extends beyond the death of the client." Colter began to stand. "I think our meeting has come to a conclusion, don't you?"

"However," Deidre interjected. "In the court's opinion, if the attorney claims client privilege to support his own interest, the privilege is revoked. Or, as in another scenario, if the client's conversation with his attorney may be key in preventing another crime, that also can negate the privilege."

Colter sat. "If that's the way you want it, go ahead. But be careful, you may be way over your head, detective, or whatever you are."

"At any rate, Gerald, I think you're right. Our meeting is probably over." She watched him begin to get up. "Don't bother, Colter. I can find my way out."

None too gently, she closed his door behind her, smiled at the receptionist, and walked out of the building. She pictured Gerald

Colter, II, sitting in his chair, wondering what this was eventually going to mean for him.

*****

BACK AT THE OFFICE, she noticed Jill seemed in better spirits. Evidently, having something to accomplish took her mind off whatever had been bothering her.

"Did you get any results from the hospital?" Deidre queried as she took a seat at her desk.

Jill spun to face her, a paper in hand. "I got through to the hospital. They were able to give me the name of the pediatrician and the psychiatrist treating our little Jane Doe." She handed the sheet of paper to Deidre. On it were two names, along with phone numbers.

Dr. Jan Bilka, Pediatric Medicine – 555-1422
Dr. William Selenka, Psychiatry –555-3673

"Each doctor wants to visit with you in person. They sounded disturbed about what they've observed as far as the girl's condition and seemed willing to cooperate with you as best they can. I told them you were busy for the remainder of the day, but I set up appointments with them tomorrow morning. Grand Chief Musio is expecting you at three this afternoon in Thunder Bay. Charles Freeman will be there as well. Is that okay?"

"Jill, I'm beginning to wonder how I'd manage without your help." Deidre was truly beginning to appreciate what her receptionist was able to do.

"Thanks, Boss Lady," Jill mumbled as she turned back to what she was doing at her desk.

Deidre looked at her watch and sighed. "I'd better be out of here if I'm going to make it to Thunder Bay by three. While I'm gone, will you research what's happened to Judge DeMarcus since his arrest?

133

It's been nearly two weeks, and I haven't read anything about him in the newspaper. I hope this isn't a matter of the good-old-boys-club sweeping their sins under the carpet. See you tomorrow."

"Bye, Boss Lady."

The road to Thunder Bay was becoming too familiar, and Deidre was lost in thought, her vehicle on automatic pilot. Suddenly a deer, a doe, leaped across the road only fifty yards ahead of her. Deidre's reaction time was a little slow, and she had hardly stomped on the brake pedal, when a buck, chasing the doe, shot out of the ditch.

It was toward the end of their mating season, but that hadn't dampened the buck's hormones, and he was oblivious to everything but the scent of the doe. During the two seconds between when the doe crossed the highway and when the buck emerged from the ditch, Deidre's vehicle covered nearly fifty yards, and the buck's form was broadside to her path.

She could feel the automatic braking system of her SUV pulsating, and she nearly pushed her free foot through the floorboard. At the last instant the deer gave a desperate lunge, and through her driver's-side window she saw the white flag of his tail. She continued on for another quarter mile and then pulled over to the side of the road.

Deidre's legs felt as though they were made of Jell-O, and her hands were shaking. She realized how close she had come to hitting a two-hundred-fifty-pound deer and perhaps killing herself.

She pulled back onto the road, this time not using her cruise control and vowing to be more vigilant. She crossed through customs with no incident and at 2:45 pulled into the usual parking ramp in downtown Thunder Bay.

"Deidre," the chief greeted her, shaking her hand. "It's good to see you again. Have a seat. Can I get you anything? Coffee? A soda?"

He pointed to the other person in the room. "You remember Charles, our chief of police?"

Deidre thanked Henry for his offer of a beverage but declined. "Charles, I'm glad you could see me on such short notice. I'm sorry to tell you I need your help again. It's almost the same scenario as the last, but this time the victim is alive . . . barely."

The men glanced at each other, and Henry said, "We know you want to see us for that reason. Your secretary wouldn't reveal much to us, stating that here was a confidentiality issue with her giving out too much information. She said you would rather turn it over to us in person. She seems to be on top of things."

Deidre just smiled and nodded.

"We know you are very busy on the last case we discussed and that you need to get back tonight, so let's not waste your time with chatter. How can we help you?"

Deidre went into detail about following tracks to the top of Palisade Head, sparing none of the details of the ensuing struggle. She explained what had happened to the girl she and Jeff rescued, but never referred to her as Jane Doe. The girl deserved more respect than that, she thought.

The two tribal leaders listened intently, bowing their heads in disgust at times.

"The real reason I've come here in person is that we have an ID of the man who was trying to throw her off the cliff. His name is Jason Leder, and his address is listed as Thunder Bay."

Both men shook their heads. "The name doesn't ring a bell," Charles admitted. Henry agreed. "Of course this is a big city and the outlying area is heavily populated for a ten-mile radius."

"Jason hasn't been an angel while in the States. He has quite a record following him."

"Then why hasn't he been deported?" Henry wanted to know.

"That's where the waters become muddy. He's been brought up on charges four times, appearing before the same judge each time. Every time he's been released for one reason or another. He has no convictions against him. We've found through court records that the same attorney from Two Harbors represented him. Can you access Leder's record while I'm here? I've brought copies of his fingerprints and samples of his DNA, if that will be of help. I also have fingerprints of the girl and samples of her DNA."

The chief looked over at Charles. "That's your area. Can we place a rush on this so Deidre might have some answers today?"

The head of the NAN police force shrugged. "We can surely try. Naturally, the DNA will take longer. We also have a photo file of missing people. It's computerized so we can narrow it down by characteristics. My office is two floors down. Let's go there and get started. Maybe you can be on the road by early evening."

Henry Musio did not accompany the police chief and Deidre, and as the two walked to the elevator, he expressed what Deidre had been thinking. "Do you believe the dead girl and the girl in the hospital are separate cases, or do you think they're connected?"

She thought a moment. "I don't know. It certainly appears they're connected. On the other hand, I don't want to go with any preconceived notions. Are there any ways your laws concerning attorney/client privilege differ from ours so that you can apply pressure to Gerald Colter, the attorney I spoke of in the chief's office?"

Charles shook his head. "I'm afraid not. Our laws and yours concerning that issue are about the same, even when it pertains to a deceased client. He seems pretty protected at the present."

By that time they were at the floor which housed the investigative offices of his force. He strode to the desk of one of his people. "We need a rush on this set of prints. I'd appreciate your dropping what you're doing and see if you can find a match. It's terribly important."

They walked further into the room and stopped at another desk. Without introducing Deidre, he asked for the DNA sample she had brought and handed it to a technician. "Run a profile on this as soon as possible. See if we can come up with a match. I know it'll take a while, but what's your estimated time table?"

The technician calculated it would be at least a week before they could have anything.

"Let's go back to my office and wait for the print results. I have a computer we can use. I'm able to access a file we have on missing persons. Maybe we'll get lucky."

The chief booted up the PC on his desk. "I've accessed our missing person file. Now we have to begin winnowing out the chaff. "Female," and Deidre heard the click of a key as the chief clicked on that subject. "That got rid of a few. Still leaves us with over six hundred possible choices. How old do you think the girl is?"

"About fourteen at the most."

"Let's try ten to fifteen then." She saw his hand move and heard the click. "That narrows the field to three hundred ten. From this group, I can select specific ages. I'll try fourteen." Again his hand moved, followed by a click.

"Now we're down to ninety-six." He turned the monitor so they both could see it. "You can advance the photos one at a time using the mouse. Spend as much time on each picture as you need. If nothing rings a bell in this group, we'll try another."

Deidre began working her way through the file. In most cases she could eliminate the subject at a glance. Some were way too heavy, some too thin, others had faces marred with acne, still others had features that didn't match. It took her a half hour to finish the file.

"Sorry chief, none of them matched our girl."

The chief took the mouse, canceled out of the file, and brought up those missing girls who were thirteen. Deidre began another search, beginning to grow weary. She clicked the mouse. "This is the one!" she almost shrieked. "That's her!"

The chief of police sat stoically staring at the screen. "How can you be so certain?" he asked in a non-confrontational tone.

"Everything fits: the shape of her mouth, her nose, her ears, even her hair line. But what makes me so certain are her eyebrows. She's so traumatized that she hardly blinks and stares straight ahead. Her eyes have a spooky look to them, but her eyebrows arch upward, giving her an exotic look. Look at the eyebrows of the girl in this picture. That's her, I'm sure of it."

Charles double clicked on the picture and another file opened. This had a smaller picture of the girl in the upper right hand corner. The remainder of the screen was filled with data.

Name: Kimi Thomas
Mother: Alicia Thomas
Birth date: August 6, 2000
Father: Unknown
Date missing: June 25, 2013
Next of kin: Sally Cloud, Aunt
Identifying marks: Two-inch crescent scar on right hip, evidence of broken medial malleolus of the left tibia, evidence of an appendectomy.
Notes: Kimi Thomas disappeared on June 25, 2013, but was not reported missing until two weeks later. Her aunt filed the report. The whereabouts of her mother, Alicia Thomas, is unknown.

"I'm afraid this is something we run into too often. The girls who disappear often had tough times at home and are on the streets to avoid the unpleasantness of their domestic situations. They're easy prey."

Someone knocked on his door, and Charles called for him to come in. The person requested to look up Jason's record handed Charles a sheet of paper. Charles scanned it for a few seconds.

"It looks like our Mr. Leder is not our most upright citizen. He has a long record of petty crime in Thunder Bay. He is, or should I say *was*, a mechanic at a local repair shop up to eighteen months ago. He fell off our radar after that. His crimes range from petty theft to assault on his aged grandfather to fifth-degree sexual assault of a juvenile. For that crime, all he had to do was pay a fine, because he had no prior history of sex crimes. It says here he pleaded for leniency on the grounds he was intoxicated and thought the girl he fondled was his girlfriend."

"How in the world did he get through customs with that record? Deidre inquired.

"That's a question that needs to be answered. I suppose we could chalk it up to an administrative error, or worse, to a corrupt system. Either way, it's inexcusable he was allowed passage from our country to yours, or vice versa. Perhaps Mr. Leder walked that fine line between misdemeanors and more serious charges and never raised a flag when he applied for a passport. We may never know the answer." He shook his head in disgust.

"Is there any chance I can speak with Kimi's aunt, Sally Cloud? I want to be back in Two Harbors tonight, and if I leave Thunder Bay by eight o'clock, I'll be okay."

Charles reached for his phone. "I had one of my staff look up her number. I'll give her a call. If she cooperates, I think we can have you on your way much sooner than eight." He dialed a number, and Deidre listened to his conversation, trying to fill in what Aunt Sally was saying on the other end by the chief's response. Finally, he hung up.

"She says we can come to her place, but we can't stay long. Said her husband will be home soon, and he's usually drunk. She advised us not to be there when he arrives."

Deidre followed Charles from his office to the underground garage and climbed into his vehicle. When they were outside on the street, she was dismayed to see how heavily it was snowing. They maneuvered the side roads until they came to a rundown bungalow.

"This is where Sally lives and where Kimi spent most of her time. Let me initiate the conversation."

Deidre stood slightly behind him as he knocked on the door. It was opened by a much younger woman than Deidre had expected.

"I'm Charles Freeman, Chief of Police of NAN. I called earlier. Are you Sally Cloud?"

The woman nodded, pushing a hank of hair that drooped over her left eye into place on top of her head. "Come in," she said softly, never making eye contact. "So you're here about Kimi. Is she all right?"

"She's safe," Charles responded. "She's getting treatment in a hospital in Duluth, Minnesota."

"Oh," was all Sally said.

"This is Deidre Johnson with the Minnesota Bureau of Criminal Apprehension. She's assisting the Lake County Sheriff on Kimi's behalf. Actually, she saved her life. Will you answer some questions for her?"

Sally nodded and looked at the floor. Deidre cleared her throat. "I'm terribly sorry to have to bother you, but Kimi might still be in a great deal of danger. Thank you for speaking with me."

"Poor kid. She hasn't had much chance at all. Her mother was pretty wild and got pregnant by lord knows who. Then she kept using drugs after Kimi was born. I more or less raised her. She stayed with me when her mother was off on her highs. Finally, Alicia took off, and I haven't seen her for two years. I took Kimi in, but this house is no place to raise a kid. She spent more time on the street than she did here." Sally turned her head as if she wanted to hide her face.

"You said she'd been gone two weeks before you reported her missing. Can I ask why you waited so long?"

"This was her pattern. At first I'd report her missing right away, but they'd always find her at a friend's house or some other place she was staying. After a while, I quit bothering the police. This time, when she didn't come home after two weeks, I thought something must be wrong. The police never found her." Sally turned away from them again.

"Sally, can you tell me if Kimi had any friends who might know what happened?"

"All I know is she said she had a boyfriend who, according to her, treated her very well. She wouldn't tell me his name, so I can't help you there. All she said was that he was interested in the woods and had a canoe. Sometimes they'd go to a lake and paddle around.

Now you'd better leave. My husband'll be home soon, and he wouldn't like it if he knew I was talking to you."

Deidre and Charles thanked Sally for her time, knowing that staying longer would cause her trouble.

She and Charles discussed the situation. "Did you notice that Sally never once asked when Kimi was being released from the hospital? I don't think she'll have any place to go when and if she recovers."

Deidre had picked up on that issue as well. "I don't think Sally wants her to come back. After seeing what we saw, I don't think I do either. She's probably safer where she is than back here."

The two rode in silence for several blocks. "I was just thinking," Deidre said, "Anna and Kimi came from vastly different homes. Anna's parents were caring and involved in her life, perhaps a little too much so. But we really don't know. Teenagers rebel against what they see as controlling parents, even if the parents are really quite grounded. On the other hand, Kimi was left to raise herself. Yet, they both ended up in the same situation. Except for a few seconds, she would have been dead too." After a pause, Deidre added, "Sometimes there are no answers." This was more to herself than her companion.

Charles pulled into the parking lot, and Deidre got out. She leaned back into his SUV. "Thanks so much for all you're doing to help. I guess this is a battle we both want to win." With that she backed out, shut the car door, and walked to her vehicle.

Not until she pulled onto the street did it dawn on her that it had quit snowing. On the way back to Two Harbors on Highway 61, she remained vigilant, not wanting another close encounter with a deer. It was just before eight when she parked her SUV behind Inga's.

She let Pete out of his kennel and ruffled his ears. "Sorry, boy. I know the days must be long for you, but nothing lasts forever. We'll get through this and back to our cabin soon." And to herself she added, "I hope."

Chapter
Eighteen

"I'M BACK," DEIDRE GREETED JILL as she entered the office. She hadn't had breakfast or even a cup of coffee yet.

"Hi , Boss Lady. Looks like you had a long night. Anything good come from your meeting yesterday?"

"Jane Doe has a name. Kimi Thomas. She's pretty much an orphan with nowhere to turn for help. I spoke with her aunt who appears to be in an abusive relationship herself, certainly not a situation I'd want to release the girl back to. We're getting a few pieces to this picture, but so far none of them are fitting together. It's going to take some time, but they will. Anything new for me today?"

"It's on your desk. You have an appointment with Dr. Bilka, the pediatrician who's treating ... what did you say her name is, Kimi? That's at ten. Then at eleven-thirty, you'll be meeting with Dr. Selenka, her psychiatrist. Oh, I didn't have time to put this down. The phone was ringing when I came in this morning. Gerald Colter wants you to call him as soon as you have an opportunity. He sounded quite disturbed."

"Colter," Deidre stiffened at the name. "What does he want from me, to rub my face in his legal technicalities some more? That smug SOB can walk off the end of the breakwater as far as I'm concerned."

"Calm down, Boss Lady. This isn't the Gerald Colter you're thinking of. This is Gerald Colter, *III*, his son. He said you'd remember him. Do you?"

Deidre sat down, and let her vitriol ebb away. "I had a run-in with him a few years ago. The head of the Drug and Gang Task Force of the area and I executed a search warrant at an address in Two Harbors. Gerald was there, stoned. He had a mouth as smart as his dad's, the sarcastic little punk. Anyway, when we took him home, his father raised the roof, not with him, but with us for accusing his son of being a junkie. That was the incident that caused Colter, II, to begin a recall petition that forced me from office. Yeah, you might say I remember Gerald Colter, III. He wanted me to call him?"

"His number is on this sticky-note. Do you need it on better paper?"

Deidre shook her head and stuffed it in her pocket. "I'd better be heading for Duluth if I'm going to make my first appointment. Take care of the shop."

On the way, she speed-dialed Ben on her phone. "Hey," she said when he answered, knowing he had caller ID. "I'm on my way to your town. Would you mind if I stopped to see the girls later today? I'll cook, if it's okay with you."

"A home cooked meal? Are you kidding? That'd be great. What are we having?" Then he added, "Of course it'll be good to see you again. After Thanksgiving with my mother, I wondered if you'd ever call back."

Deidre laughed. "It'll take more than your mother to keep me from my two favorite kids. See you after work."

She parked across the street from the hospital and walked to the entrance. The city crew had draped garlands from the light poles, and they hung motionless in the cold, early-winter air. The lobby was decorated for the holiday season: a Christmas tree in the center of the foyer, its colored lights flashing in time to a carol being played, a pile of faux presents piled at its base, and a six-foot wreath on the wall.

Christmas had never meant much to Deidre. Most of her memories of the season were of her drunken stepfather knocking over their tree or passing out on the floor. Her mother tried as best she could to be festive, but there never was money to buy gifts, and their Christmas meal was usually nothing special.

When John, her fiancé, was alive, she had gotten a taste of what a joyful time of year December could be, but that had been taken from her when he was gunned down.

She hoped for Megan's and Maren's sake she could recapture some of the joy.

Dr. Bilka had asked that they meet in a conference room in the hospital, and Deidre stopped at the information desk to ask directions. The volunteer pointed her to an elevator at the end of the hall and instructed her as to the floor and room number. She was about to enter the room when a woman in a white coat bustled down the hall.

"Hello. I'm Jan Bilka. Are you Deidre?" Before Deidre could answer, the pediatrician opened the door and indicated for her to go in. "Please have a seat. I've just finished rounds and don't have to be to my office for an hour, so we have some time to talk. Do you have any specific questions for me?"

Deidre realized the doctor hadn't even checked to see if she was Deidre or if she had any credentials. She reached in her pocket for her ID. "I thought you'd like to verify that I'm with the BCA before we started," and she held out her tag.

The doctor blushed, embarrassed that she had been in such a rush to get started that she had broken protocol.

Deidre continued. "First, I believe we have a name for your patient. Did you find any marks on her that can be used for identification purposes?"

Doctor Bilka booted up a small laptop computer she carried. "What exactly are you looking for?" she asked. "I have her medical record here."

"If she is who I believe she is, the girl should have a two-inch crescent-shaped scar on her right hip. She should also have a scar from an appendectomy. You might not have the last marker. When she was a young child, she broke her left ankle quite badly. Her missing persons' information said it was the left medial malleolus of her tibia."

144

"That one I remember," said Dr. Bilka. "Because of the condition of her feet when she was admitted, I ordered x-rays. I remember her previously broken ankle because it is not too common for a break to occur to the medial malleolus. Most frequently it's the fibula that breaks. Let me check her record for the others. Yes, she has a scar similar to what you described. And, yes, she had an appendectomy. All three markers coincide with what you said would be there. What's her name?"

"Kimi Thomas. She's of Cree Indian descent and is from Thunder Bay, Ontario. She's been missing since late June. She's only thirteen years old."

"My God! I knew she was young, but I didn't suspect quite that young. She's experienced a great deal of trauma, more than you can imagine and more than I've ever seen in a child. Who did this to her?"

"That's what we have to find out. So far we're not making much progress, but many cases begin like that. It's like a snowball, starting with a small core and gaining mass as it rolls along, but we're not going to rest until we find the person or persons responsible."

Dr. Bilka went on to explain what Kimi had suffered, and Deidre could only listen with revulsion. Finally she asked, "Will she recover?"

"Physically yes. Emotionally, probably not. And when I say physically, she will heal, but her not-fully-developed reproductive system has been severely traumatized. How that will affect her as an adult is impossible to say, but we can make a pretty accurate assumption."

Dr. Bilka looked at her watch. "I'm sorry to cut our meeting off at this point, but I really must go. I'm late for office hours as it is. Thank you so much for seeing me. Please, catch whoever did this. I want to see what the animal looks like."

Deidre drove to Doctor Selenka's office. She parked across from the Medical Arts Building and rode the elevator to the fifteenth floor. At the end of the hall was an office with a sign, DR. WILLIAM SELENKA, M.D., PSYCHIATRY. Other than his receptionist, the office was empty, and Deidre was relieved to think he would not be rushing to get to his next patient.

"You must be Deidre Johnson. Dr. Selenka's waiting for you. He's cleared a block of time. Do you have proper identification?"

Deidre presented her card with her photo attached.

"Please, come this way." The receptionist led her down a hall to the doctor's inner office.

Doctor Selenka was an older gentleman. He had a full head of gray hair and a sad but kindly look in his eyes. When he spoke his voice was soothing.

"Have a seat, Deidre. Is it okay if I call you Deidre? And, please, call me Bill. I hate formalities." Immediately, Deidre felt comfortable with him.

"What can I do to help you?" he asked.

"First, I'm quite certain I know the girl's name," Deidre began. "DNA results will be the final confirmation, but everything else points to a girl missing in Thunder Bay, Kimi Thomas. She's been missing since the end of June."

Doctor Selenka, Bill, showed surprise by raising his eyebrows. "So, you have a name. That may be one of the keys to opening her mind.

"So far she has shown no sign of responding to the nurses, except for the male nurses. When they enter her room, she flies into a panic. We've had to restrict her care to only females. As for myself, she tolerates my presence, barely, but she simply turns me off. She will make no eye contact whatsoever."

"May I ask what psychiatric treatment she's receiving? I won't understand it in medical terms, so just give me the layman's overview."

"Under these circumstances, I think I can share with you. We have her on a mild sedative to take the edge off her anxiety. I also started her on an antidepressant. At night we give her Ambien to help her sleep. Other than that, we're trying to get her to take nourishment, although her appetite is very poor. Her pediatrician, who by the way is one of the best with abuse cases, says her physical healing is progressing nicely. Have you spoken with her?" Deidre told him about her meeting with Doctor Bilka. "Good, then you know about her physical condition. But the mental and the physical are so entwined, it's sometimes impossible to separate the two. I believe, of course, I'm a psychiatrist," he chuckled, "that her mind must be healed first. Her body will follow. I think you're one person whose presence might allow her to begin to crawl out of her pit. As I said, I have set aside a block of time today to speak with you. Will you be willing to come with me and see the girl, Kimi is it? That's an unusual name. Any significance to it?"

"Kimi is Cree. I'm sure it has a meaning, but I don't know what."

Bill nodded, and escorted Deidre out of his office. "I can drive. I have a reserved parking spot in the hospital ramp. Doctor's privilege." He chuckled again, and Deidre knew she liked him.

They passed through security, and he softly knocked on her door. "This is Doctor Selenka. We're going to come in now." He slowly opened the door to Kimi's room, enough so he and Deidre could slip inside. He silently closed the door behind them.

Kimi was sitting in a wheelchair near the window, and from her vantage point, she had a view of the Duluth/Superior harbor. She didn't turn to look at them.

Bill moved in front of her. Still, she didn't move a muscle but sat staring straight ahead.

"I have someone to see you," he said in his steady voice and rotated the chair so she was facing Deidre.

"Hello, Kimi," Deidre said as tears welled up in her eyes. "Do you remember me?"

All Deidre could see was the image of Kimi lying in a catatonic state, her eyes blank and urine spilling onto the snow when she had totally given up.

Kimi stirred, and then Deidre spotted what she would describe as instant recognition. The girl grabbed her arm and clutched it to her chest, nearly cutting off the circulation to Deidre's hand. Then Kimi placed her face against the arm she was squeezing and began to sob.

"Anna, Anna," she said over and over. Deidre looked into her eyes and could see a plea, the first expression Kimi had shown since she was rescued.

"Do you know Anna? Was she your friend?"

All Kimi could do was repeat, "Anna."

Deidre knelt down beside her and placed her arms around Kimi. For a time they stayed that way, Deidre cradling the child, Kimi resting her head on Deidre's shoulder. She reached up and swept the girl's long, black hair off her face. *She's beautiful*, she thought.

"Kimi, I have to leave now." She saw instant panic shroud Kimi's eyes. "But I'll be back whenever I can to see you. We can talk. Okay? But Doctor Selenka, you know him, will see you every day. He's a good man and won't hurt you. You can trust him."

Deidre had to pry Kimi's hands from her arm. She stooped and kissed the girl on her forehead. "I'll be back, I promise."

The doctor and she stepped into the hall. "I can't believe what I just witnessed," he said. "I thought you might be one of the keys, but I didn't think you'd be *the* key. I hope we can move on from here. But who is this Anna she kept asking for? Do you have any idea?"

"Unfortunately, I do," Deidre said, and then she related the story of the murdered girl she had found.

Bill took her hand. "Thank you for all you've done today. I just hope we can keep making progress now. You'll continue to see her, won't you? And if the time comes when I think it would be beneficial for the three of us to be together, may I call you?"

Deidre assured him that would be all right. The doctor gave her a ride back to the Medical Arts Building and she drove away in her own car. She was headed to Ben's, and all she wanted was to hold the twins close.

Megan and Maren were playing outside in the snow when she pulled into the driveway. Dropping everything, they rushed pell-mell to greet her. Deidre dropped down on her knees, and wrapped her arms around them. She could feel the coolness of their cheeks when she kissed them. Then, laughing, she wrestled them into a snow bank, pretending to let them pin her down.

"Okay, okay. You got me," she complained in mock fear. Deidre looked up and saw the sitter watching them out of the window, a broad grin on her face. She waved and Deidre waved back.

"Come with me girls. Let's go inside and have hot chocolate. Are there any cookies left from Thanksgiving?"

"No, Daddy ate them all. But we can still have cocoa. Sometimes, we have it with cinnamon toast. Do you know how to make cinnamon toast, Deidre?"

By that time, they were in the vestibule of the house, stomping off the loose snow and stripping off their outerwear.

The sitter said, "You girls sure love Deidre, don't you? And I can tell she loves you right back."

Deidre hugged them. "You two are so precious." She turned to the sitter. "Is it okay that I'm here before Ben? I know it cuts into your hours."

The sitter assured her that it was no problem, and prepared to leave. "They need someone like you in their lives. You're more important to them than you know. Your name must come up a hundred times a day."

With that she left the three alone. They had hot chocolate and toast with cinnamon, sang some songs together, played dollies, and cooked a simple supper.

"Daddy's home!" they called out in unison when they heard the door open. "Deidre's here! Come see what she made for supper. Doesn't it look good, Daddy?" Maren asked in her excited little girl voice.

"Umm," he responded. "I can hardly wait.

Deidre stood back, strangely feeling she should rush up and give him a hug—or something. Instead, she waved a half wave and said, "Good to see you so soon again. Hope you don't mind that I've shown up." She smiled an awkward grin.

"Mind? What's to mind? You're always welcome here. You know that. Isn't she girls?"

His invitation received a rousing, "Yes!"

After supper, the four of them played a game of Old Maid and then got the girls ready for bed.

"I have to leave now kids. Got a busy day tomorrow, but I'll see you soon. Okay?"

They grumbled and clung to her arms. Too much, they reminded her of Kimi and the way she had not wanted to let go.

"Hey, let Deidre go now," Ben said. "She has a job to do, just like I do, and she needs her rest."

"Tell you what, maybe if you ask really nice, she'd come back this weekend and help us decorate the Christmas tree. How would you like that?"

Maren looked at her through serious eyes. "Would you do that, Deidre?"

Deidre's heart melted. "Oh, that would be lovely. What time would you like me to come?"

"How about Friday night?" Ben interjected. She looked at him, and he had a crooked grin on his face.

"Friday night it is."

Chapter
Nineteen

DEIDRE WAS ALMOST TO THE EAST END of Duluth when her cell phone rang. She pulled over to the side of the road and reached for it in her coat pocket, but it wasn't there. She tried another pocket with the same result.

I hate all these clothes we have to wear in winter. Never can find anything when you need it, she thought. She located the phone in an inner pocket and pulled it out, along with a slip of paper. Disregarding the paper, she saw a message waiting light blinking on the phone. After listening to it for a few seconds, she cut it off.

"Telemarketer," she muttered to herself.

Suddenly, she remembered what the scrap of paper was about, turned on the reading light above the dash, and unwrinkled the note. Written on it was a name, Gerald Colter, and a phone number. Although it was getting late, she decided to call.

The phone rang several times before it was answered. "Hello," she heard a tentative voice on the other end. "This is Gerald speaking."

"Hi, this is Deidre Johnson returning your call. I know it is rather late. I can call back tomorrow, if you wish."

"No! No, this is all right. I was afraid you wouldn't want to talk to me. After all, the last time you saw me, I wasn't exactly Mr. Charming. I apologize for the way I acted."

"Well, thank you for taking the time to tell me that, Gerald. It's nice of you." She wondered why, after so much time, he would want to unburden himself.

"But that isn't why I called," Gerald continued. His voice sounded choked up. "I'm a student at St. John's University near St. Cloud."

151

"Yes, I know where that is," Deidre interrupted, thinking he wanted to let her know that his life wasn't a waste after all.

"I subscribe to the local newspaper and read about the girl who was murdered in Silver Bay. As I read the article, I discovered that you were working on the case. I need to speak with you immediately about it. I have information that's imperative you access. Will you meet me so I can show you what I've got in my possession?"

Deidre was dumbfounded. Finally she came to her senses. "Why, certainly, but where are you?"

"I'm in Collegeville, where the university is located. I don't want anyone to see me talking with you or knowing that I've contacted you. It's asking a lot, but would you drive down here to see me. It's only a three-hour drive from Duluth, at least half of it's on freeway. That way chances are no one will see us. I know this is strange, but I have to get this into your hands as soon as possible."

Deidre hardly knew how to respond. "Well, sure, if it's as important as you say. But I'm terribly busy on the case and don't have time to waste."

"Believe me, this won't be a waste of your time. When can you be here?"

Deidre did some rough calculations in her head. "Probably ten o'clock tomorrow morning at the earliest. Where can I find you?"

"I'll be waiting on the steps of the Abbey church. We'll be able to find a place we can meet privately without interruption. Believe me, what I have is so important that I must get it to you."

After the phone call, and while she was driving home, Deidre had the strange feeling she was somehow being set up. But Gerald's voice carried with it such a sense of urgency, she decided he couldn't be faking it.

After letting Inga know she was home, Deidre took Pete for a long walk. The temperature had moderated, and the thermometer registered closer to the seasonal average, twenty degrees above zero.

Pete ran ahead of her, checking out every new smell and marking every light post. She wondered where all that marking material came from. He never seemed to run dry.

Deidre thought she would be able to sleep after a three mile walk in the fresh air, but she was wrong. The last time she looked at the red numbers of her digital clock it was well after midnight.

When the alarm sounded, she was sure she had just fallen asleep. She reached for the snooze button, and then bolted upright, remembering she had to be at St. John's University in three hours.

After a quick cup of coffee and a piece of peanut butter toast, she was on her way out of town. A little after seven she called Jill at the office.

"Jill, I've got something important going on. While I'm gone, I want you to search for any business that has the initials RRR. Begin with Lake County and expand your search. If you run across any that seem to be fronts or not totally legit, flag them. I'm not too sure what you'd be looking for. I guess use your intuition. Anyway, pay attention to any that might be associated with our case." She smiled when Jill responded in her usual irreverent manner. "Thanks, Jill. See you tomorrow."

Deidre made a mandatory stop at Tobie's Bakery and bought a caramel roll and a cup of coffee to go.

She turned west on Minnesota Highway 23, a twisting two laner that made for an exasperating trip, especially because the driver in front was in no hurry to get where he was going. Deidre wanted to push the gas pedal to the floor, but had to follow the string of cars in front of her.

At exactly ten o'clock, she stopped in front of the steps of the church at St. John's Abbey. Gerald saw her and waved as though she were his long-lost friend. He slid into the passenger seat of her SUV.

"I'm grateful you came to see me. I've struggled over this thing for three days, and I've concluded we have to talk. I've reserved a small conference room nearby. Keep going around this loop," he instructed. "Go back down the hill three blocks and turn right. You'll find a parking lot."

Deidre looked over her shoulder to see if anyone was preparing to follow them. She still couldn't believe that Gerald was legit, but she drove to where he said, and they entered a building, going down a flight of stairs to the lower level. Part way down a hall, he stopped at a door and motioned for her to enter.

The room was small, containing a rectangular table and six chairs arranged two on each side and one on each end. Deidre sat on one of the side chairs. Gerald chose an end seat near her.

From his pack, he produced a laptop computer and took a flash drive from his pocket. As the machine booted up, Gerald started to apologize again.

"I know I was a real jerk the last time we met. I also know what I was doing was wrong, knew it then, too. But people change and that was a long time ago. Well, long for me."

Deidre interrupted. "Look, this was a long way for me to drive to hear your apology and confession. While I appreciate your efforts, you didn't need to say that to me face to face. I took what you said over the phone to heart, and, for what it's worth, I'm glad you're remorseful, and I'm happy for you that your life seems to have direction. Why all the secrecy for that?"

Gerald's face clouded. "That's not why I called you. Please let me explain how I arrived at this place in my life. My dad insisted I follow in his footsteps and study law. He has a way of imposing his will on everyone around him."

Deidre nodded in agreement, and Gerald continued. "At first, I was resentful and was only going through the motions at the university. In my second semester, I was mandated to take an ethics class taught by one of the brothers. I was intrigued from day one. Never in my life had I been forced to look at the consequences of the actions of others, let alone the consequences of my own actions. I was so taken by that man's teaching that I took another of his offerings. And so here I am, a senior who's become committed to trying to make a difference in the world. I look at my father and how he takes from everyone and gives so little in return. The problem is, I see all his potential for doing good swallowed by his greed and power grabbing. Believe it or not, I want to study law, not to take, but to give. It's obvious to me that money buys privilege. I want to level the playing field. I may not become a bulldozer, but I can do what I can. That's why I called you."

Deidre was baffled. It was as though Gerald had something to say, but he had to first justify why he was doing it. She was totally unprepared for what came next.

"I was home for Thanksgiving weekend and wanted to check my e-mail messages. Dad had been working in his study but said he needed to get some fresh air. In reality, I think he wanted to get out of the house when Mom and me were both home. He always seems uncomfortable around the two of us, as if he is afraid we might gang up on him and tell him to stuff his autocratic ways. Anyway, I was going to use his computer, but, when I hit the space bar to bring it to life, a file was open and on the screen." He stopped and swallowed hard. Deidre waited for him to speak when he could.

"This is what I found." He turned the screen so she could see.

SHIP	FLAG	DATE IN	DATE OUT	ORDER
Espiranto	Liberian	November 10	November 12	3
Star of India	Liberian	November 20	November 21	1
Moscvia	Liberian	November 26	November 29	3
Vestavias	Liberian	December 1	December 4	4
Ishat	Liberian	December 10	December 11	2
Aegean Sea	Liberian	January 3	January 5	3
Soo Locks close		Shipping season over	Saturday, January 11	

155

Deidre studied the list, but it meant little to her. "Do you understand what this is about?" she asked Gerald.

"At first, it meant nothing. Dad was never interested in boat traffic, not even at the docks in Two Harbors. I found this strange. I know it was wrong of me, but I started to snoop around his files. He hadn't logged off, so I didn't need his password to open any of them." Gerald closed that file and opened another. "I found this."

Again he turned the computer screen toward Deidre. The file was labeled "Expenses." It was a spreadsheet, and the columns were headed by men's names, three of which stood out to Deidre as though they were neon signs: Billy Evers, Anthony DeMarcus, and Jason Leder. Down the left side of the spreadsheet were consecutive dates spanning four years.

She followed the judge's column down to the first entry, April 7 of four years previous, about the time the judge's courtroom management began to change. In the corresponding cell was the sum, *$5,000.* She traced her way back up the column, noting that the monetary amounts became more numerous and more generous.

She noted the same pattern for the other two, except that Billy Evers's payments ended the month before he was sentenced and sent to prison. Deidre was certain this record was meaningful, but she still couldn't connect the dots.

Gerald opened another file, this one marked "Shipments." Again the spreadsheet went back some four years. Deidre noticed that during the dead of winter—January, February, and March—no entries were made. They started again in April.

Each column was headed by what appeared to be the name of a ship, and Deidre read across. She realized in an instant that some of the ship names she had seen in the first file appeared in the headings.

Down the left side were dates, the same as she had seen in the previous file. This time the entries in the corresponding cells were much larger, ranging from $15,000 to $60,000.

"Go back to the first file." Gerald did. Deidre looked at the date November 20 and then the order, one. She jotted that down on a note pad. She looked at November 10. The order was three.

"Return to the last file you showed me." Deidre compared what she had written to what was recorded in the cells for that date.

Where the cell coordinates for *Espiranto* and November 10 intersected, the figure *$60,000* was entered. Where *Star of India* intersected November 20, the cell contained *$20,000*.

"What do you think of these figures?" Deidre asked, looking at Gerald for a clue as to what he was thinking. His brow furrowed.

"What do you think?" he answered her question with a question.

Deidre thought for a moment before answering. "I think the orders filled refer to human beings, women. The going rate is $20,000 per individual, and they're delivered to the various boats docked in Duluth. There is absolutely no evidence to base my suspicions on from what I see here, but something inside me says this is what the payments are about. You tell me what you think."

Gerald closed the file and opened another. This was not a spreadsheet. Instead, it was a picture folder. Gerald opened the first frame, and the images of a young girl filled the screen. There was a head shot, another of her partially clothed and sitting in a chair, the third was a far more explicit frontal shot.

He screened through photo after photo until Deidre shouted "Stop!" Gerald paused the rolling pictures. Deidre gasped. On the screen was a picture of Anna, stripped naked.

"My God, what have you discovered?" she asked, not needing an answer. Under the picture was a notation: *Ishat—December 10, 6:00 A.M.* Gerald, do you know what you've uncovered?" she asked, still not believing what she was seeing.

"My father is a human trafficker, that's what I've uncovered. We never got along, but I never thought he was an animal, until now. I want to see him out of my life and my mother's life as quickly as possible. He has taken the spark from mom, and now he is responsible for the ruination of the lives of how many innocent people? He doesn't deserve to be called human."

Deidre was stunned by his outburst. "I'm so sorry you had to find this. But I'm also grateful you did. And I applaud your remarkable sense of rightness, and your calling me. That was an act of true courage. What you have here is so incriminating, I honestly don't know where to go next. Because of the manner I have come across this evidence, I don't know if it can be used against your father. I have to talk this over with the district attorney and get his advice. I do know who I'll contact first thing in the morning, the FBI. They need to be brought in on this case immediately. There's plenty of evidence of kidnapping and trafficking. I do need to take this flash drive with me. Do you have a copy?"

Gerald nodded.

"I don't think you should be around your dad until this comes to a head. I don't want him picking up any vibes from you, and I certainly don't want you placing yourself in jeopardy."

Deidre could tell by the way his pupils dilated that the thought never occurred to him that his father might do him bodily harm. "I suppose you're right," he mumbled. "I never go home anyway, except for a few holidays. Damn him." Gerald turned his face away, trying to stem the tears that rolled down his cheeks.

Chapter
Twenty

DEIDRE REACHED THE TOP of Thompson Hill, where I-35 drops down to the city of Duluth. She pulled into the parking lot of an overlook and sat for a few minutes. The blue of the lake contrasted against the white snow made for a beautiful sight. Outside the harbor, three ships lay at anchor, and Deidre could tell by their outlines they were "salties," ships that were built for ocean travel rather than Great Lakes sailing.

The thought struck her that one of them might be the *Ishat*, the ship due in harbor on December 10, but then she decided probably not. That would mean a six-day layover, and every day a ship wasn't moving cost its owners thousands of dollars. She wondered where they were from and where they were headed.

Deidre reached for her phone and dialed the number of the Lake County sheriff.

"Hi, this is Deidre Johnson. Will you connect me to Sheriff DeAngelo, please?"

The phone rang twice. "This is Sheriff DeAngelo. How can I help you?"

"Jeff, this is Deidre. Glad you were in to take my call. I've got some very interesting news concerning the case I'm working on, as well as that of the girl we found on Palisade Head."

Deidre went on to explain as briefly as she could what Gerald had shared with her about his father. Every once in a while she heard Jeff mutter into the phone, and she thought she knew what he was thinking.

"I'm sitting in that rest area atop Thompson Hill, and I wanted to let you know I'm stopping at the FBI office to show them what's on this flash drive. I'd guess they'll take it from here, given the severity of what's been going on and the implication it has to human trafficking, let alone kidnapping, and the international involvement of the individuals."

"You have no choice but to notify them. In a way, I'll be glad to have them take over. A community as small as Silver Bay and a county department the size of mine is hardly set up to handle cases of this magnitude. Hope all goes well when you meet with them."

Deidre said goodbye and dialed Ben's number. "Hey," she heard his familiar voice. "I hope you're not calling to cancel for this weekend. I've told the girls, and they are making a special surprise for you. They'd be disappointed if you can't make it."

"No, I'll be there. No problem on that front. However, I do have some big problems, work related. I'm calling in the big guns on this case and need your help. I suppose I could have gone through a receptionist, but you'll provide a more direct line to the person I should see."

She briefly explained why she was calling, and she heard Ben exhale. "Sounds like you found the mother lode," he said. "You're at the top of the hill? That means you can be in our building in fifteen minutes. I'll have a meeting set up for you when you get here. Check in at the front desk, and the receptionist will tell you who you'll be meeting with. Will you stop and see me before you leave?"

I-35 dropped almost seven hundred feet to the level of Lake Superior in about a mile, and as Deidre drove down the steep grade, she could feel her ears pop because of the change in elevation. In minutes she was at the bottom of the hill and driving near the slips of the harbor. Several ships were taking on cargo, and she couldn't help but wonder if there were people being smuggled aboard as well.

The Federal Building, which housed the FBI offices, loomed over her like a granite castle. As she walked up its time-worn stairs, she wondered if this would be the end of her involvement in the case. If that were so, she'd be able to retreat to her cabin in the Superior National Forest, but she worried that, after this experience, she could ever be content with its isolation again.

Deidre didn't have time to mull the idea in her mind. The elevator had her to the sixth floor in seconds, and she stepped out into the reception area. After identifying herself, she was escorted to an office down one of the halls. Her guide knocked on an office door and she heard a man's voice answer, "Come in."

He stood and introduced himself as Zak Burton, district agent in charge of human trafficking. He offered Deidre a seat and pulled up a chair diagonal from her.

"Ben tells me you have in your possession some very incriminating evidence. How did it come to your attention?"

Without disclosing too much of her personal history, Deidre related in detail her initial conversation with Gerald Colter, the attorney's son. Zak wanted to know why Gerald chose to contact her rather than the FBI. In the end, the story of her history with the Colters was told, and the agent was satisfied that Gerald had selected the familiar rather than the FBI.

"Ben tells me you have a data storage device. Is there any reason you'd balk at sharing the information with me?"

The question irritated Deidre. That was why she'd come to him, not to play hide-and-seek. "Of course not," she answered rather sharply.

"I wanted to ask. Too often we're accused of bullying our way because of our backing. I certainly don't want you to think we're going to take what you have and push your agency aside. My goal is to work together with whoever is involved. Are there other agencies?"

Deidre had difficulty not saying, "Let's just get to the point," but she answered, "The Silver Bay police force is made up of one full-time officer and a part-time assistant. He's already relinquished authority to the BCA. Jeff DeAngelo is sheriff of Lake County. He was with me when we rescued a girl from her assailant, so he's involved. He's a good man, a team player who'll be an asset to you, if you allow him to be."

Agent Burton smiled. "So it'll be you, me, and Sheriff DeAngelo working together. Did you say his name is Jeff?" He wrote the name on a pad. "Show me what you have."

Deidre felt relieved to be getting to the heart of the matter. She wasn't convinced why Zak had questioned her about who was involved in the investigation to date, but his tone had been non-threatening.

He placed a laptop computer on the table between them, booted it up, and Deidre inserted the flash drive. The computer made the usual working sounds, and a message appeared on the screen, among the choices, *open files*. She clicked on those words, and a menu of the files in the flash drive was displayed across the top of the screen. She opened the first file, the spreadsheet showing names of ships, their arrival and departure dates, and what country's flag they flew.

Deidre explained to him that the list ended on a date that would roughly coincide with the last day of the shipping season. The locks at Soo St. Marie would close because of ice conditions, and the salties, if they weren't out by that time would be trapped until spring.

The second file held little interest to the agent. He remarked that the judge was being paid for an undisclosed service but there was no indication what that service was. He admitted it was a bit unusual for an attorney to have a record of payments to a sitting judge, however, that would be a matter for the State Bar Association to investigate.

She closed that file and opened the third. Zak looked thoughtfully at the rows and columns. "No doubt there's a correlation to when a certain ship was in the harbor and an amount of money that exchanged hands, a considerable amount of money. Once again we can't ascertain for what reason the exchange took place. We can surmise, but that's about all."

Deidre was concerned about his dismissive tone. She opened the fourth, and clicked on Anna's picture icon. The screen lit up with photos of her. Deidre sat silently, waiting for a reaction.

"'*Ishat*–December 10.' It doesn't take much imagination to tie this file into the others, does it? But a good lawyer would tear us to pieces with this as our only evidence. First, it was stolen from the attorney's personal computer. It doesn't matter that it was his son who committed the theft. Second, there's no direct link between the files other than they are on the same flash drive. If I were an attorney for the defense in this case, I would claim the files were downloaded from separate sources and placed in this sequence on this data storage device. And, too, I'd link it to you and to the fact that you have a motive for framing the defendant. I'd even bring up the strained relationship between the son and his father."

"As for the pictures. I'd claim they should be considered privileged information, obtained from when my client was representing Mr. Leder. I'd claim they were really Leder's work and had been accessed by you during your investigation into his background. That'd be a stretch, I admit, but then I'd give the jury a more plausible explanation. I'd say my client had them on his computer from when he represented Leder in that juvenile sex case. I'd say my client wanted to examine them to decide whether Leder should plead guilty to a lesser charge. That's thin, I admit, but I would try to place doubt in the jurors' minds."

Deidre's shoulders slumped in anticipation of being dismissed. Zak continued. "However, there's no doubt in my mind, or yours I'm sure, that we have a large scale human trafficking operation happening on the docks. We've known about it. Port security has known about it. The media knows about it, but until now we've had few inroads. Now we do. What you have here is invaluable."

Deidre perked up. "But with all the loopholes you pointed out to me, where do we go from here?"

For the first time Zak laughed. "We catch them, that's where we go. I'm going to download these files into my computer. I want you to take this flash drive with you, and share its contents with Sheriff DeAngelo. We're going to be attacking the situation on the docks, but I want him informed. It's only fifteen miles from here to the southern edge of Lake County, and I want him ready for anything that spills his way. I plan to meet with our trafficking division tomorrow. I'll share with them what you've brought me, and get back to you on Friday. Will you be available to meet with us that morning?"

I wouldn't miss it for the world, Deidre thought. "Of course," she answered.

She turned the wrong way leaving his office and walked the distance of the hallway before she realized her mistake. Backtracking, she walked past Zak's office. The door was open a crack, and she heard him on the phone, speaking to someone.

"Hi, Sammy? I'm calling about a ship, the *Ishat*, scheduled to arrive in port on December 10."

She didn't dare stop and eavesdrop on his conversation. She hoped he was on her side.

*****

THURSDAY MORNING, DEIDRE ALLOWED herself some extra minutes to visit with Inga.

"I can't tell you how much I appreciate all you're doing for me. I'm just sorry I haven't been a good guest. I come in at all hours, sometimes not at all, and you're taking such good care of Pete. I think he's gained five pounds since he started his stay in your kennel."

Inga patted her hand. "Think nothing of it. It's nice to have something to do besides putter around the house. I do wish you'd take better care of yourself. Pete might have gained five pounds, but I think you've lost ten. You won't be good for anything if you run yourself into the ground. Here, have another caramel roll." She pushed the plate toward Deidre, who eyed it for a second.

"Who could resist this treat?"

The women chatted a few more minutes. Deidre stood to leave.

"Tell you what, I should have a short day. Would you like to cook supper together tonight? I'll pick up groceries on the way home."

Inga's eyes lit up, and she left no doubt that was what she'd like.

Deidre was late getting to work, and when she walked through her office door, Jill, very pointedly, looked at her watch. Then she laughed. "Good to see you relaxing a bit. How did your meeting go with Mr. Colter? Did he have anything productive to offer?"

"Some." Deidre evaded the question. "Now about you? Did you come up with anything on those initials?"

Jill took a swig from the coffee cup on her desk. "Locally, nothing. When I widened the search to the Arrowhead Region, I still drew a blank. Next, I went state wide. There I had two hits. The first that came up was the Rochester Region Rowing Club. I think we can disregard them. They're a small group with no facility or set meeting place. They wouldn't have need for a key like you found. The second is the Red Rooster Restaurant in Belltown, Minnesota. It's a tiny village in the far southwest corner of the state. It's a mom and pop place. Hardly a crew you'd suspect of being murderers. As you would expect, a national search turned up countless possibilities. So many, in fact, that I doubt it'll be helpful. I copied the list to your computer. You can wade through it, if you really think it'll be of use."

Deidre thanked her, not wanting to say that she had discovered a lead that would probably break the case wide open. "I'm running upstairs to talk to Jeff. Be back soon. Mind the store while I'm gone."

She sprang up the stairs to the top floor, taking two steps at a time. Fortunately, Jeff was in, and he welcomed her into his office.

She walked out of his office an hour later, leaving Jeff shaking his head and being thankful someone else was leading the charge on this case. Jill was on her lunch break, but on her desk was a note: *Call Zak Burton as soon as you get back.*

Deidre dialed his number, expecting the recorded message of an answering machine.

"Deidre," Zak answered excitedly. "I've just come from a meeting with the division members. I want you to meet them tomorrow morning, if you can free up the time. We want to get your opinion on a plan we've drawn up. Also, they want to meet the person who did the footwork to give us our big break. Can you make it?"

Deidre was a little surprised. When she had first gone into law enforcement, the competition between agencies had been fierce. That seemed to be lessening, at least at the local level. A spirit of cooperation was evolving.

"I'll be there. What time?" She made an entry into her phone's reminder function.

For the first time in many days, Deidre was at a loss for something to do. She shuffled through some papers and considered calling the hospital to ask if Kimi had shown any improvement.

When she could find nothing more to occupy her time, she picked up her phone.

"Melissa, do you have time to talk?" Her call was greeted with a friendly, "Deidre. Great to hear from you. We've been receiving your reports. Seems this is a tough one. Any new developments?"

She wanted to tell Melissa everything, but decided she better wait for the fallout to clear from her latest discovery.

"Nothing of any significance right now. I've alerted the FBI to the possibility we are dealing with the trafficking of young women. Other than that it is pretty much status quo. I just wanted to hear your voice, and let you know I'm on the job up here. I didn't realize this would be such a lonely job when I took it. Tell me, have Anna's parents been able to claim her body yet?"

"Yes, Judy released it over a week ago, and the parents had her shipped back home, at considerable expense I might add. The laws are tougher when it comes to transporting a body across the border than if a reprobate like that Leder crosses with a passport. A testimony to our legislative leaders, if you ask me."

The women chit-chatted for several minutes about nothing in particular, just two friends checking in with each other. Eventually, Melissa announced she had a meeting to attend, and Deidre apologized for monopolizing her time. Melissa told her to call any time. The break from work might do both of them some good.

Deidre finished her work, wrote a note to Jill, and left it on her desk. *See you in the morning*, it said.

On her way out of the Law Enforcement Center, she crossed the courthouse parking lot. As she neared her vehicle, she almost bumped into Gerald Colter, the father of the young man who had given her the flash drive.

"Good afternoon, counselor," she said with a nod.

"Deidre," and the two went their separate ways.

That evening was as pleasant a time as Deidre had experienced since she moved back with Inga. They had a leisurely meal, cleaned the kitchen together, and sat in the living room, sipping tea.

"I don't want to snoop," Inga began. "But do you have a man in your life?"

Deidre laughed at her bluntness. "That's the last thing I need. For the first time since John's death, I feel like I'm in charge of my life. My decisions are my own, and I'm not reacting to loneliness or to a need to be with someone. No, I'm perfectly happy with my life the way it is."

Inga swirled her cup and stared into it as if she were a Gypsy tea-leaf reader. She looked up, and Deidre could see a sense of longing in the older woman's eyes.

"Don't close the door on another romance, my dear. I did that, thinking I would dishonor Eric's memory by being with another man. In my grief, I isolated myself, became an island. Now, in my later years, all I have left is to snoop on my neighbors, tend to my flowers, and hope that someone like you needs me. Don't close the door on happiness. You're too young to let it pass you by."

Deidre said nothing. Inside, she knew Inga was speaking through the voice of experience and with wisdom, and she knew she wanted to have back the happiness she and John had shared. But she knew she was afraid to allow herself that kind of joy again. What she didn't have, couldn't be taken from her.

Chapter
Twenty-One

Deidre felt at peace like she hadn't in a long time. The idea that she had done her job, had brought evidence to the FBI who were far more capable of raising the manpower to tackle the complex problem, had turned over the case to them, all of that lifted a huge burden from her shoulders. She no longer felt isolated and alone. For the first time in ages, she thought she could get back to her old way of life.

At ten o'clock she met Zak Burton in his office. Together they walked to the conference room down the hall. She was surprised that only a half-dozen men and women were waiting for them, expecting a much larger group.

"Folks, this is Deidre Johnson, the person who brought in the evidence we've been searching for."

To her surprise, they stood and gave her a brisk round of applause. One of the women offered her a cup of coffee and invited her to take a seat. Deidre felt a little like a reluctant celebrity.

Zak took his place to the side of a projection screen in the front of the room. He began a power point presentation.

"This is a photo of the *Ishat* the last time it was in port the summer before last. Notice that there are two gangways, one fore and one aft. Our intent is to cover both of them when our operation begins.

"I checked with Port Authority. Its ETA is December 10 at approximately 6:00 a.m. Of course that's highly variable at this time. We'll update the information when the ship clears the Soo locks and as it makes its way down the lake."

Deidre had not thought much about the snippet of conversation she had overheard when she took a wrong turn after visiting with

Zak. Even so, she felt a relaxation of her muscles when she learned he had been speaking to Port Authority.

"It'll be docking at grain elevator nine on the Duluth side of the harbor to take on a load of wheat bound for the Balkans. It's expected to be in port only a day and a half, departing at 6:00 p.m. on the 11th. They'll be pushing to get out of port as quickly as they can, because the weather is so unpredictable this time of year. We're going to stake out the pier from the time its mooring lines are cast ashore until they are hauled in. Here's the plan."

Zak put the next frame up on the screen, a diagram showing the probable location of the ship, the location of warehouses, the grain silos, and the location of each member of the team.

"There'll be two teams, four people positioned in sight of the aft gangway, and the others near the fore gangway. Each team will have a leader, and we'll be linked by a secure line of communication. That way, no one can distract us while they enter the opposite end of the ship."

Deidre looked around the room. Along with Zak, she counted seven people, yet on the screen the diagram showed eight. She thought someone must be missing.

She was jolted from her thoughts when Zak said, "Deidre, I assumed you would want to be with us. I've included you among the four watching this location." He pointed at the fore of the ship. "I hope I didn't take unwarranted liberty in assuming this."

Her peace was shattered. Suddenly she was thrust into the middle of what she thought she would be avoiding. So she wouldn't stutter or seem too surprised, Deidre nodded.

"Good. I couldn't imagine you'd have wanted to miss the excitement. We'll get together on Monday the ninth, to prepare."

The meeting broke up, each agent returning to whatever work they were assigned. On the way out, Zak said to Deidre, "Be sure to bring your body armor. We don't know what we'll be up against."

Thanks a lot, Deidre thought, but she smiled.

*****

THE WAY TO BEN'S HOUSE was becoming second nature, and she gave the turns no thought. In minutes from leaving the meeting at the Federal Building, she was pulling into his driveway.

A Christmas tree was propped against the garage, an eight-foot balsam fir. Deidre bent over and inhaled its aromatic vapors. She could imagine the smell it would produce in his house.

The realization hit her that she had never experienced Christmas with children, or as a child for that matter. All she remembered was her drunken stepfather ruining everything. She remembered the Christmas Eve he came home drunk and threw the tree out the door, decorations and all. After that, her mother never tried to celebrate the season.

She and John had talked about what it would have been like to have their own children, and she wondered then what kind of mother she would make. She hoped she could give Ben's daughters the kind of Christmas they deserved.

As she walked past the picture window facing the street, she peeked inside the house. Megan and Maren were playing with their dolls, and when Deidre tapped on the window, they sprang to their feet. By the time she made it to the door, they were waiting for her, their arms outstretched to receive a hug. They showered Deidre with kisses on her cheeks.

"Daddy will be home from work soon. Can we play dollies until he gets here?"

"We sure can. First let me get my coat off and get comfortable, then we'll play."

The sitter had stood by while the girls fawned over Deidre. "They certainly love you. Whatever I do, they tell how you do it differently." She smiled a warm smile, and Deidre knew she wasn't bothered by being one-upped. "I'd better be going. My husband will be needing supper when he gets home. He's retiring this spring, and we've made a deal. He promised to do the cooking and give me a break from meal preparation when that time comes."

As she was leaving, Ben came up the walk, supper in hand and ready to put in the oven. Tonight they were having gourmet ready-to-bake sausage pizza. Deidre thought this was about as good as it got. She sat down on the floor and held a doll while Ben set the table and poured milk for the girls.

After supper she helped clean up, put the dishes in the washer, and wiped off the countertop. Then, after playing another game of Old Maid, she helped tuck Megan and Maren into bed. As Deidre pulled the quilt up around her shoulders, Maren reached up and wrapped her arms around Deidre's neck. "I love you," she said and kissed her cheek. Tears formed in Deidre's eyes as she said goodnight.

As she and Ben enjoyed some quiet time, they shared what was left of a bottle of wine.

"I don't think the girls remember Jenny," he said, sadness in his voice. "Once in a while they talk about their mother, but their conversations are almost always about heaven where their mommy is."

He held his glass up, almost like a toast. "You have no idea how we appreciate you being a part of our lives. They have more awareness of you than they have of Jenny. She was special, but they were so little when she died."

Ben swirled the wine in his goblet and stared at it as it stopped rotating. "I worry about them sometimes. We don't seem to be making any progress in cutting out the cancers in our society, and I wonder what lies ahead for them. By the way, how was your meeting with Zak? He told me you were in the building today."

Deidre briefly outlined the plans Zak had in the works. "Did he tell you he wants me to be a part of the team when they stake out the ship?"

Ben's eyes widened. "No, he didn't say a word about that. That's highly unusual, you know. Zak's a good man, and he tackles every case like it is a personal vendetta. He must see something that makes him believe you'll be an asset. Otherwise he'd never ask you to come along. But, Deidre, be careful. The twins can't absorb another loss in their lives. Promise?"

"Promise," she said.

By Saturday evening, the excitement had built to the point the two girls could hardly be still. Supper had been an early affair. During the mid-afternoon, Ben brought the tree in from outside and placed it in its stand.

It stood in its allotted corner, emitting the smells of Christmas as it thawed in preparation to being decorated. At five-thirty, Ben announced it was time, and the girls cheered. He put a CD into its player and the voices of Christmas carolers filled the background.

Everyone stood back, offering advice, as Ben strung the lights on the tree, burying some deep near its core and stringing others near the tips of the branches. He showed the girls how to pull the corners of their eyes to form an exaggerated squint.

"It makes the lights all streaky," Megan exclaimed, and she and sister kept pulling at their lids until Ben said, "Enough. Your eyes will stay that way."

Deidre boxed him on the shoulder. "Don't scare them like that." Then she tried to give a better reason. "If you squint like that, you can't see as well, and you might stumble over a box."

Somehow, she thought, Ben's threat had a greater effect.

After an hour of working together, Ben stood on a stepstool and placed an angel at the top of the tree. They stood back to admire the adornments. Not intending to do so, Ben and Deidre said at the same time, "I think this is the best tree ever."

They looked at each other and laughed out loud.

"Sit over here and close your eyes," Megan instructed the two adults. Deidre heard them rummaging in some wrapping paper and then heard the sound of the stepstool being dragged across the floor.

Amid whispers and giggles she heard them struggling to accomplish some sort of task.

"Don't open your eyes, but stand up," Maren directed. Each child took one of the adult's hands. "We're going to spin you around, but don't open your eyes."

The girls led the way, and Deidre felt small hands positioning her.

"You can open your eyes now." Deidre was surprised to find herself no more than a foot from Ben, facing him. Ben looked puzzled as well. "Look up!"

They did.

"That's mistletoe! Grandma gave it to us last year. She said whoever stands under it has to be kissed."

Ben and Deidre looked at each other.

"Well?" the girls asked in unison. Ben laughed nervously, and Deidre blushed her usual shade of red.

He placed his arms around her, careful not to be too aggressive, and she stood on her tiptoes. For an instant they kissed, and then Ben backed away.

Megan and Maren stood back, their hands covering their mouths and giggling like Deidre had never heard them giggle.

"Was that what you meant?" he asked. They were speechless, still covering their mouths as though they held an important secret. Ben grabbed them and nibbled at the nape of their necks. "I love you so much, I could eat you up!" They clung to his shoulders as he carried them to bed.

It had become a pattern for Deidre and Ben to have a glass of wine and visit after the girls were in bed. They talked about many things that evening, their fears and worries, what Deidre planned to do after her job was done, what her plans were for Christmas. Ben told her he really would like her to spend it with him and the twins, although he had to admit his parents were celebrating with him.

They had a good laugh about how his mother had reacted to Deidre being invited to Thanksgiving. About eleven o'clock, they decided they better retire for the night, and Ben went to the kitchen. Deidre heard him rinsing out the glasses.

She stood in the doorway, and when he turned to come back into the living room, he almost bumped into her.

Deidre put her arms around his neck, stood on her toes as she had done before, and kissed him on his lips. She felt his arms encircle her and pull her toward him, and they held that pose for many seconds. Finally, Deidre pushed away.

"I'm sorry, Ben. Forgive me." She rushed up the stairs and closed the door to her room, fell on the bed and wept, being thankful she didn't have to explain why she was crying. She had no answer herself.

Deidre was up early the next morning, and was eating a piece of toast and drinking a cup of coffee when Ben came down the stairs.

"I thought I'd better get an early start," Deidre explained. "Pete needs to go for a good walk, and I have to get things together for Tuesday." She had a difficult time looking at Ben's face for fear of what she'd see.

Before he could respond, Deidre was at the door, pulling on her jacket. Ben took her hand.

"First of all, there's no need to be sorry. Second, thank you. And third, I know you're meeting at the Fed on Monday and then have to be back early Tuesday morning. I'd like you to stay here Monday night, if you will. Bring Pete. The girls will have fun playing with him, and we can take him for a walk in the evening. Will you?"

Deidre reached up again and kissed his cheek. "Yes." And she ran to her car.

Chapter
Twenty-Two

THE SKY ON MONDAY MORNING looked ominous, and Deidre felt chilled as she took the scenic highway to Duluth. She had plenty of time. Zak had called the meeting for two that afternoon, and until then, she had little to do. She pulled into one of the many spots overlooking Lake Superior, and sat in her SUV, allowing its engine to idle. The thermometer on the dash registered an outdoor temperature of ten degrees, not dangerously cold but, nevertheless, bitter, considering the wind-chill factor.

She watched the streamers of steam rise, evidence of warmer water interfacing with colder air. In the distance, steel-blue clouds lay in windrows over the horizon, giving the lake an icy-gray color rather than blue. Normally, this was a time of year Deidre liked above all others.

For some reason the way the shades of gray held contrast to the water intrigued her, made her feel comfortable. She wondered if that was because it was a part of nature's rhythms, a predictable cycle providing her an anchor in a continually shifting world. She decided the lake was nurturing.

Her thoughts turned to the weekend. *Did I make a fool of myself?* she wondered. *What came over me? I've never behaved like that.*

Finally, Deidre convinced herself that her kiss given to Ben was more a reaction to being with his girls than anything else. They made her feel as though she were family, and she wanted them to be happy.

Perhaps that's why she put her arms around Ben's neck. It wasn't about him. It was about them. After twenty minutes of rationalizing, she looked at her watch, one-thirty. Only a half-hour before the meeting. She put the shift lever in reverse and backed out of the space.

Almost everyone was present when she walked into the meeting room. Zak was in front, pacing, and he held the control for his power point presentation in his hand as if it were a weapon. Seeing that almost everyone else had a cup in hand, she poured herself coffee and took a seat. The same woman who sat next to her at the last meeting plunked down beside her.

"Well, here we go," was all she said.

Zak cleared his throat and everyone became attentive.

"You may have noticed there are two ships anchored outside the harbor, waiting to dock. One of them is the *Ishat*. It arrived last night at midnight and will pass under the lift bridge at five Tuesday morning. We estimate she'll be docked at the Orton Grain elevator by six, and loading will begin immediately. You know we're expecting two females to be smuggled aboard sometime during its stay. We haven't a clue when. But you know as well as I do, most clandestine operations take place when it's dark. Prime times would be from 6:00 p.m., when it ties up, to 7:30 a.m., and from 4:30 p.m. to 7:30 a.m. the next day. The ship is scheduled to leave at 6:00 p.m. on the eleventh. That means another window will open from 4:30 p.m. Wednesday, until they pull away from the pier. If I had to put my money down, I'd bet on the last window. There's always a hubbub at the last minute, and my gut feeling is that would be the opportune time to get someone aboard. Unfortunately, that's only a guess. Wear warm clothing. Layer it. Thermal underwear, sweaters, your parka. Be sure to wear pacs on your feet, and well insulated mittens for your hands. Stocking caps will be mandatory. All of this is agency issue. Deidre, we'll see that you're equipped. Do not wear parkas with the FBI logo, but underneath have your vest with the initials front and back. At the last minute throw the parka off and identify yourself as FBI. Deidre, I assume your vest is labeled BCA." She nodded.

Her insides were in knots as she drove to Ben's, not so much because of tomorrow's action but more so because she knew seeing Ben was going to be awkward. She hesitated getting out of her car.

Then, she squared her shoulders and walked to the door to receive her usual welcome from the girls.

They mobbed her. Ben stood in the background, grinning from ear to ear. "Good to have you here again, Deidre," and he gave her a quick kiss on the cheek. Deidre looked at the girls. They were beaming.

"Do you like Daddy," Megan asked, her eyes searching Deidre's face.

"Yes, I like your daddy." She looked at Ben, and he winked at her. *Not too awkward after all,* she thought.

"Come look at the tree," Maren asked as she pulled Deidre to the masterpiece they had created on Saturday. Hanging from strings were four paper dolls, gaudily colored the way an almost five-year-old would.

"This is me." She pointed to one of the small figures. "And this is Megan." She pointed at the other paper doll. "And this is you, and this is Daddy."

Deidre fought back the tears. The paper dolls were arranged in order from the man doll, to the woman doll, to the two children. The girls had taped them together in order: Daddy, Mommy, Megan, and Maren they had written in crooked letters on each doll.

It's a family, she thought, but didn't verbalize the words. She wouldn't allow herself to imagine such a scenario.

After the nightly ritual of baths and hair brushing, the girls were tucked in for the night.

On the way down the stairs Ben asked, "Wine?"

"Sure, but make mine a short one. I've got a big day ahead of me tomorrow."

She sat on the sofa while Ben opened a fresh bottle and poured the Clos DuBois. He handed her the glass and took a seat in the chair across from her.

"Can you tell me what you expect to happen tomorrow?"

"I know it's going to be cold." She laughed nervously, almost afraid to be alone with him. "Seriously, we're beginning a stakeout tomorrow that may last as long as eighteen hours. Zak says there'll be a place nearby where we can get warm, and we're going to take shifts being in the cold. He thinks he has it arranged so we look like workers, and our rotation will look as if we're a team trading off warming ourselves. I guess we are, but it's going to take an acting job to convince anyone we should be there. If and when it looks as though someone is being smuggled aboard, whoever is on outside duty will be closer to the action and can lead the charge. From there we have to react to the circumstance."

"Are you worried," Ben asked, his brow furrowing so his eyebrows almost met.

"Worried? No, I'm scared shitless," Deidre admitted and took a sip of wine.

Ben got out of his chair and slid next to her on the sofa. He wrapped his arms around her, and she slumped so her head rested on his shoulder. They sat that way for a long time, and Deidre felt safe.

"Don't take any foolish chances," Ben said softly. "The girls couldn't live without you." He hesitated, "And I'm beginning to think I can't either."

Deidre finally moved. "I wish I could sit here all night, but I have to get some sleep."

She took her empty wine glass to the kitchen and stepped onto the first step of the stairs leading to the bedrooms. Then she turned. Standing that way she was almost his height, and she put her arms around his neck, kissed him on the forehead, and said, "Goodnight, Ben."

Together they made their way to the top of the stairs.

In her room, alone, Deidre prepared for bed, brushing her teeth and washing her face. She seldom wore makeup, especially when she was working, so it didn't take much time to clean up. She peeled back the comforter on the bed and crawled under it, clutched an extra pillow to her chest and curled around it. She fell asleep almost as soon as her head hit the other pillow, a slight smile on her face.

Chapter
Twenty-Three

As the weatherman had promised, Tuesday, December 10 was clear and cold with the morning temperature bottoming out at two degrees above zero. Deidre made her way downstairs before anyone else was awake. Between what Ben had said to her last night and what lay ahead, she couldn't sleep any later.

She picked up the daily paper from the outdoor steps, made a cup of coffee, and placed a sliced bagel in the toaster. She had just settled into a kitchen chair, when she heard Ben coming down the stairs.

"Good morning," he said, bent down and kissed her cheek, and poured himself a cup of coffee. He separated the sports page from the rest of the paper and began reading.

"Look at this. The editorial writers are after the Viking's coach again. Why don't they ever go after management for not giving him any players?" He shook his head.

Deidre laughed. "If only that was the biggest problem in the world today." She felt comfortable.

They fixed breakfast for the girls, and the sitter arrived, which caused Deidre to feel a little uncomfortable even though nothing was happening between her and Ben. They both left in their own vehicles, heading to the same building.

They parked side by side in the lot, and as they walked to their jobs, Ben said, "Be careful, please." Deidre squeezed his hand.

She was directed by the receptionist to report to the staging area in the lower level of the building where she met Zak and a few others of the team. Deidre was beginning to feel butterflies in her stomach, and the reality of what was going to happen began to sink in.

As the rest of the team straggled in, a few cracked jokes, but most of them were dead serious. Deidre found a stack of clothes she was to wear: agency issued sweaters, boots, even long underwear. She and the two other women suited up in the next room. Then Zak asked them to take a seat.

"We've got things set up on the dock where the *Ishat* will be moored. The Port Authority has been extremely helpful by giving us information about the site. The dock workers know nothing of our sting, but the location of the loading chutes of the grain elevator pretty much dictates where the ship must be berthed. It'll be docked in the right spot, give or take a couple of feet.

"You've seen those tents that electrical and phone line workers use on cold, windy days? We have one of those set up opposite where each gangway will meet the dock. We'll be playing the part of workers doing repair work. The colder it is, the better to convince people of the need for the shelters. Inside each is a closed-circuit camera that will transmit real time images to our post inside the building behind the shelters. Those of us inside will monitor what's happening on the dock."

Zak handed out a schedule. "Here are the times you'll be in the shelter. They are blocked off in twenty minute shifts. That will be about how long you can stand the cold without becoming too uncomfortable. Wait inside the shelter until your replacement scratches on the canvas. When you come out, don't be afraid to gab a little bit as though you are friends making a switch. Then come inside the warm building. We'll have coffee and other hot drinks around the clock, plus food. It won't be gourmet, but it'll keep you going in the cold. Speaking of which, there are toilets inside." Everyone gave a nervous laugh. "Any questions?"

One man raised his hand. "Do we have any way of knowing how the exchange will be made? And when we're sure it's happening, how are we going to respond?"

"Thanks, Jim. In my mind I thought I had covered that, but I guess I wasn't clear at all."

Several members of the team shook their heads.

"We have no idea what to expect. There is room for a car to be driven onto the pier. Or, we could see them escorting the women as they walk toward the ship. They might even be transported with a forklift and in a container.

"We just have to not become fixated on what we think it'll look like. As to your second question. I'll give the signal to move. We'll be in teams of four separated by a couple hundred feet between the two gangways. That means one team or another will be in action before the other can respond. The safety of the girls who will be under duress is paramount. One member of each unit will be equipped with a high-powered rifle to cover the scene. I'd be extremely surprised if our perpetrators aren't armed, so have your weapons drawn and ready to fire. We know the fate of the girls who are trafficked, and the traffickers have no scruples. They won't hesitate to shoot to save their own skins."

"When we get to our post, we'll run through possible scenarios. But by all means, we can't develop a mindset as to how this is going to happen. Whatever we plan, we'll probably be wrong."

The team drove to the site, singly or two to a vehicle, and they arrived at odd intervals until everyone was inside a small shack that was dwarfed by the towering grain silos behind it. Almost a block down the pier was a building similar to the one in which they gathered.

Zak instructed four members of the team to make their way to that site. The woman in the group was the leader. Zak stayed with Deidre's group. He sent one of the men out for the first shift in the shelter. It'd be over two hours before the ship docked, but he wanted it to look as though the utility company had been working on a problem for most of the afternoon.

Twenty minutes later, another agent was sent out. The man who had spent time in the shelter joined them, poured himself a cup of steaming coffee, and said, "This is the easiest stakeout I've ever been on. The sun shining on the canvas is absorbed and the greenhouse effect inside is unbelievable. I almost fell asleep it got so warm. Took off my parka so I'd stay awake." He slurped the hot coffee.

Zak chuckled. "I hope you remember that when you're on a shift just before dawn. The forecast is for zero by morning, and the sun won't be shining. Enjoy it while you can."

Next, it was Deidre's turn. As Zak had requested, she spent a couple of minutes chatting with the person she was relieving. Then she playfully punched his arm and crawled inside the shelter.

There were no wires to fix, only a camera mounted on a tripod and placed against a barely visible hole in the canvas. From her vantage point, she could peer through a small opening. Best of all, she could hear what was happening outside, even the conversations of the workers.

She had heard foul language before and was no prude, but during her shift, she heard words used in ways she'd never encountered. Deidre decided she wouldn't want to be in this part of town alone at night.

Her predecessor was right, the shelter was almost too warm, and when she heard someone scrape the back door, she didn't feel the need to go inside to be warmed.

The shortest daylight period occurs on December 21 in the northland, and the sun set at around four-thirty. By the time five-thirty came, the temperature had dropped so the team members were more than ready to be spelled after twenty minutes. Each had served five rotations in the shelter, and it was Deidre's turn again.

She had just made herself comfortable when in the distance she heard the deep baritone pitch of a ship's horn. Seconds later, the lift bridge operator responded with several high pitched signals. The ship was preparing to enter the harbor.

She couldn't see the canal from where she sat, but she could picture the ship entering between the concrete abutments with only a few feet to spare on either side. Deidre knew that, because it was a foreign ship, a U.S. pilot was on board, guiding the vessel to its berth.

It took until the end of her shift for the lights of the ship to come into her field of vision, and she watched it glide into position in front of where she was hidden. She was so intent on the process that she jumped in surprise when the person relieving her gave the signal.

Deidre exited the shelter, and the two of them stood for a few seconds, watching the activity. Mooring lines were heaved onto the pier and secured to the pilings. The engines of the ship became almost silent as the captain ordered the boilers to be damped.

Inside the warm warehouse, she realized how chilled she had become, and she shivered while gulping a cup of steaming coffee. She was going to have to catch some sleep between shifts as best she could, but right now she wasn't concerned about the caffeine keeping her awake.

By the time she warmed up, she could hear the whoosh of grain flowing through chutes into the holds of the ship. The sound was pleasant and lulled her to sleep.

It seemed as though she had just closed her eyes when she was awakened by Zak shaking her shoulder. She looked at her watch, six-fifty. Deidre was thankful she had slept a little. It was going to be a long night.

The surveillance continued around the clock. Nothing out of the ordinary happened. She drew the 7:00 to 7:20 a.m. shift, the coldest part of the night. Deidre remembered learning that just as the sun was rising, the temperature would take a nosedive. It didn't make sense, she thought, but the explanation had been that the first rays of the sun caused a drop in the relative humidity and cooled the earth.

She wasn't sure if that was correct. What she did know was that there was a sudden drop in temperature inside the shelter. By full daylight, she was more than ready to end her shift.

When her replacement came to the shelter, she stepped outside and, for the first time, saw the ship in daylight. Its railings and guy lines were encrusted with icicles hanging from every location possible. She heard the thud of hammers or axes and looked up to see crewmembers dislodging chunks of ice from the deck. It was a surreal scene, like a ghost ship had been brought to anchor.

Zak decided to lengthen the shifts during the day. He had experienced the warming factor of the sun's energy being trapped inside the shelter, and he thought it best to give his team members an opportunity to sleep for a longer interval than he planned.

Deidre found a place inside the building where she could stretch out, took one last gulp of coffee, swallowed the last bite of sandwich she had been chewing, and lay down. In minutes she was asleep.

The next thing she new, she was being awakened. It was noon, and she had slept four hours. She stretched, feeling stiff and cramped but was due in the shelter in fifteen minutes.

After using the facility, Deidre grabbed a bagel and cream cheese, a cup of coffee, and an apple. She sat on one of the chairs against the wall and quickly downed her lunch.

The air outside was warmer than it had been when she finished her last shift. Now, she would spend the next two hours in the shelter. It would be two-thirty before she could use the bathroom again, and she wondered if she should have had that second cup of coffee. *Too late now*, she thought.

It was a struggle to stay awake. The day was clear, and the sun heated the shelter to the point that she had to remove two layers of clothing. Nothing much was happening on the dock, only a solitary worker passing by every so often. She realized that the sounds of ice removal had stopped and surmised the ship had been rid of its burden while she slept.

According to her watch, her replacement should be making an appearance very soon, and right on time she heard the sound of someone tapping on the canvas. They stood in the mid-afternoon sun, chatting. Deidre commented on how soon it would be dark, and her counterpart noted that the weather prediction was for the wind to begin to pick up and the temperature to drop by evening.

The routine was becoming boring, and Deidre wondered if this was going to end up being an exercise in futility. She was tired of coffee and bagels, tired of sleeping on a makeshift cot, tired of waiting.

Zak got off his phone and came over to where she and the other agent were sitting. "Bad news. There's a storm, a heavy nor'easter, scheduled to blow in later tonight, and the ship's captain persuaded the Port Authority to speed up the loading process so he can clear the harbor before it hits. It's scheduled to leave at seven tonight."

Deidre didn't think that was bad news. It meant she wouldn't have to spend another minute in the shelter. Its current occupant's shift was to run until five o'clock, and then Zak and the other agent would take their turns. By then the ship's gangway should be up and the mooring lines readied for castoff. She had another bagel, this time with jelly and peanut butter.

At five, the shift changed and the agent who had been outside stepped through the door. "The weather's really changing out there. I think the temperature dropped twenty degrees during my shift, and I can't guess how strong the wind's blowing. It's going to be a brutal night on the lake. I don't envy those sailors who will be on it."

Zak was in the shelter. Deidre said a word of thanks to herself that the schedule had worked the way it did. She glanced at the monitor sitting on a stand by the coffee pot. The docks were empty. She was debating whether she should indulge in another stale bagel when she saw a strange vehicle move into the picture, and then she recognized it as a mini-crane, a self propelled hoist frequently used on the dock to lift heavy objects such as repair parts for the ships.

"I think this is it," Zak's voice sounded calm as it was projected through a small speaker set by the monitor. "Get ready."

185

The three of them tightened their vests and checked their weapons. On the monitor they saw two men get down from the cab of the vehicle. They wrestled what looked to be two large duffle bags from a compartment, threw them over their shoulders, and headed toward the gangway.

"Let's go!" Zak shouted, and the team burst out the door of the shed.

Deidre took in the scene with a sweep of her eyes. In the halo-like glow of the dock lights she could see two crewmembers making their way down the stairs from the ship. The men with their duffle bags were near the base of the gangway, and Zak was running toward them, the FBI logo of his flak vest reflecting the dim light. He was yelling, "FBI. Stop and put your hands on your heads."

In that instant, Deidre saw the men throw their bundles over the side of the dock, and she heard a delayed splash when they hit the water. Zak was chasing the men, and the other two agents were following suit. She saw the other team running toward them, sandwiching the fleeing suspects.

Instinctively, she realized what was happening, and as she ran to the dock's edge, she stripped off her belts and her vest. By the time she reached the brink, she had removed what clothing she could, and she jumped into the water. In the time between when she leaped and the time she entered the lake, she heard a series of gun shots from atop the pier, but the sounds didn't register in her brain.

In December, the temperature of Lake Superior was about thirty-seven degrees. When her body hit the water, she involuntarily gasped from the shock. In seconds her fingers became numb. She saw one of the bags sink below the surface, and she grabbed it with all the strength she could muster, dragged it over to the wood pilings and kept it near the surface.

"Deidre, grab this buoy!" She looked up in time to see a ring being thrown to her. The agent was descending a ladder attached to the dock. He wrestled the bag from her grasp and carried it on his shoulder to the top.

Deidre, life buoy in one hand and stroking with the other, moved away from the pier. She had been in the icy water scarcely five minutes, but already her feet and lower legs were numb. She kicked as hard as she could.

After another five minutes, she located the other bag, suspended a foot or two below the murky surface of the harbor water. Her core temperature was dropping, although she had no awareness of that. She was beginning to feel an overpowering sleepiness, along with a sense of peace. She no longer felt the cold.

As Deidre was jumping into the water, the two suspects realized there was no way out. They decided to take a stand. One crouched behind a piling and fired at the oncoming agents, and an agent let out a gasp as he crumpled to the deck.

From a way off, the agent with a rifle and a night scope placed its crosshairs on the shooter's chest and pulled the trigger. He saw a body fall behind the piling.

In desperation, the other suspect stepped out in full view and emptied his pistol, hitting no one, but the return fire riddled his body. In the end no one really knew whose shots hit home.

At that moment, they realized they had all reacted to the gunmen, and they rushed to the spot from where Deidre had leaped. One of them hurried down the ladder to water level and hefted the bag she clutched onto his shoulder. When it was carried to the decking of the wharf, two agents cut it open, exposing the limp body of a young girl.

By that time, Zak had made an emergency call, and ambulances were on their way. Two arrived, their lights flashing and sirens blaring.

One agent remembered seeing a hook hanging on the wall, meant for retrieving objects from the water. She rushed to where Deidre clung to the life ring with her right arm and the other bag with her left. The agent threw the hook attached to a line and snagged the bag on the first try. Deidre felt herself being pulled toward the pier, and then her world went black. With the help of two others, Deidre and the duffle bag were dragged to the base of the dock and carried up the ladder.

The duffle was cut open. Inside the canvas bag lay another girl. She wasn't breathing, and the woman agent started CPR, continuing chest compressions until a third ambulance arrived. The EMTs took over.

When Diedre opened her eyes, she was in an ambulance and the EMT was trying to get her to respond to his voice. He kept repeating, "Stay with me, girl. Don't give up. Stay awake. Fight it." She lay her head on the pillow and wondered if she would see Ben that night. In minutes the ambulances were on their way to the hospital.

Above, from the ship's railing, the sailors looked down with amusement. It had been quite a show, but now it was over, and they returned to what they had been doing.

Zak checked on the fallen agent. His vest had saved him from serious injury, and he was sitting on a timber, holding his ribs.

"You okay to ride to the hospital?"

The agent nodded and struggled to rise. With two of his companions supporting him, he slowly made his way to a police car that had arrived at the tumultuous scene.

Zak and another agent walked to where the suspects lay. "I wish they hadn't died so quickly," the female agent said. "They should have suffered more."

She walked away, turned, and looked up the hill at the city lights. "Just a bunch of damned animals," she said, and wiped her eyes.

Chapter
Twenty-Four

DEIDRE WAS AWARE OF BEING whisked through the hospital ER doors and being transferred to a bed. She was aware of her wet clothing being removed and of the blessed feeling of a warm, dry blanket being tucked around her. She tried speaking, but her words sounded garbled to her ears, and she felt an overpowering urge to close her eyes and sleep.

She became irritated with all the people rushing around, asking her questions, urging her to stay awake and to not drift away.

A doctor came in and mumbled something about ninety-four degrees, and then left. A nurse entered, carrying a bag that she hung on a stand, and Deidre felt a warm trickle enter her vein through an IV port.

After several hours she was able to focus her eyes somewhat. She felt warm and secure under the layers of blankets, but she was far from secure in her mind. As she lay in her hospital bed, she tried to force the recollection of what had happened, but all she remembered was rushing from a building and removing her jacket.

She looked around her dimly lit room and spotted someone sitting in a chair across the room. He was looking at her, and she wondered if she was hallucinating.

The man's image came into focus. "Ben," she murmured as though she were drugged. Her lips felt parched.

Ben pulled his chair closer to her bedside. "So much for being careful," he said and a wide grin split his face.

"How does it feel to be a hero?"

She stared at him, a confused look on her face. "What do you mean?"

Ben got up from his chair. "Just a minute." He left the room for a moment and returned with Zak. "She's back with us."

Zak sat down next to her bed and took her hand, and Ben stood behind him, still grinning.

"So you don't remember much of what happened?"

"Virtually nothing."

"Do you remember getting my call to come out of the warehouse?" Deidre nodded.

"Do you remember why I made that call?"

Deidre thought for a moment. The cobwebs cleared, somewhat. "There were two men carrying bundles. I remember that." A look of recognition came into her eyes. "They threw the bundles into the water." She paused. "Oh, my God, there were women in those sacks." A look of shock crossed her face. "What happened?"

"We came under fire from the men, and everyone went after them, everyone but you. While we lost sight of our first obligation and engaged the shooters, you dove into the harbor. You must have known those bags contained the girls being sold to the ship's crew."

Deidre tried to grasp what he was saying, but her thoughts were muddled. "Did I . . . are they going to be all right?"

Zak smiled. "Yes. One of them is about where you are now. The other is in pretty tough shape, but the doctors say she'll recover.

"It took you almost ten minutes to locate the second girl. That's a long time to be under water. But, and again this is the doctor speaking, we were told the body has some unusual reactions to being submerged in ice water. It shuts down and breathing is suspended. That's why she didn't drown. This was an extreme case. She was placed on a ventilator, and her body was gradually warmed with a heart-lung machine regulating the body temperature. The second girl is still in ICU, but her brain functions look good, and she's expected to make a recovery, although it'll be slow going. Asking you to come along on this mission was the best thing I could have done."

Deidre relaxed so her head rested fully on the pillow. She wanted desperately to remember, but all she could do was take Zak at his word.

"Gotta run," he said. "But be prepared for some reporters to visit you this afternoon. They smell a story, and it's a good one."

Ben hovered over her, tucking the blanket under her chin. Then he bent down and kissed her forehead. "You scared the crap out of me. Try not to do that again."

"What time is it?" she asked.

"Seven-thirty."

"In the evening?"

Ben laughed. "No, in the morning, and here comes your breakfast to prove it." A hospital worker placed a food tray on her table. "Would you like coffee or tea?" she asked.

As predicted, two reporters and a camera crew visited her later in the morning. It was easy for her to not reveal much about the case. She didn't remember. All she could say was that she was glad the team had rescued two girls from a life of prostitution, probably a short life.

That afternoon she was pronounced fit to go home, and Ben was there with her civilian clothes and a blanket. She felt babied as he wheeled her chair to his car and helped her get settled inside. He had left the engine running and the heater on, and it felt good.

When they arrived at his home, he and the girls fawned over her until she had to say, "Enough, already."

The six o'clock news came on, and Deidre was chagrinned to see herself on the screen, propped up by pillows and in a hospital bed. She decided she didn't look too bad, considering what she had endured.

*****

THE NEXT MORNING, Ben told Deidre that Zak had left a message. He was calling a meeting to review the operation, and if she was up to it, he'd like her to attend. She felt stiff all over, as though she had been steamrollered, but it was nothing so debilitating she couldn't function.

They met in the Federal Building, all eight members of the team, and Zak gave his heartfelt thanks for having such a great group of people covering his back. He was especially complimentary to Deidre, and she shrunk down in her chair, not liking being singled out.

"The first girl Deidre pulled from the water has recovered enough to speak with one of our women agents. She's pretty banged up, shows evidence of having been sexually assaulted, but is recovering nicely from the hypothermia. She's given us a great deal of information, but unfortunately it leads to a dead end.

"Last July in the evening she was sitting by Lake Superior, smoking weed, as she put it, and an older man she didn't know sat down beside her and started up a conversation. He offered her a drink from a bottle of liquor he had in his pocket. The next thing she knew, she was in his pickup on some dirt road. He took her to a boat landing on a lake, and there she was forced into a canoe with another girl. Their hands and feet were bound, and their mouths were duct taped so they couldn't shout or scream. She said it was getting dark, and two men paddled the canoe. Evidently they knew the wilderness very well, because they made their way in the dark.

"They traveled all night, and the next morning, pulled the canoe into the brush where they spent the day. At dusk, their journey continued. Just before dawn, the canoe crunched up on a gravel landing, and she and the other girl were taken to a waiting pickup where they were transported a distance—she's not sure how far—to a place that had a number of log cabins by a river. All she can remember is that they were old and rundown.

"The two of them were shoved into a cabin and discovered there were six other girls already inside. All of them were shackled to makeshift beds by an ankle bracelet and a chain.

"She has no idea where the cabins are. She didn't even know she was in the United States. You see, the kidnappers must have come through the Quetico Provincial Park, crossed the unmarked border into the Boundary Waters Canoe Area Wilderness, and then departed from one of the entry points on our side of the border.

"I checked. It is only a two-and-a-half-hour drive from Thunder Bay to lake Saganaga. They could have paddled to the U.S. side of the lake and from there made their way to Knife Lake. It would have taken them another six hours or so to get to Moose Lake landing, from where they could travel by pickup anywhere south.

"It's evident that we have stumbled onto a well-organized human trafficking ring. Unfortunately, we are at somewhat of a standstill right now for lack of evidence, and lack of knowledge. For now this is all I have for you, but hopefully we'll be called together again to continue our work on this case. I hope that time is days from now rather than weeks."

Zak dismissed the group, except for Deidre. "Can I see you in my office for a few minutes?"

She followed him down the hall.

"One of our only links to what our girl has told us is Kimi. Will you stop and see her today? See if she's talking at all about what happened. The other two girls are in the same hospital. I'd like you to try to interview them today. You have a link to them that our people don't, and if anyone can get through, I think it'll be you.

"Also, because you have a relationship with the leaders of the Nishnawbe Aski Nation, I'd like you to be the liaison between our two offices."

Deidre wasn't quite sure how to react. She'd assumed that because the case was now under the FBI's jurisdiction, her job would be done. She was glad it wasn't, because she had some unfinished business with a certain attorney.

"What about Gerald Colter, II?" she asked.

"We have to be a little patient at this point. I'm thinking once we get this onion peeled to the core, he's going to be found near the center. We'll get him if he is."

Deidre drove the few blocks to the hospital where the girls were patients. She went to the room of the first girl she had pulled from the water.

"Hi, Allison," she said as she entered the room. "You don't know me, but my name is Deidre Johnson."

The girl's eyes widened, and then filled with tears. "You rescued me."

Deidre was a little flustered. "Well, we all rescued you. And there's a young man you don't even know who gave us the information that allowed us to step in when we did so we could rescue you."

The girl motioned for her to come by her bedside, reached up and hugged her. "Thank you so much. I'll never be able to say that enough."

Deidre sat down. "You can thank me by trying to answer some questions as honestly as you can. Was there a girl in the camp where you were held named Anna Woodsong?"

As soon as she asked the question, she saw Allison go rigid. "Yes, she was there."

"Can you tell me about her?" Deidre pressed.

"Anna was strong, stronger than the rest of us, I suppose. She refused to give up. All day and night she worked on ways to free herself. Because of her struggles, she developed a bleeding sore where her shackle fit around her ankle. Another girl was just as determined to get free. One night, Anna worked a nail free from the frame of her bed. Somehow, she used the steel of her shackle to hook its head. Over a few days she managed to work it loose. She used the nail to rid herself of the piece of steel. I remember her asking who else wanted to go with her. One other said she would. The rest of us were too afraid. We didn't have jackets, and it was winter outside. We didn't even have shoes."

Deidre stopped her and asked, "Was the other girl named Kimi?" Allison's eyes widened. "Yes. How did you know?"

"She's in the hospital, one floor up from you. Do you know what happened to Anna?" The girl nodded. "Can you tell me about it?"

Allison shook her head and began to sob. All she could say was, "They killed her. They made us watch what they did, and they killed her. They tortured her, and then they killed her. After she was dead, one of the men who guarded us said, 'This is what happens if you try to get away.'"

Deidre was so shocked and repulsed she had difficulty asking her next question. Evidently, Anna was so traumatized that she appeared dead to the other girls. They didn't know she was alive when the torturing was over.

"Tell me, Allison, do you remember a man named Jason Leder?" Allison shook her head.

Deidre opened a folder she had brought and produced a picture of Jason, and panic overtook Allison's expression. "He was one of the men who kept us locked up. He's the man who picked us up at the canoe landing last summer. He's the man who killed Anna." She began to shake.

Deidre said, "Allison, you don't have to be afraid of him anymore. He's dead. I want you to know I think you're incredibly brave, Allison. Thank you so much for answering my questions. I do have to go now, but may I come back in a day or two so we can talk again."

Allison nodded.

"I'll arrange so we can go up to Kimi's room and see her. Would you like that?"

Again Allison nodded and buried her face in the bedcovers.

Deidre climbed the stairs to the next floor and knocked on a door. It was open a crack, and she inched it open a little more, enough to stick her head in the room.

"Hi, Kimi. Is it okay if I come in?" The girl was standing by the window. When she heard Deidre's voice, she quickly turned and almost ran across the room. Her hug lasted several minutes, and finally, Deidre led her to her bed and sat down, still holding her closely.

"Kimi, you'll never guess who's in a bed one floor down."

"Anna?" Kimi asked excitedly.

Deidre hardly knew how to respond. "No not Anna, but Allison is down there, and she says she knows you."

Kimi slumped, dejection evident in her posture. "Not Anna?"

Deidre shook her head.

"Do you remember Allison from the cabin." Kimi nodded. "Was she your friend?" She shrugged.

"Well, I just stopped to see how you were. I can't stay long, but is it okay if I come back in a day or so."

Kimi looked into her eyes, and answered, "Yes."

"Can I bring Allison to your room?"

Kimi looked at the floor and nodded.

*****

DEIDRE WAS BACK IN TWO HARBORS before Jill's quitting time, and she hoped her secretary didn't have a day's worth of interviews lined up for her the next day.

"Hi, Boss Lady," Jill chirped. "You look like hell!" She laughed at what she had said. "But you're still pretty. It's been quiet around here the last couple of days, and I've sort of run out of work to do with you gone. Anything that needs doing?"

Deidre couldn't think of anything and was about to tell her to take tomorrow off.

"Oh, I almost forgot," Jill said. "This call came in yesterday from the women's shelter. It's a request for you to stop and visit one of their clients." Jill picked up a piece of paper. "Her name's Jessica Sobranski. Do you recognize the name?"

Deidre grabbed the back of a chair to steady herself. "I know her mother. But you said the woman wants to see me? Do you know why?"

"The director of the shelter called on her behalf. She asked that you stop over as soon as you can."

Deidre could hardly believe what she was hearing.

"Call the shelter and tell them I'm on my way. Oh, and Jill, why don't you take the day off tomorrow. I won't be in the office." She rushed down the stairs and out the door, ran the two blocks to the woman's shelter and burst through the front door.

"Someone called and asked for me to come to the shelter. They said a Jessica Sobranki wanted to see me. Is she still here?" she asked, still quite out of breath.

"Deidre, great to see you. We have a young lady who came in the other day. She saw you being interviewed on TV and asked if I could reach you. I think she believes if you helped the girls at the dock, you'll be able to help her. I'll go to Jessica's room and let her know you're here," the volunteer at the front desk announced. "Why don't you wait in our conference room where the two of you can have some privacy."

She waited impatiently, wondering what to expect. The volunteer returned, escorting a tall, thin young lady.

"This is Jessica Sobranski. Jessica, Deidre Johnson. I'll leave you two alone for as long as you'd like." She closed the conference room door behind her, and the two women stood looking at each other, neither knowing quite what to do next.

Finally, Deidre broke the ice. "Jessica, you look just like your mother."

Jessica puckered up and tried to speak, but all that came out were squeaks. She rushed to Deidre and hugged her while she sobbed. Deidre held her until she felt the girls body stop shaking.

"Come, let's sit over here so we can talk. I've heard about you, you know. A few weeks ago, I was working a case with your mother,

Melissa, and she told us about you being missing from her life. She misses you terribly."

"Are you sure?" Jessica questioned. "After all I've put her through, she still misses me?"

Deidre nodded. "She does, and she's never given up trying to locate you. It's none of my business where you've been and what you've been doing, but I can assure you, your mother wants you back, unconditionally. The fact that you came to this shelter and that you called me, says that you want to go home. Am I correct?"

Jessica looked at the floor but managed to nod.

"Do you want me to contact your mother and set up a meeting?"

Again Jessica gave a slight nod as though she was too ashamed to raise her head.

"Where do you think would be a good place to meet?"

"Home."

Deidre promised her that she would set up everything that night, and they would be on their way to the Cities the next day. They walked to the front door of the shelter together.

"Thank you for calling me. Believe me, your reunion will be better than anything you can possibly imagine."

That evening she dialed Melissa's personal phone.

"Hello. This is Melissa speaking," Deidre heard the familiar voice.

"Hi, Melissa. Deidre here, making a social call for a change. I'm planning on being in Minneapolis tomorrow, and I was wondering if I could stop over for a visit in the evening, that is if you have no plans."

Melissa didn't hesitate. "Have anything to do? My evenings are so boring, all I try to do is fill the hours until bedtime. Of course you'll be welcome. Would you like to stay over? It won't be as exciting as your cabin, but I have a bottle of good wine."

Deidre laughed. If only she knew. "I'm bringing a surprise. Just be prepared."

After Melissa hung up, she called the shelter and told Jessica to be ready about three o'clock the next day. The remainder of the night Deidre spent going over in her mind possible scenarios of the reunion. They all had a happy ending.

*****

JESSICA WAS A BALL OF NERVES as they sped along I-35 to the Twin Cities. Deidre could see the panic in her eyes, and she was sure that if they had not been trapped inside a car traveling seventy miles per hour, she would have fled. Deidre reached over and touched her hand. "It's going to be wonderful. You wait. I just know it is."

"Did you tell my mother I was coming with you?"

"No. I knew if I did, she would get in her car and race to Two Harbors, and I didn't want her taking chances, especially driving at night. And I knew that if she waited for us to come to her, she would agonize over our meeting until we arrived. Believe me, I gave it a lot of thought, and I think this is the best way."

They rode in silence for a long ways. "I wasn't a saint, you know," Jessica volunteered.

"You don't have to confess to me. All your mother told me was that you were troubled before you ran away."

"No, I mean after I ran away. When Mom finds out the things I did to survive, I'm afraid she won't want me around." Jessica began to cry, softly at first, then more uncontrollably.

"Please, Jessica. I know you're frightened, but your mom is going to be so happy that you're alive. Nothing else is going to matter. Knowing her, she'll let you tell what you want with your own timing. She loves you, Jessica. It will be all right. I know it."

Jessica took a deep breath and sat up straight in her seat. She wiped her eyes and resolved to face her mother, no matter the consequences.

Deidre sensed the girl begin to tense up even more as they drove the residential streets, eventually stopping in front of her home.

"You stay here while I say a few words to your mom. When I give you the high-sign, you can come to her."

Deidre rang the door bell, and Melissa opened it immediately. Evidently, she had been waiting.

"Hi, Deidre. Welcome. Well don't just stand there, come in."

Deidre beamed. "Remember I said I had a surprise for you? Are you ready? You'd better hold my hand, tight."

Melissa looked confused, and Deidre motioned toward her car. Its door opened and Jessica stepped out.

"Oh, my God, my baby," Melissa shrieked, and she ran down the sidewalk.

Jessica hardly had time to move before her mother reached her. She wrapped her arms around her daughter and buried her face in the girl's hair, all the while repeating over and over, "Jessica, you're home, you're home."

After several minutes, Deidre approached the two and led them toward the door. "Let's move this party inside. I'm getting cold, and your tears are going to freeze into icicles on your face." Mother and daughter couldn't let go of each other.

The reunion was what Deidre had hoped for, and by ten o'clock, she decided all was going to be well.

"I've got to be going. Love you both, but I want to get back to Two Harbors before morning. Call me soon and tell me how things are going."

Melissa tried to talk her friend out of driving home in the middle of the night, but Deidre had made up her mind. On her way home the realization hit her, eleven days until Christmas, and she had yet to buy anything for the twins. She resolved to take the weekend to do her shopping.

She wanted to get a small gift for Jill, something for the twins that they could play with together, and perhaps a token gift for Ben. It was going to be a good Christmas, better than she had been expecting.

Chapter
Twenty-Five

IN THE EARLY MORNING HOURS of the fifteenth, Deidre arrived at Inga's, then spent the morning sleeping. She went to her office in the afternoon, hoping Jill had taken the day off and that she would be able to spend some time alone, thinking. No such luck.

"Good afternoon, Boss Lady. Just wake up? How'd it go with Melissa and her daughter?"

Deidre more or less avoided the question. "Well. It went well. Anything happen I should know about?"

"Zak Burton called, wants you to return his call as soon as you can. Jeff wants to meet with you, but he said it can wait until you have time, even next Monday would be okay. Other than that, everything is pretty quiet. Do you mind if I take the rest of the afternoon off? I've got something I want to do at the women's shelter."

Deidre let Jill go with her blessings. She wanted to be alone, but first she had to call Zak. She reluctantly dialed his number.

"Hey, Deidre. Thanks for getting back to me. How you feeling?"

Deidre shrugged, even though she knew Zak couldn't see her. "I'm okay, good in fact. What's so important it can't wait?"

Zak cleared his throat. "On that file you gave me, the one from Gerald Colter, there was one more delivery scheduled. Remember? The ship named was the *Aegean Sea*, the delivery number was three. It is due in port on January 3. I would guess after our raid last week, they'll be reluctant to make that delivery. But to be safe, I think we have to set up like we did before, if for no other reason than to assure ourselves that the three women aren't shipped out because of our lack of follow through. Are you with us?"

Deidre didn't have to think. "Of course I am. We can't allow one more woman to be violated."

"I guessed that'd be your answer, but I had to be sure. We're meeting tomorrow at nine in the morning in the same office as last time. See you then."

The next day, she sat through the meeting, not being surprised that the plan was pretty much the same. Zak said they'd be using a different ruse to camouflage their presence. He wasn't sure what excuse they would use for their being on the docks, but plans would be in place by the time they met for final instructions on the twenty-eighth. Now, Deidre had a more difficult assignment—find a special present for the girls.

*****

THE STORES WERE CROWDED, every aisle choked with shoppers growing more frantic by the moment. Deidre really had no idea what she was looking for, and she aimlessly wandered through the store. As she turned to leave the toy section of the department store, she spotted what she knew she would buy.

It was a dollhouse, built to scale. One wall was missing so she could look into the house that was divided into an upstairs and downstairs. Each level was partitioned into several rooms, each of which was completely equipped with furniture and appliances.

She was able to find a set of people to go along with the house, her eyes being drawn in particular to two blond-haired dolls representing children. They came complete with changes of tiny sets of clothing.

She had everything packed in a very large box and gift wrapped. Then she realized she should get something for Ben. That was a problem. She wanted something special but without any romantic connotation, not cheap but not terribly expensive either. Then she remembered that, when he returned from his last camping trip into the BWCAW, he lamented the fact that some coals from the campfire had landed on his sleeping bag and burned a hole in it. The stuffing was spilling out. After putting the dollhouse in her SUV, she headed to sporting goods.

A young lady who seemed to know what she was talking about, guided Deidre through the various models. Finally, she decided on one filled with artificial down that had a temperature rating of ten degrees. It cost more than she expected to pay, but what didn't these days?

That, too, she had gift wrapped, and as she carried it to her vehicle, she hoped Ben would admit if it wasn't what he wanted. She made up her mind to offer a disclaimer. He could return it if it wasn't the kind he wanted. She'd save the receipt in case.

It took her several minutes to get to Ben's, because the shopping mall was outside the city limits. She pointed her SUV downhill, carefully applying the brakes to avoid sliding into cars in front of her. She was relieved when she pulled into the driveway.

As usual, the girls answered the door.

"Get your coats on," Deidre ordered. "I need help bringing in some gifts." The girls scrambled to get dressed for the outdoors, Megan putting her boots on the wrong feet in her haste.

"Here, let me help." Deidre bent down and switched the boots. "That will feel a lot better," she laughed.

She looked up, and was startled, embarrassed, really, to see Ben staring at her. "What?"

"Nothing, just looking at you," was all he said.

Amid squeals of delight and questions that came faster than she could answer, Deidre guided the moving of the wrapped dollhouse inside.

"I don't think there'll be room under the tree," Maren complained, sounding almost alarmed.

"Oh, sure there will be," Deidre said as she moved some of the wrapped presents already in place.

"Be careful!" Megan warned. "That one's yours." Then she covered her mouth with her hands, panicked that she had given away a secret.

Ben took her in his arms. "That's okay. She'll never guess what you got her."

Deidre went to the car to retrieve the other gift. "See. This one's for your daddy. He'll never guess what I got him, either."

The rest of the evening was filled with the magic that only children can produce at Christmas, and Deidre realized she loved the girls more than life itself. That scared her, and she thought, *If Ben ever remarried, how could I give these two up?*

She and Ben each carried one of the twins up to bed, and together they tucked the girls in. "Good night you two," she said. "I love you more than you'll ever know."

"I love you, too," they said in unison.

Deidre stayed the weekend at Ben's, feeling a little guilty that she was neglecting her dog, Pete, but knowing he was being looked after assuaged her feelings. Inga walked him twice a day, and she had hired a dog sitter to come in twice a week to take him out of town where he could romp in the woods.

Most of the time, however, Deidre was having too much fun with Megan and Maren to be troubled. The excitement of Christmas rapidly approaching kept the twins in a constant state of anticipation, and their joy was contagious.

Every time she looked at Ben, saw the love in his eyes for his daughters, the more she wanted a repeat of what she had experienced under the mistletoe, and she wondered if he felt the same.

Saturday night, after the girls were in bed and a movie was playing on TV, Ben sat down beside her, put his arm around her shoulders, and drew her close to him. She allowed herself to rest her head on his chest. They sat in silence for several minutes, then Ben reached for the remote and turned the TV off.

"This case has been tough on you, hasn't it?" he asked as he looked straight ahead. Deidre nodded, and tears formed in her eyes as she pictured the girls with whom she had been working, pictured Anna's ravaged body.

"I see it in your expression every time you look at Megan and Maren, and I sense your fear that something like this could happen to them."

Again Deidre nodded. "Sometimes I look at them and wonder how I can make a difference in their lives, how I can protect them from the world," she lamented. "Ben, I look at what society has become, and I wonder what chance do they have?"

Ben thought for a minute. "We have to be careful, Deidre. Day in and day out, you and I come in close contact with the evil in this world, and it's too easy to become jaded, thinking the whole world is like that. But it isn't. The world is filled with good, decent, loving people whose only wish is to live peacefully with their neighbors. You and I are doing everything we can to make sure those two little girls have a chance at that kind of life. We can't do any more. Today was a wonderful day. Chances are tomorrow will be too. The day after, well, let the day after take care of itself. If we don't, we rob ourselves of the joy of living."

Deidre had no way of responding. Had those words really come from the mouth of the man who had been an egotistical jock in high school?

Ben gently tilted Deidre's face toward him and kissed her forehead while he stroked her hair. Then he kissed her like she wanted to be kissed ever since that evening when the girls had set them up in the doorway.

Sunday dawned one of those perfect December days. The sky was blue and cloudless, the snow was fresh and powdery, and the forecast was for temperatures in the mid-twenties.

The four of them went sliding again on the Zoo hill, and afterward, they returned home to have hot chocolate with miniature marshmallows bobbing in the brown foam.

Ben said, "Girls, I have a surprise for you after we eat supper and clean up the kitchen."

They begged him to tell what it was, but all Ben would say was, "If I told you, it wouldn't be a surprise, would it?"

It was dark by four-thirty, and they ate early, tomato soup and grilled cheese sandwiches, something easy to make and quick to clean up. By five-thirty they were on their way to Lakeside Park. As it came into view, Deidre could hear the girls inhale, followed by an "Oooh!"

Acres of parkland were lit up by millions of tiny lights. Ben parked, and they got out of his car. Deidre made sure the girls were bundled up and wrapped a scarf more securely around Maren's neck. Then they set out on the trek, a paved path that led them through a maze of animated figures made of wire outlined with lights: figure skaters and snowmen, Santa and elves, leaping reindeer and scurrying bunnies, all choreographed to move to the rhythm of Christmas carols.

The place was alive with families and singles, grandparents and lovers, all enjoying the free cookies and cocoa being handed out by real, live Santa's helpers. Everywhere she looked, Deidre saw people having fun, laughing and slurping hot drinks, their cheeks pink from the cold and their eyes a-sparkle with the season of giving.

She looked up at Ben. "You are right." was all she said.

That evening she drove home, happier than she had been for several years.

*****

DEIDRE SAT AT HER DESK. Monday morning—she felt a letdown from the high she had experienced over the weekend. Two cups of coffee later, she was still feeling out of sorts.

After the burst of excitement on the dock in Duluth with its huge shot of adrenaline, she looked at her meager office and was at odds ends. The FBI had pretty much taken over the trafficking investigation, and her days with the BCA were numbered. She wondered why she was even occupying office space.

What affected her most was the realization that they really had not dried up the stream of girls being transported down Highway 61 from Thunder Bay, through Two Harbors, and to the ships arriving at the harbor in Duluth.

Jill sensed her situation. "What will you do after this is over?" she asked Deidre, the tone of her voice telling of her concern.

"I don't know. Go back up to my cabin, I suppose. Wait out the winter and then see what summer brings."

Even as she said it, Deidre knew she would never be able to return to cabin life as it had been. She needed people. "How about you, Jill?"

"I'll go back into the secretarial pool. We're hired on temp duty, filling in for vacations and special needs like this. I'll volunteer at the shelter. Read a lot. That's about it."

"You really don't have anyone, do you?" Deidre asked without thinking.

Jill shook her head and looked at the floor.

"Want to talk about it?"

"Not much to say. I don't get along with my mother, and my dad always takes her side. I left home when I was sixteen, because I was using drugs, and they finally gave me an ultimatum, either get treatment or they were going to turn me over to Social Services. I ran away and lived on the streets for a while. Now I'm here."

"What made a difference in your life. You're extremely capable. You're not on the streets. What happened to lift you out of your situation?"

"I finally couldn't stand who I was any longer, and tried to take the easy way out."

"Suicide?" Jill nodded.

"I was taken to a hospital in Duluth to get help. There I met a most marvelous chaplain. He had experienced much of what I had. He spent hours with me, letting me talk and sharing his story with me. He got me into a women's shelter in Duluth and lined me up to get some training in a business school, and, well, here I am. End of story."

"I hope not, Jill. I hope not."

Deidre got out of her chair and gave Jill a hug. "I really believe better days are ahead for you."

For the remainder of the week, Deidre felt as if she were in limbo. There wasn't anything that made time drag like having nothing to do and no direction for the future. She was getting as antsy for Christmas Eve to arrive as were Megan and Maren.

Evenings, she visited with Inga, took Pete for walks in the snow, and tried to wade her way through a tome written about events leading up to World War II. She wondered if people then thought society was getting so perverse that it could not endure.

Deidre put the book down on her lap and pondered that question. She concluded that, if she had been alive then, she would have had the same feelings she had now. *The world has always experienced turmoil*, she thought, and she vowed to begin trying to concentrate on the good rather than the bad. Ben's words from the other night had had a remarkable effect on her thinking.

On Friday, she gave Jill the small present she had bought and wrapped. "This is for you," she said as she handed the gift to her secretary. Tears welled up in Jill's eyes as she carefully unwrapped what seemed to be a fragile object.

"Oh, Deidre. This is lovely," she gushed as she draped the silk scarf around her neck. Deidre had attached a pin to the scarf, and it gathered in and reflected the bright colors of the cloth.

"Thank you from the bottom of my heart."

Deidre was delighted by Jill's reaction. "Have a wonderful Christmas, Jill. Are you doing anything special?"

Jill looked a little embarrassed to answer. "I'm spending the holidays with a friend. We graduated from high school together and have reconnected through Facebook. He invited me to spend Christmas Day with him and his family. I'm worried sick about what he'll think when he sees me in person."

Deidre tried to reassure her that he'd be crazy if he didn't get to know her. They walked to their cars together, Jill to go to the shelter and Deidre to go to Duluth for the weekend and then Christmas.

She never had been a good singer, but today she couldn't help but sing a carol along with a crooner on the radio. In Duluth, she decided to stop at a coffee shop on the east end of town and debated about going by the drive-through window but decided to go inside to order. That way, she could doctor up her mocha the way she wanted it.

Standing at the counter to place her order, she looked over her shoulder at the customers sitting at tables. Her heart dropped.

At a corner table sat Ben and a very attractive young lady. He was holding her hands between his and was leaning forward. By his expression, she could see that he was talking intently to her, never breaking eye contact. Deidre offered up a silent prayer that he not look up and see her staring.

The server handed her the cup of mocha she had ordered, and as she moved to put her money on the counter, the loose coins slid through her fingers and clattered on the floor. Her hands trembled so she could hardly hold the cup, and some of its contents splashed out.

"Are you okay, lady?" the worker asked, shocked.

"Yes ... yes, I'm okay," she said and hurried out the door.

On the way past a trash can, she threw the half-full cup in the bin. In her car, she put her head on its steering wheel, choked back her sobs, but couldn't stop the tears from dribbling off her chin. She held no anger, only an aching hurt.

Wiping the tears from her eyes, she managed to make it through the Christmas rush traffic and arrived at Ben's before he did.

"Were you crying, Deidre?" Megan wanted to know.

Deidre answered honestly. "Yes, I feel sad today, but I'll be okay. Let me go wash my face before Daddy gets home."

She climbed the stairs to her room and ran cold water over a washcloth, wrung out the excess, and placed it over her tear-swollen eyes. After several minutes, she looked in the mirror. Some of the swelling had subsided and the redness was not quite as noticeable as it had been. She put on a new layer of makeup and went downstairs.

Just as her foot hit the bottom step, Ben came through the door, stomped the snow from his boots, and took off his jacket.

"Daddy," Maren said when he stooped to give her his ritual kiss, "Deidre is sad today."

Ben went over and wrapped his arms around her. "You've been crying. Your day must have been as bad as mine." Deidre couldn't help her reaction, and she felt her body stiffen as he touched her.

"That bad, huh? Well, I'll go first. I got a call this morning from my uncle's granddaughter. Her father is the same age as my dad, so even though she's officially my cousin, twice removed, she's only three years younger than me. Because of the similarity in our ages, we grew up together more like sister and brother than second cousins. To make a long story short, she wanted to have a cup of coffee with me and talk about a problem she's having with her boyfriend. We met at that little place on London Road on the East End. When she told me he had hit her during a recent argument, I told her to pack her bags and run, told her if she needed a place to stay, she was welcome here. So, what was so wrong with your day?"

Deidre felt her face flush, and she hid it on his chest. Finally, she murmured, "Nothing. Just me behaving like a foolish schoolgirl. Give me a minute for attitude adjustment, and I'll be right down."

She turned tail and ran up the stairs to her room, where she flopped on the bed, not knowing whether to laugh or cry. In the end, she became angry at herself for jumping to conclusions. She stood up, took a deep breath, squared her shoulders, and looked in the mirror. "Mirror, mirror on the wall. Who's the craziest of them all?" The mirror didn't answer, which she took as a good sign.

"Sorry about that," she apologized as she made what felt to her like a grand entrance. All three were standing at the bottom of the stairway, watching her descend. She chuckled at the thought of a grand entrance, and no one asked questions.

Chapter
Twenty-Six

BEN HAD MADE AN ADVENT CALENDAR for the girls, a stack of twenty-five compartments in the shape of a Christmas tree. Behind each compartment door was a symbol of Christmas. Today, the twenty-second of December, it was Megan's turn to open it. With great diligence, she pried the small hatch open, reached in, and took out a miniature dove.

"Do you know what that is?" Ben asked.

"I know," Maren exclaimed, wildly waving her hand. "It's a bird."

"Ah, but what kind of bird?"

The girls thought for a moment. "A pigeon?" Megan asked rather than answered.

"Close," Ben laughed. "It's a dove. What does a dove represent?"

"What does 'represent' mean?" Maren asked, her brow furrowed. Deidre covered her mouth.

"It means what does it stand for." Ben answered patiently.

After a lengthy silence he said, "It stands for peace."

"Oh, you mean like when people don't shoot each other?"

"Well, something like that." Ben decided that was enough of a lesson, and decided to leave morality to another day. "Who wants pancakes for breakfast?"

Both girls' hand shot up. "I do. Hooray!" and they ran off to get their dolls.

Somehow, everyone made it through the weekend, and Monday became a grueling day for the twins.

"Daddy, can't we open just one present today. We promise not to bug you anymore if we can open just one," they whined so many times that Ben had to make an edict.

"Every time you ask to open a gift early, I'm going to tack a half hour on to when we start opening them on Christmas Eve. Be careful what you say or it might be Christmas Day before we open gifts."

The girls' eyes widened in surprise, and they went off into the other room. Deidre and Ben could hear them whispering, perhaps wondering if they should test the law. For the rest of the day, they never mentioned the subject again, but every so often one of them, or both, would go to the base of the tree and read the labels on the presents again. Deidre watched them count who had how many gifts.

That night, Ben and Deidre allowed them to stay up an hour past their bedtime, and they made hot apple cider to go with the cookies Deidre and the girls had made that afternoon.

When they were being tucked in for the night, Megan and Maren were like "wiggly worms" as Deidre said.

"We are not wiggly worms!"

"Oh, yes, you are!"

"Are not!"

"Are too," and Deidre pretended to pin Megan down with her quilt.

"Okay," Ben had to say, "It's time for sleep. Settle down now and close your eyes."

Deidre watched as both children lay perfectly still on their backs, their eyelids closed, but behind the closed lids she could see the movement of their eyes, and she knew what would happen the instant she and Ben left their room.

He turned on the night light and turned off the bed lamp. As soon as the two of them were in the hall, they could hear giggling and moving around.

"I think we're losing the battle," Ben whispered in Deidre's ear, and they tiptoed down the stairs to the living room, where they sat and squinted at the tree lights so that star-burst patterns were created.

A perfect day is coming to a close, Deidre thought.

"An end to a perfect day," Ben declared out loud. She nodded.

*****

CHRISTMAS EVE DAY began with a chorus of voices at Deidre's door. Ben and the girls stood outside singing "We Wish You a Merry Christmas" followed by an off-key version of "Santa Claus Is Coming to Town."

She looked at her clock, 7:25, threw on her robe and opened her door.

"We get to open presents tonight!" Maren excitedly exclaimed. Megan took her hand and led her to the stairs.

"Daddy made a special Christmas breakfast for us. Come see!"

Ben had made French toast by cutting the bread slices in the shape of an evergreen tree with a cookie cutter. After frying them in the usual manner, he had decorated each tree with colored sprinkles and blue berries. Then he dusted them with powdered sugar, making his creation look like a winter scene. It had to have taken him an hour, Deidre thought.

The "family" sat down to their Christmas Eve breakfast feast, complete with crispy bacon and eggnog.

"We usually go to church on Christmas Eve. Will you join us, Deidre, or would you rather stay home?"

In her entire life, she had never attended a Christmas service, or very few others for that matter. She thought for a moment, and then saw the expectant looks in the twins eyes. "Okay, should be fun," she said, not completely sure she really wanted to attend.

That afternoon they all went to the largest mall in the city and watched shoppers frantically rushing to make their last-minute gift selections. They stopped to hear a choir singing in the mall's rotunda. It was a good choir, singing excerpts from some of the old masters, Bach, Handel, and others, and Deidre let her spirit soar with the notes. She realized she had taken Ben's hand, and he was gently squeezing hers.

Supper was a simple smorgasbord, set so everyone could fix what they wanted from several selections. It also made for a quick cleanup, and Megan and Maren were all too eager to help. By six, they were ready to gather around the tree. Ben put on a Santa cap, and began rummaging under the tree. "Let's see," he said examining a tag. "This one is for Maren. Can you read who it's from?"

Maren squinted, and Deidre could see she was trying to sound out the name. "Meg . . . an. Megan!" She ripped the wrapping from the gift her sister had so carefully wrapped.

The scene was repeated over and over, everyone taking a turn while the others oohed and aahed over the gifts. Finally, there was only one round of gifts left to open. Ben opened the one from Deidre and his eyes lit up when he pulled out the new sleeping bag.

"Why, thank you! I didn't know you were even listening when I told you about my old one having a hole burned in it."

Unexpectedly, he leaned over and kissed Deidre's cheek. That really caused the girls to giggle. He handed her the gift he had bought.

The package was quite large and rectangular. Deidre shook it, but nothing rattled. She methodically peeled the paper off and carefully loosened the tape holding the seams. The girls squirmed and shifted their positions. Megan stood by her shoulder in anticipation of what would be revealed. She lifted the top off the box.

"Oh, Ben. This is beautiful." She held up an authentic Norwegian-made sweater. Knitted into the fabric were traditional Scandinavian designs. The clasps in front looked to be handmade of silver.

She held it up to her front and felt the heft of the fabric. Deidre buried her face in the wool to hide her tears. Then she looked up. "Thank you from the bottom of my heart," and she gave Ben a hug that lasted many seconds. She felt his arms wrap around her, cuddling her and the sweater together.

"One more! There's one more!" Maren shouted. "It's from Deidre."

Ben moved the very large box into the center of the room, and the girls attacked it, pieces of paper flying in every direction. When the dollhouse was exposed, their mouths dropped open, and they sat on the floor for a moment, stunned.

Maren picked up the transparent package that held the dolls. "Look, Megan. It's a family. There's Daddy, and this one is you, and this one is me." She pointed to the female figure. "Is this you, Deidre?" she asked, her eyes pleading for the answer she wanted. Deidre wasn't quite sure how to respond.

"Would you like that to be me?" she asked. The girls nodded.

"Okay, then that's me." Her answer satisfied them, and nothing more was said.

As they were cleaning up the paper mess, Ben leaned close to her. "I'm not putting them up to this, I swear."

"That's all right. They're just children. By the way, thank you for the beautiful sweater. I've always wanted one but never afforded myself the luxury," she said, changing the subject.

*****

BUT FOR THE GLOW OF CANDLES set in every window and a collection arranged on the altar, the church was darkened when they arrived. Deidre was not comfortable in that setting, but as she sat, taking in the shadows and light patterns produced by the open flames, she began to relax. She was seated next to Ben, and he reached over and took her hand. Megan was on the other side of her and intertwined her arm inside Deidre's elbow.

Deidre held a copy of the order of service in her free hand, and she noticed that even though much was strange, she recognized the titles of the hymns: "O Little Town of Bethlehem," "It Came Upon a Midnight Clear," and "Hark! The Herald Angels Sing."

The one tune she didn't recognize was "Silent Night Benediction." She didn't recognize the name of the composer, but an asterisk after his name led her to a brief note that he was a local composer.

Before she could read more, the service began, the congregation stood, and the house lights were brought up so they could read the words to the carol. By the time they finished the song, the processional had reached the front of the church, and the pastor began to speak. Immediately, Deidre's mind began to wander, and she found herself lost in thought, wondering what the child victims were doing in the hospital, wondering if the abductors would be so brazen as to attempt one more delivery of human lives that was scheduled after Christmas, wondering how many more lives would be destroyed by the river of young women flowing from Thunder Bay to Duluth.

Her thoughts were disrupted when a box of small candles was passed down her row. She watched as everyone took one and adjusted a wax guard to protect their fingers. Megan showed her how to do it, and she sat waiting for further directions.

The pastor instructed everyone, "Please tilt your unlit candle toward the lit candle of your neighbor. That way, melted wax will not drip on the floor."

The house lights were extinguished, and the ushers lit the candles of those congregants sitting on the aisle. The next person in from the aisle lit his or her candle off the lit one and so on down the row. In seconds the wave reached Deidre, and she successfully passed on the light. Soon the sanctuary was lit by the glow of hundreds of candles.

From the front of a church, someone began to softly play the piano, and a tenor voice softly sang, "Peace I give to you, not as the world knows peace. Peace I give to you. God grant us peace."

As the singer's mellow voice led the congregation through the words, almost like a chant, Deidre felt herself being caught up in the moment. *When will the world ever know peace,* she thought. *Will there ever be peace?*

A tear ran down her cheek and dripped off her chin, and she found herself singing the words, her eyes closed, and desperately, she wanted to claim the peace she was feeling at that moment.

Without notice the song leader smoothly slipped into singing "Silent Night." After the last verse was sung, everyone extinguished their candles, and the sanctuary went dark, except for the candles on the altar and those in the windows.

Even though hundreds of people filled the sanctuary, there was not a sound, not the rustle of papers, not the sound of someone rushing to put on their jacket so they could make a quick getaway, not even a cough.

Row by row, the ushers directed the exit of the worshippers. Still, no one talked, and even in the narthex, people were speaking in hushed tones. On the way home they were silent. Megan and Maren were half a sleep in the back seat, and Ben and Deidre were buried deep in their own thoughts.

Why can't our lives be filled with this kind of peace everyday, she wondered. *Certainly humanity has made enough progress that we can cease injuring each other.*

Ben pulled into the driveway. Together they carried the sleeping children into the house and to their rooms. Deidre couldn't get past their childhood innocence as, in their sleep, they curled up and buried their heads in their pillows. She kissed each of them before leaving their room.

As they quietly made their way downstairs, Ben whispered, "Time for Santa to arrive."

He went to the basement, and Deidre could hear him rummaging around. In a few minutes he came up the stairs, laden with packages. "Santa had a good year," he laughed.

For the next half hour, they arranged the gifts. The girls had left out carrots for the reindeer and cookies for Santa. The carrots went back in the refrigerator, and Ben ate the cookies, making sure to leave some crumbs on the plate.

Six-thirty the next morning, Deidre awoke to squeals of delight coming from downstairs, followed by racing footsteps coming upstairs.

"Deidre!" Maren exclaimed, her eyes wide open. "You got to see this. Hurry! Santa came last night." They grabbed Deidre's hands and pulled her out of bed.

Ben was already in the kitchen. He emerged with a cup of coffee in each hand.

"Daddy, can we start now?"

"Go for it," he said, handed Deidre her cup, and sat down to watch the excitement.

Amid exclamations of "Look what he brought me" and "It's just what I wanted," Deidre could do nothing but grin. She looked at Ben, and he winked at her.

About mid-morning, Ben's mother and father arrived. Rebecca gave Deidre the once over look. "Looks like you've been spending a lot of time here lately," she said abruptly.

"Rebecca," Jim butted in. "We're delighted to see you again, Deidre. "You must forgive Rebecca. She fell off the wrong side of the bed this morning."

Rebecca gave him a sideways glance and stomped off to the kitchen, where Deidre heard her asking Ben if he needed her help.

Jim took Deidre's hands. "It's okay. She just needs some time to get used to things being different. She and Jenny were like mother and daughter, and I think Rebecca's still mourning her death. Be patient," and he gave Deidre a hug.

At that moment, Deidre decided her only recourse was to show Rebecca rather than tell her how easily she was fitting into her granddaughter's lives. By the time Christmas Day was history, she thought she had made some progress.

When Jim and Rebecca were heading out the door, Jim hugged her and whispered in her ear. "Hang with us. Everything's going to be fine."

That evening, after the kids had been put to bed, the two adults sat staring at the tree, exhausted.

"Do you have a lot to do tomorrow and Friday?"

Deidre looked at Ben and realized she had very little on her agenda until the next week when the *Aegean Sea* would be coming into port.

"Not really. What do you have in mind?"

Ben had an expectant smile on his face. "I've got just a few things to clear up at the office. I could be done about ten on Friday. What if you got your cabin warmed up? The three of us could be there by late afternoon. I know the girls would love being in the woods in the winter. What do you think? I'll bring the food if you want, and we could stay 'til late Sunday."

Deidre was thrilled. She wondered why she hadn't thought of the idea herself. As they sat staring at the tree again, she pictured what it would be like to be snowed in with them at the cabin.

Chapter
Twenty-Eight

DEIDRE WASHED DOWN the last bite of toast with what coffee remained in her cup.

"Well, I'd better get going. Last night I decided I would stop and see how the three girls in the hospital are recovering. See you tomorrow. I'll have a friend plow the road into the cabin, and the fire will be going."

"Whoa. Just a minute," Ben said, and he stood up from his place at the table. "You're not getting out of here without a proper sendoff. He gave her a very tight hug, and kissed her forehead. "I'm getting to dislike the wait between our times together," he groused.

Deidre smiled as she buried her head on his chest. She reached up and gave him a quick kiss. "See you tomorrow."

It was shift change when Deidre stopped at the nurses' station, and doctors were reviewing patients' charts, preparing to do rounds. Deidre spotted Dr. Bilka, the pediatrician attending the girls. She looked up from the chart she was studying.

"Deidre, you're saving me a phone call. I have marvelous news for you. Kimi has responded so positively to Allison's presence, that she's begun to come out of her shell. She has a long way to go, but she's conversing and initiating dialogue. Her appetite has even picked up. The other girl, she says her name is Jean, is out of ICU and has joined the two for daily visits. They don't laugh much, but they share their feelings with each other, and that is so positive. I wanted to invite you to meet with them. Each is so thankful for what you did for them. If you have time, they should have been served breakfast, and could get together right now."

"I was hoping I could, but tell me, what happens to them now?"

"We've been in contact with the chief of police of the Nishnawbi Aski Nation. He's arranging all of the legal papers that will be needed to bring them home. He's assured us that their social service organization will provide psychiatric assistance."

Dr. Bilka turned to a nurse. "Will you please tell Allison—she's in room 420—and Jean in room 431, that Deidre is here and would like to see them in Kimi Thomas's room? Thank you."

Deidre walked down the hall to Kimi's room, dodging workers pushing food carts, lab techs with their baskets of needles, and everyone else who made the hospital a place of restoration. She knocked on Kimi's door before entering.

Kimi was sitting on the edge of her bed, finishing a glass of orange juice while she watched a morning TV show. When she saw Deidre, her eyes lit up in a way Deidre had never seen before.

"Deidre!" but before she could say more, the other two victims entered the room.

Allison touched Deidre's arm. "Hi," was all she said.

A third girl entered. "You must be Jean. I'm Deidre Johnson," she introduced herself, and for several minutes they talked about how the hospital food was, if they were comfortable, and other mundane bits of conversation. Finally, Deidre thought she could broach the subject she wanted to discuss.

"I have an awfully big favor to ask of you girls. Maybe it's asking too much, and if it is, I want you to tell me without hesitation."

Quizzically, the girls looked at her.

"Can we talk about the place where you were held captive? Will you try to remember what the place looked like? If it's too painful, please tell me, and we can just visit for a while."

The room went silent, then Allison spoke first. "I remember the cabin had one room."

Jean broke in. "There were eight beds, four along each wall."

"They were made of boards, and the mattresses were old and smelly," Allison added.

Kimi looked out the window, a faraway look in her eyes. "We were chained by one ankle to the foot of the bed. The chain was long enough for us to reach one of the pails they set in between the rows of beds. That was our toilet."

Deidre shuddered at the image.

"There were two windows on each sidewall, and one in front," Allison said.

"And the door was heavy, like it was made of really thick boards," Jean added.

"It was locked from the outside with a large, brass padlock," Kimi volunteered. The girl's were beginning to feed off each other's memories.

Deidre thought for a moment and then asked Kimi. "Are you sure about the lock?"

Kimi nodded. "Anna and I escaped through the front window. It was hinged and I was able to push out the bottom and crawl through the opening. I fell on the deck of a small porch, and the door was right beside me. I saw the lock." Tears began to form in her eyes and dribble down her face. "We ran up a trail, but then we heard someone swearing and breaking through the brush. One of the men came after us. I ran one way, Anna, another. He went after Anna and caught her. I made my way to the road—it was a long way through the woods—and caught a ride with some logger going to Silver Bay. I had him drop me off at the main highway, thinking I could find my way back home. I ended up in that deserted cabin where you found me." Kimi went silent, and neither of the other two girls had any more to say.

Together, the four of them sat with bowed heads, and the winter sun shined through the hospital window.

"I hear you will all be going back to Canada very soon. Will you please keep in touch with me? I truly want to know how you are doing." She handed them her name card. "My e-mail address is on this. Contact me anytime. Perhaps when this is all over, we can get together for a picnic or a nice meal at a restaurant."

The girls took turns saying goodbye and offered their thanks one more time. It was especially difficult for Kimi to let go, and after a prolonged hug, Deidre whispered in her ear, "You're safe now. It will be okay."

Two people were in the elevator when the door opened, and they looked at her face, then looked away in embarrassment. They didn't want to stare at the lady dabbing her eyes and blowing her nose on the trip down to the parking garage.

Before pulling out into traffic, she called the person who plowed the driveway into her cabin. "Hey, Jerry," she said when he answered. I'm coming up to my cabin this weekend, and I need the driveway plowed out. It will probably take a while to clear the half mile stretch, but we haven't had too much snow yet. How much do you think, a foot? . . . Oh, that much," she answered after Jerry upped her estimate. "Anyway, do you think you could have it opened up by this evening? Thanks a million, Jerry," she said to his reply.

Chapter
Twenty-Nine

O N THE WAY NORTH, Deidre mulled over her role in what was left of the investigation. She had been in daily contact with the BCA for more than a month, and they agreed with her that because the FBI had pretty much assumed the lead, she should back out. She planned to close her office next week and file her final report with the state agency.

In a way it felt good to think of being free of the responsibility, but on the other hand, it felt like she was dropping out of a foot race. She wondered what would happen to Gerald Colter, both father and son. And what about Judge DeMarcus? Would he be implicated, or at least be barred from the courtroom? Of course, there were the three girls. Would they grow up in spite of their emotional scars?

These thoughts and many more concerning the case crowded her mind, and she was almost to Two Harbors before it dawned on her how far she had traveled. It was noon when she stopped at Inga's and picked up her dog. Inga wasn't home, so she left a note on the door saying hi and that she had taken Pete with her.

The thought occurred to her that she was only an hour from her cabin, and Jerry said he wouldn't have the driveway cleared until five or so. She decided to stop and see her old friend Pete, the logger after whom she had jokingly named her black lab.

He was outside, splitting wood for his stove, when Deidre pulled up alongside his rusted-out pickup. Pete straightened his back and shielded his eyes against the afternoon sun. His face broke into a grin and he put down his splitting axe.

"Well, Deidre Johnson. How the heck are you? And you brought Pete with you. You know I still haven't forgiven you for naming him that." He chuckled and the gaps formed by a few missing teeth showed.

A year-old lab came running in from the woods, and she circled the pair, her tail wagging and begging for attention.

"Pete, you got another lab!" Deidre exclaimed.

"Yeah. After the old guy died, I thought I wouldn't get another. At first I thought it would be foolish, because I'm so old. But then I thought, heck, I might outlive another one, so I picked up this girl at the animal shelter in Two Harbors. Somebody dropped her off, because she had too much energy for them. I was lucky. She's a great dog."

"What did you name her?"

"Deidre."

"What?" Deidre asked in astonishment.

"Fair is fair," was all Pete had to say. Then he added, "I call her Deid for short, though," and Deidre could see his shoulders shaking from suppressed laughter.

"Come on in. Bring Pete with you. He can meet Deid, and we can have a piece of pie and a cup of coffee."

As they sat at Pete's two person table, he asked, "What have you been up to? Haven't seen you for a good three months. I thought maybe you had gone south for the winter. Thought you might be wimping out on us." He slurped his coffee, but he couldn't stifle the mirth in his eyes.

"Do you remember hearing about the girl that was found dead under the Silver Bay bridge?"

"You know I don't get out much, but Terry told me that he thought you were involved in it somehow. How'd it turn out?"

"Can't tell you too much until everything is done, but it hasn't been a good scene. Somewhere up here, girls are being held and then sold into prostitution a few at a time, mostly to sailors on the ships docked in the harbor in Duluth."

Pete took another swig of coffee, got up, and spit out the door. "Those bastards. I've lived in the woods my whole life, seen a lot of things up here. I've watched a pack of wolves pull down a moose, seen a bear walk off with a newborn fawn, even seen a red squirrel climb my birdfeeder and snatch a pine siskin right off the platform. That unnerved me, I'll tell you. Squirrels aren't supposed to do that. But, you know Deidre, I've never seen animals do what humans are capable of doing to each other. I know it's not right, but sometimes I'm happy to be so isolated that I can let all this crap pass me by. I get so angry when I hear of what's happening out there," and he swept his arm toward the south and east, "I don't want to know about it." He gulped his coffee.

Deidre patted Pete's hand. "I feel that way too. But then I think, if each of us can do one thing in our lives to make a change, then the world is a little better place. Remember how willing you were to help me when I needed your assistance tracking down that gang of meth manufacturers? You're a good man, Pete. Don't underestimate your ability to make a difference. I know how you look out for the logger's widow down the road. You let it slip once. And what about the way you took care of Jarvinen the time he broke his foot getting off his skidder. You drove it for a month while he healed. If I remember, you didn't collect any pay, but had the logging company send him the check. Pete, you old goat, you can't fool me. You do what you can to help others."

Pete took a bite of his pie so he wouldn't have to answer. The two visited for a long while, and Pete looked out his window.

"Only about two hours of daylight left. You better get going if you're going to make it into your cabin with some daylight to spare."

Deidre looked at her watch. "No, it's not even three, yet. Jerry said he wouldn't be done with the plowing by at least five."

Pete's eyes lit up. "Well, then you're staying for supper."

Deidre laughed. "Thought you'd never ask." He sat down and made himself comfortable.

A thought struck Deidre. "Say, Pete. You wouldn't know any business around here that might have the initials or logo RRR? I found an old brass key that had those letters stamped on it. Looked to be from an old lock."

"Geeze, I haven't thought of that place for years. Where'd you find the key, in that antique place in Beaver Bay?"

"No, nothing like that. I just found it, and I've been wondering where it came from. It seems to be rather unique. You know about it, then?"

Pete shrugged. "I might. Suppose there are a lot of keys that were made like that, but I know of one place that used big, heavy brass locks, the Rocky River Resort."

Deidre's heart skipped a beat, and she asked, a little too excitedly, "What can you tell me about it?"

Pete looked at the log beams overhead in his cabin. "Well, let's see. It must have been 1938, no, 1939, at least that's what my folks used to say. This area was pretty wild back then, you know."

Deidre wanted to scream, "For God's sake, get on with it, Pete," but she held her tongue. She knew he would eventually get to the point.

"I've heard that a group of businessmen from Minneapolis bought two sections of land. It went cheap back then. The area had been logged off by the timber barrens twenty years before, and it had come back with scrub timber, balsam and poplar, sometimes birch. You could buy land for fifty cents an acre. 'Course nobody around here could scrape up enough money to grab it. Well, anyway, these guys from Minneapolis bought two sections, pushed a road in about a mile to the Rocky River. Then they built a hunting lodge. I've seen it, been in it. They made it out of timber they got from a small area the loggers had missed in 1910, or whenever they cut that area, huge pines."

Deidre had to stifle her desire to begin asking questions. She put another bite of pie in her mouth and sipped coffee. Pete continued rambling.

"Yep, that was quite a lodge. They hunted up here with a gang of their friends for a couple of years, and then the war broke out. My dad and most of the men who lived up here enlisted, so they were gone for a few years. I had a chance to roam the woods, and a couple of times my older brother took me with when he walked the road they had put in. Best grouse hunting you ever seen. I guess that's not what you're interested in, though. The couple of times I got back there, you could tell it wasn't being used. One window had been shot out, and somebody had broke in and taken most of the stuff from the lodge.

"After the war, you'd a thought they'd come back and fix it up, but a year later they sold it to some guy from Chicago. Believe it or not, he came up here to live. Fixed the lodge up and built a dozen cabins. Advertised he was opening a fishing resort. Used to be two-pound brook trout in that river.

"He did okay. A lot of people from Chicago came here and paid big money to experience what I had all my life. By then I was old enough to go to work, and I did odd jobs around the resort for him. Even got to do a little guiding. He had a boy about ten years older than me who he really loved, and they did everything together. Then, in 1951 his son was drafted and was sent to Korea. Got killed there. The guy was never the same after that. He asked me to go fishing with him one day, but he didn't fish much at all. Just watched me. On the way back to the lodge, he told me he was going back to Chicago.

"The place sat empty ever since. I got back there a few times. Everything was starting to fall apart. Last time I saw, it must've been ten years ago. Three or four years ago, somebody posted the land, strung no trespassing signs all around its perimeter. We thought maybe somebody was going to try to make something of the place, but I guess not."

Deidre was sitting on the edge of her chair. "Do you know who bought it?"

"No. Some people tried to find out, but the records at the courthouse show that it belongs to a trust, whatever that is. There's no way to track down the owners."

"Tell me, Pete, was there anything unusual about the locks on the doors?"

"How do you know that? They were really heavy, made of brass I think, and big. They made me think of the kind of lock you might find on a seaman's trunk, the kind that needed a big key to open it.

"Funny thing, though, they were placed on the outside of the cabin. There was another hasp inside, so the guests could lock the door from either inside or out. I still don't know why you want to know all of this. It's ancient history."

"Pete, will you tell me where this place is?"

"Sure. It's no secret. Go back a mile on Highway 1, and take a right on the Bagna Lake Road. Go another two miles, and on the left you'll see what used to be two stone and concrete pillars that mark the driveway entrance. It's mostly grown up now, but I think you can still make it out."

Before he could say anymore or ask any questions, Deidre stood up and began to put on her jacket. "You make supper. I'm going to take a drive. I'll be back by five or so," and she started out the door.

"Don't get caught back there after dark," Pete warned. "Everything looks different once the sun sets, and I don't want to have to come looking for you. It's supposed to be below zero tonight. Do you have a flashlight? And make sure you take some matches with you. How about a compass? Do you have one?"

Deidre turned to face her friend. She was almost as tall as he was, he being stooped from his many years of working in the woods.

"Got them all. And don't worry, I just want to look around the place. Be back soon." She gave his sinewy arm a squeeze before she left.

Pete shook his head after she closed the door. "Got a mind of her own, that one," he muttered to himself, and went to his stove to check the pot of stew simmering on the front burner.

Using a large serving spoon, he scooped up a piece of venison that was cooking in the broth and sampled it, added a pinch more salt, and turned the burner off. Pete heard Deidre back up and drive away. He looked out the window, wishing she hadn't gone off on her own.

Chapter
Thirty

D EIDRE DROVE INTO THE SETTING SUN and had to shield her eyes from the glare off the pure snow. The clock on her dash showed it was 3:05. In an hour and a half, it would be dark. She remembered that the moon was in its full phase, and she was comforted by the thought that she could make it back to her SUV in the moonlight.

Traveling on Highway 1 was easy because the county workers had plowed it and spread a mixture of sand and salt to melt the ice. However, it was a different story when she turned onto Bagna Lake Road.

As she made the turn, she felt the rear end of her vehicle begin to yaw, and it swung first one way, then the other. She spun the steering wheel in the opposite direction of the skids, and after two or three oscillations, her vehicle straightened out, and she continued on her way but at a slower pace.

As Pete had predicted, two miles down the road she came to large fieldstone columns by the side of the road. In places, a rock or two had been dislodged by frost and time, but for the most part, they were intact.

Deidre pulled as far off the road as she could without becoming stuck in the snow banks piled up by a county plow. She stepped onto the frozen road, and a gust of arctic air hit her in the face. It was going to get very cold as soon as the sun set, she thought.

She removed her pistol from its holster, checked the magazine, checked to make sure a round was chambered, and set the safe. She returned the pistol to her belt and zipped her jacket before pulling up its hood, and last, she pulled on heavy winter mittens to protect her hands from frostbite.

As she approached the two cairns that used to guard the entrance to the resort, she noticed a no trespassing sign with an ominous message, VIOLATORS WILL BE PROSECUTED, attached to each.

Most surprising to her were snowmobile tracks leading up the trail from the road. They were covered by a dusting of snow, indicating the trail hadn't been traveled since last week. The footing underneath was packed and frozen solid, so walking was not difficult.

Any other day, she would have enjoyed the hike. A snowshoe hare had crossed the path, leaving behind a distinctive trail of elongated footprints. The tracks told a story of struggle and death, but also survival. It ended in a patch of blood stained snow bordered by the imprints of large wings, and Deidre knew that a great horned owl had descended on its prey in the middle of the night. The rabbit died; the owl lived.

As she observed the evidence of the battle for existence, Deidre carried no ill feeling toward the owl. It did what it had to do to survive the harsh Minnesota winter.

On the other hand, she wanted nothing more than to find and punish those people preying on young women, people who weren't doing it to survive, but to fulfill their evil need to dominate and to satisfy their own greed.

She trudged on through the snow for another twenty minutes until she reached a spot in the trail where it curved to the right while going up a steep hill. Before Deidre reached the top of the grade, she was forced to stop and rest her hands on her knees. Her breath came in gasps from the exertion, and when she exhaled, it formed a cloud of condensation before her face. She could feel perspiration mat her hair under her parka hood, and when she threw it back, a cloud of steam rose in the air.

She rested for two or three minutes, allowing her body to regain its rhythm. A few more steps brought her to the top of the hill, and she stopped once more. From her vantage point she could see the layout of the defunct resort.

Straight ahead, the main lodge was nestled under the cover of towering white pines that had seen their better days. The tops of most were dead, their dried limbs reaching like scraggly arms ready to snag anything that passed by.

The porch attached to the lodge was partly collapsed, and one of its main corner posts had given way. A portion of the roof had fallen, although not all the way to the ground.

To the right, following the banks of the frozen Rocky River, a dozen cabins stood side by side. A few of them had the glass missing from their windows, and with one, the roof had caved in, probably from the weight of some forgotten heavy snowfall. Everything was silent. No birds sang, nothing moved except the tops of the trees that swayed in the wind. Deidre could hear the soft whisper of the wind as it passed through the pine tree needles. It should have been a peaceful sight, but the hair on the back of Deidre's neck bristled ominously.

She knew when a person had that feeling, there was usually a reason, but she disregarded her gut reaction. She unzipped her coat to have better access to her pistol.

Deidre kept to the edge of the trail, partially shielded by a dense stand of balsam fir trees that stood like a wall. When she was less than fifty yards from the lodge, the wind shifted slightly, and she caught the odor of wood smoke. At the same time she saw the plume rising from the lodge chimney.

Deidre froze in her tracks, realizing she was not alone. She knew she should back out, return to her SUV and call for help. But she had a problem. This far from civilization, her cell phone would register no bars. She knew that without checking.

The nearest phone was several miles back, past Pete's place and near a small community, Finland. It would take her twenty minutes to walk back to her SUV and another twenty minutes to reach Finland. Against her better judgment, Deidre crept forward while trying to maintain a low profile. As she moved closer to the lodge, she looked across the clearing at the row of cabins and saw smoke rising from one cabin's chimney.

She paused to gather her thoughts. The driveway made a loop past the cabins and in front of the main lodge. In the center of the loop was a stand of trees where stately paper birch had grown in three or four clumps, but that had been years before. Now, rotting stubs waited to be toppled by the next heavy storm, the remnants of their once white bark flapping in the breeze. In the place of birch, tag alder brush and cedar trees were growing, forming an island of protection.

Deidre held her breath, listening for any sound. Hearing none, she dashed from the edge of the road to the safety of the island of trees. Once there, she stopped and held her breath, trying not to let a cloud of vapor rising from her mouth in the cold air give away her position.

Her heart was pounding against her ribs, and she couldn't decide if it was from fear or exertion. Probably both, she guessed. Again she waited for any telltale sound: a voice, a cough, the crunch of snow under someone's foot. Nothing.

She moved to the other side of the dense copse and paused. Still no movement or sound that she could detect. Deidre made a dash across the road to the side of the cabin with the fallen-in roof and worked her way around back and out of sight from the lodge. From there she was able to walk undetected to the back of the cabin from where she saw smoke rising.

As quietly as she could, and sticking to the shadows, she felt her way along the side of the building until she was standing under one of the side windows. It was too high up for her to see inside, and Deidre looked around for something to stand on.

Near the next door cabin was a small drum that looked as though it had held oil at one time, and she managed to reach it, staying in the shadows, which were lengthening in the afternoon sun. In a half hour it would be dark, at least for the time before moonrise. Deidre dragged the barrel over to the window of the apparently occupied cabin.

She climbed upon it, making more noise than she intended, and peered through the sagging glass. Her heart skipped a beat, and she sucked in a gasp of air.

A dimly lit, bare light bulb hung on a cord suspended from one of the rafters. Eight beds lined the walls, four on one side and four on the other. In the center, between the two rows were placed two five-gallon plastic buckets.

On each of three of the beds lay a young girl, a shackle on her ankle and the shackle chained to the foot of the bed. They looked lethargic, emotionally beaten, although they didn't appear to be bruised or otherwise physically damaged.

Their bedclothes were disheveled, and each seemed to have just one blanket covering the bare mattress. Each girl wore a sweatshirt and a pair of jeans, socks but no shoes. They weren't talking to each other. In fact, Deidre noted that they weren't even looking at one another. In the corner of the cabin stood an old-fashioned oil burner, which she surmised was the only source of heat for the room.

As quietly as she could, Deidre got down from the drum, and began to make her way around to the other side of the cabin. She didn't want to alarm the girls and cause them to call out or in any other way announce her presence.

On the other side of the cabin, she was completely out of view from the lodge, and she peeked around the corner of the building. She could see the lodge, see the light in the window because of the deepening shadows. She could clearly see the smoke continue to rise from its central chimney, however, she could see no sign of life in the lodge, and there were no snow machines outside.

She could plainly see a beaten down path leading from the lodge to the cabin, but even that didn't look like it had been used today. In one place, snow had drifted over the tracks, and where it had, it was pristine.

At that moment she decided to approach the door to determine if there was any chance she could get inside.

Deidre removed her pistol from its holster, checked the safe, and with her weapon in hand quietly slipped around the corner.

Chapter
Thirty-One

PETE HAD KNOWN BETTER than to ask Deidre if he could come with her. She might have said yes, but then, he knew, she would have made him wait out of sight. She probably would have made him stay in the truck, keeping the motor running and the heater going.

After he was sure Deidre had left, Pete took down his heavy jacket, and went to his closet. He picked up an elongated case and took a small package down from the overhead shelf. After checking the stew one more time and making sure the stove was turned off, he went to his battered pickup.

When he turned the ignition key, the starter motor ground so slowly it seemed as though it would stop mid-crank. He tried again. This time the engine coughed once. On the third try, the engine spun over and the motor came to life.

The inside of the windshield was completely frosted, and Pete scraped a small opening through which he could squint. He had parked facing out, so he could drive away without turning around.

By the time he was a mile down the road, the truck's defrosters had melted a slim margin of the frost where the window met the dash, and Pete scrunched down so he could peer through the growing opening.

The windshield was nearly clear by the time he came to where Deidre had parked her vehicle.

Pete got out of his truck and surveyed the scene, noticing that Deidre's were the only visible tracks. He hoped that was good news. His gate was easy as he followed where she had walked, and he covered ground at a surprisingly rapid rate.

He noticed where his friend had stopped to look at the site of the kill, and smiled to himself, pleased that she would be observant of the stories that animal tracks can tell. Pete moved on.

At the top of the hill, he saw that Deidre had paused, and he stood in her tracks, silently watching as though he were a hunter on a deer stand. His back stiffened and his senses became more keen when he saw movement by one of the cabins. He was only a hundred yards or so from the lodge. Pete saw Deidre poke her head around the cabin's corner. He watched her slink along the front of the building and step up to the door.

She bent down, evidently looking closely at something, and Pete wanted to yell at her to get the hell away from there, but it was no use. He watched in silence, waiting to see how this scene would play out.

Chapter
Thirty-Two

WHEN DEIDRE REACHED THE DOOR of the cabin, she saw it was locked from the outside by a large, brass padlock similar to the one described by the girls in the hospital and later described to her by Pete. She wished she had the key they had found on the bridge near the body of the murdered teen. She lifted the lock in her hand, being careful to not make it rattle against the hasp. She had an idea.

Holstering her pistol, she reached inside her vest pocket and felt for her key ring. It held three keys of varying shapes and sizes, and she hoped the keyhole in the lock was large enough that one of her smaller keys could be wedged inside and used as a lock pick.

Beads of sweat formed above her brow and trickled past one of them, the salty perspiration stinging as it contacted the delicate tissue of her eye. She had to stop what she was doing and wipe her eyes.

Deidre tried again, and she felt her key catch on something inside the padlock. She thought she felt it move but then felt her key slip past whatever it had been hung up on. She tried again.

She heard movement inside the cabin, and then heard one of the pails being moved slightly, followed by the sound of liquid splashing on liquid. After that, there were no sounds from inside.

Deidre was so intent on what she was doing that she lost track of her surroundings, lost track of the fact that the sun had nearly set, lost track of the fact that her presence was exposed to the lodge.

"Keep your hands above your head," she heard a man calmly say from behind her.

Involuntarily, she spun around.

"Uh, uh, uh," he said in the same even tone. "Don't make another move."

Deidre could see that he had a gun in his hand, and he had it pointed directly at her chest.

"Very slowly, move away from the door. Now, with your left hand, reach across your body and with your thumb and forefinger, take your weapon from its holster."

Deidre did as he said, being careful to not make any sudden moves. She withdrew her side arm.

"Toss it into the snow over there," and he motioned with his head where he wanted her to throw it. Deliberately, she did as she was told.

Without taking his eyes off her, the man hollered, "LaTourell, come out here, right now!"

Deidre saw the door of the lodge open, and steam billowed out as the warm air from inside contacted the outside cold. Another man quickly strode across the yard to where the gunman stood.

"Look at what I found. She's kinda cute, don't you think. A little old, but cute." He addressed Deidre. "Honey, you got yourself into a world of trouble."

Never taking his eyes off Deidre, he addressed the man he called LaTourell. "She won't bring a prime price, but I'll bet somebody will want her."

Panic swept over Deidre, and at that moment she knew what it felt like to be looked at like an animal meant for slaughter, simply a piece of meat. She knew her situation was helpless. She thought of Pete, knowing he was her only hope, and she prayed he wouldn't wait too long to call for help. He knew where she was and how to find her. She closed her eyes.

"If you're thinking somebody is going to come to help you, don't. As soon as it gets dark and before the moon comes up, were taking you and the girls you saw in there for a ride. Ever ride in a sled pulled by a snow machine? Well, if you haven't, you will tonight. By morning you'll be in Two Harbors. The snowmobile trail runs through the woods only a mile from here, and it goes through wilderness right to the town. It's just a quick car ride from there to Duluth. Enjoy the scenery along the way." He laughed at his own attempt at humor.

Deidre still had her eyes closed when she heard a gunshot that sounded as though it came from directly in front of her. Her knees buckled, and she nearly fell to the decking of the rotting porch. It took an instant, but she realized she hadn't been hit, and she tentatively opened her eyes.

The man who had been holding the gun pointed at her had a confused look on his face. At his feet lay the pistol he only seconds before had held in his hand. As though she were seeing in slow motion, Deidre saw him bend over to pick up the gun, but every time his hand reached the ground, it flopped the way a rag doll's hand would.

Both Deidre and the one he had called LaTourell were too stunned to react, and the man kept trying to will his fingers to work, frantically groping for the side arm. Then the snow-covered ground beneath his useless hand began to turn pink, a little at first and then bright red. A stream of blood began to drip from his lifeless limb.

He looked at Deidre with an expression that begged for an answer. Then he dropped to his knees in the snow, clutched his wrist in an effort to make his hand work and moaned, "Oh, God, no."

At that moment, LaTourell came to his senses and snatched the gun off the ground. He came up from a crouch and was bringing the sights to bear on Deidre.

"You'd better put that thing down if you know what's good for you," a voice rang out in the cold, clear air. "Set it on the deck and keep your hands away from your sides."

Deidre looked up the trail, and in the twilight, she could make out the figure of a person walking toward them. She squinted, trying to regain her bearings. Then she recognized the movement of the person.

"Pete! How did you get here?" She realized when the words left her mouth that it was a stupid question, but she was so rattled nothing else came out.

LaTourell appeared to be thinking over his options, because he hesitated in carrying out Pete's order. The thought flashed through Deidre's mind that he was going to kill her and take his chances on Pete missing with his first shot.

"Don't even think about it," Pete said in a calm voice, as if he were used to having a human in his sights. He kept walking slowly forward, his gun sight trained on the center of LaTourell's chest.

By this time Deidre could plainly see the rifle Pete had to his shoulder, and to her, it looked like a cannon. It had an unusually long octagonal barrel, and it looked like it must weigh several pounds. Pete held it without wavering. From where she stood, the bore looked as though it were an inch in diameter. She thought it must look even larger to LaTourell, who was looking directly into it.

"Damn you, drop it now, or I'll drop you," Pete barked. "No court in the land will convict me if I shoot you on the spot. I really wouldn't care if they did, you sack of shit!"

There was no doubting from the look in Pete's eye that he meant what he said. LaTourell slowly placed the gun on the deck and backed away. "Help your friend up. He ain't hurt as bad as he thinks, only got nicked under his arm. He'll live, but if he don't, that's okay, too."

The cold look in Pete's eyes frightened Deidre. "Pete, don't do anything you'll regret later. The courts will take care of these two. Don't create a mess for yourself."

Pete lowered his rifle but kept it ready in case one of the men made a run for it, or worse, tried to disarm him. She heard a click as he lowered the gun's hammer into the "safe" position.

"What do we do now?" he asked Deidre, realizing he had no answers.

She became aware of a commotion inside the cabin and heard a voice call, "Who's out there? Can you help us?" And then a plea, "Please, help us, whoever you are," followed by muffled sobs.

Deidre put her face by the door. "It's okay. I'm with law enforcement, and my friend is guarding the two men. Should we be looking for anyone else. Are there others?"

The same voice answered back. "Once in a while they bring someone in to use us, but almost always one of them comes along. I don't think anybody else is around."

"Do any of you need help right away. Will you be okay in there for a few more minutes?"

The now familiar voice responded. "We'll be okay. Just don't leave without taking us with you."

"We won't. That's a promise. I'll come back in a few minutes. Do you have a clock in there?"

"No."

"Take turns counting to one-hundred. By the time you each have done that five times, I'll be back." Deidre wanted to give them something to do that was concrete, something that would mark the passing of the minutes. "Okay?"

"Okay."

"We're going up to the lodge. You two walk side by side in front of us, slowly. Don't make any quick movements."

The men had seen Deidre pick up the gun from the deck, and they knew both she and Pete were now armed. LaTourell and the unnamed man led the way, he, staggering every few steps and cursing at no one in particular.

Once inside the lodge, she told LaTourell to sit in a chair and had Pete guard him. Then Deidre told the wounded man to remove his jacket and shirt. She waited, her pistol half raised while he struggled to extract his lifeless arm from the coat sleeve.

He grimaced and cried out in pain. Deidre was somewhat appalled to realize she gained a degree of satisfaction from his

242

discomfort. When he was shirtless, Deidre could see that he had been hit near his armpit in a muscle weight lifters call the lats.

The wound was oozing blood, but had quit bleeding heavily. Blood was caked on his forearm, where it had run down, coagulated, and was beginning to dry. His side was covered with blood, and she looked at his wound without getting within his reach.

The bullet had entered at an angle from his back left side. She could see that a chunk of flesh had been blown away from the lat, but because of the angle from which the shot had come, the bullet had also creased the inside of his upper right arm.

The wounds were turning a dark black from dried blood, and she could see that the entire area was bruised.

Deidre recognized that was why he couldn't pick up his pistol after he dropped it. The damaged muscles were the ones responsible for flexing his upper arm and controlling his fingers. She imagined the nerves, if they weren't damaged, were at least shocked.

"You'll live," she said unsympathetically.

"Keep watch over these two so I can find something to use to tie them up," she instructed Pete, and she heard the distinct sound a gun hammer makes when it is cocked. She looked at her friend. The rifle barrel was pointed at them, and Deidre knew he was ready.

Deidre went into the rustic kitchen and rummaged around in the cabinet drawers. She came out with a handful of plastic ties.

The wounded man was still standing, swaying on his feet and looking very pale.

"Don't pass out on me, you SOB," she snapped. "Put your hands behind your back, wrists together." She looped a tie around each wrist and hooked a third through both of them, cinching it tight and drawing his hands together so they touched.

"Sit down over there." She pointed at a wood bench against the wall.

"You, stand up," Deidre ordered LaTourell. Not being wounded, he was the more dangerous of the two. "Belly up to the wall, and put your hands behind you."

With his face pressed against the logs of the building and his hands behind his back, LaTourell was rendered practically immobile.

Deidre repeated the same process she had used on his accomplice. "Sit down on the bench next to him."

LaTourell shuffled across the floor and dropped down onto the bench, the wall to his back.

"Where's the key to the lock on the cabin," she demanded. The men responded by sneering at her. Neither said a word.

"Watch these two," she said to Pete. "But don't even think about shooting either one of them. There's no way they're going to overpower you from where they're at." Deidre looked at the heavy rifle Pete had in his hands. "But if one of them is stupid enough to come after you, crack him over the head with your gun barrel. It looks thick enough to split his head open pretty good." She glared at Latourell, who shifted his eye contact away.

Deidre ran from the lodge to the cabin. Even before she reached the door, she could hear one of the girls counting: seventy-six, seventy-seven, seventy-eight . . .

"Are you doing okay?" she shouted.

"Yeah, we're okay," someone answered, her voice quavering.

"I don't know where to find a key to this lock, so I'm going to try to find a hammer or something I can use to break it. If I can't find something, we'll break out a window, and I'll come inside and free you. Okay?"

"Okay."

"I'll be back. I promise," she reassured the captives.

She heard a weak, "Okay."

It was getting so dark that Deidre was having difficulty seeing the outlines of the buildings, but she noticed a set of tracks veering off the trail between the lodge and the cabin. She'd gone only a few yards off the main trail when she came to a what was left of a woodshed, and she could see it was in use. Using her flashlight, she was able to explore inside and found a splitting maul leaning up against the far wall.

Deidre shouldered the heavy implement and jogged back to the cabin.

"I've got a maul, and I'm going to break the lock off the door. Don't be alarmed."

She took a swing at the lock but in the dark, she missed and struck the door. The sound reverberated inside.

By feel, Deidre placed the head of the maul on the lock, set her feet a measured distance from her target, and swung again. This time she felt the heavy hammer strike the lock and heard something snap. She felt where the lock had been and discovered it was loose but not entirely opened.

Deidre repeated the process, this time with more effort, and she was rewarded with the sound of metal hitting the deck's floor. She released the hasp and pushed the door open. At first, the stench stung her senses, but she recovered in time to force herself to enter the room. The girls looked at her through hollow, expressionless eyes.

"It'll take me a minute to get these off your ankles. Be patient." Deidre bent over the bed to which the nearest girl was chained.

"This shouldn't be too hard to break," she said more to herself than to them.

She spoke directly to the girl. "The chain is long enough that you can scrunch up near the head of the bed while I cut one of the links. Move up now. Good."

Laying the chain over the four-by-four timber which served as a bedpost, Deidre swung the maul as hard as she could. The axe-like side of the head bent one of the links and made a cut partway through. She set the link on edge and hit it with the hammer side of the maul. The link doubled in half and snapped where it had been partially cut. The first girl was freed.

Deidre moved to the next bed and repeated the process. In minutes she completed the task.

"Do you have any other clothing?"

The girls shook their heads.

"Shoes?" Again a head shake was all she got.

"I'm going to the lodge to get something for you. Stay right here. Promise?" They nodded, still not believing what was happening.

On the way to the lodge, Deidre was wracked with fear that they would panic and make a run for the woods, and she thought that perhaps she should have locked the door from the outside by shoving a stick through the hasp lock. There was no way she could have locked them up again.

In minutes she was able to return with several pairs of wool socks, which she instructed them to pull over their feet. When each of them wore a double layer, Deidre told them to wrap their blankets around their shoulders, and she led them up the path to the lodge.

Chapter
Thirty-Two

W HEN DEIDRE AND THE GIRLS entered the lodge, they had to walk in front of the two bound men, and one of the girls began to sob uncontrollably. Deidre placed her arm around her skinny shoulders, and she could feel the girl trembling. She was sure she knew why the girl was terrified at being in the lodge and in their presence.

She whisked them past the two men who were sitting on the bench and leaning against the wall and ushered the victims into a separate room.

"Don't worry at all. Their hands are tied so tightly they'll never get loose. Not only that, my friend has a very large gun, and I think he'd like a reason to use it. I'm here too, and believe me, I can take care of them if I have to. Can I get you anything? Water? Food? Anything?" She looked at their eyes and saw nothing but fear.

In a weak voice, one girls asked, "Can I go to the bathroom?"

The question stumped Deidre, and she went to the other room.

"Is there a toilet around here?"

One of the men shifted his feet. "There's an outhouse in the back. Knock yourself out."

Deidre escorted the poor girl out the backdoor and to the outdoor toilet. She waited outside while the girl did what she came to do and heard the girl whimper from pain as she passed her liquid.

Those damn animals she thought as the door opened and the girl looked at her, tears in her eyes. They made their way back into the lodge.

"Stay in this room. I'm going to make arrangements to get us all out of here. I'll be in the other room. If you need anything, need to know I'm still here, call my name, and I'll answer you. My name is Deidre. Do you understand?" All three nodded.

She moved into the other room, leaving the door half open. "Pete, we've got to get some help. My cell phone registers zero bars, and I don't think we can get any reception until we reach Highway 61. That would take way too long. Do any of your neighbors have a land line?"

Pete didn't have to think. "Mrs. Ostberg has one. She's about five miles on the other side of me, off Highway 1. Do you want me to go?"

"I think that'd be best. You know the way, and the girls would probably feel safer with me than with another man. Do you mind?"

Pete turned to LaTourell. "Where's the snow machine?"

"Don't know what you're talking about."

"Don't play stupid with me," Pete snapped. He was a different person than Deidre was used to. "You didn't walk in from the road, and I saw the snowmobile tracks on the trail. Where is it?"

Deidre heard the hammer on his rifle click into firing position, and she was stepping forward when LaTourell, his pupils dilated with fear, answered. "It's out back. There's a small shed beside the toilet. We keep it there. The key's in the ignition." He glared at the floor.

Deidre found a scrap of paper, and using a pen she had in her pocket, she scribbled three numbers.

"Call this number. It's the sheriff's number. Tell him I need a couple of deputies, and they should get here as soon as they can. Then call 911 and have them send out two search and rescue units. Tell them to bring sleds and transportation for three girls and an injured man. Finally, this is the home number of Zak Burton. Identify yourself by saying you are calling at my request. Tell him I need him here as soon as possible. Give him the directions. He'll be able to find it on a map."

Pete walked out the back door. In minutes the roar of a snowmobile engine disrupted the winter silence of the wilderness, and Deidre saw the taillights of the machine disappear over the hill.

She stood at the window a few seconds. The moon had risen, and under normal conditions, she would have turned out the lights and watched the muted shadows produced by moon glow as it reflected from the pristine snow. Tonight, however, she was in a tenuous position and turned back to face her prisoners.

She pulled up a chair so she could face them and kept the pistol on her lap. It was difficult for her to look at the men, difficult to remain silent, but she knew it would be futile to say anything. They looked at the floor. She watched them for any threatening movement. The stalemate lasted for nearly an hour before she saw the single headlight of the snowmobile bouncing up and down and side to side as Pete returned to the lodge.

He walked in and stomped his feet to dislodge the snow from his boots. Deidre noticed a ring of frost on his parka hood, and his nose was red and running.

"It's bitter cold out there," he announced. "Looks like it will be the coldest night of the year."

Pete relieved Deidre of guard duty, and she checked on the girls.

"How you doing?" They shrugged. "Do you know Kimi Thomas?" All three girls jerked upright.

"How do you know Kimi?" one of them asked.

"I thought you'd like to know she's safe in a hospital in Duluth."

"Is she alive? I mean is she okay?" another girl blurted out.

Deidre nodded. "She's fine and will be returning to Canada very soon. How about Allison. Did you know her?"

"Yes. Yes, what about her?"

"She's with Kimi. You must know Jean, too? She's also there. All three are doing fine, and they're going to be so happy to see you. I know they will."

Tears of joy and disbelief ran down their cheeks, and they spent the next fifteen minutes questioning Deidre. She answered as best she could, then left the girls to talk among themselves about their friends.

Pete sat back in his chair and rested his rifle across both knees.

"What kind of rifle is that," Deidre asked, wanting to relieve some of her tension by talking about a subject that didn't much matter.

"This old thing," Pete said as he laid his hand on the gun's breech. "I got this from an old-timer years ago. I was only nineteen but was already working in the woods, so I had a few bucks to spend at the time.

"He had a son he wanted to give it to, but the kid wanted a new 30-06. Well, the old man got mad and offered it to me. I traded a beat-up chain saw and ten dollars for it, even up. Best gun I ever owned. It's only a 30-30, but it shoots real straight, and see the extra long magazine? Holds ten shots, counting the one in the barrel. You can really crank them off in a hurry if you know how to work the action. I've dropped more deer with this rifle than I can remember."

Deidre was surprised it was only a 30-30 caliber, but she supposed the octagonal barrel gave it the appearance of being larger.

"Can I have a drink of something?" the wounded man growled.

"What is there?" Deidre asked.

"There's a bottle of brandy under the counter and beer in the kitchen."

"No water?" Deidre asked.

"None fit to drink," he answered.

"Well, then I guess you're out of luck," she said. He spat on the floor and mumbled something under his breath.

Suffer, you bastard, she thought and went in the other room to check on the girls. She sat on one of the beds. "How you doing?" she inquired.

One girl smiled tentatively. "We're okay. Can you tell us what's going to happen to us?"

Deidre realized she had been so wrapped up in dealing with the suspects, she had neglected the victims, something she believed happened too often in the system.

"I've called for help. They should be here very soon. Search and Rescue will take you out to the road on sleds. From there, you'll be transported to the hospital in Duluth." She looked at the girl who had used the outhouse. "You're having some trouble peeing, aren't you?"

The girl nodded, and crossed her legs at the thought.

"They'll get that cleared up for you in no time. Do any of you have problems that need attention right now?"

The other two shook their heads.

"Okay. Then depending on how much care you need in the hospital, I think you'll be back in Thunder Bay in a week or so. Do you have families?"

One girl began to cry. "I have a mother. Don't know where my dad is. She and I used to fight a lot, because she didn't like my friends and what we did. The last time I saw her she told me I couldn't go out, but I did anyway, went to a party. The next thing I knew, I woke up in a canoe. It was dark, and I had no idea where I was or where I was being taken. My hands and feet were tied together, and they put duct tape over my mouth. I ended up here."

"Do you know when that was?" Deidre wanted to know.

"August. There were seven other girls in the cabin, but every few days some would disappear, and then they would be replaced. I don't know why I didn't get taken."

Deidre looked at her youthful beauty and her shapely body. The thought crossed her mind that perhaps the traffickers were saving her for a special client.

"Were Anna and Kimi in the cabin with you."

The same girl answered. "Anna was able to pry the chain loose from the bed, and she offered to help free us. Kimi was the only one who had the courage to go with her. They were gone only a couple of hours, when LaTourell and Jameson dragged Anna back to the cabin."

"Is he the other guy out there?" she asked, motioning with her head.

"That's him. Like I said, they dragged her into the cabin. She was so scared, she couldn't talk, we all were. LaTourell said to watch what was going to happen to Anna and learn what happens to girls who try to run away." She looked at the floor and swallowed hard. "I guess I can't tell you what they did to her." She wept openly, her body convulsing with each sob. The other two girls wrapped their arms around themselves.

"I know. I found her body and was present when the medical examiner finished her autopsy. It was brutal. I'm so sorry you had to endure what you have. What about you two? Do you have family waiting for you?"

"I was living on the streets," one of the other victims said with flat affect. "What will happen to me?"

Deidre smiled at her. "The head of the Nishnawbe Aski Nation has assured me that you'll be well taken care of. Their social service network is already working on behalf of Allison and Jean, and I'm positive they'll work for you, too. You're going to be okay." She wished she believed her words.

The third girl looked away and stared at the wall.

"They're coming," Pete shouted from the other room.

Deidre hurried to the door and stepped outside. She counted four single headlights bouncing along the trail leading to the lodge.

In minutes, she was meeting with four members of Search and Rescue and two sheriff's deputies.

She directed the EMT trained rescue members to where the girls were, and stepped aside to allow them to enter the cabin. One looked after Jameson, the others cared for the girls in the bedroom.

"Let me take a look at your back," he said to Jameson. The man stood and turned around.

"Take these damn straps off my wrists, so I can move my arm."

"Oh, sure, right away," the EMT said, sarcasm dripping from the words. "Stand still so I can get a better look."

He could see where the slug had entered his back, about four inches from the left of his spine, but because of the angle of the shot, it hadn't penetrated the rib cage. Instead, there was a neat puncture wound where it had entered, but the exit point had blown out a piece of flesh the size of a golf ball. It had also removed some skin and a little flesh from the inside of his bicep.

"You're lucky that old man is a good shot, mister, or you'd be dead by now. 'Course, maybe he isn't that good and missed where he was aiming. Either way, you'll live. Always going to have a reminder, though."

He placed a gauze compress on the open wound and bound it tightly with a bandage. Jameson winced and cursed, and Deidre thought the EMT was being none too gentle.

The rescue squad had brought sleeping bags with them, and they helped each girl into one. Then each was gently lifted and carried outside to a waiting ride.

As they went by her, one of the girls asked, "Will we get to see Allison and Jean?"

Deidre smiled. "Of course you will," and she brushed a lock of hair from the girl's eyes.

Now she had to decide what to do with the two suspects, because, technically, she had no authority to make an arrest. She addressed one of the deputies.

"In the confusion, I didn't read these two their rights, although, I actually tied them up for my own safety. I'm requesting that you arrest them for kidnapping, assault with a deadly weapon, battery, and anything else you can think of."

A look of disbelief crossed the deputy's face. They had almost created what would have been a major faux pas.

He began, "You have the right," and continued until the two men had been read their Miranda rights. Deidre breathed a sigh of relief. Neither man had said anything that would have been used in court, and now anything they said could be used against them.

Not only that, now they were in the custody of the Lake County Sheriff's Department and were no longer her responsibility.

"Do you need a ride out?" the deputy asked.

"No, you go do what you have to do. We'll walk."

She put her arm around Pete's shoulders. "Come on, friend. Supper's getting cold."

Chapter
Thirty-Three

THE MOON WAS NEAR FULL and high in the sky as she and Pete trekked through the silence. What sounded like the crack of a rifle shot split the icy air, and both she and her companion spun around to see who was behind them. They burst out laughing, because it had only been the sound of a tree, splitting from the extreme cold. Deidre took in the beauty of the moonlight reflecting off the snow, and she thought she could have read a book it was so bright.

As they neared the road, they could see lights and hear the voices of people. The deputies hadn't driven off with their prisoners, neither had the rescue people pulled away. Evidently, they were taking their time, making sure all was in order. She walked up to a group huddled around a car that hadn't been there when she had started in and elbowed her way through the knot of bodies.

"You sure have a way of being in the middle of things," Zak Burton said, a huge grin cutting his face. "I can't believe you did this. It was pretty stupid—or gutsy. I'm not sure which." He paused. "But I'm sure glad you're okay. We decided the deputies will take the suspects in. Jameson will be housed in the jail and LaTourell will go to the ER. My guess is that he'll join Jameson by tomorrow. Is there any place we can go to talk?"

Deidre was exhausted and hungry. "Tell you what, Zak. Come with me and Pete. We'll have a bite to eat at his place, and then we can go to my cabin. We can talk as long as you want. I'll give you the good bed, and you can stay the night, then leave in the morning. I've got company coming in the afternoon. What do you say?"

Zak looked please. "How can I turn down an offer like that?"

By the time they arrived at Pete's, the stew had hardly had a chance to cool, and he reheated it in a few minutes. Deidre had little appetite, and picked at the meal. As she raised her fork to her mouth, her hand trembled, and she hoped the other two didn't notice. She was relieved to see that they were engrossed in the food.

"This stew is incredible," Zak said as he ladled another helping into his bowl. Deidre left hers half full and pushed away from the table.

"Finish up, Zak. I need to get home." She called her dog over to her and pet his head.

"I bet you want to go home too," she said, scratching his ears while he looked at her through sad eyes as only a Labrador retriever can.

*****

ZAK WAS ENTRANCED by Deidre's cabin. "Most of us would give anything to have a place like this," he said, a little envious of what she had.

"Yeah, it's nice, but it can get pretty lonely up here, especially during the winter."

"No one in your life, then?" Zak questioned, not meaning to get personal.

"Not really, just me and Pete," was all she answered, and looked at her dog who raised his head at the sound of his name. His tail thumped on the floor, but he didn't get up from his spot near the stove.

"How are you doing?" Zak asked, concern in his tone.

"Okay I guess. Shit! I'm not okay. I couldn't eat my supper. I'm a ball of nerves, and I'm angry, angry at those men, angry that I didn't figure this out sooner, angry that I know we haven't stopped the abuse of women." Deidre's feelings spilled out.

She went to her cupboard. "Want something to drink?"

"What are you having?"

"Brandy-coke. Want one?"

"Sounds good."

Deidre dumped a few ice cubes in each of two glasses, added brandy from a half-empty bottle, and topped the drink off with a little Coca-Cola. Zak took a sip, and shuddered and coughed.

"Too strong?" she asked.

Zak cleared his throat. "Just right."

"I know we haven't drained the headwaters of their operation, but we sure have cut off one of its feeder streams. Because of you, six girls are still alive and have a chance at a new start. There'll be no more women funneled to Duluth down this route.

"All we can do is to keep working and making a difference one life at a time."

"What happens to the attorney, Gerald Colter?" Deidre needed to know. "And Judge DeMarcus?"

"You didn't read this morning's paper?" To her, this morning seemed like last month. She shook her head.

"The judge was last seen drinking at a bar Christmas Eve. Yesterday, friends checked on him at home. He was on lying on the floor, dead. Shot himself through the mouth with a thirty-eight-caliber pistol.

"He left a three-page suicide letter. I haven't seen it yet, but a copy will be on my desk when I get back. Would you like to read it?"

Deidre had to think about the question. "The next time I'm in Duluth," she affirmed.

"As for Colter," Zak continued, "On Monday, I'll turn over the files we have on him, along with a copy of what was on the flash drive you gave us. We're dealing with a federal offense, and we'll let a federal prosecutor handle the case against him. Hopefully, that investigation will lead to others who are involved. How about you? What are your plans?"

"Retire—again." Deidre laughed halfheartedly. She didn't have a plan. "I suppose I'll spend some time alone. Try to sort things out. Maybe I'll move back into civilization, Two Harbors, maybe even Duluth."

She stopped talking. Why did she say Duluth? The thought had never crossed her mind before. Deidre looked at her watch.

"My God. It's one-thirty. I have to get some sleep. Towels and washcloths are under the sink. Help yourself, just don't borrow my toothbrush." She wobbled as she stood up. The drink had been potent.

Zak placed his hand on her arm to steady her. "Take care of yourself, Deidre. The world needs people like you."

She looked at him and was struck by the sincerity expressed by his eyes.

"Thanks, Zak." She made it to her bed and crawled beneath the covers, still clothed but shoeless.

Deidre was awakened by Pete's cold nose nudging her hand that was draped over the side of the bed. He whined and pranced toward the door. She sat up, squinted her eyes to make out the numbers on her digital clock, 6:31.

"Ah, Pete. This early?" she mumbled but climbed out of bed to let him out to do his thing.

The cold, late December air cleared her head. By the time she threw a couple of billets of wood in the stove, she was almost awake, almost. She made a pot of coffee and sat so she could look out her living room window. Cedar Lake was frozen solid, and along the far shore she saw two timber wolves following what she suspected was a deer, or maybe a moose had passed that way. She picked up the binoculars kept by the chair for times like this. Watching the animals lope along, their easy gait eating up distance, she was at peace, but in seconds, peace was replaced with a wave of loneliness. She realized she needed more than what this wilderness had to offer.

The toilet flushed, and she remembered she wasn't alone. Zak came out of the bathroom, looking the way she imagined she must look.

"Whoo. That was quite the night," he exclaimed as he flopped down in the chair that matched the one in which Deidre lounged. "Got a cup of coffee?"

"Over there." She jerked her head toward the kitchen counter. "You'll have to serve yourself," she said in a voice still hoarse with morning clog.

Zak forced himself out of the soft chair and returned with a cup of brew. "Got any brandy to put in it?" He laughed. Deidre looked at him through bleary eyes. "Never mind," he said and arranged himself in the chair again.

"You gonna be okay?" He took a sip of the coffee and winced. She watched him blow over the top of the cup, trying to cool the liquid enough so he could comfortably drink it.

"Yeah, Ben and the girls will be here by evening. He said he had to work this morning, and by the time he gets them packed up and ready to go, it will be at least six before they arrive. I'll be okay."

"I've got to get back as soon as I can. Called my wife last night and told her I was staying with a good-looking blonde. She didn't think that was funny. I might need you to vouch for me." He chuckled, and Deidre was beginning to see the humor in the day.

"Anyway, if you're sure you'll be okay, I'm going to take off for home. I promised my wife and kids we'd go skating this afternoon. There's a real nice pond open to the public at a place up on the hill, Chester Park. You and Ben should take his girls there sometime. It's a great place to slide and have a good time. Has a warming house where they serve snacks and cocoa. Maybe we'll see you there sometime."

Zak stood and was making his way to the kitchen. Deidre followed him, handed him his jacket, and took his hand.

"Thanks, Zak."

"For what?"

"For including me, for not cutting me out of the action, for accepting me for my skills."

"It was our gain," he said matter-of-factly. "You sure you'll be okay?"

"I'm sure."

Deidre watched Zak drive away, and a surge of profound loss swept over her, almost panic. She walked to the window. The wolves had vanished into the frost-filled air, the tree line was muted in the cold, and she was overwhelmed with the silence. Somewhere in her cabin, the frost forced a nail to push out, and the resounding snap made her jump. She decided the first thing she needed to do was clean up.

The hot shower felt wonderful on her bare skin, and she shampooed her hair, rinsing it in the spray. Normally she conserved water, especially in the winter when she had concerns about her country wastewater disposal system, but today she allowed herself the luxury of standing in the hot steam.

Eventually, she had to give up, and she turned off the faucet, wiped the fogged-over mirror with a towel, and combed out her tangled hair.

In her reflection, she could still see the outline of the wound from when she had been shot in the chest several years ago. It had healed, but she would always carry that reminder. She touched it with her fingers, then ignored the scar as she dried herself. After donning a robe, she opened the bathroom door, allowing the steam to escape into the rest of the cabin. Her eyes widened.

"Surprise!" the girls cried out, and came running to greet her. Ben stood by the table, waiting for them to finish their greetings. When Megan and Maren had received their kisses and hugs, he stepped forward and wrapped his arms around her.

"Deidre, Deidre, Deidre," he repeated. "What am I going to do with you? Every time I let you out of my sight, you're doing some foolish thing. Am I going to have to sit on you to keep you out of trouble?"

He kept her engulfed in his arms, swaying from side to side as though rocking her. Deidre felt his warm body, and cuddled up to his chest. She was so choked up she couldn't say anything.

"What do I have to say to make you believe that we need you? Doesn't that mean anything to you?" Without looking up or pulling away, she nodded.

Finally, Deidre could speak. "What are you doing here so early? How did you find out?"

"Zak called me last night from his car. He told me what had happened, and he suggested I take today off and get up here as soon as I could. I told him I'd be coming here tonight and would be staying through New Year's. He was worried about your mental state and didn't want you to be alone any more than you had to be."

Ben didn't let go of Deidre, and the girls recognized that something was wrong. They stood in one place, staring at the couple.

"Is it going to be okay, Daddy?" Megan finally asked.

Ben looked at the girls and let go of Deidre, although he kept hold of her hand. "It's going to be okay, I promise. Why don't you girls go give Pete some attention. Look at him. He's wagging his tail and wants you to scratch behind his ears."

The girls scrambled over to Pete and soon were wrestling with the Lab, he mouthing their small hands and they hung onto his neck.

Ben led Deidre to the couch, and they sat facing the lake. "Tell me what happened."

She began from the beginning, recounting how Pete had known about the resort. He had made the connection between it and the key she had found near Anna's body. She hadn't thought through the consequences of her actions, putting herself in mortal danger.

"If I was that terrified of LaTourell and Jameson, imagine how helpless those poor girls must have felt in their hands. Think of being abducted and trussed up in a duffle bag, transported in a canoe without knowing where you were being taken, and then being locked up and held like livestock waiting your turn to be used." She shuddered.

Ben held her close. "It turned out as well as it could have. There's no use looking back. They're safe. You're safe, and those two will never victimize girls again."

Deidre curled up next to him as the twins crawled into their laps.

"And we're going to celebrate the New Year." He stroked the back of Deidre's hair, and the four of them watched as a woodpecker landed on a tree outside the window and began hammering away at it.

"Do you think woodpeckers ever get headaches?" Maren asked, and they all burst out laughing.

Chapter
Thirty-Four

Two days after they ushered in the new year, Deidre made one last trip to the Federal Building in Duluth and looked up Zak.

"When we were in my cabin, you said I could read the suicide letter left my Judge DeMarcus. Does the offer still stand?"

Zak opened his file cabinet and shuffled through a few folders, extracted the right one, and laid it in front of her.

"Don't let it out of this office," he reminded her. "I've got to take a walk down the hall for a few minutes," and he left Deidre alone to read the judge's final verdict. She tentatively opened it, wondering what a suicidal person would reveal.

> *To My Family,*
>
> *I'm going to try to explain how I have arrived at this place. It will do no good to those who I have harmed, won't do you any good, probably. But I feel I must tell you.*
>
> *At one time, I was a good husband, a good father, and a good judge, and we were happy. I hope the memories you hang onto of me will be of those times. I know what pain I have caused you, and I know what I've lost.*
>
> *Somewhere, I lost my moral compass, or at least forgot how to read it. The stress of the job was sometimes almost overwhelming, not that I'm using that for an excuse. Most judges cope, but a few of us from the office began to stop at a lounge after work to have a drink and unwind. It became a daily ritual.*
>
> *As time went by, the drink we had became two, three, four. After a few drinks, a few more don't matter. I'm sure you saw the change in me, and don't blame yourself for not intervening. I always was a stubborn ass.*
>
> *About four years ago, when I was drunk, I met this guy at the bar who asked me if I wanted a real ride, a real thrill. At first, I didn't*

understand, but then he showed me a picture of this woman, girl really, and said he'd set me up with her.

Like a fool, I went with him to a place he said was his. Well, I'm sure I don't have to tell you the details. He had a hidden video camera set up and taped the whole thing.

I tried to forget about what I had done, but several weeks later a case came before me involving a prostitution charge. I received a video CD in the mail with a note telling to look at it. The note said I'd know what to do about the prostitution case I was hearing. I don't have to tell you what was on the disc.

From that time on, they had me. I drank more to ease my conscience, not that it helped, but finally I reached the bottom. You left, the kids don't want to be associated with me, and I have lost my career. What remains of my life? Nothing.

I can't ask you to forgive me, and I won't ask. Only know that I deeply regret what I have done to you, to the kids, to myself. May you find peace when I am gone from your lives. I love you, Tony

Deidre slowly closed the folder as Zak returned. "I don't understand how someone can be so self-destructive. It's a shame."

Zak slipped the paper into its proper slot and closed the drawer. He shook his head.

*****

Deidre closed up her office the first week of January. She worried about Jill and where she would go. Jill was the most efficient secretary she had ever worked with, and she wanted more than anything to help her find a more permanent position. That wasn't possible, she thought, because she no longer had any influence with the county system. She dreaded having to say goodbye.

Jill waltzed into her office. Several of her piercings were missing and her hair was died monochromatic, light brown. Instead of looking downcast because she was no longer needed, her head was held high, and she had a sparkle in her eye.

"Deidre, I want you to know, you're the best boss I ever had, and you've been more of an example for me than you can ever believe.

Here, I want you to have this." She handed Deidre a small rectangular package.

Deidre peeled the wrapping away, exposing a pasteboard box, which she carefully opened. Inside was a nameplate for placing on a desk. Deidre read the inscription: BOSS LADY.

They both laughed and hugged each other. "I'm so glad you were assigned to work with me," Deidre said, her eyes beginning to mist. "I couldn't have asked for a better person. But I worry about you. I think you should set your sights higher than being a temp and a volunteer. Think about it. Will you?"

Jill's face lit up even brighter than it had been. "That was the next thing I wanted to tell you. I received a call from your friend, Melissa. She wants me to apply for a secretarial job with the BCA. She'll try to pull some strings," she said.

Deidre looked directly into Jill's eyes. "Go for it," They walked out of the door together, Jill turning the key in the lock for the last time.

*****

DEIDRE SPENT THE REST of January at her cabin, hauling firewood, cleaning the place, snowshoeing with Pete trailing behind on the trail she packed, and catching up on some reading.

Two weekends each month, she traveled to Duluth to be with Ben and the girls, and they came to spend the other two weekends at her cabin. It became more difficult to say goodbye each time.

February arrived and with it Valentine's Day. She bought special gifts for Megan and Maren, and she spent that day and night in Duluth with them. Ben surprised her with a night on the town, beginning with a fancy meal at a hotel having a revolving restaurant perched fifteen stories atop its rooms. It made a complete revolution every hour. Twice, they saw the same street pass below them.

He had purchased tickets to a magnificent ice show at the entertainment center, and following the show, they were treated to a concert by the symphony, celebrating the occasion with music fit for the Boston Pops.

Afterward, they went to a quiet lounge where they each ordered a drink.

"And so I propose a toast." Ben raised his goblet and waited for Deidre to raise hers. "A toast to times gone by, to memories and to our successes, even to our failures. Here's to the joy we had in Jenny and in John. May they rest in peace." Deidre was shocked by his solemnity at the moment, but he continued. "And here's to the future, our future. Happy Valentine's Day, Deidre," and he kissed her on her lips.

*****

In March they celebrated Megan's and Maren's fifth birthday. Each girl had her favorite birthday cake, and they were allowed to invite a few girls from their pre-school class to spend the night on a so-called sleepover.

The weekends kept starting sooner and lasting longer for Deidre, sometimes beginning early Friday morning when she arrived at Ben's house and lasting until Monday evening, after the girls had been tucked into bed and she left for her cabin.

One sunny day near the end of March, she was alone at her cabin. The early spring sun was shining through her living room window, and outside, animals and birds were becoming active again, a few having begun to move north from more southerly climes.

The night before, Pete had wanted to come in, but he carried with him the distinct smell of skunk. Deidre was reminded by the odor that still clung to his fur, that March was skunk mating season, and they had come out of their winter's hibernation to carry out their courtships. Pete slept in the nearly empty woodshed that night.

As she soaked in the rays trapped by the window glass, she watched droplets of water drip from a row of icicles hanging from the cabin's eaves, and she realized this was not the life she wanted.

She needed people. Not just people. She needed friends, companions who would share her joys and her sorrows. She needed people she could touch, people for whom she could lend comfort. She needed to be in the lives of Megan and Maren.

Deidre struggled with the thought that she might have fallen in love with Ben. She tried to convince herself that it wasn't true, and she almost succeeded. She vowed she was going to have to confront that possibility, but the thought scared her.

Her excuse was that she was afraid to give herself, emotionally or physically, to anyone again for fear that he would be taken from her like John had been. Then too, she couldn't face the possibility that he might not feel the same way she did, and by using the word "love," she might destroy what they had.

Confused, Deidre fell asleep in the sunshine, and the sun was setting when she woke. After supper, she strapped on her snowshoes and took Pete for a walk across the frozen lake. She stopped and rubbed snow into his fur until it smelled fresh and clean, knowing that when he warmed inside the cabin, the smell would return, but it would be faint.

As they turned toward home, Deidre looked straight up at the stars. Polaris lit the way north, and she could clearly see Orion, his belt of stars twinkling around his middle and she was captivated by the expanse of the Milky Way. It was then she made up her mind.

She wouldn't risk alienating Ben with that four letter word, and she decided the status quo was better than nothing. She vowed to make the most of the situation, loving the girls like a mother, being with Ben as a companion, and loving them all as much as possible.

*****

APRIL WAS TYPICAL for northern Minnesota. During the night, temperatures dropped to the mid, or even low, twenties. Twice, snow dusted the area, and an early April blizzard dumped a foot of snow across the region. It melted in three days, but still, it dampened spirits, but not Deidre's.

She'd heard a forecast of the impending storm, and packed up Pete, a few clothes, and her toiletry case. She reached Duluth as the first sticky flakes of wet snow had started to fall, and all four of them, Ben, Megan, Maren, and Deidre, were snowed in for two days while the wind whipped off Lake Superior and lake-effect snow piled up outside.

As soon as the storm subsided, they dressed in winter garb and went out to build a snowman. When it was complete, they flopped in the snow, moving their arms and legs back and forth, spreading their legs and sweeping their arms from their sides to over their heads.

Ben stood up as carefully as he could and helped the others to their feet. Deidre looked at the "angel" imprints left in the snow. She choked back her tears, and resisted the urge to print Mom, Dad, Megan, and Maren above the figures.

"Come on. Hot chocolate for everyone," Ben called out, and he held the door open for them to go inside.

As they sat around the table, the children trying to fish the miniature marshmallows out of their cocoa with their fingers, Ben pulled out a bright yellow map marked with blue patches, red dots, and black lines. Deidre recognized it as a Fischer Map, one commonly used to navigate in the Boundary Waters Canoe Area.

"I'd like to take the kids on their first canoe trip," he said. "Would you come with us? I'd really like that."

Deidre had been into canoe country a few times, and each time she was thrilled by its remote beauty. She jumped at the opportunity. The rest of the evening they studied the map, choosing routes and picking out possible campsites.

"I've been to this lake so many times," Ben said, pointing to a blue area on the map labeled Bald Eagle Lake. "This campsite has a sand beach." He placed his finger on one of the red dots. It's really isolated. We might camp there for three of four days and not see another person. "I think it would be a perfect place to take the girls."

It was bedtime for the soon to be campers, and Deidre and Ben performed the often repeated ritual of carrying them upstairs and tucking them into bed. Life was comfortable for the four of them.

Easter was late that year, falling on the last weekend of the month. Deidre, feeling a natural part of the family, helped pick out outfits for the girls. They dyed Easter eggs, and she helped cook

Easter dinner. She even sat in the pew at church with them. Church was not seeming so foreign to her.

The Easter Bunny was good to everyone, and Deidre was at peace with her world.

*****

THE FIRST DAY OF MAY was a rarity for Duluth. The wind was from the west, not off Lake Superior, and the temperature soared into the low eighties. Buds on tree branches were swollen and ready to burst, and robins seemed to be everywhere, cocking their heads sideways in search of unaware earthworms.

Deidre had come to Duluth in the middle of the week and was at Ben's. While she waited for him to come home from work and while the girls were upstairs playing with their doll house, she made a cup of tea and sat down. The TV had been left on, and she thought she'd watch the five o'clock news. She instantly became absorbed.

Gerald Colter II was seen exiting the Federal Building in downtown Duluth. He was flanked by his attorney on one side and his wife on the other. A reporter blurted out a question. "Mr. Colter, is there any truth to the rumor that you're being charged with being accomplice to a sex trafficking ring?"

Before he could answer, his attorney answered for him. "Mr. Colter has nothing to say at the moment."

"Then, is it true that authorities have searched your home and have confiscated your personal computer?"

Once more his attorney answered in his stead. "I'm sorry. Because this case has not been resolved, Mr. Colter will not be able to answer any of your questions at this time."

The same reporter pressed on. "Mrs. Colter, do you have anything to say at this time?"

"Again, due to the point we are at in this case, Mrs. Colter has nothing to say."

"Oh, but I do." The attorney and Colter were taken by surprise, and they looked at her incredulously. Mrs. Colter had a demure smile on her face.

"No. Don't you dare say you are standing by your man," Deidre blurted out, not realizing she had verbalized her own feelings.

"I've been married to this man for twenty-five years," Mrs. Colter said, the same naive smile on her face. "And during those twenty-five years, I have never known him . . ." She paused for effect. ". . . to be anything but a complete ass."

The attorney looked like he was about to have a stroke, and Colter's jaw clamped shut. There was nothing they could do to shut her up, and the camera kept rolling.

"He is an arrogant SOB who tries to dominate everyone around him, and I'm not going to take his philandering and lying anymore. This is for you, Gerald." She handed him an envelope she had discreetly carried in her hand. "It's notice that I've filed for divorce. Have a nice day, sweetie." She confidently strode down the steps of the courthouse, holding her head high and still wearing a smile.

Deidre applauded the performance, and the girls came running downstairs to see what the excitement was about.

"It's nothing, girls, just an old friend of mine getting what he deserves. Go on up and finish playing. Daddy will be home soon."

She turned off the TV, and contemplated what she had just witnessed. Gerald Colter had his tail in a ringer, and it was pulling him ever closer to disaster. Then she thought of the judge. He had taken care of his problem in his own way.

LaTourell and Jameson were in jail, not able to post bail, their trials set to take place during the coming summer. The thought hit her that she should make good on her promise to look up the girls she had rescued. Not only that, she wanted to visit with Melissa and her daughter, and she hadn't heard from Jill for many weeks.

Chapter
Thirty-Five

THE LAST TIME DEIDRE TRAVELED to Thunder Bay, the roads were covered with snow, and the trip had taken four hours. Today, the sun was shining brightly, the temperature was in the seventies, and she was cruising along a little over the posted speed limit. As she rounded a curve, she was treated to the sight of a bay of Lake Superior, and she thought how lucky she was to be able to enjoy the scenery without having to be worrying about a murder or kidnapping.

Two days before, she had called Charles Freeman, the chief of police for the Nishnawbe Aski Cree Nation. He had given her information about the girls: Allison, Jean, Kimi, and the others who had been rescued. After calling the people at Social Services, and with the aid of Charles, Deidre was able to set up a meeting with the six of them. A picnic had been scheduled in one of the parks near where they were receiving care.

She parked her car in a small lot, and walked across the newly mown lawn, and the smell of the cut grass reminded her of how sterile winter was in the northland. Across the park, she could see a group readying a table for a picnic, and she recognized Kimi, who was waving at her.

"Deidre! Deidre, over here," the girl called out excitedly. She was beautiful, Deidre thought. The others turned and all waved at her.

When Deidre was closer, she could see the meal she had ordered from a caterer had arrived, and the girls and a social worker had everything laid out.

They hugged and stepped back to look at each other. A few tears were shed, and finally, the social worker said, "I think it's time we ate this great looking food."

One of the girls extracted a pinch of tobacco from a pouch hanging from a lace on her belt and, scattering it in the breeze, gave thanks to the Creator for his provision. She felt a kinship with the girls who bowed their heads for an instant.

Then everyone rushed for her plate and began loading it with standard picnic food. Deidre watched as they giggled like school-age girls should, and she marveled at how healthy they looked. Someone, probably many people, were making a difference in their lives.

Time passed swiftly. Too soon, Deidre had to say it was time to leave.

"Will you girls clean up the area? I want to talk a moment with Deidre," the social worker said. They walked toward a paved path, and the girls began their task.

"I know you came here to find out how they are doing. Kimi is having the most trouble. She still has nightmares, and at times becomes very withdrawn, but she's getting better. Allison and Jean carry a great deal of guilt, because they think if they had been courageous enough to leave with Anna and Kimi, they might have been able to overcome Jason Leder when he grabbed Anna.

"The three you found at the camp don't know you as well. One of them had a terrible urinary tract infection that had traveled to her kidneys. It took a while, but with antibiotics, the infection was cured. Doctors think there was no permanent damage done.

"All of them are receiving psychological help, and two will be going home to their families next week. The other four have become wards of the state because their parents can't be located or are deemed unfit. Their psychologists agree that it will be years, if ever, before they can put this behind them. Each of them will have to exorcise their demons in their own way and in their own time. All we can do is walk with them on their journey and give them all the support we can. I know you might have wanted better news for all of them, but we think they are far ahead of the game." She was silent for a few steps, then she stopped and faced Deidre.

"Our nation owes you a great deal. We struggle every day, trying to undo the damage that's been done to our people going back two hundred years when our tribes were conquered by the Europeans. But we are making progress. As you saw when an offering was made to Manitou, we still hold onto many of our beliefs, at the same time living in the twenty-first century. People like you are making it possible for us to gain back our lives."

For a moment, Deidre was speechless. She shrugged. "They are strong, aren't they?" The social worker nodded.

*****

DEIDRE MADE ARRANGEMENTS to meet Jill at a cozy eatery off Waterfront Drive in Two Harbors, Louise's Place. She arrived earlier than intended and was browsing the collection of rolls and cakes in a display case when Jill walked in. Deidre would not have recognized her had she not anticipated Jill's arrival.

Jill's hair, which had formerly been rainbow colored and then light brown, was dyed black, as were her eyebrows. For the first time Deidre noticed that she had dark-brown eyes.

"Jill. It's great to see you," she said. Then added, "I wouldn't have recognized you with your new hair color."

Jill selected a chair at a corner table. "Yeah, well, it's a long story if you're interested."

Deidre could tell there was something Jill needed to say.

"I know I looked a mess when you met me. You must have known I was hiding behind my weird hairdo and dress. I really hated myself for what I was doing."

A waitress asked them what they wanted to drink, and they both ordered coffee. Deidre asked Jill if she wanted anything to have with it, and they both ordered a Danish pastry.

"There's something I've tried to hide since I was a little girl, and it nearly destroyed my life."

The waitress returned with their order, and Deidre's mind conjured up a raft of thoughts, including incest, rape, or an alcoholic mother.

"My mother is a full member of the Anishinabe Indian Nation. She's a good woman, but I was always ashamed of her and my heritage. In high school, kids, especially the boys, called me smoked meat and said I was a tarpaper blonde."

Deidre looked at her former secretary. With her black hair, her skin color did appear more swarthy than most. But so did some Finns of Saami descent, or even some whose relatives had immigrated from the northern part of Norway.

"What hurt almost as much were the kids from the rez, who called me an apple, red on the outside, white on the inside. I became rebellious and bitter. Look where it got me."

Deidre reached over and touched Jill's hand. "I'm sorry. But it seems as though you've pulled things together. Right? Are you going to take Melissa up on her offer to help you apply at the BCA office?"

Jill smiled. "No, I've decided against it."

Deidre looked startled.

"As we worked on this trafficking case, my eyes were opened to the plight of those girls and the uphill battle they were fighting. See this black hair. It's dyed, but when it grows out, this will be its natural color. After seeing you work so hard to help those kids, and after seeing their will to survive, I thought, 'Who am I to deny my heritage? I am Anishinabe. We were a noble people once, most still are. Those who look down on us are wrong. Why should I be ashamed of my heritage?' No, I'm not going to go to the Cities to be a secretary. Not that there's anything wrong with being a secretary. It's just that I need to be close to my mother's people. I've enrolled for next semester's program at the Tribal College near Duluth. Because of my Anishinabe blood, I'll receive quite a bit of financial help. In the meantime, I'll do temp work and continue to volunteer at the women's shelter in town."

Deidre asked about the guy Jill had seen over Christmas, her former classmate.

"Him," Jill said with scorn. "All he was after was a quick fling while he was in town."

"I'm glad you turned him down," Deidre consoled her.

She wholeheartedly endorsed Jill's plan, and for the remainder of the time they spent together, they talked about their hopes and dreams, Deidre not being explicit about hers.

*****

AFTER SPENDING THE WEEKEND with Ben and the girls, on Monday morning Deidre drove to Minneapolis. She was to meet Melissa and Jessica at a small, out-of-the-way eatery, and they were already seated in a booth when she arrived.

Jessica looked refreshed. The black circles under her eyes were gone, and she had a smile on her face.

Melissa slid over to make room for Deidre, and took her hand.

"So, how are things," Deidre asked, not quite sure how to begin the conversation.

Jessica shrugged, but smiled. "It's been an adjustment—for both of us. The difference this time is that when one of us is bothered, we talk about it without snapping at each other."

"I have to remember that Jessica has seen more of the street scene than I ever will."

"And I have to remember that mom runs the house," Jessica finished her mother's sentence. "But it's working, getting better every week. I can't say every day, because we have our moments. But it's going to work."

Deidre didn't quite know where to go from there, but before she could say anything, Jessica continued. "I want to thank you for being there for me. I know, without a doubt, I couldn't have returned home on my own. During the ride down, I wanted to open the door and jump out. If you'd have stopped at a rest area, I planned to make a run for it."

Deidre was surprised. She knew that Jessica was struggling with her decision, but she hadn't been aware just how much.

"I don't think I could screw up the courage to do it again." Jessica fished a tissue from her pocket and blew her nose. "Anyway, thanks for being there when I needed you."

Up to that point, Deidre had said nothing. Now she asked, "What are your plans? School? Sports? Music? Right now, what interests you?"

Jessica looked a little embarrassed. "I'm so far behind in school, there's no way I'll ever graduate with my class. I'd be an old lady of twenty-one if I went the conventional route." She smirked at the thought.

"I'm attending an alternative school, trying to make some progress, although most kids at that school are just killing time. I might be able to attend summer school and take extra night classes. If I can't graduate by the time I'm nineteen, I've decided to go for my GED. From there, maybe a community college or tech school. But who knows, I might even continue on to a four-year school. My life is up in the air, and I'm not sure where it is going to land."

Deidre slouched a little so she could look Jessica, who had her head bowed, directly in her eyes.

"Everyone messes up sometime. You're one of the lucky ones. You screwed up early, and you have a lifetime ahead of you. You have the support of your mother. You have a short-range plan in place. You're sheltered, fed, clothed. You have a second chance. I have confidence you'll complete your schooling, you'll find your niche, and you're going to make a difference to others. You're a strong young lady, a survivor."

The three of them sat in the booth for a long time. The clientele turned over at least twice. Before Deidre knew it, she had to wish mother and daughter the best and say her goodbyes.

On the way home she wondered if Jessica would adjust or if the day would come where some voice called her to bolt again. For Melissa's sake, she hoped that all would be well, but Deidre knew that the recidivism rate among runaways was high. In an awkward way, she said a prayer for the two of them.

Chapter
Thirty-Six

DEIDRE LABORED UNDER THE STRAPS of a Duluth pack, a traditional way of carrying supplies and equipment over the portage trails of the Boundary Waters Canoe Area. Mosquitoes bored holes in her bare arms, deer flies became entwined in her hair, and sweat streamed down her face. It was June sixteenth, and through breaks in the overhead canopy, the sun was beating on the four campers.

A refreshing breeze was blowing, but for those on the trail, the trees and brush didn't allow it to reach the hikers, and the humidity from the decaying duff on the ground created a sweltering microclimate.

"Are we almost there yet," Megan asked, and she stumbled over a root in the trail.

"Almost," Ben encouraged. "Look. You can see the lake through the trees. If we walk over the next hill, we'll be there."

"You said that two hills ago," Maren complained.

"This time I mean it," Ben chuckled. "We're almost there."

Deidre licked her lips, and wished she had an ice-cold bottle of anything to drink, but just when she thought she could go no farther, she crested the hill. A panorama stretched out before her that stopped her in her tracks. It was one of the most beautiful lakes she had ever seen. Bordered by jack pines and cedar trees, it was the purest blue she could remember, and the breeze moving across its surface caught her sweaty hair and blew it off her face. Deidre picked her way over the rocks in the trail and descended the drop. She drew in a deep breath, enjoying the smell of the lake, and set the pack down by the water's edge.

Ben lifted the canoe from his shoulders and set it down on shore, the twins shed their small packs, and all four campers flopped down in the green grass of the canoe landing. They lay on their backs for several minutes, and then the girls jumped up, raced to the waters edge, and began trying to catch minnows with their hands.

"Okay everybody, time to load up and move out," Ben announced.

Ben pulled the canoe into knee-deep water, and Deidre handed him two large packs, the one she had carried and the one he had toted while he also carried the canoe. He placed them strategically in the bottom of the canoe, making sure the craft remained balanced, and then they stowed the small packs the girls had brought.

"Lifejackets, everyone," Ben commanded, and they were ready to shove off.

The girls were tucked in among the packs. Deidre sat in front, and Ben in the stern. The adults paddled, and the girls dragged their fingers in the water. The day was as perfect as it could get.

They crossed three lakes, being able to pass from one to the other through narrows just wide enough to allow the canoe to be navigated. Late in the afternoon, the canoe scraped its way up on the gravel shore, and Deidre stepped out, steadied the canoe while the girls crawled over the packs and jumped to dry ground, and held it while Ben stepped into the shallow water.

"We're home," he announced, and Deidre could sense the peace in his voice.

She surveyed the site where they would camp for the next two nights and three days. A small river ran past, a short connecting waterway between two lakes, and the rocky channel flowed near the shore where she stood. Deidre would have perched on a rock and allowed the river to cascade around her feet, but Ben had another idea.

"Come on, gang. We've got to get the camp set up before dark. Girls, help me with our tent. Deidre, why don't you set yours up right here?" He pointed to a spot of flat ground.

"And who made you boss?" Deidre asked as she jokingly jabbed him in the ribs. But she unrolled the tent that was made for one person. She thought two could squeeze in if they had to. Perhaps she'd invite the girls to cuddle a while before they fell asleep.

By late afternoon, the place felt like home in the wilderness. Their tents were set up, Ben had a small cooking fire going, a coffee pot was on the grate, and everyone had taken a dip in the river to cool off and wash away the day's dirt.

Deidre leaned her back against a pine tree while she sat on her lifejacket. Ben was in his element, cooking supper, feeding the fire, and trying to keep a chipmunk from stealing from their food pack. She and the girls tried to get a jay to eat from their fingers. It would come within inches of their hands but then become alarmed, flying to a low-hanging branch while it screwed up its courage to try again.

After supper, they took a ride in the canoe, following close to the shoreline. Not far from camp a disturbance in the water, a black hump that was moving toward them, caught their attention. When they were too close, the beaver slapped its tail on the surface and dived underwater, much to the girl's delight. In the distance, two loons called to each other. Deidre wished the tranquility would last forever.

"Time to go back to camp," Ben decided, and he pointed the canoe toward their temporary home.

When they arrived, Deidre mixed a cup of mocha with hot coffee and instant hot chocolate. Ben was in the tent, trying to get his daughters settled in for the night, and twilight had turned the sky purple as Deidre stood by the water flowing past their campsite, her cup in hand.

She thought she heard the sound of paddles in the water but wasn't quite sure. Then she heard a muffled voice. It was a man's, and it sounded like he said there was someone at the campsite they wanted to use.

A canoe painted with camouflage markings rounded the bend of the river, and two men were paddling as fast as they could. Deidre waited for them to come closer and called out. "Care to stop for a cup of coffee?"

"No thanks, we've got to get to the next campsite before dark," the man in front growled at her.

Their canoe shot by, aided by the stream's current, but in that flash, Deidre got a good look at the bottom of the canoe, and a shiver jolted her body. An olive-drab duffle bag lay between the paddlers, and Deidre was sure she saw movement inside it as they whisked by.

Before she could react, the canoe and its occupants disappeared around the bend, and she heard one of the men curse. Five minutes later, the canoe scraped on the beach, and she heard the sounds of a camp being hurriedly set up.

Not thinking of the consequences, Deidre quietly slipped her canoe into the water and slowly worked her way downstream. In the distance, she saw the flicker of a campfire, revealing the location of the travelers.

She steered the canoe near a large rock, and soundlessly stepped out. After wedging the canoe between a tree that had fallen in the water and the rock, Deidre began to creep toward the men, stopping only when she was close enough to observe their actions and hear their conversation. One of them was untying the duffle bag.

"That's the biggest damn northern I've ever seen," one said. "Must be close to forty inches long," the other answered.

He reached into the bag and pulled out a huge fish that flopped in his hands. It was still alive.

"If we put it in the water on a stringer tonight we might be able to keep it alive until morning. This baby's going on my wall as soon as I can get a taxidermist to do the job.

"But let's get our stories straight. I don't want anybody to know where we caught it. Let's say it was in Ojibwa Lake. That's not too far from here, and once in a while, somebody catches a good-size fish there."

Deidre sat in the brush, her heart pounding and feeling weak as the adrenalin in her system dissipated. She listened as the fishing buddies recounted to each other the experience of catching a lunker. Then, as quietly as she had approached them, she slunk off through the woods, reached her canoe, and paddled back to camp.

Ben was standing by the water's edge, anxiously waiting for her to return.

"Where the heck were you?" he asked. "I was getting worried that you had gotten lost."

"No," Deidre said as nonchalantly as she could. "The water was so calm, I just wanted to float downstream a ways and listen to the evening sounds without any background noise. Are the girls asleep?"

Ben nodded and took Deidre in his arms. She was still shivering, and he thought she was cold. "Come, let's warm you by the fire." He led her to the blaze.

The two of them talked until the drone of mosquitoes leaving the underbrush in search of prey began to sound ominous. "Sleep tight," Ben said, and kissed Deidre good night. They went to their separate tents.

She had just crawled into her sleeping bag, when she heard scratching on her tent, and she lifted her head to see what was making the noise.

"Deidre, is it okay if I come in with you for a few minutes?" It was Ben.

"That'd be okay, I guess," she answered. "Are the girls still asleep?"

She heard the zipper of her tent come undone, and Ben crawled in and lay beside her. It was a tight fit, and she could feel his body next to hers, although she was inside her sleeping bag and he outside.

"There's something I want to talk to you about," Ben began, and Deidre detected the nervousness in his voice.

"What's that?" she asked, wondering what to expect.

"I just wanted you to know before somebody else told you that I've met someone I'm going to ask to be my wife. I didn't want you to hear the news through the rumor mill or before the girls spilled the beans."

Deidre's mind spun, and she bit her lip to keep from blurting out the question, "Who is it?" Instead, she took a deep breath. "How long have you known her?" was all she could think to ask.

"Quite a while. She was awfully hard to get to know, I'll say that, but when we did, our love for each other just grew, at least mine did."

Deidre was silent for many seconds. "What will become of the girls if she says yes?"

"I suppose they'll learn to call her mom. I think it'll work out really well. She tells me she loves them."

But not like I do, Deidre wanted to say.

Ben continued. "She was a high school classmate of mine."

But that means she was a classmate of mine, too. I wonder . . . It's got to be Jolene. That tramp. Ben, you could do better than that.

"We couldn't stand each other back then. In fact, years ago she hurt me, bad."

Deidre turned to face Ben, but the interior of the tent was too dark to make out his expression. "Oh. You mean she jilted you?"

"No, I mean she hurt me. Broke my foot when she stomped on it."

Finally, the light bulb came on in Deidre's head. "But of course you didn't deserve it."

"I deserved it. I was a jerk."

"Yes, you were," Deidre said, and tried to suppress a laugh.

"Deidre, will you marry me?" He choked up and couldn't say any more, but he took Deidre's hands and held them between his.

"Yes!" was all Deidre could squeak out as her throat tightened around the words. She leaned forward and kissed Ben, and from the other tent she heard two high-pitched voices call out in unison.

"Good night, Mom."